Crime nove

Non-fiction by Susan Fleet

Women Who Dared: Trailblazing 20th Century Musicians

Volume 1: Violinist Maud Powell and Trumpeter Edna White

Praise for Absolution

Best Mystery-Suspense-Thriller -- 2009 Premier Book Awards

"A New Orleans killer thriller." -- Arts Journal

"Relentless tempo and sharp writing." -- Kirkus Discoveries

"Creole-flavored suspense, colored with musical connections which Fleet handles with particular deftness." -- The Attleboro Sun Chronicle

"Fleet has created a crime drama that stands far above the ordinary whodunit. A wholehearted bravo!" -- The Florida Times-Union

"First class writing! Fleet goes inside the head of the killer with a rare talent. An 'I couldn't put it down' thriller." -- C. J. Gregory

Praise for Diva

"Great character development [and] an absolutely fascinating ending ... a very suspenseful book!" -- Feathered Quill Book Reviews

"Fleet subtitles *Diva*, her new killer thriller, a novel of psychological suspense. That's an understatement." -- Jan Herman, *Arts Journal*

"NOPD detective Frank Renzi returns in a relentless hunt through ravaged, drug infested neighborhoods in search of murderous thugs and a psychotic stalker. Fleet weaves a web of danger [charged] with raw emotion ... another nail-biting page-turner!" -- K. G. Hunt

"Fleet takes us inside the head of the obsessed stalker as he lusts after his victim ... one a must-buy book." -- Tom Bryson, author of *Too Smart To Die*

DIVA

A novel of psychological suspense

It is not the idol but the worshippers that are to be dreaded.

-- William Hazlitt

SUSAN FLEET

Music and Mayhem Press

Diva is a work of fiction. All names, characters, businesses, incidents and events are either products of the author's imagination or used fictitiously. Any resemblance to actual persons, living or dead, is entirely coincidental.

DIVA

A Frank Renzi Novel

Copyright © 2011 by Susan Fleet

Second Edition published in 2012 by Music and Mayhem Press

This book contains an excerpt of Susan Fleet's next Frank Renzi Novel, *Natalie*, copyright © 2012 by Susan Fleet

All rights reserved. This book may not be reproduced or distributed, in whole or in part, in any printed or electronic form without written permission except in the case of brief quotations in articles or reviews. For information, review copies or permissions, contact the author at www.susanfleet.com

ISBN: 978-0-9847235-2-2

Back cover author photo by Pete Wolbrette

ACKNOWLEDGEMENTS

Several people shared their expertise with me and I am very grateful to them. To better understand the world of flute playing and flute repertoire, I spent a delightful afternoon with New Orleans flutist Anne Chabreck. Anne also owns two dwarf rabbits. I had fun watching them and even got to hold one!

The Bear, a former NOPD Homicide Detective, shared his memories of the difficulties New Orleans police faced in the dark days after Hurricane Katrina. New Orleans attorney and former prosecutor Michelle Magill Smith explained how juveniles are treated within the Louisiana legal system. My conversation with security consultant Monty J. Curtis, president of the Corporate Intelligence Group, about stalkers and stalking scenarios was also helpful.

I also consulted two books. *The Gift of Fear*, by security expert Gavin De Becker, aided my understanding of the stalker mindset and the difficulty of deterring them. *Mozart in the Jungle: Sex, Drugs and Classical Music*, by oboist and Julliard graduate Blair Tindall, shed light on the cutthroat competition encountered by students at Julliard and in the professional music world.

However, this is a work of fiction and I have taken a certain amount of dramatic license. Any errors or inaccuracies in the book are mine.

Heartfelt thanks to my fellow writers Carolyn Wilkins and Jaimie Bergeron. Their suggestions on early drafts improved the book tremendously.

Thanks also to you my readers for choosing *Diva*. I hope you enjoy reading it as much as I did writing it. Many of you wrote to me after reading *Absolution*. I hope you'll do so again. Please visit my website www.susanfleet.com and drop me an email. I'd love to hear from you.

This book is dedicated to stalking victims everywhere, and especially to A.M., a friend and fellow brass player, who finally escaped the man who stalked her.

CHAPTER 1

Thursday, 12 October 2006

With military precision, he thrust his torso upward, arms rigid, palms pressed to the floor. Oblivious to the dingy carpet that reeked of cigarette smoke from the previous tenant, he feasted on the slick color brochure that lay below him. Belinda Scully, celebrated soloist on the cusp of stardom.

Gazing up at him. Enticing him with her come-hither smile.

Admiring his naked hard-body.

Audiences loved her fiery passion, her magical way with the flute.

He loved her, too. Desire flamed his groin. He lowered his body and brushed her photograph with a kiss. He wanted to lick every inch of her, wanted to make her moan with ecstasy and make her beg him for more.

A final burst and his pushups were done. He sprang to his feet, bathed in sweat. Even in October the New Orleans humidity was a killer. He'd shut off the air conditioner. Paying for this shitty studio apartment was bad enough; he didn't need sky-high electric bills to boot. His money paid for more important things: air fares and hotel rooms and concert tickets.

He toweled sweat from his face and sank onto his cheap metal futon. Large posters on the opposite wall hid cracked plaster and chipped paint: Belinda at Tanglewood, Belinda at the Hollywood Bowl, Belinda in St. Louis. The first two he had obtained after the concerts, asking nicely. The third he'd stolen from a glass display in a quick smash and grab.

The photos didn't do her justice. She was far more beautiful in person.

The insistent throb in his groin became a full-fledged erection.

"Dazzling technique and a sensuous dulcet tone," the *Times-Picayune* reviewer had gushed. A rave review—justly deserved—of her performance with the Louisiana Philharmonic last weekend.

From his fourth row seat he had watched his beloved pour her emotion into the music. Thirteen years of heartache. He knew what that was like.

At the after-party, he'd watched the LPO benefactors fawn over her, rich old men lusting after his beloved, seduced by her captivating smile, sapphire-blue eyes and the coppery hair cascading in waves to her shoulders. Watched them and hated them. Lurking behind her, aching to touch her, he had edged closer, close enough to smell her favorite perfume, Mambo.

He flexed his fingers. It had been ages since he'd touched a piano. Years since he'd talked to his beloved. She hadn't responded to any of his messages.

How dare she ignore him? A sea of burning acid roiled his gut.

Tonight he would send her a different message.

―――――

"Damn it to hell!" Frank Renzi stared at his computer screen: *Ink Cartridge Empty*. Two hours writing reports, the last thing he needed was a dead printer. He wanted to go home. Not that anyone was waiting for him, but he could have a beer and chill out with a Clark Terry CD.

He strode to a metal supply cabinet, opened it and cursed again. No print cartridges. SOS, fourteen months post-Katrina, half the residents still gone, violent crime off the chart and NOPD short 400 officers, not to mention money for equipment. The thugs were winning.

The sweet scent of jasmine wafted through the window bringing sounds of the night: the rumble of a delivery truck, the honk of a taxi, the clangor of Bourbon Street one block away, bars and strip joints bursting with workers who'd come to New Orleans to rebuild the city.

He returned to his gunmetal-gray desk, one of four jammed together in the center of the Eighth District homicide office. They were short a detective, and stacks of unsolved case files stood atop one desk. He cancelled the print run and yawned. It had been a backbreaking day, starting with a homicide at Iberville, a public housing complex north of the French Quarter plagued by gangbangers and drug dealers. When he and his partner arrived, a crowd encircled the victim, a young black male with two GSWs to the head, the body count climbing in an eruption of drug-related hits. A second teen had taken slugs in his legs. No wits, of course. Nobody knew nothin'.

Any kind of luck, the second kid would live to see another day.

Any day without a murder was a good day in New Orleans.

His internal phone line buzzed: the desk officer calling.

"Sorry, Frank," said Bill Poche. "I hate to bother you this late."

During his four years with NOPD, Franklin Sullivan Renzi had acquired a certain reputation thanks to his ruthless pursuit of thugs, and his expletive-laden tirade at the Deputy Chief one day when the fool tried to tell him how to do his job. "What's up, Bill?"

Please, not another homicide. He was ready for a beer, not another corpse.

"I got a young couple here want to report a possible murder attempt."

He heard a male voice in the background: ". . . tried to kill her."

"Yes, sir," Poche said, "you can tell Detective Renzi all about it." To Frank, he said, "By the way, don't forget that *big bash* tomorrow."

Big bash. NOPD-code for VIPs. Just what he needed, nine-thirty at night. He set an Incident Report form on his desk, went to the door and played Who's-the-VIP. No shortage of show-biz celebrities in New Orleans: John Goodman, Nick Cage, Brad and Angelina roaming around the Big Easy.

A door at the end of the hall opened and a well-dressed couple, early thirties tops, approached him. The woman was a knockout, five-seven and willowy in her skimpy aqua dress. Great legs, except for the scrape on one knee. Her companion was six feet tall and skinny, his lips a grim line between his dark moustache and beard. Frank didn't recognize them, made a bet with himself: Whoever speaks first is the VIP.

The woman dazzled him with a smile that lit up the dreary hallway. Raised her chin like an Olympic gymnast, as if to say: *Watch me! I am the best.*

"Belinda Scully," she said.

The name didn't ring a bell, though she looked vaguely familiar, even features, copper-colored hair skimming her shoulders. Attractive. Amazing eyes. Great bod. Maybe this wouldn't be so bad after all.

"Jake Ziegler," said her companion. No smile, a worried frown and a limp handshake.

He led them into the office and gestured at two visitor chairs beside his desk. "Looks like you scraped your knee, Ms. Scully."

"Please, call me Belinda." Claiming the chair nearest him, she crossed her legs and arranged her skirt. "I'm fine. This is a big fuss over nothing."

Ziegler folded his gangly frame onto the other chair, his dark eyes smoldering. No wedding rings, but it seemed clear that Belinda wore the pants in the relationship, whatever it was.

"Tell me what happened," he said.

"We had dinner at Trattoria Bella," she said, gazing at him with her startlingly blue eyes. "It's a great restaurant. Have you been there?"

"Yeah, home-cooked Italian," he said, and realized she was staring at his chin. Fourteen hours since he'd shaved, the two-inch scar was probably a white zigzag amidst his dark stubble.

Radiating annoyance, Ziegler fidgeted in his chair. He cleared his throat, an ugly rasp, but said nothing. Was he waiting for her permission to speak?

Frank looked at Belinda. "Did the incident happen in the restaurant?"

"No. In the parking lot."

"We were walking to the car," Ziegler said, agitated. "I heard a high-pitched whine and screeching tires and this car came out of nowhere—"

"And then the headlights came on—"

"Right, Belinda. And then the bastard tried to run you down!"

Frown lines formed between her eyes. "He wasn't trying to—"

"Yes, he was! He drove straight at us." Like a Cocker Spaniel begging for a treat, Ziegler gave him an imploring look. "Detective Renzi, if I hadn't pushed Belinda aside, the car would have hit her!"

"Jake, it was just some kid—"

"Hold it." He rubbed his temples to ease a budding headache. Was this a lover's quarrel? Was Boyfriend working on his Hero merit badge? He fixed Ziegler with a hard stare. "What makes you think it was deliberate?"

Zeigler tugged his beard with long slender fingers. Every nail was bitten to the quick. "Belinda's a public figure. Don't you know who she is?"

He spread his hands, a weary disclaimer. "Sorry. You got me there."

Ms. Celebrity smiled. "Not everyone is a classical music fan, Jake."

Then he remembered the photo-spread in the *Times-Picayune* last week. "Oh, right. You're the flutist that played a solo with the LPO last weekend."

"Yes. Seven years ago the LPO gave me my first break, a solo performance with a professional orchestra, and I fell in love with the city. Four years ago I moved here from Boston."

"Me, too," he said, and wished he hadn't when he saw the spark of interest in her eyes.

"Why did you move to New Orleans?"

Because my wife divorced me, and a little girl died that shouldn't have.

"I hate shoveling snow."

She gazed at him, somber-eyed. Her eyes were stunning, deep pools of emotions he couldn't decipher, a hint of pain, then nothing.

"I bet it's more complicated than that."

The comment surprised him. Had she seen something in his face, some remnant of the anguish he'd felt when he decided to leave Boston? Maybe there was more to Belinda Scully than celebrity-hood. Maybe a real person lurked beneath her carefully groomed exterior: aqua eye shadow, lip-gloss, not a strand of coppery hair out of place.

He started to print her name on the Incident Report.

"Don't put my name on that," she said, her voice edged with steel.

"Use mine then," Ziegler said. "I don't care. Someone tried to kill her."

This was getting tedious. "Can you describe the car, Mr. Ziegler?"

"No. It happened too fast. It was dark."

"The car was dark?"

"Yes," Ziegler said, his voice rising in exasperation. "Dark and big. A big dark sedan. We were walking along, talking the way you do after a meal, and a car came out of nowhere and homed in on us like a . . . like a *missile!*"

"Did you get a look at the driver?"

"No. I was too busy looking out for Belinda." She shot Ziegler a nasty look, but Ziegler ignored it. "Whoever it was tried to *kill* her."

For the briefest instant, he saw a flash of fear in her sapphire-blue eyes. Then her carefully crafted mask reappeared. No window to the soul through those baby-blues now. She kept denying Ziegler's assertion that someone had tried to kill her. Maybe she wasn't so sure.

"What makes you think someone wants to kill Belinda Scully?"

Ziegler stared at the floor, clearly uncomfortable.

He's hiding something and so is she. They both have secrets. Hoping to jolly it out of them, he said, "What? You think someone didn't like her solo?"

Belinda grinned at his flip remark, as though they were co-conspirators. They weren't. She wanted to flirt. He wanted to go home.

"There's more to it than that," Ziegler said. "This is an anniversary of sorts. We have dinner together every Columbus Day, the day her parents—"

"Jake! Stop. Detective Renzi isn't interested in hearing my life story."

He felt the beginning of headache build behind his eyes. Then his cell phone chimed, always trouble at this hour.

It was Kenyon Miller. "Frank! Cop down in Lakeview. Where y'at?"

Cop down. His heart hammered his chest like a drummer bashing cymbals. "At the station. Call you back when I'm on the road."

He opened the bottom drawer of his desk and took out the leather holster that held his SIG-Sauer.

The well-dressed couple beside his desk stared at him, wide-eyed.

"Leave your contact information at the front desk, Mr. Ziegler. I'll call you tomorrow."

CHAPTER 2

Tires screeching, Frank barreled into the I-10 exit at sixty miles an hour and swung north on West End Boulevard, the main drag through Lakeview. Before Hurricane Katrina decimated the city in August 2005, Lakeview had been an upscale predominantly white neighborhood. Now it was dark and deserted, no street lights, abandoned homes lining the street. The Katrina floodwaters had reached the eaves of some houses and shoved others off their foundations, scenes reporters likened to war-torn Kosovo, filming a sign on one flood-ravaged home that said: I AM HERE. I HAVE A GUN.

West End ran three miles north to Lake Pontchartrain. Thirty yards to his left Pontchartrain Boulevard ran south. Between them was the neutral ground, shrouded in darkness, cleared now of the fifty-foot mountains of debris dumped there after Katrina. Piercing the inky-black shadows of the two-lane street, his headlights revealed a boulder-sized pothole. He swerved to avoid it, got on his cell phone and called Kenyon Miller.

"I'm on West End heading north. Lay it out for me."

"Off-duty cop goes in a convenience store to buy cigarettes," Miller said. "He's in civvies but carrying, you know, 'cuz Lakeview's a ghost town these days. He sees a kid holding a gun on the clerk and a female customer, goes for his piece and the kid shoots him. He makes it outside to his car and calls for backup. I called you soon's I heard."

"How's the cop?"

"They took him to City Hospital, no word yet. What happened, one of the maggots used the woman as a shield. Him and another kid piled into a black Cadillac, probably boosted, and split. The cop didn't dare shoot with the woman in the car."

"You got a description on the scumbags?"

"Two black males, late teens, early twenties. Cop only saw one gun, but you never know. Gunslinger's a wide-body in cargo pants and a hoodie, driver's a skinny guy with dreads."

"There's trouble, two black kids take a white woman hostage."

"No shit. Only black folks came back are the thugs. My wife and kids gotta stay in Atlanta with Tanya's mother, and I'm bunking in a goddam FEMA trailer 'cuz our house took seven feet of water and I can't find a contractor to work on it."

Miller called his family every night to quiz his son and daughter on their homework, trying to be a good dad, long distance.

"You can bunk with me anytime, Kenyon. I told you that."

"Thanks for the invite, Frank, but I gotta stay close to my house, you know? Goddam looters."

The looters came out after dark like roaches, stripping homes of plumbing, light fixtures, copper flashing, anything they could sell.

"How's the clerk?"

"Shook up but he's okay. The scumbag told him to stay put, fired a shot to scare him."

"Okay, I'll check the side streets over here. Keep in touch." He turned right onto a street lined with gutted homes and mounds of debris piled at the curb. He rolled down his window and putrid odors filled his nostrils.

An instant flashback to Katrina: the horrible stench of raw sewage and dead bodies floating in waist-high water, a tragedy so profound that some residents hadn't recovered. Some never would. The first week fires burned unchecked for lack of water and the manpower to fight them. Frantic parents looted Wal-Mart for diapers and baby formula. The thugs looted pharmacies and stores with guns.

A barking dog drew his attention. He trained the cruiser's spotlight on a house: gaping windows without glass, a crumpled carport tilted against a fence, no signs of life. Or a dog.

He drifted into the next block, heard faint sirens in the distance. Here there was only silence, unlike the desperate days after Katrina when the sound of helicopters, chainsaws and sirens filled the daylight hours. Nightfall brought inky darkness and a scary silence punctuated by gunfire. No one shaved or bathed for days, pissing in toilets that didn't flush, living on MRE's and water. And beer if they could get it.

More yelps from the dog. He swung left at the next street and put the spot on a two-story house with a basketball hoop on the garage. No lights in the FEMA trailer out front, but that didn't mean it was vacant. After Katrina, he'd seen hard-eyed men with shotguns and attack dogs on the porches of Garden District mansions, protecting their property. The French Quarter had survived almost unscathed and Canal Street morphed into media alley. Secure and well fed, Geraldo, Ted Koppel and Anderson Cooper had beamed their reports around the world.

A flash of movement caught his eye. He hit the brakes and studied the dark hulk of a house, letting his eyes absorb the gloom.

There it was again, shadowy movement in the darkness. He trained the spot on the left side of the house. Saw a dark form jump out of the bushes and run toward the rear of the house, arms flailing.

The metallic taste of adrenaline flooded his mouth. He sprang from the cruiser and vaulted several trash bags on the sidewalk. Dug out his SIG-Sauer and ran alongside the two-story boarded-up house. Stopped at the back corner. Heard footsteps pound on gravel. Charged into the next yard.

Moonlight revealed a skinny kid in a hoodie, racing away from him toward the street, arms and legs pumping.

He ran faster, his lungs on fire, his thighs burning, his forty-plus legs accustomed to a daily run, not a sprint like this. He whipped around the corner of a house and spotted the kid. The kid saw him, whirled, tripped over some sheetrock and staggered.

A surge of adrenaline, a quick sprint and he grabbed the kid's arm, put him on the ground and straddled him. "Police! Put your hands on your head."

Gasping for breath, the kid didn't move.

"Put your hands on your head!"

The kid slowly laced dark skinny fingers around the back of the hood.

"I'm gonna frisk you. You got anything sharp that's gonna hurt me? A knife? Any needles?" Silence. He swatted the kid's head. "Answer me!"

"Ain't got nuthin."

He patted him down, found nothing hard and metallic, and searched his pockets. No weapon, no needles, no drugs, and no ID. He holstered the SIG and yanked the kid's arm. "Get up, and don't try anything or I'll smack you."

As the kid struggled to his feet his hood fell off, revealing close-cropped hair, a smooth coffee-milk complexion and a narrow face with a delicate nose. No telling about the eyes, the kid staring at the ground, lips clamped together. He cuffed the kid's hands behind his back and marched him back to the cruiser. Halfway there, penned inside a wire-mesh fence, a German shepherd snarled at them. When they reached the cruiser, the kid tried to run.

Frank twisted his arm. "Don't be stupid!"

"You're breaking my arm!" A soprano voice rising to a shriek.

He studied the long eyelashes, thinly arched brows, large doe-eyes in a too-pretty face. Realization hit him like a head-on collision.

The kid was a girl.

He took her to the Eighth District station, the girl not saying word-one on the way, and marched her down a hall to a funky-smelling interview room. A three-foot-square wooden table with two chairs sat in the center of the room. A fluorescent light in the ceiling made the pale-green walls look putrid. On purpose. Nothing like a nasty environment to get the thugs talking. Shit green walls, no air-conditioning, and the odor of stale urine from some moke who'd wet his pants.

He removed the handcuffs, sat the girl down and told her to stay put. His female juvy, no doubt about it. Not good. He was supposed to contact her parents and get permission to interview her, but that could take hours. Hell, he didn't even know her name.

And the scumbag-robbers had taken a woman hostage.

He propped open the door, went around the corner to a one-way window and watched her. Rail-thin, she hunched her shoulders inside the hoodie and massaged her bony wrists. Set her elbows on the scarred tabletop, her lips moving, muttering to herself. He put a fresh tape in the camcorder, hit Record and returned to the room.

She looked up, her expression as bleak as if she were facing a firing squad, her dark eyes unfathomable. He sat down opposite her and flashed his you-can-trust-me smile. "I'm Detective Frank Renzi. What's your name?"

Her eyes shifted away and her leg jiggled up and down, nervous knee belying her stone-face demeanor.

He let the silence build for a minute, his irritation mounting.

"Listen, Miss No-name, we know you and your friend robbed that convenience store. You're in big trouble. Your buddy shot a cop."

Her head jerked up. She gazed at him, eyes wide and fearful.

"What were you doing in Lakeview?"

Her face settled into a sullen mask.

"Maybe you didn't rob the store. Maybe you were the lookout."

She gazed at him, eyes baleful. "Don't know nuthin 'bout no robbery."

"Why were you in Lakeview?"

"Ain't no law against it, is there?"

"There's laws against people casing abandoned houses at night looking to loot them."

"I ain't no looter."

Making great strides with his hard-hitting questions, unidentified girl lobbing denials at him. He gave her an encouraging nod, not quite a smile, and said in a quiet voice, "Best thing for you to do right now is tell me your name. That'd be a start."

"No start for me," she mumbled, plucking at the folds of her hoodie with skinny fingers. "You just wanna pin something on me."

"I'm your best shot at getting out of here tonight. I don't want to put you in the lockup with the whores and the crackheads. What's your name?"

She hunched her shoulders and gazed at him, chin cupped in her hands, a glimmer of hope in her eyes. "You can get me outta here?" Her voice rising in panic, knee jiggling faster.

"Gotta have a name to do that."

"You gonna let me go if I tell you?"

He was on dangerous ground, threatening to charge her and not giving her the Miranda. He pushed back his chair and stood.

"Stay there while I get you a bottle of water. Maybe that will loosen your tongue. I don't want to be here all night."

The understatement of the year. He'd been working fifteen hours.

"You got any cigarettes?"

Smoking inside a police station these days was strictly forbidden for cops, never mind teen witnesses and suspects, but hey, whatever worked.

"Maybe," he said. "Don't even think about leaving that chair."

He went to his office and took a stale pack of Marlboros out of his desk drawer. On the way back to the interview room, his radio handset crackled with chatter. But not about catching the robbers.

Maybe he had one. Maybe the wounded cop was mistaken and the second kid was this girl. Except she didn't have dreads.

When he put the pack of cigarettes and the lighter on the table, her expression softened. She lit up, inhaled and blew a cloud of smoke.

Anxiety zinged his gut. He was breaking every rule in the book. Not that breaking rules bothered him, but if they wound up charging her, this interview would be useless in court without a Miranda warning. And if she was under eighteen, he shouldn't even be talking to her without her parents' consent. Double trouble.

"Chantelle," she said, puffing her Marlboro.

Keeping her end of the bargain, a pleasant surprise.

"What's your last name?"

"Wilson, okay? Can I go?" Gazing at him, hopeful.

"How old are you?"

"You said I could go if I gave you my name! Just about broke my arm, shoving me into your damn car." An angry flick of her wrist sent ashes to the floor. Chantelle emboldened by nicotine.

"You don't look much over sixteen to me, that about right?"

She looked away. "Be sixteen next month."

Acid chewed his gut. Not even sixteen.

"You got a sheet? Don't lie. I can check on you."

"Ain't got no sheet for nothin! You lied. You said I could go if I gave you my name. You can't keep me here. I didn't do nuthin!"

"Where's your folks, Chantelle? Where's your Mom?"

"Gone." She puffed her cigarette and stared off into the distance.

"Gone where?"

"Gone on crack. Gone to the Superdome after Katrina. Gone to wherever they took her."

An all-too-familiar story. "Where's your father?"

She flicked ash off her cigarette onto the floor. "I got no idea."

Another familiar story. "Where you living, Chantelle?"

"Nowhere." A forlorn smile parted her lips. "That's a nice tune. You know it?"

He shook his head and smiled. "Can't say I do."

"I sing it sometimes . . ." She clamped her lips together, dropped the butt on the floor and mashed it under her dirty sneaker.

"You a singer?"

Her eyes teared up, bright and shiny. She sucked in air, a half-sob, turned her head away and mumbled, "Sing to myself sometimes."

"You go to NOCCA?" The prestigious high school for the arts served the talented teen population of New Orleans.

"I wish. Went to McDonogh Senior High before Katrina." She sucked in a shuddery breath, gazing at him with her large doe-eyes. "What happened to the policeman? He okay?"

He studied her, moved by the concern in her eyes. She might not have pulled the stickup, but his gut told him she knew something.

"Tell me where you're living, Chantelle."

Her eyes shifted away and she ducked her head. Big lie coming up.

"Already tol' you. Nowhere."

"You got no relatives here?"

DIVA

A tear trickled down her cheek and ripped out his heart. She was only fifteen, scared out of her mind. He couldn't put her in the lockup.

She arched her graceful neck and looked at him. "Got nobody."

"So you have no permanent address."

She shrugged her shoulders. "I guess."

"Best thing I can do is charge you with criminal trespass and—"

"No! You said I could go home . . ." She trailed off in a sob.

"You don't have a home to go to. I'll get you a place to stay until we straighten this out. Better than living on the street." It would also allow him to run her name through the system and see if she had a sheet.

But if he expected gratitude for keeping her out of the lockup, forget it. Chantelle looked at him as if he were a cockroach crawling over her Big Mac.

She bit her lip to keep from crying. Here she was for the second time tonight in a cop car, not handcuffed this time but just as trapped, the cop driving her God knows where. Antoine might be in worse trouble.

If they caught him, the cop would have told her, wouldn't he?

Knees to her chest, she squirmed into the corner of the back seat so he couldn't watch her in the rearview with his bloodsucking eyes. The man was scary-looking. A hawk-nose and a stubborn jaw. A trickster, acting sympathetic, making bullshit promises, then charging her with trespassing.

Tonight had been a disaster from the get-go. Antoine didn't want to rob no store, but AK said he had to, like it was some kind of test. Smiling his evil gold-toothed smile. AK was the one shot that cop, for sure. Antoine didn't own a gun, would never have touched one.

Her heart beat fast and hard. Damn AK to hell!

The cop stopped at a red light on Esplanade Avenue at the edge of the French Quarter and turned to look at her.

"How you doing back there?"

"Fine." *Not gonna give you no satisfaction, Mr. Trickster. Not about to tell you my heart is breaking, my boyfriend's in trouble and I got nobody to help me.*

Her stomach rumbled with hunger. Last time she'd eaten was breakfast, rancid peanut butter on stale bread, the only food she kept in the apartment she'd once shared with her mother. She looked out the window as they passed a Circle-K convenience store, heading north toward Rampart Street.

Please God, don't let him get on the I-10 and take me miles away.

Arms clenched around her knees, she dug her fingernails into her thighs.

No way was she staying in some foster home with a bunch of teen bitches. She'd bust outta there and get home so's Antoine could find her.

Tears burned her eyes. Antoine loved her even if nobody else did, smiling when she sang to him, his eyes full of love, and later, in bed, holding her tight, telling her everything would be all right, they'd be together soon. Then she wouldn't have to worry about crackheads and dope dealers and pimps busting into her apartment. Wouldn't need AK to protect her.

As if AK would protect her. Try and jump her was more like it.

The cop turned right at Rampart Street and headed toward the I-10.

"Where we goin'?" Hearing the tremor in her voice and hating it.

"Mama LeBlanc's. You'll get along fine as long as you follow the rules."

Where is it? She wanted to scream. *Is it far from here?*

But screaming at cops got you nowhere. Found that out five years ago when they arrested her moms, said they had her on a security video at some dress shop, her moms boosting clothes so she could sell them and buy crack.

"Don't take my moms away," she'd wailed. "I don't wanna be alone."

Didn't wanna be bawling in front of no cops either, but she couldn't help it. So they put her in foster care—some pissy-assed woman in it for the money. For a whole year she'd slept on a lumpy mattress, hardly any food to eat, stupid woman couldn't cook for shit.

They turned onto a side street, going slower, seemed like the cop was hunting for a house. *God be praised!* If the foster home was near here she'd only be two miles from home.

The cop pulled to the curb, laid his arm along the seat back and looked at her. "I know you're not happy right now, Chantelle, but this is the best deal I could get you."

Best deal woulda been to let me go like you promised.

But she didn't dare say this.

The cop gave her a hard-eyed stare. "Don't cause trouble for Mama. Don't try to run away. I'll do what I can to get this trespassing charge dismissed." Speaking softly in his musical voice, a deep baritone, the only thing she liked about him. She knew she should act grateful, thank the man for keeping her out of the lockup, but she couldn't make herself do it.

He held out a card, gazing at her, not hard-eyed now, more like he cared about her. A little bit anyway.

"My daughter's only eight years older than you and she cried on my shoulder a few times. If you need to talk, call my cell phone anytime, day or night. Detective Frank Renzi."

She reached out and took the card, seeing the concern in his eyes, wishing she could trust him, wishing she had someone strong to lean on. Someone grown up and in charge. Antoine was strong but he wasn't in charge of things any more than she was.

"Thank you," she whispered, had to work to get the words out, her throat so choked-up she could barely speak.

He smiled. "You're welcome, Chantelle."

CHAPTER 3

Friday, 13 October

She stood at the music stand, studying Khatchatourian's *Concerto for Flute*. In 1940, flutist Jean-Pierre Rampal had been so taken with Khatchatourian's violin concerto he had asked the composer to rework it for flute. The result, thirty-six minutes of musical and technical challenges, was considered one of the most difficult in the flute repertoire.

But not too difficult for Belinda Scully.

She ripped off a three-octave chromatic scale, relishing the glorious acoustics in her first-floor studio. The room had sold her on the house, a stately two-story Victorian on a tree-lined side street near the New Orleans Museum of Art. She'd paid a ridiculous price, but the luxury of practicing in a room like this was worth every penny. No rugs or curtains to suck up the sound. Sunlight poured through tall windows onto the polished-oak floor, and twin fans on the fifteen-foot ceiling twirled cool air through the room. A Steinway baby-grand stood near the back wall, shielded from the sun. Along the side wall were shelves for her sheet music, beside them the cherry-wood ladder-back rocker—her mother's—that she used during breaks.

She set the music aside. She used it for practice, never in performance. Humming the accompaniment that preceded the passage, she took a huge breath and leaped into it, fingers flying over the fiendish pyrotechnics Khatchatourian had devised for the cadenza that ended the first movement.

Everything was perfect: rhythm, intonation, a big fat glorious sound . . .

A missed note. She stamped her foot. How could that happen? She'd played it flawlessly hundreds of times.

Then she remembered. Today was Friday the 13th. But next week it wouldn't be. She never scheduled concerts on Friday the 13th.

She studied the passage with the note she'd missed. Two or three notes, actually. She closed her eyes and made her mind go blank as she did during concerts. Reviewers sometimes commented on this, conjecturing that she'd been swept away by the orchestral accompaniment. Nonsense.

She silently chanted her lucky mantra. *Never give in to fear. Act successful and you will be successful. Believe in yourself and you cannot fail.*

She began again, breathing easily, fingers flying over the keys of her platinum Haynes flute. She negotiated the offending passage and finished the cadenza. Perfect. All perfect.

Until the door opened and Jake stepped into the room.

"Jake, I'm practicing. You know I hate being disturbed—"

"I know," he said, advancing toward her, "but we need to talk."

His grim expression said it all. Forget practicing. Jake had a bug in his ear. But then he surprised her and smiled. "I just saw a juicy tidbit on the Internet. Nick Philopolous got the principal bassoon job with the Cleveland Orchestra. Wasn't he at Julliard when you were there?"

Nick. She crafted a bland expression, but her body betrayed her. Heat flooded her cheeks. She turned away, hearing Nick play the solo in Dukas' *Sorcerer's Apprentice* with the Julliard orchestra, hearing him ace the impossible opening to Stravinsky's *Rite of Spring*. Hearing his words when she told him she was pregnant: "You'll make a fabulous mother!"

As if he expected her to abandon her career while he pursued his.

She beamed a smile at Jake. "Good for him. He's a fabulous bassoonist." And after a slight hesitation, "I'll bet his wife is thrilled."

"I don't know. Cleveland's a far cry from San Francisco."

I don't give a damn whether his mousy violinist wife likes Cleveland or not.

She picked up her flute. "Can I get back to practicing? I've got a big concert next week, remember?"

Jake's dark eyes sparkled. "Right. A week from today we'll be in London. I can hardly wait. All the top critics and managers will be there."

"What about the hotel rooms? No unlucky thirteen's, I hope."

"Belinda, I've made your travel arrangements for years. No rooms on the thirteenth floor, no plane seats in row thirteen. I don't know why you're so fanatical about it. It's only a number."

No, it's not. She raised her flute and noodled some notes.

"I got an email from Guy St. Cyr's manager this morning. Guy's coming to the concert."

Guy St. Cyr. Renowned flute soloist. Her former teacher.

Another heartbreak.

"Jake, I really need to practice."

His frown returned and his eyes grew serious. "Okay, but there's something we need to talk about."

At last, his real agenda. Jake hadn't interrupted her practicing to tell her about Nick or discuss hotel reservations. "Well? What is it?"

His face darkened and he cleared his throat. Damn, she hated that sound. The nervous tick grated on her ears worse than chirping crickets.

"Look at this." He thrust a newspaper at her. "It's outrageous!"

Her heart pounded. Had someone had written a negative article about her? She studied the huge headline: **WOMAN DEAD IN LAKEVIEW HOLDUP**. Relieved that it wasn't some malicious article about her, she said, "That's terrible, but is it so important you had to interrupt my practicing?"

"Yes, damn it! Two black kids robbed a store, shot a cop and took a woman hostage. They found her later, badly injured. She died at the hospital. They never found the robbers."

Guilt-stricken, she said, "That poor woman. I'll bet that's why Detective Renzi ran off last night." She pictured his craggy face, the jagged scar on his chin, his dark sexy eyes. An attractive man with a deep melodious voice. Intriguing, but she couldn't afford romantic distractions now, not with the most important performance of her career coming up next week.

"Renzi never called me back. Black-on-white crime gets all kinds of attention, but ordinary folks like you and me—"

She laughed, the melodious trill she used when someone said something incredibly annoying. "I may be many things, Jake, but ordinary is not one of them. Belinda Scully is not *ordinary*."

He plucked at his dark beard with long skinny fingers. "I'd be the last person to call you ordinary. You're an amazing person and a marvelous musician. The *point* is Renzi doesn't seem to think an attack on a famous flute soloist is important enough to merit his attention."

"That's fine by me. If my name's in the report, some reporter will make a big deal about it because—"

"It is a big deal! It's a *big fucking deal* when somebody tries to run you down—"

"Damn it, Jake, I will *not* be portrayed as Little-Miss-Victim. You saw the sob stories they used to write." She gave him the icy stare she used to quiet detractors. "That is not my image. We shouldn't have bothered to report such a silly incident—"

"It was not a *silly incident*. Someone tried to kill you!"

His words pierced her like a dagger. "Stop it, Jake! You're upsetting me. I can't afford that now, not with London coming up."

Not with all these nasty convergences. A car attack on the thirteenth anniversary. The day before Friday the 13th.

What next? Everyone knew bad things came in threes.

An icy chill wracked her. Thirteen years ago her brother, a talented composer with his whole life ahead of him, had died. Ever since she had secretly harbored the secret belief that she would die young too. Die before her time. Die before her musical ambitions came to fruition.

"If Renzi doesn't call today, I'll go to the station and *make* him listen!" Jake stalked out of the room and slammed the door.

Her heart pounded. Why were these horrible things happening now, just when she was on the brink of stardom?

She hadn't told Jake about the note she'd found on the front porch or the creepy message on her voicemail from a man saying he knew all her secrets. The raspy whisper had thrown her into a panic.

Did he know why she'd left Julliard and driven to New Jersey that day twelve years ago? No. How could he?

No one knew about New Jersey. No one.

Saturday, 14 October

Jake entered the Creole cottage he shared with Dean Silva, inhaled mouthwatering aromas and hurried down a short center hall to the kitchen.

"Home by four at the latest, huh?" Dean said without looking up, stirring something in a saucepan on the stove. "It's almost six."

His stomach roiled with acid, a reflex reaction to the verbal zinger. He put his arms around Dean's waist and nuzzled his neck. "I'm sorry, Dean. I was tending to last minute details for the London trip and lost track of time. You've been busy, too. Something smells fantastic."

Dean squirmed out of his embrace and slugged down some wine. "Not much else to do on a Saturday afternoon."

His unspoken words hung in the air: *Without you*. Jake grabbed the half-empty bottle of chardonnay on the counter, poured himself a glass and took two gulps. The wine hit his stomach with a painful sizzle.

Dean plucked a fat blunt from an ashtray, took a hit and held the smoke in his lungs. After a moment he let it out and resumed stirring. "This is lemon butter sauce for the pecan-crusted trout."

Cooking was Dean's passion. He loved trying elaborate new recipes. Well-worn cookbooks lined the counter: Julia Childs, James Beard and a recent one by New Orleans' own Emeril Lagasse.

"Yum. I can hardly wait." Anything to placate his angry lover.

Darkly handsome in a muscle T-shirt and tight jeans, lean and muscular from workouts at the health club, Dean held out the blunt with a lazy smile.

He didn't care much for pot, but took a quick hit to please Dean. The love of his life. He adored Dean's bottomless-pools-of-chocolate eyes and his impish grin, which appeared when it suited him. Right now it could go either way: pissed off or lovey-dovey.

"Stir this while I take a piss." Dean kissed his cheek and handed him the wooden spoon. "And you better open another bottle of wine."

He watched Dean walk down the hall, admiring his magnificent butt. They'd been together five years. He hoped it would last forever.

They had met at an organ recital at Brown University. Goosebumps rose on his arms at the memory: the magnificent sound of the organ in Sayles Hall, a cavernous wood-paneled room with a high ceiling. Dean had been sitting two rows ahead of him. Partway through the concert their eyes met and something clicked. Later, it seemed natural that they should talk over a glass of wine. It also seemed natural that they would go to bed together and, in a matter of weeks, fall deeply in love.

He set his wine glass on the counter and swirled the spoon through the bubbling sauce. If it burned there'd be hell to pay. The Creole cottage was a hundred years old, but the kitchen was state-of-the-art. Dean wanted to buy it, but given Belinda's moods, he was reluctant. Three years ago she had suddenly decided to move to New Orleans. She could just as easily decide to move somewhere else.

Dean crept up behind him and stood on tiptoes to kiss his neck. "Guess what's for dessert?"

"What?"

"Me, if you're lucky," Dean chortled, and danced away when Jake pinched his butt.

"Best dessert I'll ever have," he said, and meant it. Dean flashed an impish grin. Maybe they wouldn't fight after all.

"This sauce smells fantastic. I don't know how you do it."

Dean shrugged, his nonchalance belied by the warm glow in his eyes. "I love to cook. If you love something, you should do it well."

"You should open your own restaurant."

"Never. Then it would be work, not fun."

"But you're so creative and artistic. You should go to art school."

"Where?" Dean said, somber-eyed. "There's no art school in New Orleans." He picked up his empty wine glass and frowned. "You forgot to open another bottle of wine."

He hadn't forgotten. Too much wine and Dean could get confrontational. While he set about opening another bottle of chardonnay Dean carried platters of sautéed trout and fresh asparagus to the dining table. He popped the cork on the wine and went in the dining room.

The oval table looked like something out of *House Beautiful.* Suffused in the rosy glow of two tall candles, gleaming silverware and fine china sat on a white linen tablecloth. He filled their wine glasses and sat down.

Dean flashed his impish grin. "As my Portuguese grandmother used to say: If you don't clean your plate I'll never cook for you again!"

He laughed, a laugh quickly silenced by the ring of the telephone.

"Ooooh, I wonder who that is? Wait. We're about to have dinner. The Queen Bee must need Jake to do something for her."

Acid burned his stomach. He left the table and went in the kitchen to take the call. Maybe it was his mother. But he knew it wasn't; on Saturday nights his parents watched Great Performances on PBS.

When he answered it was Belinda, of course.

"Jake, where are the plane tickets? I can't find mine."

"In the office on my desk. You were practicing when I left. I didn't want to disturb you."

"You're such a dear. Hold on while I make sure I can find them."

"Dean and I are eating dinner. The tickets are right on my desk."

"Oh. Okay. Sorry to interrupt. Give Dean a hug for me."

Fuming, he ended the call. Belinda could be incredibly self-centered. He loved her like the sister he'd never had, but she was beyond irritating sometimes, calling him anytime day or night about inconsequential things.

When he got back to the table, Dean was topping off his wine glass. "What did she want this time?"

"She couldn't find her plane tickets. Sorry for the interruption."

Ignoring the food, Dean lit another joint, his expression morose. "Why don't we get on a plane and go somewhere? You know . . . like the old married couple we're not."

"You know I can't do that. Not now. Not in my position."

"What position is that? Belinda's step-n-fetch-it? God forbid anyone should think her manager is gay."

Unwilling to look at his angry lover, he gazed into the orange-red flames of the candles. They'd had this argument before and the outcome was always the same. Dean went to bed angry. He sat up all night on the sofa, wishing he had the guts to do what Dean wanted.

"Dean, you know I love you more than anything in the world."

"So why can't we take a vacation? You and Belinda go places together."

"That's business."

"Out and about, but not *out*, right, Jake?" Leaning on the word for emphasis. "People think you're her lover. That's what she wants. You're the decoy. She fucks around with married men, because she's got no time for a husband. She's too busy being a star."

He gulped some wine. "It's part of my job, okay? And I love my job." He could be honest about that at least. He'd long ago concluded he was no soloist. He couldn't handle the performance anxiety. But he loved traveling, loved hobnobbing with orchestra managers, distinguished conductors and celebrated musicians like Andre Previn and Yo-Yo Ma.

"The money's good, too."

Dean said nothing, piercing him with a belligerent stare.

"Dean, you know how I feel about Belinda. She's like a sister—"

"No! She's like a mistress only you're not fucking her!" Dean's eyes blazed with fury. "You're thirty-four, Jake. You figured out you were gay when you were ten! What's the problem?"

"Easy for you to say. Your parents accept you—"

"Now they do, but my Catholic mother threw a fit when I came out. It took Dad a year to bring her around, with a lot of help from my sisters."

He reached across the table and squeezed Dean's hand. "You know how my mother is."

"No, I don't." Dean's eyes glistened with tears. "You met my family and they love you like a son. I've never met yours and I never will."

"Dean, you mean everything to me. I want us to be together forever. I love you more than you could possibly know."

"I love you too, but I hate that we never go places together."

He rose and circled the table, and kissed Dean on the lips. "Come on. Your magnificent meal's getting cold. Let's sit down and enjoy it."

"We never even go to a movie! You're too busy fawning over Belinda."

"We'll go tomorrow, I promise. No Belinda, no cell phone. You pick the movie."

Dean's eyes lit up. "It's a deal! No more wine for me, Jake. No more pot, either, dammit. I'm fresh out. I better go see my supplier on Monday."

"Be careful. If you get busted for—"

"I'm always careful and so is the kid. He's a NOCCA student. If he got caught, they'd expel him."

Silently, they devoured the gourmet dinner Dean had prepared, but Jake knew the truce was only temporary. Nine years he'd worked for Belinda. Maybe Dean was right. Time to find another job. He'd be perfectly happy as a church organist. Why not please himself for a change, instead of always making other people happy?

Dean gazed at him from across the table, his eyes liquid puddles of desire. "Want your Chocolate Tort now?"

How could he resist those eyes?

"Forget the tort. You're my dessert, Dean."

CHAPTER 4

Frank ordered a family-sized bucket of Popeye's chicken, extra mashed potatoes and cornbread, and swung around to the drive-up window. A siren whooped in the distance, a police car judging from the sound. Just another Saturday night in New Orleans. Thugs didn't take weekends off.

He didn't either, unless he had visitors. No visitor tonight, though.

An iron fist put a stranglehold on his gut. He wouldn't be seeing Dana this weekend or ever again. He'd met her during a homicide investigation last year. An adolescent psychotherapist, Dr. Dana Swenson lived in Omaha. Long distance romances were tough enough, brutal since Katrina. Last week she'd called to tell him she had reunited with her ex-husband. Her hot-shot attorney husband, hospitalized with a heart attack, had wooed her back.

He scratched the jagged scar on his chin, a gash that had taken ten stitches to close on his sixth birthday after a kid dared him to ride no-hands down a hill on his new bike. With predictable results.

The scar was his emotional barometer, itching whenever his thoughts were in turmoil. The end of a relationship was always gut-wrenching. From past experience, he knew that work was the antidote. It didn't end the pain but it kept him busy, too busy to fixate on what might have been.

Two days after the Lakeview robbery they had hysterical headlines in the media, politicians demanding an arrest, and no leads. The cop was in guarded condition, unable to be questioned. Their only description of the robbers was from the clerk: a wide-body gunslinger and a skinny kid with dreads. Useless. The hostage had died after the thugs dumped her out of the getaway car, a fact the media had pounced upon, playing up the black-on-white-crime angle.

He'd dug up some background on Chantelle. Pre-Katrina she had lived with her mother, a known crack addict, at Iberville. Six years ago her mother had born a son by the man who'd lived with them until Katrina. The man had taken his son to Birmingham. Chantelle's mother wound up at the Superdome, then the Convention Center, finally got bused to Houston with the other refugees. Without Chantelle, no record of the girl on file.

No arrest record, either. That was a plus, but he would never forget her desolate expression when she thanked him. Nobody gave a damn about a teenaged girl on her own or the black kid gunned down at Iberville. His parents were AWOL too, all kinds of teenagers roaming the city these days unsupervised by any adult. Nothing but bad news all around.

The takeout window slid open, emitting odors of deep-fry cooking oil and chicken. "Big bucket of fried chicken," said a young black woman in a Popeye's cap, "extra mashed and cornbread."

He paid for the order, set the Popeye's bag behind the passenger seat and drove off. At the next corner he turned right and parked behind a beat-up Chevy sedan. Angela hopped out and scurried to his car, a slender black woman with corn-rowed hair, dressed in cutoff jeans and a T-shirt.

She got in and flashed him a smile. "Somethin' smells good."

"The usual. Fried chicken, extra mashed potatoes and cornbread."

Three years ago Angela had been arrested for hooking, got off with probation and got out of the life. She was a high-school dropout, but she didn't do drugs, so he'd recruited her to be his CI, told her to get her GED and find a decent job. Now she was twenty-four, with two-year-old twins and no husband, cleaning rooms at a hotel. He never paid her for information, but he often bought her food. She and the boys lived with her mother.

"Thanks, Frank. The kids love Popeye's chicken." She pulled out a cigarette and lit up.

"How are they doing? They must be getting big."

She chuckled. "Doing great. Jamal's talking up a storm. Rasheed, he's into everything. Got a mind of his own, like his daddy."

The guy that left you holding the bag.

"What's shaking on the street these days?"

"Not a whole lot, far as I know."

"You know anybody that lives at Iberville?"

"Nah. I grew up in the St. Bernard project. We didn't hang with the Iberville kids." She puffed her cigarette. "But I know who runs it."

"Who?" He already had a name, but he'd let her tell him, make her feel important.

"AK-Forty-Seven. He run it before Katrina, he runs it now."

"Him and his crew selling drugs?"

"What I hear, you get most anything you want over there. Weed, crack, uppers, downers, X." She looked at him. "I don't do that stuff, Frank."

"I know you don't and you better not start."

She smiled, teeth gleaming white against her dark skin like a model in a toothpaste ad. "No drugs for me. Got my boys to think of."

"A kid got shot at Iberville two days ago."

"What I hear, things are tough over there."

"What do you hear about the Lakeview robbery?"

"Ain't heard nothin."

"There's a big reward out to finger the robbers. Ten large."

"Can't spend it in hell. Don't need it in heaven."

"Somebody put the word out to keep quiet?"

She stared straight ahead, puffing her cigarette.

"Who wants it kept quiet?"

"I dunno, Frank, honest. I just, you know, talk to my friends. They say the cops gonna pin it on some black kids, white lady died, white cop in the hospital." She tossed the butt out the window. "Be hell to pay, anybody finds out I'm talking to you."

"No one's going to find out." He pulled out a photo of Chantelle. "You know this girl?"

She tilted the photo to let the streetlight shine on it and shook her head. "Never seen her before. Pretty girl. She a hooker?"

"No, just a messed-up teenager. She's fifteen. Chantelle Wilson."

Angela gnawed her bottom lip. "She mixed up with that robbery?"

"She's missing. Her mother's worried." He didn't want to lie to Angela and rarely did, but he needed information.

"Uh-huh. Okay, I'll ask around." Facing him with a flirtatious smile, she said, "How come you working on a Saturday night, Frank? We could go someplace and have a good time."

"Angela, I've got a daughter your age. You're smart and attractive. Find some guy your own age and—"

"Get real, Frank. Guys my age be doing drugs, selling drugs or in jail." She heaved a sigh. "My moms never married my daddy, and I ain't never gonna find a guy to marry me, neither."

His heart ached for her. Much of what she said was true. Few black men wanted to take responsibility for another man's kids. He reached behind the seat for the Popeye's bag. "Get your GED and find a job at Target or Starbucks, some guy comes in, sees you at the register he'll fall in love with you." Hoping this would actually happen.

She took the Popeye's bag and opened the car door. "You best get yourself a girlfriend, Frank. Working on a Saturday night? You need some lovin', baby." Her high-pitched giggle trailed her to her car.

He smiled ruefully. Angela was right: Get a new girlfriend because Dana Swenson had kissed him off.

———

He checked the side-view mirror and eased away from the curb outside Arrivals. Tons of traffic on a Saturday night, people eager to party in the Big Easy. The sleek black limo was insured but his boss had made it clear he'd have to pay the deductible for any damages. A thousand dollars.

Fuck-all! That would wipe him out. He was already mired in debt.

"Hotel International," his passenger instructed from the back seat.

"Right-O, sir. I'll have you there in a jiffy." He studied the man in the rearview, a sourpuss with horned-rim spectacles and lots of luggage. He sucked the knuckle he'd scraped heaving the two heavy suitcases and matching suit-bag into the trunk. "First time in New Orleans, sir?"

"No."

"Too bad. I was hoping to show you around." *And get a big tip.* "I showed Nick Cage a few hot spots." A lie, though he had seen the actor once outside his Garden District mansion. "When Sean Penn was here filming *All the King's Men* I was his driver." He wished.

"I'm really tired. It was a long flight."

He got the message: *Shut up and don't bother me.* Fine. Let Sourpuss find his own way around. And if he wanted his bags schlepped into the hotel, he'd better have a big tip ready. Alert for careless drivers, he eased onto the I-10 and focused on London. The airfare had maxed out one credit card and reserving a hotel room for three nights had cost 420 pounds.

"That's nine-hundred-thirty dollars," the silly twit had said in her cheery voice. As if nine-hundred bucks were a pittance to stay in her precious hotel.

"Could you turn the AC down? It's freezing back here."

"Certainly, sir. Whatever makes you comfortable."

No thank-you from Sourpuss. His fists clenched reflexively around the wheel as he pulled into the high-speed lane. Forget Sourpuss. Focus on Belinda. He envisioned the smooth white flesh of her breasts, imagining how her nipples would stiffen when he rubbed his cock through her coppery hair, imagining the other delights he had in store for her.

By the time he pulled up to the hotel, his crotch was throbbing with desire. He opened the door for Sourpuss and muscled his luggage out of the trunk. Sourpuss gestured for him to carry the luggage inside. As if he was a servant. He hauled the bags inside and set them beside a plush sofa. If this didn't merit a big tip, what did? "That will be forty dollars, sir."

Sourpuss handed him two twenties and added a two-dollar tip.

A flush burned his neck, flamed upward and blazed his cheeks.

He wanted to kill the bastard. Wanted to stick a dagger into the bastard's eye and watch it burst and spew fluids and blood.

He pasted on a smile. "Thank you, sir. Enjoy your stay."

CHAPTER 5

A faint sound floated down the hall.

Chantelle froze, one foot in the kitchen, one in the hall, her heart beating her ribs like a drummer in a Mardi Gras parade. Mama would whup her ass if she caught her out of bed at this hour, the woman no bigger than a flea but had murder in her eyes, anybody screwed up.

She held her breath. Heard it again. A soft footstep. Then another.

A floorboard creaked.

Please, God, don't let it be Mama.

A ghostly shadow appeared in the shadowy darkness of the hall—her roommate—the little bitty Hispanic girl who'd run away from home, fifteen years old, knocked around by her uncle before he knocked her up, belly swollen, seven months along now.

"Wha' you doin', Chantelle?"

"Shh. Ain't doin' nuthin. Go on back to bed 'fore Mama hears us."

Ramona gazed up at her with sad brown eyes.

"G'won," Chantelle whispered, gesturing with her hand.

Ramona shook her head, eyes sorrowful. "Don't leave, Chantelle."

Last night Ramona had blurted out her sad story, said she couldn't talk to the other two girls, one busted for shoplifting, the other selling pills, hard-ass bitches thinkin' they were hot shit 'cause they'd been here two months and had the biggest room. She only spoke to them at the dinner table to be polite. *Please pass the beans and rice, Tameka. Please pass the milk, Linyatta.*

'Bout made her sick, the bitches giving her hard-eyed stares and fake-smiles. Ramona was different, a sweet little girl, a baby about to have a baby. Going nowhere. Getting knocked up was a dead-end, forget about singing. She and Antoine always used a condom when they made love.

She gripped Ramona's arm, whispered, "I'm outta here. Don't you dare snitch on me. Morning comes you didn't hear nuthin, didn't see nuthin."

Bright shiny tears glistened in Ramona's dark eyes. "Good luck, Chantelle. Go with God."

"You too, baby. Now go on back to bed real quiet so's you don't wake nobody." She gave her a shove and Ramona shuffled back down the hall toward their room.

She slipped into the kitchen, the moon shining through the window over the sink, enough light to see her way to the back door. Sweat dampened her palms. If the cops caught her, they'd put her in the lockup. She felt in her pocket for the card the cop had given her.

Detective Renzi wasn't so bad. Not like some of them.

Silent as smoke, she drifted toward the door, tracing her fingers along the counter. *Lord be praised!* There was Mama's cell phone plugged into an outlet, charged up and ready to go, a sign from God calling out to her! She unplugged the cord, wrapped it around the thick plug, stuffed it in one pocket of her jeans, put the cell phone in the other.

Bust out of here and call Antoine, halleluiah!

She got the deadbolt open no problem. Hard part was the Yale lock. She twisted the knob with one hand, worked the little button with the other to keep it open. Gave the door a gentle tug so the wooden door wouldn't creak.

A shrill alarm sounded, *Jesus-God,* loud enough to wake the dead!

Fear clawed her throat.

She blasted through the screen door, down the steps and ran like the wind, didn't stop till she rounded the corner on the next block, heart pounding, gasping for breath, wanting to scream: *I'm free! I'm free!*

But she wasn't. Not with Mama's alarm shrieking, cops headed this way right now probably, or a National Guard hummer full of men with machine guns. She touched Mama's cell phone, aching to call Antoine, desperate to hear his voice. *Please God let him be safe.*

No. Better wait till she got home. Better stay off the sidewalk too, so nobody in a passing car saw her. In the distance a dog barked. She hated dogs, sensing you were near and yapping.

That's what tipped off the detective up in Lakeview.

She ran in the opposite direction, cut through a yard between two dark houses. At Rampart Street she stopped to catch her breath, Interstate traffic thundering above her head, lights blazing in the Shell station on the corner, stay away from there, cops stopping in all hours of the night to buy coffee.

Sheltered by the overpass, she darted across one lane of Rampart, hid behind a concrete abutment, let two cars go by and crossed to the opposite side.

A siren whooped, coming her way.

Her heart slammed her chest. She ducked around a corner onto a side street, ran past two boarded-up houses and spotted a bike leaning against the porch of a dilapidated cottage. No fenders, but the tires looked okay. The windows of the cottage were dark, no light inside, not even a creepy blue flicker like when you watched TV in the dark.

She ran up the walk and grabbed the bike and wheeled it to the street, teeth clenched, heart pounding, expecting a shout any second: *Stop thief!* She ran beside the bike to get it going, hopped on and peddled away. Get herself home fast as her legs could pump, call Antoine and see if he was okay.

Didn't want to think what she'd do if he wasn't. She'd read the story in Mama's newspaper. AK had shot a cop and taken a white lady hostage. Now the lady was dead. Bad news. About as bad as it could get.

Tears burned her eyes. *Please God, let Antoine be safe.*

The sirens wailed, louder now, and closer.

———

Monday, 16 October 8:30 A.M.

"Thanks for coming in, Mr. Ziegler. I was about to call you," Frank said, a preemptive strike to pacify the visibly angry man. "Sorry I didn't get back to you, but it's been hectic around here."

Ziegler gazed at him, stony-faced. "I read the papers."

Like everyone else in the city.

He glanced at Jim Whitworth, a white-haired florid-faced man seated at the desk to his right, the veteran detective working the phone, putting his own caseload on hold to troll for leads on the Lakeview robbery.

He took out the Incident Report, the one with Ziegler's name on it because Belinda didn't want him to use hers. A beautiful flutist with secrets.

Ziegler fingered his beard with long slender fingers, his nails bitten to the quick. "There are some things you should know. Things I didn't want to say in front of Belinda."

He said nothing, waited for the bombshell.

"Belinda's parents and her brother were killed in a car accident."

Not what he was expecting. "I see. When was this? Recently?"

"No. On Columbus Day in 1993. Last Thursday was the thirteenth anniversary. That's why we had dinner together. We do it every year."

Thirteenth anniversary. He did a quick calculation. Belinda had to have been a teenager when her parents died. "Where was the accident?"

"In Connecticut. Her parents were taking her older brother back to Yale after the Columbus Day weekend. A drunk driver got on I-95 going the wrong way and hit them head-on. Belinda's brother and father died at the scene. Her mother died at the hospital."

Such tragedies happened all the time, but the self-confident women he'd met Thursday night had given no hint she had survived one. She was focused on her career. Belinda had big ambitions. There were a million flute players, not as attractive as Belinda maybe, but competition in the music world was fierce. Only a handful of soloists achieved stardom.

"Blaine was a prodigy too, on French horn. Belinda was devastated, but she won't talk to the press about it. She doesn't want to be viewed as some sort of pathetic victim." Ziegler shrugged. "Her words, not mine."

"And Thursday's incident is related to this how?"

Ziegler gnawed what was left of his thumbnail. "I screen Belinda's mail. I didn't want to say this in front of her, but she's gotten some creepy notes."

"Creepy in what way?"

"Saying how he loved her lips and her hair and . . . sick stuff like that."

He said nothing, digesting the information. Over the weekend he had visited her website. The photos were stunning: Belinda posed with her flute in a low-cut gown, lips parted seductively. Sexy. The Internet was great for some things, not so good for others. Lots of weirdoes out there.

Beside him, Whitworth slammed down the phone and muttered, "Useless." Whitworth looked over and shook his head. "Nobody's talking."

"Par for the course," Frank said. Except for Ziegler. Ziegler wanted to tell him Belinda's life story. He wanted to go talk to Chantelle.

"When did the notes start, Mr. Ziegler?"

"A few years ago when we were in Boston. In one note, he asked her to meet him outside the stage door entrance to Symphony Hall. It's on—"

"I know where it is, I used to work that district. Were they signed?"

"Yes. *Your adoring fan, B.* Just the initial."

"I need to see them. When can you bring them in?"

A flush rose on Ziegler's cheeks. "I threw them away." He spread his hands in supplication. "I didn't want Belinda to see them. It would have been too upsetting, you know? Like, B is for Blaine."

Maybe. Or maybe Boyfriend was a conspiracy nut.

"She got a note last week postmarked New Orleans."

"Did you throw that one away too?"

"Yes." A muscle worked in Ziegler's jaw. "A week before the anniversary? It would have put Belinda over the edge! She's a high-strung soloist. Under enormous pressure."

Frank wanted to smack him. "Tell me what it said."

"*You know how much I love you, Belinda. Soon we'll be together. Love, B,*" Ziegler said. "Postmarked New Orleans, a week before the anniversary. And the night of the anniversary a car comes out of nowhere and almost hits Belinda. Someone tried to kill her!"

Whitworth looked over, cocked an eyebrow that said: *You got a problem?*

Frank waved him off and gave Ziegler a hard stare. "You seem ultra-protective of Belinda. Is she your girlfriend?"

Ziegler blinked rapidly and swallowed, his Adam's apple bobbing up and down. "No. More like a sister. We met when I was a grad student at New England Conservatory. Belinda was studying flute there. We met in the hall one day, got talking and became friends. After her family was killed in the accident, Belinda was terribly distraught. She poured her heart out to me."

He tried to make sense of the blitzkrieg of information. Was someone stalking Belinda? Or did Ziegler have an overactive imagination? He didn't buy the *like-a-sister* disclaimer. He studied Ziegler's well-groomed mustache and beard, the long slender fingers, the dark sorrowful eyes. Maybe Ziegler was gay. That would explain the odd interactions he had observed: tension between them, but no sexual vibes, none of the usual touching by lovers.

Ziegler leaned back, looking relieved, as though he'd gotten a ten-ton truck off his chest. Maybe he had. Or maybe the notes were a fairytale.

"I want you to tell her about the notes."

"Now?" Ziegler gasped. "She's got a huge performance in London this weekend!"

"Listen," he said, leaning on the word. "If someone is stalking her, she may be in danger. I'd like to see *all* the notes to determine if they came from the same person, but you threw them away. Tell her about the notes. *Today.* If she gets any more, bring them to me. *Right away.*"

His cell phone chimed. He checked the ID and answered.

"Detective Frank?" Mama LeBlanc said in her something's-wrong voice. "I know you not gonna like this, but Chantelle? She's gone."

"Gone?" A sick feeling invaded his gut. "When?"

"She was here for bed check at midnight, but my security alarm went off at three this morning. When I roust the girls outta bed, Chantelle's gone."

He didn't want to think about where she'd gone or what she was doing. If Chantelle was mixed up in the Lakeview robbery, she was running with some bad hombres, a fifteen-year-old girl on her own in a city full of thugs, with no one to protect her.

"Okay, Mama. I'll be right over." He punched off, silently cursing.

Whitworth looked over. "The girl split?"

"Looks like it." To Ziegler he said, "I've got to deal with an emergency. When I get back, I'll write an Incident Report about what you've told me."

Ziegler gnawed his thumbnail. Worrying about how to tell Belinda about the notes, he assumed. If they even existed. He had worse things to worry about. He handed two business cards to Ziegler.

"Give one to Belinda. If she gets any more notes, I want to see them. Tell her to call me if anything unusual happens. Anything at all."

———

"Someone's been sending you weird notes," Jake said in his doom-and-gloom voice, his dark eyes somber.

She stared at him, horrified. First the note on her doorstep, then an ugly voicemail message, now weird notes? Had that awful man revealed her secret to Jake? "Why didn't you show them to me? What did they say?"

"I didn't want to upset you."

"Tell me what they *said!*"

"They were nice enough at first, typical fan mail, raving about what a great flutist you are. Then he started saying how much he loved your eyes and your hair and your . . . lips."

A sick feeling cramped her stomach and her palms grew sweaty. Thunder rumbled in the distance as she sank onto her mother's rocking chair. Afternoon thunderstorms were frequent in New Orleans. She hated rainy weather. Nothing good ever happened when it rained. Thirteen years ago her family had died on a rain-slicked highway.

"Show them to me."

Jake cleared his throat. "I can't. I threw them away."

"You threw them *away*? Why?"

"That's why I screen your mail, remember? To weed out the crazies and send form letters to your fans. I was just doing my job!"

Gooseflesh crawled down her arms. "How many were there?"

"Fifteen or twenty, I guess, over the past four or five years."

"Four or five *years*?"

Jake nodded.

"And you threw them away. And told me nothing."

"Belinda, I stood by you when your family died, and when you begged me to work for you, I chucked my own career to be your assistant or whatever the hell it is that I am. Tour manager, publicist and chief cook and bottle washer!"

His anguished expression made her melt. "Please, Jake, I can't stand it when you get upset. I'm making a fuss because, well, it *does* upset me if someone's sending me notes and—"

"The last one was different. The others were mailed in Boston. The one last week—"

"On the anniversary?" Her heart slammed her chest, vicious hammer-strokes pounding her ribs.

"No, the week before. Postmarked New Orleans. It said *You know how much I love you, Belinda. Soon we'll be together. Love, B.* Just the initial."

She felt like a horse had kicked her. Impossible. How could it be?

"I know this is upsetting but—"

"Upsetting! It's fucking unbelievable! Did you throw that one away too?"

Jake ducked his head, avoiding her gaze. "Yes. Detective Renzi wasn't happy about it, either."

Aghast, she said, "You told Detective Renzi? Why?"

"Bee, you don't get it. At the restaurant some maniac tried to kill you."

She clenched her hands around the arms of the chair and rocked harder. How could this happen right before the biggest concert of her life?

"Jake, you really let me down."

He flinched as if she'd slapped him. "I let you down? When have I ever let you down? I sacrifice my own happiness for you all the time. You call me at home anytime of the day or night. You did it on Saturday. Dean and I can't even eat dinner together in peace."

She stared at him. Really, did she make that many demands?

"Ten years ago I had a good job in New York, organist and choir master at a cathedral. I've got a Masters degree from New England Conservatory. Maybe it's time I pursued other options."

Pursued other options. A Titanic-sized iceberg lodged in her stomach.

Jake would never leave her, would he?

"Detective Renzi said to call if anything unusual happens." Jake handed her a business card. "We're both upset right now. Finish practicing. Let's talk later when we've calmed down." He turned and left the studio.

Finish practicing? How could she practice with all these hideous distractions? Voicemail threats. A note on her doorstep. Weird fan mail, signed with Blaine's initial. And now Jake, her oldest and dearest friend, her only friend, was threatening to abandon her.

Her throat closed up and tears fogged her vision. She blinked them back and studied the card Jake had given her. Frank's card.

She pictured him seated at his desk. His craggy features, rock-solid jaw and penetrating eyes gave him an aura of strength. Always a turn-on. If Jake told him about the notes, he must have told him about her family, too. The thought galled her. Maybe she should talk to Frank herself, and tell him about the note and the voicemail threat. But not until she returned from London.

London was crucial, the biggest concert of her career.

If she gave a perfect performance—and she had no doubt that she would—it was sure to win her a fabulous recording contract and the international fame that went with it.

CHAPTER 6

Mama LeBlanc had a nasty gleam in her eye when she waved him into the tidy kitchen of her Creole cottage. A big stainless-steel pot on the stove gave off a delectable spicy odor, whirled through the room by a ceiling fan. Barely five feet tall, Mama had a big heart, sixty years old and still a bundle of energy, nary a wrinkle on her milk-chocolate skin.

It never ceased to amaze him how a woman so tiny could manage four delinquent teens at once, as she often had. But not this time.

"Chantelle ran away," Mama said, frowning up at him, her hands on her hips. "Stole my cell phone, too. Brand new one I got last month, left it on the counter overnight to charge."

"That might be a break. Can you write down the number and provider for me?"

"Sure can." Mama gestured at a wooden stool by the door to the dining room. "Take a load off, Detective Frank. Want coffee? I made a fresh pot."

"No thanks, but you go ahead." On the wall above the stool, a cork bulletin board held a list of emergency numbers, his included. Tacked beside it was a chore schedule—Take out trash, Clean bathrooms, Do laundry—mapped out in a time-grid with penciled-in names.

"What about the other girls? Do they know anything?"

"They do, they ain't telling me." She came over and gave him a slip of paper with her cell phone information, then leaned against the counter and sipped from a mug of coffee. "Ramona might give you something. She's young, pregnant and scared. The other two girls got, you know, at-ti-tude."

"Tell me about Chantelle. How did she act while she was here?"

"That's the thing, Detective Frank. I thought we were gettin' on okay. Chantelle seemed like a nice girl. Polite, you know, please and thank you, no backtalk like some of 'em. When I asked about her family, she said her moms was in Houston, last she heard."

"Last she heard. Sad."

"You got no idea the sad stories I hear." She went to the stove and lifted the lid on the big pot, releasing a steamy aroma. After stirring the contents with a wooden spoon, she replaced the lid.

"Something smells good," he said.

"Creole gumbo. Want some?" Mama grinned. "Nah, you're too busy. The attitude twins are in their room watching TV or listening to the crap that passes for music these days. Ramona was bunking with Chantelle in the back bedroom. Come on, I'll take you."

As they walked down the hall he heard television voices. Mama stopped at the first door on the left and opened it without knocking. "Shut off the TV, girls. Detective Renzi wants to talk to you, so be polite and speak up."

He stepped into a large square room with two neatly-made twin beds, the corners of their blue bedspreads squarely tucked. The whole room was shipshape, no clutter on the dresser, no dust on the mirror above it. An older-model TV sat on a metal stand. Slouched on blue-plastic armchairs facing the now-dark television screen were two girls, one dark-skinned, the other lighter. Neither looked happy to see him.

He gave them a reassuring smile. "Hello, ladies. Let's start with names."

"Tameka," said the dark-skinned girl with the dreadlocks and the round chubby face.

"Linyatta," said the other, gazing at him with mistrustful eyes.

"What time was lights out last night?"

"Midnight," Tameka said. "Mama came in and tol' us shut off the TV and go to sleep."

"Uh-huh. Did you?"

An insolent smile appeared on Linyatta's face, quickly suppressed.

"What'd you do, hit the mute button and stay up all night watching a silent movie?"

"Not all night," Linyatta said. "Just till the movie was over."

"What time was that?"

"Around one-thirty," Tameka said.

"What happened after that? Did you hear anything?"

"We went to sleep, woke up when the alarm went off."

"Did Chantelle talk to you about running away?"

"Didn't talk to us 'bout nuthin," Linyatta said. "Snotty bitch."

He believed it. These girls had rap sheets. Chantelle wasn't likely to have confided in them. "Thank you, ladies," he said. "Don't get any ideas about going AWOL like Chantelle."

Linyatta waved the TV remote at him. "Can we watch TV now?"

"Sure." He left the room, depressed beyond measure. Both girls were high-school dropouts, nothing to look forward to but lives of crime and dope and making babies with gangbangers.

And that's how Chantelle would wind up if he didn't find her.

At the far end of the wood-paneled hall Mama stood outside another door. "Told you nothing, right? Hard cases, those two, but you might get something from Ramona."

Mama opened the door and they entered the room. A Hispanic girl with an angelic face and large dark eyes lay in bed, propped against two pillows, wearing an over-sized cotton shirt with a big bulge, clearly pregnant.

"This is Detective Renzi," Mama said, "here about Chantelle. If you care about your friend, you best tell him what you know about where she's at."

He sat on the empty bed opposite hers. "Did you see Chantelle leave?"

"Didn't see nuthin, didn't hear nuthin," Ramona said, twisting the white bed-sheet with thin bony fingers.

"Uh-huh. But I bet you got to know her a little bit, rooming with her for a few days. Did she talk to you? Tell you about her friends?"

The girl shook her head, hugging her swollen belly with stick-thin arms, gazing at him. Tears filled her large dark eyes. "She gone."

"Did she say where she was going?"

Ramona's eyes overflowed and tears ran down her face.

"She jus' gone. Left me all alone."

At one-thirty Frank drove into Iberville and parked his unmarked Chevy Caprice in front of a three-story red-brick building. After Katrina many of New Orleans' public housing projects had been scheduled for demolition. Not Iberville, a two-block collection of buildings grouped in around cement courtyards. It reminded him of the projects he'd worked as a Boston detective, except that here plywood covered many of the windows.

About as charming as a sardine factory.

He walked into a courtyard, absorbing the vibe, weeds peeping through cracked cement, security lights on poles with electric wires that carried no juice. At night the complex would be pitch dark. A scary place for a teenaged girl on her own. Now the midday sun baked weedy grass littered with empty beer cans, crumpled candy wrappers and fast-food containers. On the cement were spray-painted gang tags, Day-Glo squiggles marking their territory.

A dilapidated swing-set stood in the center of the courtyard, no kids on the swings. No plywood on the windows facing the courtyard, either. Some were open, but the courtyard was eerily quiet. No babies crying, no kiddie voices, no music floating through the windows.

A creepy sensation crawled down his neck. How many eyes were watching him through those windows? His SIG-Sauer was a reassuring weight in the holster strapped to his right ankle, but it wouldn't help much if some banger decided to pop him from a second-floor window.

Sudden motion caught his eye, jumping his heart rate.

Two black kids emerged from between two buildings, shuffling along in their Nike's or whatever footwear the 'bangers favored these days, heads bobbing to sounds from the I-Pods plugged into their ears. Both wore loose T-shirts and baggy pants that hung off their skinny asses.

Baggy enough to conceal a gun.

They saw him but feigned disinterest, assuming slouched postures as he approached. He'd changed into scruffy jeans and an old T-shirt, but they knew he was a cop. A spiderweb tat covered the taller one's neck. The other had tattoos on each forearm, ugly daggers dripping crimson blood.

"Hey, guys, I'm looking for someone. Maybe you can help me out."

Got back dead-eyed stares. He showed them Chantelle's mug shot, the full-face version with the height-chart background edited out.

"Seen this girl around here lately?"

"Uh-uh," grunted the tall one, Spiderweb, avoiding his gaze.

"How about you?" he said to Dagger. "She lived here before Katrina."

Dagger pointed, extending his forearm to display his bloody-dagger tat. "That her pitcher?"

"Yes. Do you know her?"

"Don't know nuthin, Mr. Po-leece-man," Spiderweb said. He jerked his head at Dagger and the pair sauntered away.

After watching them swagger across the courtyard, he mounted the steps of the nearest building and entered a dark hallway that stank of every foul odor imaginable: stale cigarette smoke, spoiled food, vomit and urine.

A swarm of gnats buzzed his head. He swatted them away.

Halfway down the hall he came to an open door and stuck his head inside. The stench got worse. Two chrome kitchen chairs with torn plastic seats stood by a window, surrounded by mounds of trash that included a broken crack pipe. Stuck in a crevice between the filthy carpet and the baseboard was a used syringe with a bent needle.

Appalled by the squalor, he flashed on Chantelle's roommate, Ramona, fourteen-years-old and pregnant, about to have a baby fathered by her uncle. Not much older than Janelle Robinson, a black girl in Boston who'd hung out with bangers and wound up dead. Different project, same sad story.

Before Katrina, 673 of Iberville's 836 units had been occupied. Now only 200 housed legal residents. Many of the others were occupied by drug dealers and crackheads. Forget finding someone to help him locate Chantelle. The bangers wouldn't tell him anything, and the legal residents were too scared to talk. He scratched the scar on his chin. If Chantelle was hiding in one of the eight-hundred-plus units, he'd never find her.

Lost in thought, he pushed through the exit door into the sunlight.

"Yo!" a deep voice called. "Help you with sump'n?"

A young black man with milk-chocolate skin leaned against the side of the building. He was five-ten or so and barrel-chested with powerful arms and shoulders. Looked like he'd just worked out, the skin on his shaven head gleaming with sweat, approaching him now with a self-assured swagger. Over the obligatory baggy pants, he wore a white dress shirt. Gold cufflinks at the wrists glinted with diamond chips. Heavy bling. Surprisingly delicate features decorated his face: almond-shaped eyes, a narrow nose, thin lips.

Frank showed him the photograph. "Have you seen this girl around?"

The man stared at him with dead flat eyes. "You a cop?"

His voice was deep and resonant, sounded like James Earl Jones.

"Detective Frank Renzi, NOPD. And you are?"

A big smirk. "Mos' folks call me AK."

Known to NOPD as Atticus Kroll, age twenty-four, gang leader and drug kingpin. Also known as AK-47 due to his preference for that particular weapon of destruction.

"You live here, AK?"

"Hardly nobody lives here. The city ain't got no money to fix the place."

He tapped the photograph. "Have you seen this girl? She lived here before Katrina."

AK gazed at him, face closed, eyes hard. "Never seen her before."

The next moment an insolent smile parted his lips, and a gold tooth glittered at the front of his mouth.

"Nice tooth, AK. The pharmaceutical business must be good."

The smile disappeared, the eyes hardened, and AK stalked away.

Thursday, 19 October

"I better go," Antoine whispered. "It's almost midnight."

"Stay a couple more minutes." Spooned against him on the mattress, Chantelle felt his velvety-soft lips brush her neck. She loved the feel of his bare skin against hers. Loved it even more when he reached back and stroked her cheek. He'd brought her two bags of groceries, including a big package of Doritos, her sweet lover-man buying her favorite treat.

Beside them on the floor, a flickering candle sat on an aluminum pie plate, the only light in her bedroom, but enough to see the love in his eyes, the cinnamon-scented candle masking the awful stink in her apartment.

"Stay all night if I could, but Uncle Jonas be home from work soon."

She stroked his cheek. "Thank God the cops didn't catch you."

"You got that right. Jesus-God-A'mighty, thought I'd die when AK shot that cop, idiot got the brains of a flea, you know, shoot first, think later."

"Wasn't your fault, Antoine."

"Maybe not, but the cops'll blame me, just the same. Woman died 'cause AK only cares about saving his own ass. I shoulda never gone with him."

The truest words ever spoken. Only reason her lover man did was 'cuz AK had told him he'd protect her. Bullshit. AK was the one bothering her.

"I want you to go back to that foster home. You be safe there."

"No! Then I won't be able to see you."

He kissed her mouth, a soul kiss that made her tingle. "I love you, Chantelle. I want you to be safe. Call that cop and tell him what happened."

"You crazy? No way I be telling a cop you was in on that robbery. They put you in jail, you won't be playing your saxophone no more."

"You don't someone else might. You don't think AK be keeping quiet about it, do you? Be serious. Every guy hangs out here knows it was him."

She blinked back tears, felt a sick-ache blossom in her stomach. "I go back to that foster home, they bust me for running off, and that trespassing charge. Besides, I can't sing over there. Can't meet you someplace so's we can make music together. And make love."

"AK finds you here, he'll shut you up, make sure you don't talk."

"I'll live on the street then. Lots of sistas do it."

Antoine's eyes got shiny and wet, looked like he might cry. "No. It's too dangerous. I'll ask my uncle if you can stay at his house."

A warm glow swept over her. Big risk for her lover-man, telling his uncle about her. "Tell your uncle, he pick up the phone, call your Daddy in

Houston and that be the end of that." She kissed his cheek. "I'm okay here. You know me, quiet as a mouse 'cept when I sing."

Antoine held her tight and whispered, "I love you, Chantelle."

"I love you too, Antoine, love you with all my heart."

He rolled away from her and sat up. "What's that?"

"What? I don't hear nothin." But then she did, a scratchy sound, metal against metal. Her heart jolted, beating fast and crazy like a bug at a light bulb. "Somebody messin' with the lock."

With frantic haste, they put on their clothes as footsteps sounded, then AK's deep distinctive voice. "Where y'at, Chantelle? I know you in here."

Her heart exploded in a spasm of fear, her body shaking like a tree in a hurricane. Antoine wrapped his arms around her. It didn't stop her trembling.

AK barged into the room with a big flashlight. Smiled his evil smile to show off his gold tooth. "Time you and me had a talk, Chantelle."

"What we need to talk for?" Hating the tremor in her voice.

"Let her be, AK," Antoine said. "I did what you wanted."

"Where you at when the cop showed up, girl? You 'sposed to warn us, anybody comes."

"How'd she know he's a cop?" Antoine said. "Wasn't wearing a uniform."

"Neither was the one came here Monday looking for her." Smiling his evil smile. "Had a mighty fine picture of you, axed me and my boys if we seen you lately. How come?"

"I don't know, AK. Honest." Heart racing, hands wet with sweat.

"Why he looking for you, this cop? How come he knows you?"

Tears blurred her eyes and sweat prickled her temples.

"I-I-I don't know, AK, I swear."

Antoine said, "Maybe the Houston cops asked him to look for her."

"Yeah," she said. "My moms in Houston, don't know where I'm at."

AK ran his tongue over his gold tooth and smiled. "You get yo'self some nooky tonight, Antoine? Maybe I get me some, too. AK-Forty-Seven runs Iberville, gets to fuck any pussy he wants, Chantelle included."

"Don't even think about it." Antoine grabbed her arm and pulled her toward the door. "C'mon, Chantelle, we best be going."

She was so scared she was afraid she would wet her pants.

AK glared at them. At the last second, he stepped aside to let them pass.

"Either one a you talk to the cops, you dead."

CHAPTER 7

London Friday, 20 October

Applause thundered through the Royal Festival Hall, rolling waves of sound like a jet plane racing down the runway. He leaped to his feet, eyes fixed on the rise and fall of Belinda's breasts. His beloved was winded after her demanding encore. A brilliant stroke.

The Brits loved Gershwin, and her spectacular variations on "I've Got Rhythm" had won her another standing ovation. The first, after her stunning performance of the Khatchatourian, had lasted three minutes. She'd graciously asked the orchestra to rise, but the players had refused, joining the audience in applause. The Diva in all her glory.

She bowed deeply and coppery waves of hair fell over her face.

Dazzled by her beauty, he feasted on the pale flesh revealed by her low-cut royal-blue gown. Imagined those silky tresses caressing his naked body. His erection was an insatiable beast in his groin, hot and ready for his beloved. He glanced at the man beside him. White hair and a walrus mustache, lips parted in a broad smile. A glittery necklace adorned his wife's wrinkled neck. Rich Brits, able to afford seats in the fifth row. No scrimping for them, unlike the sacrifices he'd made.

The recently refurbished hall—2800 plush new seats and gleaming new walls of polished elm and walnut—had marvelous acoustics, allowing him to bask in Belinda's rich sultry sound, though at times the brasses had intruded, shrill sounds that offended his ears.

A roar from the sell-out crowd drew his attention to three little girls in white frocks tossing rose petals onto the stage at Belinda's feet. Gazing out at the audience, Belinda raised a hand to her lips. And blew him a kiss!

His heart almost stopped. Some primal instinct had told her he was here, her most loyal fan! Soon they would meet. Soon he would be with her. Soon there'd be no need to go into debt as he traveled to her concerts in the United States and around the world.

With a final wave, she gathered the skirt of her gown and swept offstage. The rhythmic clapping began, a European ritual, the sold-out crowd applauding in rhythm. But The Diva wouldn't be back. Nothing could top that encore. His beloved would greet her most important fans at a gala reception at the Royal Trafalgar Hotel.

He edged down the row toward the aisle. This afternoon he had met the man he'd contacted on the Internet. He had expected a seedy type with furtive eyes, but the man was just the opposite, a dapper well-dressed older man who resembled John LeCarre. After collecting his fee, the man gave him his documents. The name on his new credentials was not his own. He doubted Belinda would remember meeting him all those years ago but she might remember his sister.

Slowed by the mob of people in the aisle, he recalled the glorious day he'd driven Rachel to a concert and saw the gorgeous girl with the coppery hair playing principal flute. After begging and pleading—she always made him beg—his sister had introduced them after the concert. Then, the ultimate insult. Even now his cheeks burned with embarrassment. A quick hello, a smile of dismissal, and The Diva had begun talking to another musician.

Enraged by the memory, he plunged into the Royal Festival Hall lobby.

This time he would not allow her to dismiss him.

This time she would pay attention or pay the price.

———

She closed her dressing room door and sank onto the plush satin chair facing the makeup table. Solitude at last. For twenty minutes she had endured the obligatory meet-and-greet that required her to smile and be gracious, suffering the attentions of wealthy old men whose predatory eyes roved over her body while their stodgy bejeweled wives feigned smiles and made inane comments. Complimenting her dress of all things! How insulting.

But now she was alone. Her mantra had worked its magic. Before going onstage she had chanted it twice. *Never give in to fear. Act successful and you will be successful. Believe in yourself and you cannot fail.*

Now she could celebrate. She pumped her fist in the air. A perfect performance! Five minutes ago Guy St. Cyr had murmured those very words in her ear. She would never forget how his muscular body had pressed against hers the last time they made love seven years ago. Or the painful aftermath.

A flood of embarrassment crept up her neck at the memory.

"Wouldn't it be great if we were married?" she'd said. "We'd be a team."

"But I'm already married, luv. Abigail and I have a life together, and two children. You don't need me. You'll have scads of suitors. You don't have to marry them. Enjoy them and focus on your career. Married lovers are best. They've got their own wives."

And Guy still had his. Now he was headed home with Abigail, an Englishwoman with a long nose and a stingy mouth.

She would return to her hotel room and an empty bed.

She studied her reflection in the mirror outlined with blazing lights above the makeup table. Guy was right. Plenty of men had been eager to woo a beautiful young flutist. She'd sampled a few—none of them married—and stayed emotionally aloof. Until Ramon.

She slammed her palms on the table. *Forget Ramon. Focus on your career.* If tonight's performance didn't warrant a recording contract, nothing did.

She slipped off the spaghetti-straps of her gown and plucked baby wipes from a container. Wiped her underarms and freshened her deodorant. Her mascara and eye shadow looked fine. She dabbed lip-gloss on her lips, wiped her fingers on a tissue and tried to relax.

Impossible. Horrible memories intruded. The car in the parking lot. The voicemail message from a man who knew her secrets. The notes Jake had thrown away. The final frightening message: *Soon we'll be together.*

And now Jake was hinting that he might leave her. Tears flooded her eyes. Jake was her rock, the one person she could depend on. The one person she could confide in. She couldn't bear it if he deserted her.

A tap sounded on the door. "Belinda? It's Jake. Are you ready?"

She gathered herself. Rose from the chair. Pasted on a smile.

When she opened the door, Jake swooped inside and hugged her, giving off a faint odor of sweat that his aftershave and deodorant failed to mask. Jake had worked hard tonight, too.

"You were incredible, Bee. A fantastic performance. Your best ever!"

Yes, but did it get me a recording contract?

"What did the orchestra manager say?"

"I haven't talked to him yet. Come on. A limo's waiting to take us to the Royal Trafalgar. Wait till you see the Rooftop Lounge. It's fabulous."

―――

Lurking in the corner of the Rooftop Lounge, he stood by the floor-to-ceiling windows overlooking the city. He had talked his way in easily enough, flashing his concert program, just another distinguished gentleman in his rented tuxedo, black bow tie and white dress shirt.

The view outside the window was spectacular. Glittery lights on the Houses of Parliament. A spotlit statue of Lord Nelson on his horse in Trafalgar Square. But not half as stunning as his beloved. He turned and watched her greet her admirers. A half hour ago she had swept into the lounge like a goddess, accompanied by a tall bearded man in a tux.

Jacob Ziegler. His rival. Fury boiled into his throat.

Now Ziegler was deep in conversation with two white-haired older men, three bigwigs, chatting and sipping champagne.

His gaze returned to his beloved, positioned near a table with silver platters of hot and cold hors d'œuvres. The moment she arrived a swarm of sycophants had surrounded her. Now the crowd had dwindled to one couple, a young man and woman in their twenties. He started toward them, but a scrawny woman in a low-cut red gown stepped in front of him, blocking his path. He wanted to put his hands around her bony neck and throttle her.

"Great performance, hmmm?" she said, smiling at him with garish scarlet-painted lips.

When he didn't answer, the bitch snatched a shrimp canapé from a roving waiter's tray and headed for the bar. That allowed him to sidle up to Belinda, chatting now with the young couple, Brits, judging by their accents.

"I don't know how you do it," the woman said, eyes wide with admiration. "That's the most difficult piece in the flute repertoire."

"No mystery there," he said, stepping closer. "Ms. Scully is the best flutist on the planet."

They all turned to look at him, Belinda included, gazing at him with her incredible sapphire-blue eyes. He extended his hand to his beloved. "Barry Silverman. I've been a huge fan for years. Your performance was marvelous."

She smiled and shook his hand. "Thank you. You're very kind."

His erection, stoked by the silken feel of her hand against his palm, pulsed with desire. It almost made him forget his lines. Almost.

"Nonsense. You deserved both of those standing ovations."

To his great relief, the young couple turned and left.

"Thank you so much." She withdrew her hand and looked over his shoulder as though she was seeking others who might be more important. Didn't she understand that he was the most important person in her life?

Maintaining his smile, he said, "How do you like London? Have you been here before?"

Her eyes met his. "Yes. Guy St. Cyr lives here. I studied with him."

He locked eyes with her so she couldn't look away. "Marvelous city. I've been here two years working a security detail for a British industrialist. A nice chap, but he doesn't care for music."

"That's too bad. Some people don't know what they're missing."

"Quite right. I gave notice last week so I can get back to New Orleans."

"New Orleans is lovely," she said, glancing around the room as though she was looking for someone. "I played a concert there recently."

Yes you did, three weeks ago. I watched you from my seat in the fourth row.

"I operate a security agency there. If you ever need a security expert, I've got extensive experience. That's why the Brit hired me to drive him around." His fingers curled around the fake business card.

She gave him a polite smile. "Thanks, but I love driving."

Loved driving? He could change that. He pressed the business card into her hand. "Take my card, Ms. Scully. You never know when you might need a driver to keep you safe. My rates are quite reasonable."

Her smile disappeared and her sapphire-blue eyes grew distant. "I'm sure they are, Mr. . . . ?"

His cheeks flamed with embarrassment. She couldn't even remember his name. He mustered a smile. "Barry Silverman."

She turned and smiled at an older man who was approaching them, one of the white-haired bigwigs.

Anger boiled into his gut. How could she ignore him this way?

"I'm flying home tomorrow," he said. "What about you?"

"I'm not leaving till Sunday. We're going to Ronny Scott's tomorrow night. The jazz club."

We're going. Belinda and loverboy Ziegler.

"I loved your encore. Were those your own variations?"

"Yes." She gazed at him, unsmiling.

The bigwig was almost upon them. His heart plinked his ribs, a xylophone clang of anxiety. "Would you like me to drive you home from the airport? Cabs are in short supply sometimes."

"No, thank you, Mr. Silverman. Now if you'd excuse me—"

"You know," he blurted, "this has been the most exciting night of my life. Meeting you, I mean. I've been a fan of yours for years. I own every one of your CDs."

"My pleasure, Mr. Silverman," she said, and walked away.

A tsunami of rage erupted inside him. Another kiss-off.

After all his planning and preparation, not to mention his financial sacrifice, The Diva had dismissed him as if he were a flea. This he could not allow. No more friendly persuasions.

This called for action.

CHAPTER 8

Monday, 23 October

Stifling a yawn, she veered off the I-10 onto the long City Park exit road that ran alongside Metairie Cemetery. She couldn't wait to get home and fall into bed. The concert had exceeded her wildest expectations. Rave reviews in London's three biggest newspapers and a fabulous recording contract from the orchestra. But the trip home had been exhausting.

Their seven-hour flight from London had landed at JFK at four. After a mediocre meal in the food court, she and Jake boarded their flight to New Orleans. She'd tried to sleep, but a cranky infant two rows behind them had cried non-stop until they had landed at eleven-fifteen.

She stopped at a traffic light at the intersection of City Park Avenue and glanced at the dashboard clock. Ten past midnight. In five minutes she'd be home. She yawned, willing the light to change. This intersection was spooky at night, a cavernous underpass with massive concrete columns that supported the eight-lane Interstate overhead, and City Park Avenue was deserted. Not a single car passed through the intersection.

Headlights flashed in her rearview mirror.

The idiot had his high beams on. How rude.

Mercifully, the light changed. She turned left onto City Park Avenue, slowed for the next light to turn green and accelerated out of the dark underpass. The SUV followed, its headlights a blinding glare in the rearview of her Infiniti coupe as she drove along City Park Avenue, surrounded by cemeteries on both sides. New Orleans lay below sea level, so residents buried their loved ones above ground in crypts and mausoleums.

Cities of the Dead. A shiver danced down her spine.

Anxious to get home, she accelerated.

Behind her, the SUV matched her speed, an ominous presence. Blinded by the lights in her rearview, she glanced at her wing mirror. There were no cars behind the SUV. Why was it tailgating her?

A whisper of fear plinked her mind.

Delgado Community College appeared on her left. She rolled down the window, and hot humid air hit her face. In the daytime, students would be clustered outside the buildings or walking to their cars in the parking lot. Now the lot was empty, the buildings dark.

The SUV drew closer.

She hit the gas and her Infinity coupe spurted forward.

So did the SUV.

Her palms grew sweaty on the wheel and her neck corded with tension. To her left was the familiar sight of City Park where she went for her early morning runs, a sunny cheerful space with lush green grass and duck ponds, birds chirping from live oak trees and people walking their dogs.

Now it was pitch dark. She accelerated to fifty.

The SUV matched her speed.

She looked to her right. No help there, nothing but darkened homes, no porch lights, not even a car parked outside.

The sour taste of fear filled her mouth.

The SUV slammed her bumper.

Fear exploded into panic.

Her heart pounded like a sprinter nearing the finish line. She stomped the gas, and wind whipped through the window onto her face. The engine whined, matching the frantic thrash of her heart. The SUV remained inches from her bumper, its lights blinding her. She floored the accelerator, sweaty hands gripping the wheel, desperate to reach the safety of her house.

Desperate to escape the maniac in the SUV behind her.

The SUV rammed her car again and sat on the bumper, forcing her to go faster. Bile rose in her throat. This couldn't be happening. Any second she would wake up, sweaty and terrified, safe in her own bed.

But this was no dream, this was real. A living nightmare.

The idiot would make her crash, like the drunk driver who'd killed her family. Tears burned her eyes. She would die in an accident like Blaine and her parents, die before her time, her life snuffed out just as her career began to blossom. Just as she'd always feared.

She stomped the brakes. Heard them screech against the wheels.

The car bucked, but didn't slow down. The SUV backed off.

Her arms went weak with relief. She was safe.

No! Headlights glared in her rearview as SUV came at her again and hit her left bumper, pushing her toward the sidewalk.

She thought her heart would stop. She tried to turn the wheel.

Impossible. Panic sat on her chest like a grand piano, squeezing the air from her lungs. A light pole flashed by, then a fire hydrant.

A huge tree trunk loomed in front of her.

"No," she screamed. "No, no, no."

With a deafening bang and a bone-jarring impact, the car hit the tree, and her airbag deployed, hitting her face and chest, a one-two punch that drove her back against the seat.

Too stunned to move, she inhaled the sour stink of the airbag, heart pounding, unable to catch her breath, dimly aware that the SUV was speeding away. She heard a hissing sound and peered through the windshield.

Steam was rising from the crumpled hood of her car. The impact had broken her radiator. Her hands trembled.

Her hands! A broken finger might end her career. She examined each finger, went weak with relief when she found them uninjured.

Her panic subsided, replaced by outrage. The idiot had run her off the road, had almost killed her. She was alive, but her car was wrecked.

How would she get home?

Call Frank, she thought. *He'll know what to do.*

Then she thought: No. Frank would make her report the accident.

She pictured the headline: *Famous flute soloist crashes into tree.*

She reached for her purse. Before the crash it had been on the passenger seat. Not now. Frantic, she groped the floor. At last, she found the purse near her feet. She dug out her cell phone.

―――

After a nerve-wracking fifteen-minute wait, a long flatbed truck with flashing yellow lights arrived. Relieved not to be alone, she asked the driver, a courteous young man with a ginger-colored beard, to tow her car to a service station and asked if he could stop at her house on the way. He got her luggage out of the trunk, helped her into the cab of his truck and cranked her Infiniti coupe onto the flatbed.

When he dropped her off, she thanked him and went in the house.

Her empty house.

Numb with exhaustion, she went in the kitchen, drew a glass of water from the sink and sank onto a chair at the butcher-block table in the corner. The cozy table for two where she ate her solitary meals. Jake sometimes ate lunch with her if he wasn't too busy. No one else ever came to visit her.

And now Jake was threatening to leave.

A dull ache pulsed her temples. Her hand shook as she raised the glass to her mouth. Visions whirled through her mind like debris from a tornado.

The SUV behind her. The tree looming in front of her.

The bone-jarring impact. The exploding airbag. The sour stench.

The mind-numbing fear.

She began to weep, sobbing uncontrollably, torrents of tears running down her cheeks. Jake was home with Dean, the man who loved him dearly. Guy had his Brit wife. Ramon had his Spanish spitfire. She had no one.

Before she could change her mind, she went to her wall phone and dialed a number.

"Hello."

She recognized the deep melodious voice. Was it her imagination or did his voice sound wary?

"Frank, some idiot just forced me off the road near City Park and made me crash into a tree."

Silence on the other end.

"I'm sorry, Frank. Did I wake you? This is Belinda Scully. I'm afraid I'm still shaken up from the accident."

"Oh. Belinda." Sounding less wary now. "Are you hurt?"

"I'm okay, but my car is wrecked. I had a tow service take it to my service station." She drew a shaky breath. "You said to call if anything weird happened."

"Where are you?"

"At home. The tow truck driver dropped me off."

"What did the police say?"

Her worst fear. Frank expected her to report the accident. "I can't explain over the phone. Do you think you could . . . could you come over?"

Tears filled her eyes. She sounded like a helpless little girl. She hated that.

"I'll be there in ten minutes."

"Thank you." She returned to the table and drank some water, picturing his strong jaw, hawkish nose and penetrating eyes.

His aura of strength. She needed his strength.

She couldn't bear to be alone, not now.

"Please, Frank," she whispered, "please get here as fast as you can."

CHAPTER 9

She set two bottles of Arizona Iced Tea on her butcher-block table. Before Frank arrived, she had composed herself enough to wipe the streaks of mascara off her cheeks and freshen her makeup. Now that he was here she felt better. Calmer. In control. But her throat still felt scratchy and parched.

She opened her bottle of iced tea, took several gulps and sat down opposite him. His jaw was dark with stubble and his tan polo shirt was rumpled, as though he'd grabbed whatever clothes were handy and rushed out of his house to come here. Despite his disheveled appearance, he seemed alert and focused. Intense. Powerful.

"Thank you so much for coming, Frank. I'm sorry I woke you."

"I'm glad you're okay, but you should have called 911." His dark penetrating eyes were full of reproach.

"And have the media run outrageous articles about me in the newspaper and on TV?" She conjured a humor-me smile. "If Britney Spears gets a pimple on her nose, it makes headlines. Besides, what would I say? Some drunk forced me off the road? They might say I was drunk!"

He gazed at her, expressionless. "Is that what happened? Some drunk ran you off the road?"

"Of course! Do you think I made it up?"

"If someone forced you off the road, you need to report it."

"But I'm fine now. Really. It was just some idiot—"

"No, it wasn't. That's what you said about the car at the restaurant."

A tingle of pleasure rippled through her. Frank was worried about her. He wasn't handsome in the conventional sense. Nothing about Frank Renzi was conventional. He had a face you couldn't ignore: a prominent nose, angular cheekbones and those incredible dark eyes, intense and penetrating.

Frank had no trouble attracting women, of that she was certain. What would it be like to have a man like Frank fall in love with her? It had been three long years since a strong, powerful man had made love to her. Ramon.

Don't think about Ramon.

She forced herself to concentrate on what Frank was saying.

". . . willing to accept the hot-rodder theory until Jake told me about the notes you've been getting. Jake told you about them, right?"

A shiver of fear danced down her spine. Weird notes. A lot of them, notes dating back to her days in Boston. She clenched her hands, dug her fingernails into her palms. "Yes, he did."

Frank pulled a spiral notepad out of his pocket. "I don't believe in coincidences. Someone's trying to scare you. Can you describe the vehicle that forced you off the road?"

"Not really. It was some sort of SUV. The high beams were on so it was hard to see, and when my car hit the tree, the airbag deployed. By the time I recovered, it was gone."

"Anything you can tell me would help, even the color."

"I couldn't tell you if it was white, black, green or blue."

"Did you get a look at the driver?"

"No. It happened too fast," she said, and absently rubbed her cheek.

"You're going to have a nasty bruise."

"At least it didn't hit my mouth. That would have been a disaster."

To her surprise, he smiled. "I know. I used to play trumpet. Get smacked in the chops, forget playing."

"You played trumpet?" Another enticement, along with his deep melodious voice.

"In high school and college. Jazz mostly." His smile disappeared and his eyes locked onto hers, an intense look that made her body tingle.

"If I'm going to find whoever did this, I need information. I can't get the lab techs to go over your car without an accident report."

She faked a yawn. "I'm too tired to think about that now. I spent the day in planes and airports."

His expression softened. "How did the concert go?"

Grateful for the diversion, she smiled. "It was fantastic. The orchestra wants me to record the Khatchatourian with them, and my solo variations on Gershwin's 'I've Got Rhythm'."

"Nice tune," he said, and put his notepad in his pocket.

"I'm playing it at a NOOCA concert Friday night. Why don't you come and hear it?"

"I'll try, but in my business, you learn not to make too many plans." He pushed back his chair.

"Please, don't go yet. I need to tell you something." She gulped some iced tea. Now that the moment was here, the thought of revealing her secret terrified her. She'd never told anyone. Would Frank understand? She wiped sweaty palms on her skirt and tried to reassure herself. Frank was a policeman. He'd heard all kinds of stories. But not her story. Not her secret.

The secret she'd guarded so zealously all these years.

"I was pissed that Jake didn't show me those notes. But I've been keeping something from Jake, too."

"Uh-huh. What?" His eyes were laser beams, intense and unwavering.

"Two weeks ago someone left a threat on my voicemail."

"What kind of threat?"

"It's . . . complicated. Julliard granted me early admission when I was a senior. I already had enough credits to graduate, so I moved to New York."

"After your family was killed?"

"Yes." She fiddled with her napkin, folding it into tiny squares. Her heart skittered against her ribs. "I got involved with another student and got pregnant. Stupid, I know, but I didn't think—" She gave him a rueful smile. "No one thinks it will happen to them."

"You were hurting," he said, holding her gaze with his incredible warm brown eyes. "You needed someone to love you."

Her eyes filled with tears. Determined not to cry, she clenched her jaw. She couldn't afford to lose control, not now, not in front of a man she found so attractive. "Having a baby would have ruined everything I'd worked so hard to achieve. Lots of flutists apply to Julliard, but most of them don't get full scholarships." She gazed at him, willing him to understand. "I had an abortion. No one knows about it. Not even Jake."

"What about the father? Did you tell him?"

She hesitated, then said, "No. He wouldn't have understood."

Frank raised his eyebrows, a quick flick, but said nothing. Watching her with those incredibly sexy eyes.

She faked a bright smile. "He's married now, with two kids of his own. He just got a great job with the Cleveland Orchestra—"

"Tell me about the voicemail message. What was the threat?"

"He said he knew all my secrets." The thought made her cringe. She had no idea what the man knew, but if the media got wind of the abortion and certain other sordid details, it would wreck her career. It was bad enough telling Frank about the abortion. She didn't want him knowing about her affairs with married men.

"I've got a reputation to maintain. I don't want people knowing I had an abortion when I was eighteen." She studied his face, waiting for a reaction, but his expression remained unreadable.

"Was the caller a man or a woman?"

A woman? The idea shocked her. Then again, women could be vicious if they didn't like you. She'd found that out at Julliard. The school was a cesspool of bitchery and intrigue, Purgatory Prep for the hell of competition in the music business. If women hated you, they were beyond vicious.

Get out of Boston or I'll tell every reporter in town you're fucking my husband.

The Spanish spitfire's hateful words.

She swallowed some iced tea. "I'm pretty sure it was a man. Whoever it was spoke in a raspy whisper."

"What would he gain by exposing your secret? Did he ask for money?"

"No. He asked me to meet him the next morning in Jackson Square."

"Did you?"

"Of course not!"

"Did you save the message?"

"No." She sighed. "I know. I'm as bad as Jake, not saving the notes. But I didn't want to hear it on my machine, over and over."

"Do you remember what he said?"

Remember? She would never forget it. She recited it from memory.

"*I know all your secrets, Belinda. What would your fans think if they knew? Meet me outside the Cabildo tomorrow morning at ten.*"

"But you didn't go and meet him," Frank said.

"No." She clenched her jaw. "Three days later I found a note on the mat outside my front door when I was going out for my run at six that morning."

"I want to see it."

"Frank, I know you're going to kill me, but I . . . I ripped it up and threw it in the trash."

"Jesus." He stared at her. "What the hell for?"

"It frightened me."

"What did it say?"

She licked her lips and spoke it aloud. "*Stop ignoring me, Belinda. I know all your secrets. We need to talk.*"

"That's it? No signature?"

"No signature."

Frank scratched his jaw. "Where did you have the abortion?"

"At a clinic in Newark. No one knew about it. No one."

He tapped his pen on the table, frowning, as if he were trying to make a decision. "Any other secrets I should know about?"

She made her mind go blank. Don't think about Ramon's wife and her vicious threat. "No. No more secrets."

Another flick of his eyebrows and a deadpan expression. "Most security experts would tell you to put out the information yourself. You need to decide how important it is to keep your secret. He called two week ago, delivered the note himself three days later. You've heard nothing since?"

"No, thank goodness."

"Maybe you never will."

"Do you think so?" Desperately hoping he was right.

"Hard to predict. If he calls again, save the message. I want to hear it. Same with any notes you get."

She smiled. "I will. Thank you for understanding, Frank. Could you, um, could you keep what I told you confidential, please?"

"Sure." He rose to his feet. "I need to see your security system."

"Why? It's state-of-the-art. I've got flutes in the house worth thousands of dollars."

He didn't answer, striding down the hall to the foyer. He had a muscular way of walking, purposeful and confident, as if he knew exactly where he was going and why. She liked that.

He studied the keypad by the front door. "Are there motion detectors?"

"Yes, in the halls, upstairs and down." She took him around the corner to her studio. "I love the high ceilings. The acoustics are great."

He circled the room, paused at the two front windows, continued past her mother's ladder-back rocker, and ran his fingers over her gleaming Steinway baby grand. "Do you practice in here at night?"

"No. I practice in the morning and every afternoon."

"Better put up some curtains. Anyone on the street can see in here."

"But that would ruin the acoustics."

He gave her a stern look, one intended to intimidate. She knew that look. "Belinda, someone is stalking you. He's got your phone number and he knows where you live. And you live by yourself. You need to hire some security, someone trained to protect you."

She had no intention of hiring a security guard. She faked a yawn. "I'm grateful for your help, Frank, but if I don't get some sleep I'll collapse."

He went out to his car and sat there, thoughts churning. When his phone rang, he'd figured it was his ex-wife having one of her panic attacks, not Belinda Scully. He almost blew her off and told her to call the District police station. But she'd been on the verge of hysteria, her voice shaking with fear, and he was a sucker for damsels in distress. And that wasn't the only reason. She was a flute soloist with secrets. A beautiful woman. Intelligent. Talented. And hiding something. The exact sort of puzzle he couldn't resist.

She was also unwilling to admit she was scared. In the safety of her own home, she was in control, lowering her head, eyeing him with her baby-blues, lips parted in a smile. He'd seen Princess Di do that on TV, seducing millions of viewers. The vibes Belinda put out tonight were unmistakable, stronger than the vibes he'd picked up at the station. She was flirting with him.

Not that it would do her any good. Within seconds of meeting a woman he usually knew whether he wanted to go to bed with her, and he had no desire to sleep with Belinda Scully. Maybe it was her hair.

He preferred dark-haired women, sexy women with a sense of humor. Like Jane Russell. He loved the way she bantered with Robert Mitchum in the movies they'd made back in the fifties, Mitchum gazing at women with his hooded eyes, faintly disinterested, which, of course, drove women wild. He'd tried that heavy-lidded gaze on a girl once and got back a baffled look. Even now, twenty-five years later, the memory embarrassed him.

He was no Robert Mitchum and Belinda was no Jane Russell.

Like many top-notch musicians, Belinda exhibited certain narcissistic traits. Self-centered, seductive and ambitious as hell. Her rationale for hiding the abortion was understandable. But when he asked if she had other secrets, he'd seen a flash of fear in her eyes. Her terse denial didn't fool him. She didn't want people to know she'd had an abortion, didn't want them knowing her other secrets, either.

He could relate to that. He had secrets, too.

What else was she hiding? He now believed Ziegler's tale about the creepy notes was true. The messages and requests to meet sounded like a stalker. But most stalkers wanted the object of their obsession to fall in love with them. This one was trying to frighten her. Did someone have a grudge against her? A spurned lover? A disgruntled fan? Had some nutcase seen the sexy photos on her website and become obsessed with her?

He hoped not. Celebrity stalkers were fanatical.

If thwarted, some of them could be deadly.

CHAPTER 10

Monday, 23 October

Slouched in his chair in the back row of Advanced Jazz Harmony class, Antoine tried to concentrate, penciling chord changes on a sheet of staff paper as Ella Fitzgerald scatted on "Lullaby of Birdland." He knew the changes by heart, had heard it on Ella's CD a zillion times, playing along on his saxophone.

He loved Ella but listening to her reminded him of Chantelle.

A terrible ache gripped his stomach. He loved Chantelle with all his heart, but she could be outrageously stubborn, took no guff from anybody, himself included. That's one reason he loved her. She didn't do that simper-smile act like most girls. Chantelle spoke her mind. Not only that, she was beautiful, had that sexy smile, those luscious lips . . .

He caught Mr. Dawson watching him, penciled in a chord change, E-flat seven to A-flat, and stared out the window, hearing a train whistle in the distance, trains chugging by at inconvenient times, clashing with the music as they rumbled past NOCCA.

After AK threatened them, he'd put Chantelle in his car and drove away. Should have taken her to his uncle's, but Chantelle said no way was she leaving those groceries he'd brought her, said wait an hour, she'd sneak back to her apartment. He parked six blocks away and they smooched for an hour. She promised to call him, so he'd let her go.

He wished he hadn't.

The music stopped. He scribbled the last three chord changes and put down his pencil. In the front row, Marcus Goines was waving his hand. Marcus always wanted to be first. First to answer, first to take a solo, first to get into a good music school. Marcus was a decent flute player, had a nice tone and all, but he couldn't play jazz for shit. He just couldn't swing, solos coming out stiff and tentative, like he was thinking on every note.

Marcus also hated being wrong, arguing with Mr. D now, pointing to his worksheet, saying he'd heard the chord as an E-minor-seven with a flat-five.

Antoine figured Marcus was uptight 'cuz of his Baptist minister father, fire and brimstone to the max.

Reverend Goines would shit a truckload of bricks if he knew Marcus was dealing pot. Dealing dope was stupid. Marcus probably did it to make money so's he could impress girls. Marcus was homely and built like a dump truck, and girls loved when you spent money on them. He'd seen him at Iberville once, copping his supply from AK.

Mr. D turned to check another student's work, left Marcus looking angry, his lower lip stuck out in a pout. The boys in the 'hood where the Goines family lived ragged on Marcus, said flute was a sissy instrument. Selling pot might give him street cred, but it wouldn't turn him into a jazz player. To play jazz you had to act confident even if you weren't, play every note like you loved it.

Like Chantelle. She was a natural, had perfect time and a sultry low-pitched voice like Dinah Washington. Chantelle sang with feeling, put all her emotion into the music 'cuz of the trouble she'd had in her life, her daddy running off, her moms a crackhead.

He saw Mr. D head his way and composed his face into a cheery smile. Had to work at it.

Chantelle had called him when she got back to her apartment like she'd promised, so he said he'd see her on Saturday. But Friday night when he called the cell phone she'd copped from that foster mom, he got no answer.

Same thing Saturday. Same on Sunday. No answer.

It was driving him crazy.

A basketball-sized lump clogged his throat. Anything happened to Chantelle, he'd die of loneliness. After school he was going straight to Iberville and make sure Chantelle was safe.

―――――

"I don't want some stranger driving me around. I like driving."

She saw Jake's dark bushy eyebrows bunch in a frown. His office made her feel like a caged animal. Unlike her sparsely furnished studio, it was crammed with equipment. Three gray-metal file cabinets along one wall, a computer station with yellow Post-its stuck to the monitor, two high-speed laser printers, a fax machine and a state-of-the-art copier.

In the center of the room, Jake sat behind his massive mahogany desk. He rose from his chair and came over and hugged her. "Why didn't you call me last night? You must have been terrified."

She kissed his cheek. "I didn't want to bother you."

If I'm extra considerate, maybe you won't abandon me.

Jake plucked three Hershey's Kisses from the glass dish on his desk, popped them in his mouth, chewed rapidly and swallowed.

"Why did you call Renzi? Why didn't you call me?"

She turned and stared out the front window with unseeing eyes.

Because Frank has taken a personal interest in me. That's why she'd told him about the abortion. Frank cared about her. She had seen it in his eyes. Heard it in voice. *You were hurting, Belinda. You needed someone to love you.*

Speaking the words she had never allowed herself to think, much less articulate to anyone. Frank was the first person she'd had a real conversation with in years. After talking to him last night, she had the feeling Frank understood her better than any man she'd ever met.

"Renzi wants you to hire a security driver," Jake said. "He gave me some names—"

"No." She turned away from the window. "I don't want someone investigating those notes and the accident and the voicemail—"

She caught herself in time. Jake knew nothing about the voicemail threat. Or the abortion.

"Bee, it's for your own safety. You need someone to protect you."

Protect you. A sense of impending doom descended upon her, the same feeling she'd had watching Suzanne Plechette in *The Birds*, sitting on a bench smoking a cigarette, oblivious to the swarm of blackbirds swooping down to perch on the trees behind her.

Maybe she should get a driver. Maybe she'd hire that man she'd met in London. The instant he walked away she had dismissed him from her mind. But he was a security expert. And he loved classical music, especially hers. She didn't have to reveal her secrets to him.

She beamed a smile at Jake. "If we have to hire a security guard, let's hire someone who loves music. At the reception in London I met a man who used to supervise security for a British businessman. He lives in New Orleans. Let me go find his card."

———

He wandered through Dillard's lingerie department. Brassieres of every size and description dangled from the racks: underwire bras, sports bras, padded bras, white bras, black bras, flesh-toned bras. He loved the lingerie in upscale stores, not the cheap ones at K-Mart. He knew a quality bra when he saw one. He'd been handling them since he was ten. He could still hear Ma bitching at him when he did her laundry.

Don't put my bras in the dryer. The heat ruins the elastic. That mind-fucking voice giving him orders, finding fault even if he did exactly what she said.

He ran his fingers over a lacy black bra. For some reason, touching women's underwear excited him.

Across the aisle, a clerk picked up a bra someone had dropped on the floor and hung it on a rack. A young girl with strawberry-blonde hair, not as nice as Belinda's, but long and wavy.

The insistent urge in his crotch drew him toward her. No one could replace Belinda, but now and then, when thoughts of his beloved drove him mad with desire, he had taken a substitute.

He walked over to her. "Your hair is beautiful," he said.

"Thank you." She flashed a mechanical smile and stepped into the next aisle to straighten the packages of pantyhose on a display rack.

He studied her, assessing her ability to resist: petite, not athletic looking, not a jogger for sure. Joggers tended to be strong and fit. He hated to fight with his dates. It was better when they complied without a struggle. Maybe he'd get her in his van after she finished work and take her for a spin.

Careful not to startle her, he moved closer.

"Your hair is really beautiful. Girls with short hair are so unattractive. I love long hair on a woman. It's so feminine."

She looked up at him, eyes wary. "My *boyfriend* likes it too."

Anger spewed into his throat like molten lead. Why was she being so hostile? Rejecting him when he hadn't even asked her out.

He faked a smile. "I'm sure he does. I'm sure he likes everything about you." *Including your big tits and your ass.* Burning with rage, he pretended to check the price on a pair of pantyhose, fantasizing about how Blondie's hair would feel when he rubbed it against his cock.

And then, a miracle. His Belinda-phone chimed the ring-tone he'd given it: the opening of Mozart's *Symphony No. 40*.

His heart surged. Finally! He'd been waiting all day for her call.

"My girlfriend," he said to the clerk. "I'd better take it. She gets cross if I don't answer." He turned away to answer the call.

"Could I speak to Barry Silverman, please?"

The dulcet tones of his beloved. His cock throbbed. But he didn't want to talk to her in front of this bitchy clerk.

"Speaking. Could you hold, please?"

Belinda, bless her heart, said she could.

He rushed to the nearest exit and stepped outside.

"Sorry. I was in a situation that needed my undivided attention."

"This is Belinda Scully. We met in London last week and you gave me your card."

"Oh?" he said, feigning forgetfulness. "Oh, yes, now I remember. At the reception after your marvelous performance with the Royal Philharmonic. What can I do for you?"

"I'm thinking about hiring a security person. Are you living in New Orleans now?"

"I sure am, settled in and already working. What sort of security services did you require?"

"Hold on. My assistant can explain."

A male voice came on the line. "Mr. Silverman? This is Jake Ziegler, Ms. Scully's assistant."

He clenched his teeth. She'd fobbed him off onto her assistant. Her lover. He fake-smiled into the phone. "How can I help you?"

"We need to assess our security arrangements. Ms. Scully might need a driver."

"That sounds reasonable." Reasonable? It was fucking fantastic! "When do I start?"

"I need to see some references first. Ms. Scully said you worked for a London businessman. Could you fax your credentials and a letter of recommendation to me?"

"Of course. When I get back to my office I'll fax you everything you need to know about Silverman Security."

His heart drummed a thunderous tympani roll. His dream was about to come true. Why settle for that bitchy clerk? Soon he'd have the real thing.

Still, he couldn't resist going back inside. The bitch saw him and scurried away, but she couldn't escape him. No one could.

With three long strides he caught up with her.

"My girlfriend needs me so I've got to go. Pity. I wanted to get to know you. I love women."

I love sucking their tits and rubbing my cock in their hair until I come.

He wrapped his powerful fingers around her wrist.

She stared up at him, eyes fearful now that he was in control.

He loved that. But why bother with this insignificant little bitch?

Belinda wanted him. Belinda was a star, a ripe juicy peach ready to fall in love with her defender.

CHAPTER 11

Tuesday, 24 October

At ten o'clock Frank stopped at a traffic light beside the Iberville project and took a swig of his take-out coffee. Chantelle Wilson had been missing for eight days. The knot in his gut tightened. Eight days and eight long nights.

He'd posted her mug shot in every district station so the patrol officers could be on the lookout for her. Nothing so far. Using the same photo with the height chart edited out, he'd made a flyer—*Have you seen this girl?*—and put his cell phone number at the bottom. She looked indescribably sad, staring into the camera with angry eyes. He'd given flyers to three black ministers he'd befriended since coming to New Orleans and asked them to post them in their churches. On the off chance that she was panhandling, he'd posted a dozen more in the French Quarter. Other than a few crank calls from drunks and weirdoes, he'd heard nothing. No one had seen her.

The light changed and he drove into Iberville. His first attempt to locate Chantelle had been fruitless, but this time he knew where to go. It had taken him a week to navigate the Housing Authority's bureaucratic maze, locate the apartment Chantelle's mother had rented prior to Katrina and get a search warrant. Any other case the judge wouldn't have swallowed the bullshit he'd put on the application, but mounting outrage fueled by the incessant media drumbeat over the Lakeview incident had convinced the judge.

Everyone was hot on that case, the NOPD top brass and local politicians fielding calls from angry residents. Not a word about the black kids shot earlier that day. Then again, he hadn't paid much attention to the incident Jake Ziegler and Belinda Scully had reported that night either. Until someone ran Belinda off the road.

He hoped she had the sense to hire some security.

He parked in front of a red-brick building and dug his digital camera out of the glove box. A warrant search without a police photographer to document it was against protocol, but their only photographer was on another case, and the urgent signals from his gut told him not to wait.

Slinging the camera strap over his shoulder, he got out and walked into Iberville. Halfway down a cement walk littered with mangled beer cans, candy wrappers and shards of glass, he arrived at Chantelle's former abode. No sign of AK or his thugs, but the same creepy sensation on his neck he'd felt on his previous visit told him they were watching.

Inside the building the usual foul odors assaulted him. He jogged up two flights of stairs, his feet thudding on the hollow metal steps. The stench wasn't as bad on the third floor, but it didn't smell like the Ritz either. Not a soul in sight. More creepy-crawlies on his neck.

He walked down the hall to unit 314, eyed the security peephole and stepped to one side. If some thug with a gun was inside, he didn't want to take a shot in the gut. He tapped on the door and waited.

The building was eerily quiet, as silent as a cat stalking a mouse.

He used the Housing Authority key to unlock the door, turned the knob and pushed. With an audible creak from its rusty hinges, the door swung open onto a living room. No one in sight. No garbage or litter on the shit-brown carpet. Below a grime-streaked window, a dilapidated couch without seat cushions faced the door. No tables, no chairs, no TV, no stereo, no nothing. All items of value had been removed.

He stepped inside. The air was thick with humidity and the odor of spoiled food, the noxious stench Katrina had bestowed upon New Orleans.

"Chantelle," he said softly. "You in here?"

The apartment remained deathly quiet. Too quiet.

The hackles rose on his neck. He unholstered his SIG. Racked the slide. Felt his heart thud against his ribs. He and his partner had faced a similar situation up in Boston once, and all hell had broken loose.

On the wall to his right a door was ajar. At some point the door had been painted sky-blue. Now the paint was peeling and streaked with dirt. Hyper-alert for sounds or movement, he edged to the door and pushed it open. A small room, ten-feet square, a child's bedroom at some point, maybe. A tattered shade covered the lone window. No furniture, no trash.

And no occupant.

He heard a distant thud and froze. Someone was in the building.

Moving silently, he returned to the entry door and stuck his head into the hall. Saw no one. Heard nothing.

His heart was racing, juiced by adrenaline. And anxiety.

Coming here alone might have been a mistake.

He quietly closed the door and flipped the lock. Dust motes danced in the sunlight slanting through the filthy window behind the couch. He fought down an urge to sneeze. Four feet to his left, an archway opened onto a dark hall. Raising his SIG-Sauer, he eased into the hallway.

Chunks of plaster had fallen from walls painted a sickly yellow, littering the wood floor. With silent stealth, he crept down the hall to an open door on the left. An empty bathroom smelling of lavender.

The sink was dry, but a bar of soap sat in a cheap soap dish screwed to the wall above the sink. Beside a tub with serious rust stains, a raggedy blue bath towel hung from a chrome rack. No shower curtain on the tub. He checked the medicine cabinet above the sink.

The only item was a small bottle of Walgreen's acetaminophen. Whoever had stripped the apartment would have emptied the medicine cabinet. Someone was living here. He eased across the hall into the kitchen. Bits of food caked a filthy stove. No refrigerator. After Katrina the city had been infested with no-see-ums, minuscule bugs that flew out of the refrigerator the instant you opened it. Once out, you couldn't get rid of them.

Signs of life on the kitchen counter: a box of saltines, a jar of Winn-Dixie peanut butter, a table knife and a cracker spread with peanut butter.

Someone had left in a hurry.

A cockroach skittered out from under a bag of Doritos and disappeared behind a squat can of baked beans. He opened the cabinet door below the sink, closed it fast when he saw roaches scatter inside.

He stepped back into the hallway. Still no sounds, just an eerie quiet.

Sweat dampened his forehead. Off to his right, the door at the far end of the hall was shut. No telling what was behind it. Alert for the slightest sound, he edged down the hall, arms extended, hand clenched around the SIG. Five feet from the door he flattened himself against the wall.

The wooden door had been painted lavender. Like the door to the child's room, the paint was flaking and streaked with dirt. A rush of adrenaline jumped his heart rate. Was someone in there?

Slugs would penetrate the wooden door like butter.

Ready to drop to the floor if a barrage of bullets came through the door, he rapped on it. Got no response. He held his breath and listened.

No telltale sounds. No footsteps.

He waited a full minute, crouched, flung open the door and burst inside.

DIVA

The room was empty. Through a tattered window-blind, rays of sunlight dappled a thin mattress on the floor. On the mattress were a tangled sheet and a flattened pillow inside a dingy pillowcase. On the floor beside the mattress, a nine-inch aluminum pie plate held a stubby red candle. A sea of melted wax at the base of the candle gave off an odor of cinnamon.

Wire hangers hooked over the top of the window molding held an oversized T-shirt and a pair of denim cutoffs. He went over and touched them. They were damp, freshly washed. By Chantelle? If so, they were her only spare clothes. Nothing but empty hangers in the closet.

He holstered his SIG, powered on his camera and photographed the room, making sure each shot overlapped the previous one. Room by room, he went through the apartment, methodically snapping shots from all angles to document what he'd seen.

During his last visit AK had denied knowing Chantelle, but that was bullshit. Was AK one of the Lakeview robbers? Judging from the gold front tooth and the bling on his wrists, AK made big bucks dealing dope and pills. Why rob a dinky little convenience store? He hated to think Chantelle was involved, but she had been in Lakeview that night.

Eight days ago she'd run away from Mama LeBlanc's. No one had seen her since. No one he knew about, anyway. No one who would admit to it.

Certain that Chantelle had been there, he left the apartment and went downstairs, his gut churning with acid even worse than before. Something or someone had interrupted Chantelle's peanut-butter-saltine snack.

On the way back to his car he saw no signs of life, no thugs, no mothers with children, not even a stray cat. He got in the car and cranked the engine and his cell phone rang. It was Kenyon Miller.

"Frank, they just found your girl's body behind some bushes over near Bayou St. John."

His gut cramped and bile spurted into his throat, sharp and acidic. He took a deep breath. Swallowed hard.

"Chantelle? You're sure?"

"Yes, unfortunately. We ID'd her from the mug shot."

"Be right there."

He tossed the cell on the passenger seat and slammed his palms on the wheel, recalling the fear in Chantelle's eyes when he left her at Mama's, the fear and the sadness and her whispered *Thank-you*.

The memory tore at his heart. Taking her to Mama's had been a big mistake. If he'd put her in the lockup, she'd still be alive.

The man who called himself Barry Silverman entered his apartment, hung his dry-cleaning in the hall closet and glanced at the small wire-mesh cage wedged under the breakfast bar.

"Hello, Oz, you sweet thing. Happy to see me?" Inside the cage Oz hopped up and down, delirious with joy. A dwarf bunny no bigger than a three-month-old kitten, Oz had silky white fur, floppy ears and sky-blue eyes.

He dropped his keys on the breakfast bar. The yellow Formica was edged with cigarette burns from the previous tenant. The sight offended him. Everything about this shitty little apartment offended him.

But he wouldn't be here much longer. Soon he'd be working for Belinda.

He opened the cage door and his adorable bunny hopped onto the carpet. Rabbits made excellent pets. They were quiet and did as they were told. He hated dogs, always barking and asking to be walked. Cats were worse. They'd as soon scratch you as look at you.

Sinking onto the futon, he scooped Oz onto his lap and petted him, relishing the feel of the soft fur. "It's going to work out, Oz," he crooned. "Belinda wants me to protect her."

Needles of doubt crept into his mind. Why hadn't she called to hire him? He'd faxed his credentials twelve hours ago. With a glow of pride, he pictured her snatching pages from her fax machine, studying his fabulous two-page CV, the recommendation letters, and the eye-catching cover sheet he'd created with SILVERMAN SECURITY at the top.

His beloved was sure to be impressed.

He set Oz down, went in the kitchen and opened the half-sized refrigerator. Oz hopped after him but stopped at the doorway. When he adopted Oz at the shelter, he'd been amazed to learn that rabbits, unlike cats, had no pads on the bottom of their feet, just fur. His precious bunny had no traction to negotiate the slippery linoleum.

He tossed sprigs of cilantro onto the dingy brown carpet, and Oz set upon them with enthusiasm. He opened the door to the cabinet under the sink, took out a bag of dry food and filled the food container in Oz's cage. Removed the water dish and dumped it in the sink. Refilled it with fresh water and put it in the cage.

"See how well I treat you, Oz? And I'll take even better care of Belinda."

The needles of doubt returned. Why hadn't she called? So what if his credentials were bogus? His military training qualified him for the job. No thanks to Sergeant Asshole.

"Sergeant Asshole said I was uncoordinated, Oz, just because I fell once on the obstacle course. What did he know? Could he play piano well enough to accompany a violinist like I could? Fuck, no! You need good hand-eye coordination for that, and mine's damn near perfect. When I got the top score in marksmanship, Sergeant Asshole had to eat crow. And so did Pa."

The macho-man who had adopted him when he was four months old.

His lip curled with distaste. As a teenager, he used to fantasize that his real father was a renowned piano soloist, like Vladimir Ashkenazi or Daniel Barenbohm. Someone with talent, intelligence and flair.

He stroked Oz's silky fur. "Pa didn't appreciate me, either. People don't realize how much smarts you need to play piano. First you have to learn the piece. Then you have to blend with the violin. That was the hardest part, Oz. Blending with my sister, keeping up when she rushed a passage. I had to accommodate *her*. I always had to make *her* look good."

His cheeks burned at the memory.

"I hate that bitch, Oz. Sometimes you do things for people and they don't appreciate it. But you do, Oz, and Belinda will, too."

He arched his back and yawned. The past twenty-four hours had been arduous, but the crucial work was done. Something deep inside Belinda, some secret yearning, had made her realize how much she needed him. His ingenious plan was about to bear fruit.

He shooed Oz into his cage. "Be good while I take a nap, Oz. I have to work tonight." Six fucking hours of saying *Yes-sir* and *No-sir* to snotty businessmen, humping their luggage into hotels. He was sick of working for people who didn't appreciate him. He'd done that all his life for Ma and Pa and his bitch sister, always doing for them, having no time for himself. And not a word of thanks from any of them.

Pain stabbed his temples, the pulsing white-light of a migraine. If he weren't so desperate for money he'd call in sick. But an ominous notice had appeared on his last American Express bill: *This account has been given to a collection agency.* Those bastards were merciless, harassing him day and night, waking him out of a sound sleep.

But soon he'd be working for Belinda. Alone with her every day. Bliss.

He took a bottle of extra-strength Excedrin off the upended milk crate that served as his coffee table and dry-swallowed two capsules.

Please call soon, Belinda. He checked to make sure his Belinda-phone was on. He didn't want to miss her call. With loving care, he placed it on the milk crate, stretched out on the futon and shut his eyes.

Useless. Every muscle in his body was taut as a bowstring.

What if she didn't call? What if she rejected him the way she had years ago? Excruciating white-light pain seared his temples. How could she keep him in suspense like this? He rose from the futon, went to his stereo and put on one of her CDs, *The Romantic Flute*.

The sensuous sound of her flute filled the room, dragging him into a deep chasm of desire. A shiver wracked him. Her next CD was due out at Christmas. *Music for Lovers Only*. He could hardly wait.

Her brochure lay atop the file cabinet beside the stereo. Belinda, gazing at him, smiling seductively. He unzipped his fly and began to stroke himself.

Frank parked behind the line of vehicles strung out along the road. The black crime-scene van, blue-and-white squad cars and assorted crime-scene tech vehicles lined up bumper to bumper. The coroner investigator's van was still here which meant they hadn't removed the body.

Acid churned his gut like a cement mixer. In Boston the street-maggots used to call him a badass motherfucker. Right now that's what he was: A badass motherfucker driven by rage. And ready to kick ass.

He stalked along an embankment beside the murky waters of the bayou. Forty yards ahead of him, uniformed police and plainclothes detectives clustered near a clump of juniper bushes strung with yellow crime-scene tape. Kenyon Miller saw him, broke off a conversation with two detectives and hurried over, a dark-skinned, six-foot-six 240-pound powerhouse with a shaven head and a soul patch under his lower lip.

"They capped her twice in the chest, once in the face," Miller said, his expression a study in outrage. "Dumped her like a piece of garbage. Damn shame, a girl that young,"

Frank said nothing, steeling himself, knowing what he was about to see would sicken him. During his twenty-plus years as a cop he'd seen many murder victims and had mourned them all. No one deserved to be murdered. But like most cops, he had a much harder time with young victims.

He ducked under the crime scene tape and followed Miller around a cluster of stunted juniper bushes. Saw Chantelle, flat on her back, naked from the waist down, legs splayed. Her white T-shirt was stained brown with dried blood. Her eyes were open and staring, dimmed by the opaque film that settles over the eyes of the dead.

He bent down and examined her face, recalling how she'd looked in the interview room when she talked about singing, the one time she seemed happy. Now an entry wound disfigured one cheek, an ugly hole rimmed with powder burns. The exit wound on the other cheek was worse.

Sickened by the atrocity, he straightened. Fought down the bile that rose in his throat. "Somebody sending a message."

Miller nodded. "You find anything at the apartment?"

"She'd been there, looked like she left in a hurry, peanut butter and crackers on the counter."

Over Miller's shoulder, he saw Detective Sergeant Morgan Vobitch heading their way. A twenty-year NOPD veteran in his mid-fifties, Vobitch supervised the homicide detectives assigned to Districts One, Three and Eight. The day they met Vobitch had said they were birds of a feather—Yankee outsiders—Frank an Italian from Boston, Vobitch a New York Jew, with a big nose to match his pugnacious attitude. Other than his full head of wavy slate-gray hair, he resembled Sipowitz on *NYPD Blue,* and he had the same take-no-shit attitude.

Frank loved the guy.

Vobitch rolled up to them like a Sherman tank, his slate-gray eyes full of anger. "She was your girl, right, Frank? Damn shame. These fuckin maggots have no respect for life. None at all."

Frank clenched his jaw. "And I'm gonna nail them. I'm pretty sure she was squatting in Iberville."

Vobitch said to Miller, "You think AK was involved? He runs that place, right?"

"Last time I checked," Miller said. "Frank talked to him last week."

Vobitch swung his leonine head to Frank. "And?"

"I showed her picture to AK and two of his thugs. None of them knew her, of course."

"Of course." Vobitch's lip curled in a sneer. "Nobody'll know anything about this either, you ask around. You think she was in on the robbery? The clerk said the second kid was tall and skinny." He gestured at Chantelle's body. "She's about five-eight, skinny, hair cropped short. Maybe the clerk mistook her for a guy."

Frank shook his head. "No dreads."

Vobitch snapped his fingers. "Right. The second kid had dreads. You want in on the autopsy?"

The idea of watching the coroner dissect Chantelle's body sickened him.

The badass motherfucker inside him rose up like a cobra.

"No. I want to catch the sick fucks that killed her and bust their balls with a hammer."

CHAPTER 12

Wednesday, 25 October

Jake hurriedly loaded the dishes into the dishwasher and hit Start. It was later than usual. After dinner they'd lingered over Dean's latest concoction, chocolate torte with Grand Marnier sauce. Dean knew how much he loved chocolate, knew he could seduce him with it.

When he went in the living room, the sweet scent of pot filled the air. Slouched on the sofa, Dean gave him a dreamy smile and held out a fat blunt.

"Let's get buzzed, Jake. I had a helluva day. Traffic was insane, big accident on the I-10."

He took a hit and held the smoke in his lungs, waiting for the lazy feeling of lassitude to soothe him. He didn't do pot every day like Dean, but tonight he needed it. "Long day for me, too, what with the Cincinnati concert and the new security man. He's a pain in the ass. When I called, he insisted on coming right over so he could check the security system. He made me take him through the whole house and get him a key."

"To Belinda's house?" Dean gazed at him, wide-eyed. "Why?"

"In case the alarm goes off while we're away. The cops get pissed if no one's around to take care of it."

Dean's mouth quirked in disdain. "How's the Queen Bee doing?"

"She's fine. I still can't believe she called Renzi instead of me."

"Jealous, Jake?" Dean gazed at him, his eyes liquid-chocolate. "Renzi's Italian. Dark, dangerous and sexy. Maybe she'll fall for him."

"Who cares? I'm just glad she hired some security. If I bring up the accident or those awful notes, she won't discuss it. Bad luck, she says. She's so superstitious it's pathetic. I spent an hour on the phone today because some idiot at the hotel in Cincinnati gave her Room 813. When I booked it I *told* him not to give her a room with thirteen in it."

Dean took another hit, set the blunt in an ashtray and put his feet on the coffee table.

He stroked Dean's thigh. "I won't be gone long. We fly out Thursday, rehearse that night, play the concert on Friday. We'll be back on Saturday."

"Don't worry about me. I'm taking a few days off to fly to New York."

His heart quivered, a nervous tremolo. "To see your folks?"

And thought: *No, stupid. They live in Massachusetts.*

Dean mocked him with a smile. "Jake gets an F in geography. I've got an appointment at Pratt Institute. An advisor wants to show me around and tell me about their graduate degrees."

"Pratt?" he said stupidly. The pot had slowed his mind to a crawl.

"Yes, Pratt." Dean's voice crackled with anger. "You're the one that keeps saying I should go to art school."

"But Pratt's in New York City." Loathing the distress in his voice.

"Yes it is, Jake. In New York City. There are lots of organist jobs there, too. You used to have one, remember? Before you turned into Belinda's step-n-fetch-it. I'm sick of having my life revolve around Belinda."

Acid flooded his stomach. "Dean, please don't do this to me."

"I'm not doing anything to you. You think Belinda can't live without you. Bullshit. Let the security guy can be her gopher. You deserve to be happy. We deserve to be happy together."

"And I want us to be, but I can't just—"

"Yes, you can. Check the job postings on the American Guild of Organists website."

He stared at the floor, recalling the fabulous cultural offerings in New York. The Philharmonic, the Met opera, organ recitals at Riverside Church, art exhibits at MOMA. He and Dean could enjoy them together without worrying that some homophobic nutcase would see them and gossip about it. In New York they could be just another gay couple, unlike New Orleans.

Guilt crept into his thoughts like a London fog. What would Belinda do without him? He wasn't just her manager. She depended on him for emotional support. She also liked having a handsome, well-dressed man squire her around, a well-educated man who loved music. No strings attached. And what did she do for him? He couldn't confide in her, couldn't explain that Dean was six years younger than he was. Handsome and smart. Witty and fun. A joy to be with. He couldn't tell her his deepest fear: Dean might fall in love with another man.

He glanced at Dean, sitting beside him, eyes closed, head tipped back. The person he loved more than anyone in the world.

"You're right, Dean. I'll check the AGO website tomorrow."

Thursday, 26 October

He studied his beloved in the rearview, seated in the back seat of his Ford E-350XL van. He had invited her to sit in front with him, but she had refused. Disappointing, but given her recent troubles, he supposed it was natural that she'd be standoffish at first. That would soon change. Soon they'd be sleeping together in her cozy double bed.

Soon those pliant pink lips would be sucking his cock.

"When shall we sit down and discuss my security assessment?"

Her gaze met his in the rearview, eyes distant.

"I don't know. I hadn't thought about it."

"We should do it as soon as possible. How about tomorrow?"

A bicyclist zoomed out from a side street in front of him. He hit the brakes, gave the kid a nasty look and returned his attention to Belinda.

But she wasn't looking at him, intent on her stupid paperwork.

"Ma'am?" He was dying to call her Belinda as he did each night in his dreams, but he didn't want to appear too familiar. Plenty of time for that.

She met his gaze in the rearview. "What?"

"Can we discuss my security assessment tomorrow?"

"All right." Her sapphire-blue eyes defrosted a bit. "That's a nasty cut on your cheek."

He smiled at her in the mirror. "Last night at the gym I went three rounds with the local heavyweight. We were wearing helmets, but he clipped me pretty hard." A lie, but it sounded good. Yesterday, in his haste to make himself presentable, he'd cut himself shaving. But when he got to her house, Ziegler had showed him around, not Belinda. What a letdown.

"My British employer may not have mentioned it, but I had to rescue him once from a serious threat. A disturbed man tried to stab him. I put some muscle on the creep and ran him off. Damn near broke his arm."

Now his beloved was gazing at him with rapt attention. "No one will hurt you when I'm around, Ms. Scully. I'll keep you safe."

"Thank you, Mr. Silverman. I appreciate it."

He smiled. *You can show me your appreciation in bed. Soon.*

He waited for her outside in the courtyard. Belinda had four flute students at NOCCA so he'd be driving her here once a week. Before her first lesson, she had taken him to the office. A clerk printed his name—Barry Silverman—on a Permanent Visitor Pass and inserted it into a plastic lanyard to wear around his neck. He shoved it into the pocket of his tailored black suit and sank onto a gray-marble bench shaded by a two-story building.

A warm breeze ruffled raspberry-red flowers in the planters lining the rectangular courtyard. Belinda was teaching in the yellow-brick building to his right. Letters on a sign above the glass double-doors said: NEW ORLEANS CENTER FOR THE CREATIVE ARTS: RIVERFRONT. The lessons lasted forty-five minutes. Maybe she'd let him sit in on one sometime. That would be fun.

Two black students pushed through the glass doors, joking and laughing. Both wore Nikes and hooded sweatshirts. The boy's was red, the girl's green. They saw him and quieted.

"Beautiful day, isn't it?" He smiled, felt pleased when they smiled back.

Three more students emerged from the building, carrying violin cases, chattering away as they walked through the courtyard toward the parking lot. Moments later a stocky dark-skinned student burst through the doors and stomped down the steps. He looked angry: lower lip stuck out, brows knit in a frown as he marched along carrying a flute case. He didn't look much like a flute player, not with that squat chunky body and those thick fingers, holding the flute case in one hand, a music folder in the other.

"Hi there," he said. "I bet you're a flute player." Still scowling, the kid kept walking. "Seems like you're upset. I hope you're not mad at Belinda."

The kid jerked to a halt. "Why would I be mad at Ms. Scully?"

He spread his hands in a disarming gesture. "I guessed right? She's your teacher?" When the kid nodded, he said, "I'm her security guard. I'm a musician too, a pianist."

The kid said nothing, dark eyes wary, shifting his body back and forth, rocking from one foot to the other.

"My name's Barry, what's yours?" He offered his hand.

The kid had manners at least, came and shook his hand. "Marcus Goines. Ms. Scully's a great teacher. I been studying with her for two years."

"She's a marvelous flutist. I heard her play the Khatchatourian in London last week." He raised his thumb and forefinger to his lips and kissed them. "Magnifique!"

Marcus beamed and puffed out his chest. "Then you musta heard the encore, Gershwin's *I Got Rhythm*. I'm the one suggested it to her."

"That's terrific, Marcus." He patted the bench. "Tell me about it."

After a furtive glance around the courtyard, Marcus plopped onto the bench. "Ms. Scully's great for classical technique and tone, but jazz is a whole different ballgame."

"I know. I'm a pianist, remember?"

"You play jazz?" Giving him a dubious look.

"Classical, but I love jazz."

He tried to recall the names of some famous jazz pianists. Duke Ellington? No, he was dead and so was Count Basie. Finally, he managed to dredge up a name. "You dig McCoy Tyner?"

"Yeah, man, he's great. He was here for Jazz Fest."

"How come you were upset when you came outside?"

Marcus ducked his head and scuffed his sneaker over the cement.

"Did you know the girl that got murdered? I read about it in the newspaper."

"No." Staring at the ground as though he might bore a hole to China.

"Why would someone shoot a young girl like that?"

The kid looked at him, expressionless. "Lotta folks get murdered in this town. Her boyfriend's a student here, just about sleepwalked through his classes today."

"Goodness, why was he even in school? I should think he'd stay home and take time to grieve."

"Can't or he'd lose his scholarship. Besides, we had tryouts today to see who plays the solos on Friday's recital." Marcus jutted his lip. "Antoine won, like always. He's Mr. D's pet. He plays alto sax. That's why he gets all the solos. I'm just a flute player, hardly get any. How'm I gonna get into music school if I don't have a CD?"

Amazed, he said, "You need a CD to get into music school?"

"Sure. Everybody does one, like a portfolio, you know? They tape all the recitals here. If I take a solo with the jazz band, I can put it on my CD as part of my, uh, portfolio. I already taped a classical solo with piano. Ms. Scully helped me learn it."

"Who accompanied you? I've worked with lots of top-notch soloists. If you ever need an accompanist, I'd be glad to help you."

Marcus studied him for a long moment. "You would?"

"Sure. When I lived in Boston, I studied piano with a woman at NEC." Seeing mystification in the kid's eyes, he said, "New England Conservatory. It's a famous music school."

The kid gave a slow nod. "Cool."

"You know, I've got some connections at NEC. They've got a great jazz department, Third Stream, they call it. If you apply there, well, I can't promise, but I might even get you a scholarship."

"That would be great, sir." Giving him a happy-camper grin.

"No need to be formal, Marcus. We're musicians. Call me Barry."

"Okay, uh, Barry. Sorry, but I gotta go. I got an appointment."

"Check out the NEC website, and we'll talk again next week."

He had no connections at NEC, but Marcus studied with Belinda.

Who knows, that might be useful someday.

With his alto sax case slung over his shoulder, Antoine stared out the glass door, his heart a stone in his chest. Some of his classmates stood at the foot of the stairs, gossiping about him and Chantelle, probably. He didn't want to talk to them. If he had to talk to one more person today, he'd throw up. Bad enough going to class, kids asking how he was doing. How did they think he was doing, Chantelle lying on a slab somewhere, dead?

And he knew who killed her. AK. The bastard had killed the most important person in his life except for his parents. And it was his own damn fault. Never should have gone to Lakeview, never should have agreed to help AK rob that store. Since then everything had turned to shit.

Yesterday morning at breakfast he'd read the newspaper article: Chantelle Wilson, age 15, found dead near Bayou St. John. He was so shocked he didn't even cry, waited until he left the house. He had to go to school 'cuz Mr. D was auditioning soloists at today's rehearsal. Mr. D had picked him to play the best one. But Chantelle wouldn't hear it.

Tears blurred his vision. Her funeral was tomorrow. His teachers were understanding, telling him to take the day off. He didn't want to. Going to music classes and playing his sax were the only things that took his mind off the most terrible thing that had happened in his whole life. Chantelle. Dead.

Through the glass door he saw Marcus talking to some white guy in a business suit. Maybe he was one of Marcus' customers, though Antoine doubted it. Marcus didn't deal drugs on the school grounds.

He turned and trudged down the corridor. Marcus was pissed Mr. D had picked him to play the most important solo. Only way he got though the audition was thinking about Chantelle. How much he loved her.

And now she was gone. Forever. Hate burned his gut and AK's words burned his brain. *Keep your mouth shut or you dead.*

AK had killed Chantelle, might be fixing to kill him, too.

CHAPTER 13

Thursday, 26 October

Morgan Vobitch stormed into the conference room and dropped two thick binders on the table with a loud thump. Dead silence and grim faces replaced the chatter that had preceded his entrance. Eight homicide detectives from Districts One, Three and Eight sat around a rectangular oak table, its top marred by coffee-mug rings.

Frank studied his boss's expression. Vobitch had just held a media briefing on the Lakeview case. This would be a tense meeting.

Vobitch eyeballed them, his slate-gray eyes cold and merciless. "As of now we assume the Lakeview case and the Wilson murder are connected. That is not for publication. Any leaks, heads will roll."

Frank looked at Kenyon Miller to his right, then across the table at the lone woman in the room. Kelly O'Neil, mid-thirties, ten-years with NOPD. He'd heard sad stories about her personal life. Her short dark hair was styled in a Liza Minelli pixie-cut that framed her oval face. An attractive woman. He liked her direct gaze, regarding him now with her sea-green eyes.

Her District-3 colleagues sat beside her: Warren Wood, stroking the ginger-colored Fu Manchu of which he was so proud, and pasty-faced Chuck Duncan, sporting his usual sad-sack expression. Otis Jones and Sam Wallace occupied the far end of the table. The two black detectives handled more than their share of murders working out of District-1, which included the Iberville housing project and Treme, a predominantly black neighborhood.

"Let's focus on the Wilson murder," Vobitch said. "I'll summarize the autopsy report."

A ceiling fan twirled cool air through the room, but Frank's shirt was damp with sweat. The past two nights he'd slept in fits and starts, visions of Chantelle Wilson's disfigured face and vacant eyes jolting him awake.

"She took two slugs in the chest," Vobitch said, reading from the autopsy report. "One went through her heart and lodged in her spine, coroner said she died within a minute. The second one lodged in a rib, different caliber slugs—a .38 and a .45—so we got two shooters. The coroner believes the gunshot wound to the face was post-mortem."

"Sending a message," Frank said. "Her face was a mess. That means a closed casket. Word gets around fast on these things."

"A Hollywood makeup artist couldn't fix it." Warren massaged his Fu Manchu and grinned. "Not that her family could afford one."

He clenched his jaw at the gratuitous remark, felt Miller's foot nudge his under the table. Miller had no use for Warren, said he was borderline racist, useless in black neighborhoods. Miller also ridiculed Warren's Fu Manchu, said it made him look even dumber than he was.

"I spoke to the Mom last night," Miller said, flipping through his notes. "She's in Houston. She was so zonked, I was lucky to pry the step-dad's phone number out of her. He's in Atlanta. I talked to him this morning. Langston Cano, works as a bus driver."

"Any possibility he was one of the shooters?" Vobitch said.

"Not a chance," Miller said. "I spoke to his supervisor at the bus company. Cano was working during the TOD window. He said he was sorry he didn't take the girl with him to Atlanta during Katrina."

"Why didn't he?" Frank snapped. "He knew the mother's a crackhead."

Kelly O'Neil caught his eye and nodded. He was grateful for the support, but he knew blaming Cano would solve nothing. It wouldn't bring Chantelle back to life.

Vobitch raked stubby fingers through his silvery hair. "We should cover the funeral. When is it?"

"Tomorrow," Miller said. "Visitation at one, funeral Mass at two."

"I'll be there," he said. It was SOP for detectives to attend the funerals of murder victims in case the killer showed up, but even if it wasn't, he'd be there. Certain cases infused him with a rage so violent he wanted to punch his fist through a wall. The atrocities people inflicted on others disgusted him. Those inflicted on women were often worse, and Chantelle was barely a woman. Sixteen years old next month she'd told him, fourteen days ago.

Miller said, "I'll go with Frank."

"I'll go," Kelly said, gazing at Frank, her eyes tinged with sadness.

"We'll be there," said Otis Jones. The dark-skinned gray-bearded detective gestured at his young partner, Sam Wallace, a baby-faced man with smooth milk-chocolate skin.

Warren and Chuck remained silent, eyes fixed on the table.

"I'd go," Vobitch said, "but contrary to the media hype, we got other homicides, more than a hundred so far this year, two months to go. And we know what happens during the holidays. Family members get riled up and decide to kill someone. Themselves or their beloved relatives."

Chuckles rippled around the table. Dark humor about dark deeds.

"The Wilson girl had a tattoo on her left breast," Vobitch said. "A red heart with two initials. The bullet obliterated the right one. The left one was singed but legible, coroner said it's an 'A.'"

"Might be initials," Frank said. "Her boyfriend, maybe."

"Sounds deliberate," said Sam Wallace, disgust visible on his face. "First slug knocks her down, they pull up her shirt to hit the tat." He shrugged. "Maybe that's farfetched, but—"

"No." Frank leaned forward over the table to lock eyes with him. "I think they knew her, probably knew the boyfriend, too."

Otis nodded. "Maggots sending a message to the boyfriend."

Reading from the report, Vobitch said, "The coroner found evidence of sexual activity. Her hymen was not intact so she wasn't a virgin. But he found no semen, no bruising on her vagina or labia. He combed the pubic hair. We'll see what we get from that."

"Maybe the initials were her pimp's." Warren sent a sardonic smile around the table. "Teenage girls these days? Lot of them are hookers."

"Hey," Kelly snapped, "women like sex too. It doesn't mean we're all out selling it. What if it was your daughter?"

Warren fingered his Fu Manchu. "My daughter's not a hooker."

Anger flashed in Kelly's eyes. "You better hope some drunk never beats her up, rapes her and tells you it was consensual and she loved it."

Warren flushed beet-red, and a pall of silence fell over the room. Kelly leaned back in her chair, lips set in a line, a jaw muscle working. Frank was touched that she'd stood up for Chantelle. He'd heard she was the go-to female cop for interviewing rape victims. Before joining Homicide after Katrina, she had worked Domestic Violence.

Vobitch broke the silence. "Frank, did she mention a boyfriend when you interviewed her?"

"No. She didn't even want to tell me her name." He scratched the scar on his jaw, recalling her wistful expression when she asked if he knew a tune called *Nowhere*. His throat tightened.

That's where Chantelle had wound up. Nowhere.

Vobitch fixed him with a stern gaze. "When you left her apartment, did you take the peanut butter and crackers with you?"

Laughter rippled through the room, all eyes on Frank now. Knowing Vobitch was trying to lighten things up, he said, "Just copping my daily fluffernutter." When the guffaws died down, he said, "I locked up when I left. If the crackers were gone when Forensics got there, somebody's got a key."

"Seems like it," Vobitch said. "Forensics got a ton of prints but they have to eliminate the occupants and any known visitors. No telling who's been in there since Katrina."

"How about AK?" Miller asked. "We must have his prints on file. AK's been in trouble since the Civil War."

Raucous laughter erupted. Sometimes dark humor was the only way to endure crimes this sickening.

"How's Robichard?" Frank said. Robichard was the off-duty policeman shot during the robbery. "I hear he's out of intensive care."

"You heard right," Vobitch said, and cheers went up around the table. "Jim Whitworth's at the hospital now, trying to get more details. Chuck, what'd you get on the getaway car?"

Chuck pulled a long face. "Not much. I checked the stolen car reports, pulled up six late-model black Cadillacs. But a lotta Caddy's got flooded in Katrina, no telling who's driving them now. I'm checking the chop-shops, got two more to go. I'm not hopeful."

"Keep looking," Vobitch said. "Anybody got anything else?"

When no one spoke, he said, "Okay, let's work the Wilson case hard. Solve that one we might break the Lakeview case. It's been two weeks since that sucker and I need something to feed the media vultures."

As Vobitch left the room Miller leaned over and said, "Pick me up tomorrow, we go to the funeral together, okay?"

"You got it," he said. He watched Warren and Chuck leave the room, followed by Sam and Otis. Amidst the chatter of voices, Kelly O'Neil remained in her chair, pawing through her purse. He scribbled something in his notepad, marking time until Kenyon Miller left. Once Miller cleared the door, he said, "Sometimes you gotta give these guys a dope-slap. Nice job."

She rose to her feet and flashed a smile, her sensual lips parting to reveal even white teeth. "Warren can be a jerk sometimes. Good job yourself, sticking up for the girl."

He rose and approached her. Up close her sea-green eyes were mesmerizing, and he liked her perfume, spicy with a hint of vanilla.

Seemingly flustered, she twisted a lock of hair around one finger. "I was wondering if you could advise me on a rape case. Not now, but later maybe? I interviewed the victim at the hospital and—"

"You're doing double duty these days? Homicide and Violent Crimes?"

She shrugged. "They call me if they can't get another female cop. It happens a lot these days. I don't mind."

This was their first real conversation, but he'd watched her lift weights at the gym where a lot of the cops worked out. She had a rangy body, slim but muscular, five-seven, nice ass, great legs. A tempting package.

He realized she was waiting for him to speak. "I'll help if I can."

"I think we might have a serial rapist on our hands, and I know you've had experience in that area."

Word got around if a cop had taken courses at the FBI training school in Quantico. Maybe that's why she'd volunteered to go to Chantelle's funeral. She wanted help on the rape case.

"Sorry," she said, grinning at him. "That sounds like I'm calling you an experienced rapist."

"True," he deadpanned. "I knock off at least one woman a night."

Equally deadpan, she said, "That's what I figured."

"How about I buy you a beer someplace and we talk it over?"

"No, how about I buy *you* a beer. You're the one doing the favor."

"We'll argue about it over the beer. Where and when?"

And gave himself a dope-slap. He'd just agreed to have a beer with this attractive female cop, a big violation of his rules. But who was he kidding? That's what he'd been angling for when he waited for the others to leave.

"How about The Bulldog Bar?" she said. "Tomorrow night?"

"Tomorrow's Friday, right?" He mentally checked his schedule, seemed like he had something Friday night. Then he remembered. Belinda's NOCCA concert. Maybe he'd invite Kelly to go. No, bad idea. Should he ask her to have the beer tonight? No. That would seem overeager.

"I can't do it tomorrow, but Saturday night I'm meeting my CI. She's kind of skittish, likes to meet me after dark. Can we meet afterwards, eight o'clock, eight-thirty?"

"Fine," Kelly said, gazing at him with her mesmerizing eyes. "See you at the Bulldog."

His pulse increased a notch. Then he saw Kenyon Miller outside the door, watching them. Great. The rumor mill would be grinding tomorrow.

"Thanks for volunteering to go to Chantelle's funeral," he said.

Kelly's eyes turned somber, an angry squint. "Maybe the maggots that killed her will be there."

"If they are, you better cuff me so I don't strangle them."

Friday morning at eight he unlocked the front door and stepped into Belinda's foyer. His second day with his beloved. His heart sang a triumphant tune. Soon he wouldn't be walking in the front door. He'd be waking up in bed with her. "Ms. Scully," he called. "Are you ready?"

She came through a door at the end of the hall that bordered the stairs to her second floor bedroom. Her hair looked lovely, as though she'd brushed her coppery tresses an extra hundred strokes, just for him.

"I need to change. Could you wait in the foyer, please?" Dressed in shorts and an emerald-green top, she came down the hall, gave him a perfunctory smile and went upstairs.

He watched her, admiring her well-muscled legs. Too bad he couldn't watch her undress. Ziegler had been reluctant to show him her bedroom, but he had insisted. He'd expected something luxurious, a mirror lined with lights over an elegant dressing table, a plush chair to use while she brushed her hair. But there was just an oak bureau and a double bed with a gold quilt drooping onto the polished-oak floor. He couldn't wait to get her in bed.

They would have an orgy. A royal fuck-fest. His groin throbbed as he surveyed the foyer. Two black umbrellas sprouted from a metal urn beside a settee with stubby legs and claw feet. Restless with energy, he went around the corner to her studio. He was dying to play her Steinway baby grand. Belinda was sure to be impressed. Not today, but soon.

He crossed the hall to the other room that faced the street. Through the half-open door he saw Ziegler hunched over a computer keyboard. He stepped inside. "Good morning, Mr. Ziegler. Beautiful day, isn't it?"

Ziegler looked up, his eyes cold and distant. "Do you need something? As you can see, I'm busy."

"Just saying hello. Belinda's upstairs changing. We'll be off soon."

Ziegler swiveled back to the computer. "Fine. Have a nice day."

He left before Ziegler could see his flush of embarrassment. Here he was trying to be friendly and the prick was treating him like a servant. That needed to change. He returned to the foyer and studied his image in the gilt-framed mirror over the settee. He looked splendid in his black Armani suit. But it had cost seven-hundred-dollars. Another maxed-out credit card.

Hearing footsteps on the stairs, he turned, and his breath caught in his throat. Belinda had changed into a blue-knit dress that hugged her luscious body. The tingle in his groin became a full-fledged erection.

She swept past him and opened the front door. "I need to buy some shoes at a little boutique where I shop. I'll tell you how to get there."

He followed her, hurrying to keep up as she strode toward his van, trailing a hint of perfume. He slid back the door to the passenger compartment. "Any time you want to ride up front, just let me know."

"Thanks, but I prefer to ride in back. Go south on Esplanade."

Anger warmed his cheeks as he climbed behind the wheel. "Have the police found the person that caused your accident?"

"They're working on it."

"Do they have any leads?" He drove off, slowly, so he could watch her in the rearview, but she didn't look up. "Did you give them a description?"

"Please, I don't want to talk about it."

Fuming, he turned right on Esplanade and drove past two Victorians and a row of towering oaks dripping Spanish moss. She was being a Diva. He had read every article ever written about her dozens of times. Most were complimentary, but a recent one said that flute virtuoso Belinda Scully could be rather haughty. But not if he charmed her.

"I think you're very brave, Ms. Scully. You're a strong, self-reliant woman. Do you take after Dad?"

A short silence, then, "We were very close, yes."

"That was a terrible tragedy, losing your parents in that accident."

"I don't care to discuss it, Mr. Silverman." An icy tone and a frosty look.

"I really admire you for not discussing it with reporters. You're a talented soloist. That's what people should remember. Your talent."

He glanced over his shoulder. She was staring out the window. How could she be so ungrateful? Here he was lavishing sympathy and emotional support on her, and what did he get in return? Icy looks and bad attitude.

"Thank you, Mr. Silverman. That's precisely how I see it."

A crumb of appreciation. Emboldened, he said, "Remember that lunatic that ran onto a tennis court and stabbed Monica Seles years ago? It's even more dangerous for celebrities now. Not that you need to worry. I served in the military. I'm trained to take out the enemy in all sorts of situations, even hand-to-hand combat. I'll protect you."

Her sapphire-blue eyes locked onto his in the rearview. Inwardly smiling at her anxious expression, he went for the kill. "I think it's best if I drive you to your concert tonight. You never can tell. Some nutcase might be there. What time shall I pick you up?"

His clearly-frightened Diva gazed at him. "Six-thirty would be good."

CHAPTER 14

A halo of golden sunlight hovered over the bell tower of Holy Ghost Church. A stark contrast to the somber ceremony inside, Frank assumed. Bells and sunshine sure as hell didn't match his mood. Four days ago a brutal bell had tolled for Chantelle Wilson, ending her short troubled life. An hour ago her coffin had arrived in a white horse-drawn carriage driven by a black man in a tuxedo, top hat and white gloves. A heart-wrenching sight.

Seeing it now, he wished the carriage was awaiting a pair of happy newlyweds, not the body of a teenaged girl.

Beside him, leaning against the trunk of an oak tree, Miller said, "They spent some bucks on the funeral, probably been out collecting donations."

"The funeral director told me her mother didn't have enough money to buy a burial dress." A statement that had led him to write a hundred-dollar check to help pay the funeral expenses.

"I told the step-dad to ask the Crime Victims Reparations Board for help," Miller said, "but they didn't give him a dime. They said Chantelle was involved in criminal activity. Man, was he pissed."

Where was he when Chantelle needed him? Frank thought, eyeballing the houses across the street from the church. Nobody out on the stoop enjoying the cool October breeze, plenty watching from inside probably. Nothing like a funeral to liven up your day.

Nothing like the murder of a young girl to darken his mood.

"I'm glad Kelly volunteered to go inside," Miller said. "Man, I hate funerals."

"Me, too." His mother's funeral six years ago had been the most painful day of his life. The only funeral he had attended since was at another black church in Boston. Another girl dead before her time.

Miller waggled his eyebrows. "How you getting on with Kelly? Fine looking woman like that, time she got back in the saddle."

"Yeah?" he said, irritated. "You an expert on grieving widows?"

"Can't grieve forever. She's only thirty-eight."

And you never buried a spouse, Frank thought.

Solemn organ music wafted from the church as the doors opened. A white casket emerged carried by eight grim-faced young men, hands encased in white cotton gloves as they muscled Chantelle's casket down three steps. Behind them came Anna-Mae Wilson, thin as a knitting needle in a black dress with shiny black buttons, eyes hidden by sunglasses, wailing, her mouth open to reveal the gaping holes of missing teeth. Frank figured she wasn't much over forty. She looked sixty. Crack could do that to you.

The stepfather, a broad-shouldered man with a gray-speckled beard, had one arm around the mother's scrawny frame. His free hand clutched the fingers of a little boy dressed in a miniature black suit, his eyes big and round and brimming with tears.

Walking stiff-legged, the pallbearers reached the horse-drawn carriage and hoisted Chantelle's casket into the back. Unable to bear it, Frank turned away. Clumps of teenagers emerged from the church, hugging each other, the girls wiping their eyes with tissues, the boys wearing dark glasses. He marveled at how quiet they were. No chatterbox teens here, just silent mourners, wearing the memorial T-shirts that seemed obligatory at the funerals of young New Orleans residents these days.

"Dig the shirts," Miller said. "It's a cottage industry nowadays, 'banger gets shot, family takes his picture to the T-shirt joint before the coroner's released the body."

Frank's throat tightened as two sobbing girls passed them. Centered on their memorial T-shirts was a photograph of Chantelle, laughing, her eyes full of sparkle, looked like she was having the time of her life. A life cut short by a retaliatory bullet. Above it was her birth date: 11-11-1991.

The coincidence shocked him. They shared the same birthday: November 11. Next month he'd be forty-four. Chantelle hadn't made it to her sixteenth birthday.

Below the photo: **CHANTELLE "Song Sista" WILSON, R.I.P. 10-23-2006.**

Song Sista. The girl who loved to sing. The girl who loved a tune called *Nowhere*. The senseless tragedy tore at his heart. Tears blurred his vision. But he would shed no tears for Chantelle. He would find her killers and get her the justice she deserved.

Lost in thought, he jumped when Kelly touched his forearm and said, "There must have been a hundred kids in the church, but no sign of AK."

She looked trim and businesslike today in a black pantsuit that made her sea-green eyes look even more alluring. But they were bloodshot, looked like she'd been crying.

"Thanks, Kelly. You did the tough part."

"No problem," she said.

But he got the feeling it had indeed been a problem.

"The maggot's probably in some bar," Miller said. "Having a beer with his buddies."

"No," Kelly snapped. "The little maggots are crawling the bottom of some garbage pail." About to say more, she turned as toots and honks sounded behind the church, then upbeat drums.

He studied her profile. A strong chin—she was stubborn, he'd bet—and distinctive ears, shaped like seashells, with gold studs in them.

A rousing rendition of "Rampart Street Parade" cut into his thoughts. Teenagers playing trumpets, trombones and saxophones marched around the corner of the church. Ahead of them, two boys carried a six-foot banner with more pictures of Chantelle. Walking between the banner and the band was a tall slender kid in sunglasses, his hair in dreadlocks, carrying an instrument case. Judging by its size and shape, Frank pegged it as an alto sax case.

Why wasn't he playing? Frank wondered.

Two stragglers leaving the church in memorial T-shirts and baggy pants caught his attention. What set them apart: a spider web tat on the tall kid's neck, bloody daggers on the shorter kid's forearms.

He drew Kenyon and Kelly closer. "Don't turn around. I just made two of AK's thugs coming out of the church."

"You think they're the shooters?" Kelly said, gazing at him.

Mesmerized by her sea-green eyes, he said, "Could be."

Would those eyes mesmerize him tomorrow night at the Bulldog Bar, he wondered.

Inside the walk-in closet beneath the eaves of her bedroom, Belinda flipped through her gig suits and selected a pair of black velvet pants. Slinky but comfortable. Perfect for tonight's concert. Figuring the only people at the NOCCA concert would be students and their friends and families, she had planned to wear a plain white blouse.

That was before she invited Frank. Now that the London concert had won her a fabulous recording contract, she could focus on the intriguing homicide detective. And the deep connection she felt when she was with him.

She took out a teal-green top. The color complimented her hair, and the scoop neck displayed her creamy skin. It had cost plenty to erase the splotches on her neck and shoulders, ugly reminders of the hours she'd spent at the beach as a teenager, trying for a tan and getting sunburned instead.

She put the outfit on her bed, removed her robe and studied herself in the full-length mirror beside the closet. She never worried about her weight. One-hundred-fifteen pounds in high school, not an ounce more now. But her upper arms looked flabby. She needed to work out more.

A tap sounded on the door. "I'm about to leave, Bee. Need anything before I go?"

She put on her robe and belted it. "Come in, Jake. I'm getting ready for tonight's concert."

When he stepped into the room, she held up her teal-green top.

"Do you think this is too dressy for the NOCCA concert?"

"It's fine," he said, pacing the oval rug between her bed and dresser. "You know, I'm not sure Silverman is going to work out."

"Why not?" She picked up the velvet pants.

"He's getting on my nerves. He comes in my office when I'm working."

"He's just making conversation, trying to get to know you."

"He doesn't give a damn about me. He's more interested in *you*."

"That's his job, isn't it? Jake, you're the one that wanted me to hire a security man." She inspected the pants. Nothing looked worse than lint specks on black velvet. She took a lint brush out of her dresser drawer and rolled it over one leg of the pants.

"I caught him going through the file cabinet this morning. And he wants to come with us when you play the concert in Cincinnati."

She finished one leg and started on the other. "I don't think that's necessary, do you?"

"That's what I told him, but he told me to check with you."

"He's not a bad guy once you get to know him. I think he's a bit insecure—"

"Insecure? Christ, he's your security man!"

"That's not what I meant. He's an excellent driver. I meant *personally* insecure. He's not that attractive. All those acne scars and that frizzy hair. We chatted today in the car. He thinks I'm absolutely right not to talk to reporters about the accident."

She raised the teal-green top to her nose and detected a chemical odor from the dry cleaners. Maybe she could mask it with perfume. If Frank asked her out after the concert, she didn't want to smell like a chem lab.

"What accident?" Jake said.

She looked at him. "The accident that killed my family. What did you think I was talking about?"

"The accident last week when someone ran you off the road. The one in the restaurant parking lot when someone tried to *kill* you!"

"Stop saying that!" She hugged the nubby terrycloth robe against her bare skin. "You're trying to scare me, and I don't like it!"

He came closer, eyes full of concern. "I worry about you, Bee."

Then why did you threaten to leave me?

She gave him one of her high-wattage smiles. "Mr. Silverman's a bit awkward, but he's harmless. He's driving me to the NOCCA concert tonight. Go on home and have a nice dinner with Dean."

Jake gazed at her silently for several seconds, and left without further argument. How could he argue? She'd sent him home to spend time with his beloved Dean. He couldn't use that as an excuse to leave her.

Her stomach clenched. If Jake left, she'd be all alone. She felt like she'd been alone forever. Her family, killed by a drunk driver. Nick, expecting her to abandon her career to have his baby. Guy, seducing her, then kissing her off. Ramon, a virtuoso bassist, seducing her with his music and lovemaking, promising they'd be together some day. A dream thwarted by his spitfire wife, whose ugly threats had driven her out of Boston.

She made her mind go blank. Chanted her lucky mantra. *Never give in to fear. Act successful and you will be successful. Believe in yourself and you cannot fail.*

To hell with Nick and Guy and Ramon. They were ancient history. Her career was taking off. Fame was right around the corner.

She put on the teal-green top and studied her image in the mirror. She'd tell the kid in charge of lighting to kill the lights for her solo and put a green spot on her. That would get their attention.

All eyes would be on her, including Frank's. Frank wasn't married. And she was Belinda Scully, a strong woman with talent and personality and determination. A winner who went after what she wanted. And usually got it.

She could tell he was attracted to her. A delicious tingle swept her body.

Her performance was certain to captivate him. After the concert, when he came back stage to congratulate her, she would charm him into taking her out for a drink.

After that, anything could happen.

CHAPTER 15

At the last minute Frank changed his mind and went to the NOCCA concert. Maybe a dose of jazz would dispel his dark mood and take his mind off Chantelle's funeral. The Black Box Theater held maybe a hundred chairs on risers that formed a U facing the stage. By the time he got there most of them were occupied. A grand piano sat stage left; a full trap set with shiny cymbals of various sizes sat stage right. Near the back wall an amplifier powered two large speakers located on either side of the stage. He took a seat at the end of a row near the door in case he had to make a fast exit.

The lights dimmed and a tall black man with a neat goatee stepped to a microphone. Greeted by warm applause, the NOCCA music director welcomed the audience and introduced the jazz band director, Leonard Dawson, a freckle-faced redhead. Bouncing with enthusiasm, Dawson led off the concert with a lower-level quintet.

Frank was impressed with the drummer, an energetic black kid with fantastic time, but the bass player, dwarfed by his instrument, struggled to be heard. The piano player showed flashes of talent amidst clichéd jazz licks, same with the guitar player. To close the set a young trumpet player took a chorus on "Well You Needn't." Frank wanted to grab his trumpet and show him how to improvise, the kid never stopping to rest, playing a zillion notes that went nowhere. No matter. The crowd gave him a standing ovation.

The first group left the stage and NOCCA's top jazz group took their places. Frank checked the program. After their set, Belinda Scully would play. The scholarship quintet featured a chubby black kid on flute, a slender black kid on alto sax, white kids on piano and bass, and the same drummer as before. Halfway through "The Touch of Your Lips," the alto sax player stepped forward to take a solo.

He wore dark glasses and a suit jacket over a Chantelle memorial T-shirt. That got Frank's attention. The kid had talent, fluid technique, nice transitions over the chord changes, knew enough to leave some space between the notes. At the end of his third chorus, the kid faded away, the mournful sound ending in an almost-silent moan.

DIVA

The audience erupted in wild applause, but the kid didn't acknowledge it. As the band continued playing, he tipped an imaginary hat to the director and walked offstage. Frank slipped out of the dark theater and checked the program for the Scholarship Quintet roster.

Alto saxophone, Antoine Carter. First initial *A*. Last initial *C*.

He went to the foyer and looked down the hall that led backstage. No sign of Antoine Carter. The kid with the memorial T-shirt. The kid he'd seen at Chantelle's funeral this afternoon. He pushed through the glass doors onto the shadowy courtyard, hoping Antoine would soon appear. Belinda's solo was next and he didn't want to miss it.

Five minutes passed. No sign of the kid. Maybe he was still backstage. Maybe he'd left through another door. Maybe he wasn't leaving. Concealed in shadow alongside the building, Frank decided to go back inside. Stopped as Antoine pushed through the glass doors and hustled down the steps, head down, dreadlocks braided in thin strands brushing his shoulders.

Frank stepped out of the shadows to intercept him. "Nice solo. You listen to Chet Baker a lot?"

The kid froze, poised to run like a deer in the headlights.

"You dig Chet Baker?" he said softly, dark-skinned face expressionless. Sunglasses masked his eyes, so it was hard to gauge his feelings, except for his lips. His lips were set in a grim line.

"Your improv on 'Touch of Your Lips' reminded me of some things Chet Baker used to do," Frank said. "But your sound now . . . you sound more like Antonio Hart. Or Kenny Garrett, maybe."

The kid's lips twitched, almost a smile, still looked like he wanted to run.

"Didn't I see you at Chantelle's funeral this afternoon?"

Antoine's head jerked up, though his face remained impassive.

"I was there." He flashed his ID. "NOPD Detective Frank Renzi. Was Chantelle your girlfriend?"

"You the cop put her in that foster home?" the kid asked, fear radiating from him in waves.

"Yes. I caught her in Lakeview. What was she doing up there?"

"Don't know nothin about that."

"Did you know she was squatting at Iberville?"

Ten seconds passed. Fifteen. Emotion rolling over the kid's face.

"Only thing I know, she's dead."

"And you're hurting," he said gently. "I want to catch her killer, Antoine. She was too young to die. What was she doing in Lakeview that night?"

A stillness came over the kid, restrained tension, as though he was willing himself not to run.

He decided not to push it. "Go home and listen to some music, Antoine. That's what I do when I'm hurting." He held out his card. "I told Chantelle to call me if she needed help. And I'm telling you the same thing. Call my cell phone if you're in trouble. Anytime, day or night."

For a second he thought the kid wouldn't take it. After an eternity, Antoine reached for the card, turned and trudged across the courtyard.

Frank watched him, aching for the kid.

Crime was off the chart since Katrina, the good folks unable to return, the thugs back with a vengeance, dealing drugs and settling scores, which meant most of the victims were young and black and poor.

Setting his gloomy thoughts aside, he entered the building, hustled down a hallway and slipped into his seat in the Black Box Theater.

Belinda stood onstage with one of her flute students. "My student Marcus Goines inspired the piece I'm about to play," she said. "My variations on George Gershwin's *I've Got Rhythm*."

A chunky black kid with close-cropped hair, Marcus almost levitated. His chest puffed out and a broad smile suffused his face as the audience applauded. He gave a stiff bow and left the stage. As he took his seat, Belinda gazed out at the audience as though she was searching for someone.

Frank sank lower in his seat, hoping she wouldn't spot him. She looked gorgeous, not eye-candy but close, slim and trim in a pair of black velvet pants, coppery hair brushing her teal-green top.

"George dedicated *I've Got Rhythm* to his brother Ira," she said, her eyes bright with tears. "I'd like to dedicate this performance of the piece to *my* brother. Blaine Scully."

She raised her flute to her mouth and played the melody, swaying to the music, flaunting her fat silky sound. Then, an abrupt shift into double-time, playing at breakneck speed, swoops and swirls of high notes, low notes and everything in between. The third chorus she took in a slow-drag did everything but shimmy her hips, emitting low sexy growls on her flute. The final chorus was pure virtuosity as she played the melody in one octave, splashing a zillion notes in the octave above.

The ending brought whoops and applause. Belinda bowed and blew kisses to the audience. But her playing left him cold. She had great chops, but the performance seemed designed to display her virtuosity, not the music. Belinda Scully was very attractive, very intelligent, very charming and very talented. And she knew it. That's why she had invited him to the concert.

Maybe he had misinterpreted the vibe she had sent him at her house that night. Then, it had seemed like a seduction.

Tonight it felt like a love-me vibe, more needy than seductive.

Protocol dictated that he go backstage and congratulate her. But he didn't feel like it. Chantelle's funeral had put him in a funk. Talking to Antoine had made it worse. Like Romeo and Juliet, Antoine and Chantelle were star-crossed lovers, but in this case only one lover had died. The other was suffering.

He left the theater wishing he could talk to Gina and get her take on the Lakeview case. A savvy investigative reporter, Gina covered the crime beat for the Boston *Herald*. He hadn't spoken with her for two years. Gina had found someone else. He still missed her.

But he lived in New Orleans now. And so did Kelly O'Neil. Tomorrow night he would meet her at The Bulldog. Kelly with the sea-green eyes, sensuous lips, and mischievous sense of humor. Tempting, but dangerous.

They both worked Homicide. Hell, they even had the same supervisor.

Definitely against his rules.

Then again, lots of times his motto was FTR. Fuck the rules.

———

Sick with disappointment, Belinda walked along the path to the parking lot beside Mr. Silverman. She'd seen Frank in the audience, had waited for him after the concert, anticipating the admiration in his eyes when he came backstage to compliment her bravura performance. He hadn't.

She couldn't understand it. At her house after the accident he'd been so kind and considerate, soothing her anguish when she told him about the abortion. The chemistry between them was unmistakable. There had to be some explanation. Maybe he'd been called to an emergency, like that first night at the station.

She glanced at Mr. Silverman, striding along beside her, tall and muscular in his tailored black suit. Unlike Frank, he had lavished praise on her solo. Too bad he wasn't more attractive. His voice was annoying, too, an adenoidal drone. Still, he did make her feel safer. A full moon shone down upon the few remaining cars, Mr. Silverman's van and half a dozen others scattered about the dark deserted lot.

"Hey, Belinda," a voice called, "that was a great solo. Can I have your autograph?"

Her lips spread in a smile. At least someone liked her performance.

She stopped and turned to look. A burly bearded man approached her, waving a piece of paper. He looked like a lumberjack: dark beard, massive shoulders, scruffy jeans and a Minnesota Vikings sweatshirt.

"You're a hottie, Belinda." He stepped closer, looming over her, his breath reeking of alcohol, his piggish eyes devouring her body. "How 'bout a kiss for one of your fans?"

Her heart jolted. What a disgusting man. In all her years of playing concerts, nothing like this had ever happened to her. She started to turn away, but he reached out and tried to grab her, his expression angry. "Hey, bitch, gimme your autograph!"

Her knees went weak with fear. What if he stole her flute? Panic-stricken, she gripped her flute case with both hands. Mr. Silverman stepped in front of her, shoved the disgusting man away.

The man staggered back, lost his balance and fell to the ground.

Silverman grabbed her arm and hustled her toward his van. She hurried to keep up, her feet skimming the blacktop, clutching her flute case against her pounding heart. Spouting vile curses, the drunk followed them. When they reached Mr. Silverman's van, he ran up to them. With a look of insane fury, he lunged at her, swinging his ham-like fists.

Silverman grabbed his arm, twisted it hard and threw him to the ground.

"Snotty bitch," the man screamed. "I'll get you . . ."

Silverman shoved her into the van and slammed the door.

She sank onto the back seat, shaking with tremors, heart pounding like a wild thing. Through the window she saw Silverman yank the drunk to his feet and force-march him away, shoving him toward the railroad tracks. She could still hear the man's vile curses.

Unwilling to look, she put her face in her hands.

And then Mr. Silverman was opening the van door. He climbed behind the wheel, turned and looked at her with obvious concern.

"Are you all right, Belinda?"

She took a deep breath, fighting for control. "I'm fine. Thank you."

He gazed at her, his pale blue eyes intent. "I'm sorry that idiot accosted you. These things are hard to anticipate. You never know when some drunk might come along."

"It's a good thing you were here." A nervous laugh escaped her lips. "You saved me."

He smiled. "That's why you hired me, Belinda. Relax. I'll have you home in no time, safe and sound."

CHAPTER 16

"That girl wasn't just lost, right?" Angela gazed at him, eyes solemn in the dim glow of the streetlight beside his car. "I ask around, you know, show that picture you gave me? Nobody wants to talk. And now she's dead."

He locked eyes with her. "Right. Now she's dead. Somebody killed her."

"She living in Iberville, AK mixed up in it."

"You know that for sure?"

"No!" A vehement headshake. "That just be my guess." Angela wouldn't look at him now, hunched her shoulders and stared out the windshield, sank lower in her seat as a bus lumbered past them belching smelly exhaust fumes.

"I need a lead, Angela. She was only fifteen. She didn't deserve to get murdered. I want to catch the thugs that killed her."

His plea got him nowhere. "Anything you can tell me might help."

"Heard a couple girls talking in the laundry room the other day. They work housekeeping, same as me. Heard 'em say Chantelle had a boyfriend that plays some kind of instrument. Saxophone, I think they said."

"What else did they say?"

"Nothin." Angela gazed at him, fear blatant in her eyes. "And you didn't hear nothin from me." She jumped out and ran to her car.

Ten minutes later he was sitting in the Bulldog, a funky bar that catered to locals and featured a huge assortment of draft and bottled beers. This time on a Saturday night the place was jammed. On the sound-system, barely audible over the conversational buzz, Ahmad Jamal was playing some tasty jazz piano. Looking equally tasty in a V-necked paisley-print top, Kelly O'Neil was sitting beside him on a stool at one end of the eight-foot bar.

"My CI thinks AK's involved in Chantelle's murder," he said. "Angela's pretty astute about these things. She grew up in the St. Bernard project."

"But not Iberville," Kelly said, and drank some of her Bud Light.

"No, but AK's got clout in this town. Enough to scare Angela."

And Angela had pretty much confirmed his theory: Antoine was Chantelle's boyfriend. He'd seen the updated composite sketches from the wounded cop's description. One sketch looked like AK: shaven head, delicate features, deadly eyes. Unfortunately, the other one, the kid with dreadlocks, looked a lot like Antoine, a fact he would have to report to Vobitch.

"Tell me about your rapist," he said, shifting gears to the ostensible purpose of their meeting.

"I think he stalks them first, jumps them when they walk to their cars after work. He doesn't seem to care if they see his face."

"And the victims don't give you squat for a description, right?"

Her lip quirked, an unhappy grimace. "That's the problem."

"Typical. They're too scared to look at him. They don't want to be there, don't want it to be happening, don't want to think about it. Afterwards they're so happy to be alive, they block it out."

"That's what Julie said. She was positive he was going to kill her."

His mind was a split screen, one half processing details of the rape, the other focused on Kelly. When she laughed, one of her front teeth overlapped the adjacent one. When deep in thought, she rolled her lower lip over her top lip. When outraged, as she was now, her eyes were sea-green agates. "He complements them like it's a fucking date or something!"

Frank shrugged. "To him, it *is* a date. He wants her to like him, so he sweet-talks her. A gentleman rapist. So called anyway."

"He's no gentleman. He's an animal. He forces these women to do disgusting things." She stared into the distance. Bright-blue Z-shaped earrings dangled from her earlobes. Maybe she was a Zephyr's fan. The Mets Triple-A baseball team played at a ballpark on Airline Drive.

"Does he hurt them? Punch them, slap them around?"

"No, but he uses a knife to intimidate them."

He tried to focus on the case but he felt weird, discussing the sexual habits of a rapist while sitting this close to a woman he found enormously attractive. Were they here to talk about the rapist? Or did she have something else in mind? When it came to romance, he was an optimist, but he never took women for granted. Still, the buzz in his gut told him they might be headed in that direction. He could smell her scent, perfume or body lotion maybe, a delicious aroma of vanilla and spice.

"Did she leave any prints? On the door handle maybe, when he forced her into his car?"

Kelly's eyes went wide. "Damn! I didn't think of that. I'll go back and ask her." She cocked her head as a new tune came over the sound system.

"That's Chet Baker, isn't it? I love his sound."

"One of my favorite trumpet players. You like jazz?"

"Big time. Terry and I used to . . ." She twisted a lock of dark hair and shook her head. It made her bright shiny Big-Z earrings sway back and forth.

"I love your earrings."

"Thank you." She smiled, gazing into his eyes. "I made them."

"Aha! A woman of hidden talents." Damn, he loved her eyes.

"I majored in art at Loyola, thinking I might hit it big like the Blue-dog guy, Rodrigue." She grinned. "I'm saving up to start a jewelry business."

Mesmerized by her smile and her deep-sea-green eyes, he leaned closer. Caught more vanilla-spice scent. Although they were in a crowded bar, it felt like they were in their own private bubble. "Tell me about it," he said.

"My brother Sean used to spend hours in the garage, making all kinds of stuff out of metal. He taught me welding and soldering. He said I was good at it, said I had great manual dexterity. So I started making jewelry."

"Huh. I've never been out with a woman welder." Realizing he'd just implied this was a date, he quickly added, "Is Sean a cop, like your father?"

"No. Sean and Patrick—he's my next older brother—run a construction business in Chicago. When they were little, they owned every Tonka trunk ever made. Michael, my oldest brother, he's a detective like Dad. They're peas in a pod, same temperament, same foul-mouthed language." She let out a low throaty laugh. "Good thing the nuns can't hear us at Christmas dinner."

Her smile faded. She turned away, a muscle working in her jaw.

"Holidays are the toughest, right?"

She turned and looked at him. "Holidays are a bitch."

"Want to talk about it?"

"What, you want to analyze me like the department shrink?"

He touched her wrist, felt the thrum of her pulse. "They made you see a shrink? What a kick in the ass. They did that to me, too, in Boston. I hated it. They think you can't handle your problems without help from some mental health jerkoff." He traced his fingers down her forearm. She didn't pull away, but her eyes had a speculative look.

"What was your crisis?" she said.

"Work related."

"And you don't want to talk about it, right?"

"Tell me about Terry. I hear he was a nice guy. A good cop."

"He was great guy. And a great cop. I still miss him."

He wanted to take her in his arms and comfort her. Not in a crowded bar, someplace private. Someplace where he could feel her skin against his.

"How long were you together?"

"Nine years, married for seven." She smiled, a wistful smile painful to see. "We were happy, you know? Lots of married people aren't, but Terry and I were. He was the softy, always bringing home strays. I'm the practical one. I told him we couldn't afford to feed three or four dogs if I was going to start a jewelry business. I'm not wild about being a cop, but Terry lived for the job. He loved helping people. That's what got him killed."

"What happened?" He'd heard the story, but he wanted her version.

She raked her fingers through her dark spiky hair. "Terry was in Slidell, helping his brother repair the deck on his house. We were supposed to go out that night. It was a Saturday. We were going to Snug Harbor to hear some jazz. Astral Project was playing." She stared into space, lost in the memory.

"It rained that day, not a downpour, but the roads were slick. Terry was driving home on the I-10 and saw a car in the breakdown lane. The driver was changing the left rear tire. So Terry, being the good Samaritan, stopped to help him." She looked at him, eyes wet with tears. "He called me before he got out of the car and said he might be late. He didn't want me to worry. And I was . . ." She heaved a sigh, a half-sob. "To tell the truth I was pissed, because we don't go out for dinner that often and . . ."

He squeezed her arm. "Don't beat up on yourself. It wasn't your fault."

Her mouth quirked and her eyes got squinty. "No, it wasn't. It was the fucking truck driver's fault. Terry was working on the lug nuts, and this eighteen-wheeler came along and crushed him. The doctor told me Terry never knew what hit him. He didn't suffer, and I am, thank-you-God, grateful for that." She picked up her beer mug and drained it.

"I can't tell you how to deal with it, Kelly. But for me, when something like that happens, when you lose someone you love, you have to focus on the good times." She gazed into his eyes, as though he'd thrown her a life jacket. "Remember the wonderful times," he said. "Little things like laughing over a stupid joke. And big things like how great it was to make love and lose yourself in him and remember how he smelled and how his skin felt."

She traced a finger down his cheek. "You've been there, right, Frank?"

The words pierced his heart. "Yes. And I know how much it hurts."

"Thank you for listening. You're the first . . ." She heaved a sigh. "Except for my dad, you're the first person I've talked to about it."

"Yeah? And how was it for you? Was it good?" Grinning to show he was joking, wanting to lighten things up after her painful recitation.

Her eyes crinkled in amusement. "Yes, Frank Renzi, it was very good."

His cell phone rang. Bummer. He checked the ID. Not someone he wanted to talk to right now. What he wanted right now was to build on the intimacies he and Kelly had just shared.

"Sorry. I need to take this." He punched on and said, "Renzi."

"Hello, Frank? It's Belinda. I hope I'm not disturbing you."

"It's okay," he said, conscious of Kelly beside him. "What's up? You got a problem?"

"It's not an emergency or anything. I was just wondering if you, uh, if you had any leads on the jerk that ran me off the road."

"I don't. Sorry. I wish I could tell you more." Making it sound like official police business. He glanced at Kelly, saw her leafing through her checkbook of all things, pretending not to listen. But he knew she was. He would have, had the situation been reversed.

"I thought maybe you might have checked the repair shops, you know, in case someone brought in an SUV with a damaged fender."

Had he said he'd do that? "No, I haven't. It's been . . . hectic."

"Well . . . you sound like you're busy. I'm sorry to have disturbed you."

"Not a problem. I don't blame you for being concerned."

"I'm less worried now than I was before. I hired a security person."

"Good." He held up a finger to let Kelly know he was almost done.

"Did you get a chance to come to the NOCCA concert?"

Bingo. The real reason for the call. "Yes," he said. "It was terrific. I enjoyed it." Speaking innocuous words, aware of Kelly's gaze.

In a crisp voice Belinda said, "I'll be in Cincinnati next weekend soloing at a Pops concert. Can you call me if you get any leads on the accident?"

"I will. Have a good trip." He set his cell phone on the bar and turned to Kelly. "I have a love-hate relationship with this thing. Sometimes it's handy and other times . . ." He waggled his hand.

"Yeah?" She gave him a slow grin. "Depends who's calling."

"That it does." Now she was fishing, and he was dodging.

"Private detail?" Smiling faintly, a knowing look in her eyes.

"Something like that." Annoyed by the interruption, he sipped his beer, casting about for a way to get the conversation back on track.

"I'm going to re-interview that rape victim next week," Kelly said. "Want to come along? I think she'll be okay with it if I tell her in advance."

His heart thrummed his chest. "Tell me when and I'll be there."

CHAPTER 17

Monday, 30 October

He played a two-octave C-Major arpeggio and flexed his fingers, stiff and achy from schlepping luggage for asshole clients. Something he'd never do again, thanks to Belinda.

Her suitcases he would gladly carry into any hotel in the world.

After last night's concert she'd seemed a bit down but she hadn't said why. She wasn't ready to confide in him. Not yet, but soon. Soon they'd lie in bed together and he would stroke her silky hair as she whispered her secrets. Her deepest darkest desires. Desires he couldn't wait to fulfill.

A spurt of anger ruined his fantasy. Her car was outside in the driveway, repaired and ready to go. But he was her driver. They were a couple now, going places together every day. He couldn't allow her go out without him. Now that he'd rescued her from that drunk she had to know that she needed him to keep her safe. He'd paid the Minnesota biker forty bucks to fake the attack. The asshole didn't know a flute from a football, didn't know Belinda Scully from Britney Spears, but he'd delivered his lines well enough.

His fingers roamed the ivories of the Steinway and settled into the introduction of the Saint-Saens *Sonata for Violin and Piano*. He hadn't played it since he'd accompanied his sister for her Eastman School of Music audition. It was a bravura piece, full of tricky rhythms and rapturous melodies. Muscle memory got him through the introduction. His technique was rusty now, but fifteen years ago it hadn't been. Rachel had played okay, though her puny sound didn't do justice to the melodies. Even so it got her into the exclusive school. He would never forget her spiteful words when she got the letter.

Piano players are a dime a dozen. They all want to be soloists and wind up playing rehearsals for ballet companies. You'll never make it as a musician, but I will. I'll be playing in a big orchestra.

Gritting his teeth, he launched into the Beethoven sonata he'd practiced for his Boston Conservatory audition. But even the marvelous sound of the Steinway couldn't erase Rachel's malicious taunt. His bitch sister. Always the favored one, ever accurate in her predictions.

He hadn't even been accepted at Boston Conservatory, never mind the more prestigious New England Conservatory.

Swept away by Beethoven's passionate music, he bent over the keys, reveling in the sound, his right hand playing the melody, his left hand thundering the bass line.

"What are you doing in here, Mr. Silverman?"

Startled, he jerked his hands away from the keyboard. "Goodness, Belinda, you startled me." She looked lovely this morning, coppery hair swept behind her delicate ears, held by silver clips on either side.

She gazed at him without speaking, her sapphire-blue eyes accusing.

He ripped off an E-flat Major arpeggio, fingers flashing up and down the keyboard. He ended with a flourish and smiled at his beloved. Soon he'd be playing arpeggios up and down her body.

"What a gorgeous piano! A lot of the top soloists prefer a Bosendorfer or a Schimmel, but I still like a Steinway better, don't you?" Tossing off the big-name builders to show that he knew what he was talking about when it came to pianos.

"I prefer to have you wait in the foyer if I'm not ready to leave."

He maintained his smile. "I haven't touched a piano in years. But I played quite well when I was younger. One time I accompanied a violinist and helped her win a big audition with the Debussy *Violin Sonata in G minor*."

Her expression softened. "Really? That's quite a difficult piece."

"It sure is. I had to practice my ass off." He covered his mouth in mock-horror. "Forgive my language. I hope I didn't offend you."

She rewarded him with a smile. "I think I've heard that expression a time or two." She looked at her watch. "We'd better go. My appointment's at nine and I don't want to be late."

Then why weren't you ready when I got here at eight-thirty?

"Don't worry, Belinda, I'll get you there on time." Testing her first name again to see how she'd react. Nothing. Not even a polite smile. "Have you considered doing a Busoni transcription? His second violin sonata is a really meaty piece."

"Busoni. Goodness, you're quite knowledgeable about chamber music."

Waving a self-deprecating hand, he rose from the piano bench. "I'm no expert, but you really should consider the Busoni *Violin Sonata*. It's a marvelous piece." Rachel had made him learn it so she could play it on her senior recital in high school, hoping to outdo another violinist. She hadn't.

"I'm too busy right now, but I'll think about it."

"It would be fun if we played some duets. The French flute sonatas on your CD, perhaps. Your recording is fabulous, much better than Rampal's. I've got all your CDs, and I'm a quick study. If you lend me the music, I'll practice them. We'll have a lovely time."

She trilled a laugh and tossed her long coppery tresses. "My accompanist plays for all the top soloists in New York. He's got a Masters from Julliard and he teaches at Yale." She turned to leave. "But thanks for offering, Mr. Silverman. I'll keep you in mind."

Bullshit. She wouldn't keep him in mind. She wouldn't even use his first name. He was nothing to her. A cipher.

His cheeks burned with embarrassment. Thankfully, she didn't notice.

Intent on leaving, she took her briefcase off the table in the foyer and rushed out the door. Seething, he watched her sashay down the walk to his van. After all he did for her, the little courtesies that weren't part of his job, complimenting her appearance, praising her performances, rhapsodizing over her CDs, not to mention saving her from that drunk.

And what did he get in return? A derisive laugh when he invited her to play duets and patronizing jibes to put him in his place.

Her accompanist had a Masters from Julliard; he didn't.

Her accompanist taught at Yale; he was her chauffeur.

He watched her tug at the door of his van. Normally, he would have rushed to assist her, but not today. Let The Diva open that heavy door herself and see how she liked it.

But as he watched her struggle with the door, his heart melted.

He hurried down the walk to his van.

"Let me help you, Belinda. That door's much too heavy for you."

Oblivious to other students piling into their cars and peeling out of the lot, Antoine trudged through the NOCCA parking area. His mind was a fuzzball. Probably flunked his advanced harmony test last period, unable to concentrate, imagining Chantelle's beautiful almond eyes and the feel of her silky-smooth skin beneath his fingers, seeing her glorious smile the last time he made her come. Something he'd never do again.

His throat closed up at the sound of a far-off train whistle. For some reason, the whistle reminded him of what Uncle Jonas said after Grandma died, said she was in Heaven and when Antoine died he'd meet up with her on The Other Side. Antoine wasn't sure he believed it, but it was the one thing he'd clung to for the past week, the one thing that gave him hope, had to stuff a pillow in his mouth every night so Uncle Jonas wouldn't hear him cry himself to sleep.

Eyes blurry with tears, he arrived at his car and got out his keys.

"Yo, Antoine!"

His heart jumped into his throat, fluttering like a captured bird. He focused on holding onto his keys, fingers cold and numb, felt like he'd been juggling ice cubes for an hour.

AK appeared at his elbow, smiling his evil gold-toothed smile, had his two homeboys with him, Spider arching his neck to flaunt his spider-web tat, Deadeye draping his forearm on the roof of Antoine's car to display the mean-looking dagger-tat, dripping red blood.

"W'as up, my man? Cat got your tongue?"

AK doing his big-man act for his homeboys.

Fear and loathing did battle in his mind. His heart hammered like a machine gun. He wished he had one so he could blow AK away. *Why'd you kill Chantelle?* he wanted to scream. But he was too scared.

"Ain't nobody got my tongue. What you doin' here?"

"Here to make sure you not runnin' your mouth to no cops."

Desperation and fear jazzed his mind. Had someone seen him talking to that NOPD cop last Friday night?

"Ain't talking to no cops."

"That ain't what I hear."

"You heard wrong." Hot pokers of hatred burned the fear from his mind. "Why you do that to Chantelle? She wasn't gonna say nothing."

AK smiled his evil smile, challenging him with his eyes. "Do what to Chantelle?"

What could he say? Why'd you murder the girl I loved with all my heart, the girl that made me almost as happy as when I play my saxophone?

"Maybe the girl stepped outta line with somebody." AK leaned closer, huffing halitosis breath at him. "You better not get outta line, Antoine, or you know what'll happen?"

He knew better than to answer. Big mistake, mouthing off at AK.

Weevils of fear gnawed his stomach. Then he saw Spider and Deadeye back away from his car, their eyes fixed on someone behind him, their expressions wary.

"What's shaking, AK?" said a deep resonant voice. "Had to bust my hump to catch up with you. You gonna apply to NOCCA?"

AK's eyes hardened, lumps of coal focused on the man who'd spoken.

Antoine knew who it was, recognized the voice right off.

"Just having a conversation with my buddy Antoine," AK said. "What's it to you, Mr. Po-leece-man?"

AK still doing his tough-guy act, Antoine noticed, but not as confident as before, looking like he wanted to split but trying hard to be cool.

"Renzi," said the voice. "Detective Frank Renzi. Let's go over to the Eighth District Police Station, AK. I've got questions for you."

"Not 'less you carryin' paper sez I got to. Me 'n my homies got business to take care of." AK jerked his head at Spider and Deadeye, signaling them to head out. "You got paper says I gotta go with you?"

Antoine held his breath, praying the cop had a warrant. Anything to let him get in his car and drive away so AK wouldn't find out he knew the cop. Or that the cop knew him. If AK found out Renzi knew him, he was dead.

"You afraid to talk to me, AK?" Renzi said in a hard voice.

AK's face turned to stone. No gold-tooth smile now. Without a word, he swaggered after his homeboys, waiting for him in a souped-up Lincoln Town Car idling noisily in the street beside the NOCCA parking lot.

Praying for a miracle, Antoine remained rooted to the spot.

"Don't turn around, Antoine," Renzi said softly. "Make like I don't know you, get in your car and drive to the New Orleans Art Museum. I'll be right behind you so don't try and run. Don't answer me, don't look at me, just get in the car and drive away."

He got in his car, grateful the cop understood the situation, but dreading the idea of talking to him. Didn't want to wear out his head remembering which lies he'd already told the man, which lies he was about to tell him.

Ten minutes later they were sitting on a stone bench under a weeping willow tree in the NOMA sculpture garden. What was left of it anyway. Sculptures still there, but broken tree limbs and debris littering the formerly tidy walks. Before Katrina, he and Chantelle used to come here and smooch as they wandered through the peaceful garden. Not peaceful now.

He clasped his hands together to keep them from shaking. His insides were already shaking, and not from the chill in the October air.

"What was going down back there?" Renzi turned to face him, lay his arm along the back of the bench and crossed his legs.

Relaxed and confident, Antoine thought, *now that he knows I know AK.*

"We just talking." He clenched his hands so they wouldn't do something stupid like fly into the air. Planted his feet so he wouldn't run away.

"Looked to me like AK was threatening you." Renzi put a hand on his shoulder. "Talk to me, Antoine. I know Chantelle was your girl and I know you're hurting. I want to put the bastards that killed her in jail, don't you?"

He nodded, afraid to speak, afraid his voice would jump an octave and betray him.

"I think AK was involved. What's his connection to Chantelle?"

"Chantelle was living in Iberville," he muttered, and turned away so he didn't have to look into the eyes of his relentless interrogator.

"So? What did she do to cross AK?"

"I dunno," he whispered. Knowing Chantelle had done nothing to cross AK, knowing her mere existence posed a threat to the King of Iberville.

"What was she doing in Lakeview that night?"

"Don't know nothing 'bout that either." Praying God didn't strike him dead for lying.

Renzi's fingers dug into his shoulder. "A woman died, Antoine. Someone pushed her out of the getaway car. Who pushed her out?"

He shook off the man's hand. "What you asking me for?"

"The cop that got shot is out of intensive care, getting better every day."

"That's good," Antoine said. "I'm glad to hear it."

"Chantelle was worried about him too. Why was that?"

His heart pounded and his palms got sweaty. Had Chantelle told Renzi something? He doubted this but couldn't be sure. He wanted to ask what else Chantelle said, but he couldn't, not without admitting he knew why she was in Lakeview. Because he'd made the biggest mistake of his life, helping AK rob that store, thinking he was protecting his girlfriend.

What he'd done was get her killed.

Murdered. In cold blood. By AK and his thugs.

His eyes filled with tears.

"The off-duty cop helped a police artist draw some better sketches of the robbers."

His heart almost stopped. He felt like a two-ton truck had fallen on his chest, felt the heat of Renzi's eyes, probing, testing. Accusing.

"One of the sketches looked a lot like AK."

What about the other one? he wanted to scream, clamped his lips together so he wouldn't.

"Did Chantelle help him rob that store?"

"No!" The word sprang from his mouth before he could stop it.

"She had to be up there for a reason. You and I both know fifteen-year-old black girls don't go running around a white neighborhood that time of night without a reason."

"AK," he said, knowing he was edging into dangerous territory. "AK made her do it."

"AK did the robbery, right, Antoine?"

He turned on the cop. "You trying to get me killed like Chantelle? That what you want?"

"No, that's exactly what I *don't* want. But I need evidence to put AK in jail. I need a witness. Someone willing to testify in court."

His blood turned to ice. Testify in court. Against AK. A death sentence.

Renzi put a hand on his shoulder again, put some muscle on it. "We'll protect you. We can get you back to your folks in Houston after the trial."

Houston? Shit. Nowhere near far enough away to escape AK's thugs. Spider and Deadeye would find him and shoot him down like a dog.

Renzi gazed at him, his dark eyes intense and implacable. "I think AK killed Chantelle. Don't let him get away with it, Antoine."

A soft moan escaped his mouth. All this talk about Chantelle was ripping his heart out, reminding him he'd never see her again. Never talk to her again. Never make love to her again.

He clenched his hands. Gritted his teeth. Tensed his body. Rose from the bench and walked away.

Renzi would have to find someone else to finger AK.

He wanted justice for Chantelle, but he didn't want to die.

CHAPTER 18

Tuesday, 31 October

"What's wrong, Jake?" she said. "You seem upset."

What an understatement. He was gobbling M&Ms by the fistful. Jake used chocolate like worry beads to soothe his frazzled nerves.

"Silverman booked a seat on our flight to Cincinnati." He dipped his fingers into the brandy snifter on his desk for more M&Ms, tossed them in his mouth and chewed furiously.

"How did he know what flight we're taking?"

"How the hell do I know? He comes in and snoops around when I'm out of the office. This guy is a pest. Yesterday he was playing your piano, now this!" Jake waved a sheet of paper. "This morning he came in and handed me an invoice for the plane fare!"

"Calm down, Jake. Mr. Silverman is not going to Cincinnati. The orchestra will have a limo pick us up at the airport, and someone will drive us to the rehearsals. We don't need him."

"That's what I told him, but I figured I better talk to you before I did anything. I told him to go outside and wait in his van."

She turned and looked out the window. Silverman was leaning against his van, a muscular presence in his black Armani suit and sinister-looking sunglasses. He raised his hand and waved at her.

Without thinking, she waved back and saw him smile.

"I think we should get rid of him," Jake said.

"But he's only been working for me a week."

"And he's been a pain in the ass the whole time. We could hire someone else—"

"No. I didn't want to hire a security man in the first place, you did. I can't help it if you two don't get along. He's been fine with me."

Not entirely true. He had rescued her from that drunk after the concert, but she'd been shocked to catch him playing her piano yesterday. His attempt to impress her was pathetic, his suggestion that they play duets ludicrous. But she'd jollied him out of it.

"Maybe I'll start driving again," she said. "My car's been repaired. Things have been fine lately."

Another half-truth. After her perfect performance at the NOCCA concert, Frank hadn't come backstage, hadn't even called to congratulate her. She'd been forced to call *him*. How embarrassing. Even then he'd sounded as though he didn't want to talk.

"What do you want me to do?" Jake said in the gruff tone he used when he was resigned to something but didn't like it.

"You're good at managing people. Tell Mr. Silverman to cancel the plane reservation. Tell him I don't want him playing my piano, too."

Jake regarded her with a sullen expression. "Okay. He won't like it, especially coming from me, but that's my worry, I guess. Just part of the job."

―――――

Wednesday, 1 November

After they interviewed the rape victim—Julie Martin, a twenty-two year old secretary for a small engineering firm—Frank suggested they have a beer at the Bulldog and talk it over. Unlike their previous visit, the bar was relatively quiet so they grabbed a table. Kelly looked elegant in her tailored black pantsuit and royal-blue blouse. She had on a different pair of Big-Z earrings tonight, bronze with thin blue stripes.

"Do you kibitz with your father about cases?" he asked.

She had told him her father, Enrico "Rico" Zavarella, was a detective in Chicago, but not much else. Nothing about her mother.

"Not often." She sipped her Heineken draft and licked foam off her lip. "It sickens me, the horrible things people do to each other."

A perfect segue to discuss the interview, but he didn't feel like it. Earlier, Julie's apartment had felt like a fortress, new locks on the door, every light blazing, the windows covered by heavy drapes. Julie was scared. Her life wasn't going to be the same for a long time. Maybe never. He'd known rape victims who'd been plagued by flashbacks for years.

"I bet your dad likes your big-Z earrings."

Kelly grinned. "He does. He wants me to make him a tie clip. The letter Z is elegant, design-wise, but having a last name that starts with Z sucks.

You're always last on the list, assigned to the last row of the classroom, the last one to get your diploma."

"Kelly Zavarella, huh? Were you the only kid in your class with a Z name?"

"No. Me and Benny. Benedetto Zeppetella."

"Now there's a name!"

She grinned and he caught a glimpse of her crooked front tooth. "Benny's mother loved Tony Bennett and his actual last name is—"

"Benedetto."

She wet a finger and drew a "one" in the air. "Poor Benny. The nuns always gave him a hard time. They said he wrote too big. He could never fit his name on one line."

"You went to Catholic school?"

"With an Irish mother and an Italian father? What else? Didn't you?"

"No. My mother refused to send me to parochial school." And when his Irish mother put her foot down, she'd usually gotten her way.

"Maybe she had a run-in with a nun like me. In third grade a nun rapped my knuckles with a ruler for bad penmanship. I don't know why the nuns were so obsessed about penmanship."

"That's easy. Pens are phallic symbols."

She rolled her eyes. "Trust you to think of that. When I told Dad, he pulled me out of there and sent me to public school."

"What about your mother?" he asked. "Was she mad, too?"

Kelly's eyes grew somber and her mouth quirked. "She was too sick to make a fuss. She died the next year. Ovarian cancer."

He could tell she didn't want to talk about it. "And you never saw Benny again?"

"Not till high school."

"Yeah? Did you date him?"

She gave him a flirty smile and batted her eyelashes. "Nah. I didn't date Italian guys. I got enough of that at home with my three brothers."

I'm your first? he thought but didn't say. It seemed like she was still pretending this was all about work. Reluctantly, he eased into the purpose of the meeting. "We didn't get much out of Julie tonight."

More like nothing. Julie, a small-boned wisp of a woman swallowed up by an overstuffed chair, couldn't even remember the color of the rapist's car. All she remembered was the terror and humiliation, a forlorn figure, twisting a tissue in her hands, saying: *I was afraid he'd kill me. He said he wouldn't hurt me, but he lied! He did hurt me!*

"She's blocking things out," Kelly said. "Disgusting things. What is *wrong* with these guys?"

"Rape isn't about sex, Kelly. You know that. It's about power."

"And preying on vulnerable women." Her eyes blazed with anger.

He pictured Julie, weeping as she recited her nightmare: *He said he loved my boobs. And after he . . . afterwards, he asked if I enjoyed it. I knew he expected me to say yes. So I did.* Staring at the floor as she spoke, cheeks flushed with shame.

He fingered the scar on his jaw. He knew most rapists had been abused as children, but he couldn't imagine treating a woman like that. He had told Julie it wasn't her fault; the important thing was that she was alive. Even so, tears had continued to pour down her cheeks, an image that would stay with him for a long time.

"You care a lot about the victims," Kelly said, gazing at him with her mesmerizing eyes.

"How could anyone not be appalled by what she went through? I'd like to put the guy in Attica, let him find out what it's like to be raped."

"Me, too, but we've got nothing, no description of him or his car."

"Maybe the next victim will be able to help you." When he saw her face register dismay, he said, "I know you don't want to think about the next one, but guys like this don't stop."

She guzzled some beer and toyed with a lock of dark hair that curled behind her ear. He traced a finger down her forearm. "Can we get off the rape case for a minute? I get the feeling you're pretending this meeting is all about work. Is it?"

Her eyes widened. She tilted her head and her Big-Z earrings swung back and forth. "I don't know, Frank. I'm not sure. Or maybe I just don't want to think about it."

"You're comfortable talking to cops, because of your dad and your brother." *And your husband.*

"I feel comfortable talking to most guys. Growing up with three brothers gave me a front-row seat on how guys act." Her eyes crinkled at the corners as she smiled. "I got used to figuring out what guys mean when they say one thing and mean something else."

He drew a "one" in the air with his forefinger.

His cell phone chimed. Not what he needed now that the conversation was going in the right direction. He checked the ID and answered.

"Hey, Kenyon, what's up?"

"Good news, bad news," Miller said. "They found the Lakeview getaway car. Fuckers dumped it out in New Orleans East, tow truck's hauling it to the police garage right now. We get Forensics on it maybe we'll ID the bastards."

"Great," he said. "What's the bad news?"

"Jim Whitworth's in the hospital with chest pains."

"Damn! How's he doing?" Everyone loved Jim. The veteran detective went out of his way to help rookie cops. He'd helped Frank out a few times during his first year with NOPD.

"They're running all kinds of tests, you know, a guy over fifty they take no chances."

He wrapped up the call and told Kelly about the getaway car and Jim's heart problems. She grimaced, as if to say *Life's a crapshoot.*

Or so he imagined. That's what he was thinking.

Forget trying to resume their conversation. The intimate mood was gone, and Kelly was yawning. Vobitch had called an early meeting tomorrow. If they didn't solve the Lakeview case soon, Vobitch might have a heart attack. After three weeks, the reporters were still hot on it.

Ten days since Chantelle's murder, not a peep since, nobody making waves about a dead black girl, seemed like he was the only one mourning her death. Except for her boyfriend. Antoine Carter.

He wasn't looking forward to telling Vobitch that Antoine might be getaway driver at tomorrow's meeting.

Friday, 3 November

Antoine copied down the chord progressions Mr. Dawson had written on the white-board in blue Magic Marker. Advanced Jazz Harmony class was one of the few things that kept his mind busy these days.

Don't think about Chantelle.

He focused on the changes, looked up when Georgina entered the classroom. Georgina worked in the office as a student aide during her free periods. Acting self-important, she strutted across the front of the classroom, the little white rings at the ends of her cornrowed hair bouncing off her shoulders. Georgina was a decent singer but chubby, like her pal Marcus, didn't get to sing with the best bands like the sweeter-looking girls. Not half as pretty as Chantelle.

Damn! Why did everything remind him of Chantelle?

Mr. D studied the slip of paper Georgina gave him and said, "Antoine, you're wanted in the office."

Double damn! Nothing good ever happened when you got called to the office. He stuck his pencil in his shirt pocket and rose from his desk. Felt Marcus's eyes on him. Made sure he didn't look at the little drug-dealing flute player as he left the room.

Sure enough, bad news was waiting in the office. Detective Renzi.

The office lady waved them into a counseling room that smelled of aftershave and burnt coffee. Antoine tried to act cool, perched on a folding chair in front of the desk. But his pulse was racing.

Looming over him, Renzi set his butt on the desk and gave him the laser eye. "Have you given any thought to what we talked about, Antoine?"

He kept his face blank, but his heart pounded. What could he say?

Thought on it every night since, don't see any way out of the jam I'm in.

"Yes, sir."

"Good. Anything more you want to tell me?"

"No, sir." *Ain't giving up AK to no cop, don't wanna wind up dead.*

Renzi's eyes grew distant, like he was thinking on something important.

"We found the getaway car."

His heart skittered inside his chest like a jackrabbit.

"We lifted some prints off the steering wheel."

Jesus God, no! His Adam's apple bobbed up and down. He couldn't swallow for spit, felt like Godzilla jumped on his chest.

"We ran 'em through the criminal data base, but we didn't find a match."

He let out the breath he'd been holding, as winded as if he'd played a whole chorus of *Sweet Georgia Brown* in one breath. The cop gazed at him, expectant, seemed like he thought Antoine was about to tell him something important. He wasn't.

"We got prints off the left rear window, too. They matched the prints of the woman that died." Renzi's eyes went hard as granite. "Someone pushed her out of that car, Antoine. Her head hit the pavement and she died of a fractured skull."

The words hung in the air like a horrible stink.

"I'm sorry she died," he said. And he was. Sorrier than he'd ever been about anything in his life except for Chantelle being dead. But he wasn't the one shoved that poor lady out the car.

"Who pushed her out of the car?" Renzi said.

Seemed like the man could read his mind. Scary. "I don't know, sir."

"I think you do. Why was Chantelle in Lakeview that night?"

The cruelest question of all, one he had no intention of answering. He blinked back tears. No way was he gonna cry in front of this cop. But he wasn't going to betray Chantelle, either.

"I think she was involved in the robbery. Maybe she was the lookout. Is that it?"

He shook his head, unwilling to speak the lie aloud.

"Someone killed her and I think you know who it was. I want to nail the bastard and put him away for good. Don't you, Antoine?"

He nodded, unable to speak.

"Chantelle was squatting in her old apartment in Iberville. She must have known AK." Renzi lowered his voice. "I think AK pulled that stickup, but I can't prove it. Help me out, Antoine."

He looked away, avoiding the man's gaze. "You gonna get me killed, you know that? Come here and pull me out of class." *Lady sends Georgina to get me, Georgina knows a cop's waiting in the office, sure as shit gonna tell Marcus.*

"Why were AK and his homeboys bothering you in the parking lot the other day? AK knew Chantelle was your girl, right? He killed her to make sure she didn't talk about the Lakeview robbery. And the *murder*. That's what it was, Antoine, cold-blooded murder, shoving that woman out of the car. AK was threatening you to make sure you keep *your* mouth shut, too."

He took a deep shuddering breath. "You gonna get me killed."

"We'll protect you, Antoine. Tell us what happened in Lakeview and we'll cut you a break."

He looked the man in the eye. "I'm not the only NOCCA student that knows AK."

Watched the cop's eyes, saw the wheels turning in the man's mind.

No way was he gonna give up a name.

He was in enough trouble already, hiding from AK, hardly stepped foot outside his uncle's house except to go to school.

If Marcus told AK he'd talked to this cop, he was toast.

CHAPTER 19

Saturday, 4 November   Cincinnati

Relaxed and jubilant, she changed into her satin baby-dolls and sat down at the dressing table in her hotel room to brush her hair. An hour after the Cincinnati Pops concert her cheeks still had a rosy glow. A standing ovation and two curtain calls thanks to her perfect performance. Best of all, PBS had videotaped the concert, which meant added revenue and wider exposure.

Things were looking up. No more threats to expose her secrets.

Her lips tightened resentfully. If reporters got wind of her affair with Guy, it would ruin her image. But not Guy's. Men could screw around. Women couldn't. Ramon's wife had threatened to tell every gossip columnist in Boston that she was a home wrecker. Nonsense.

Ramon had seduced *her*, not the other way around.

No more ugly car incidents, either. She still thought the parking lot episode was some kid hot-rodding around. But being forced off the road and crashing into a tree was different. Different and terrifying.

Still, that didn't mean someone was out to get *her*. She gazed into the mirror at the sapphire-blue eyes that stared back at her, recalling how caring and considerate Frank had been that night, his intense dark eyes focused on hers as they sat in her kitchen. But that had been an illusion, too. He hadn't even come backstage to compliment her NOCCA performance.

Three taps sounded on the door of her room. "Bee? It's Jake."

She set down the hairbrush, put on her white terry-cloth robe and opened the door. "Come on in, Jake. I was just brushing my hair. Want a nightcap? There's wine in the mini-bar."

"Uh, sure, that would be good." Jake gazed at her, solemn-eyed.

"What's wrong? The concert went well, but you don't seem very happy."

He flashed a perfunctory smile. "Your performance was fabulous, Bee." He perched on one of the easy chairs grouped around a low table and cleared his throat. "Now that the concert's over I was hoping we could talk."

Now that the concert's over. Jake hadn't come to her hotel room for a cozy late-night chat. He had something unpleasant to say.

She took two splits of Merlot out of the mini-bar, poured them into glass tumblers and carried them to the sitting area. "What did you want to tell me?" Keeping her voice calm though her heart was racing.

Jake gulped some wine. "I may be moving to New York City."

Her heart slammed her chest. "Jake! No!"

"Please try to understand. This isn't about you. You know I'd do anything for you—"

"If you move to New York, what can you do for me?" Hearing the reproach in her voice, knowing how selfish she sounded. But what would she do without Jake?

"Bee, this is difficult enough. Please don't make it worse. Dean wants to go to art school. He interviewed at Pratt Institute, and if he gets accepted—" Jake heaved a sigh and gave her an imploring look. "I can't stay in New Orleans if Dean's living in New York."

A sick-ache invaded her stomach. "Can't you fly up on weekends?"

"I've been with you for nine years, and all those years I put my relationship with Dean second. But I can't do that forever. I love him, Bee. I don't want to lose him."

She fought back tears. These hideous problems were piling up like snowdrifts in a blizzard: the thirteenth anniversary, voicemail threats, creepy fan mail, car accidents. And now Jake, her dearest friend in the world, her only friend, was abandoning her.

Gripping the glass tumbler to stop her hands from shaking, she forced herself to speak in a calm even voice. "When will you be moving?"

Jake visibly relaxed. He even smiled. How could he?

"Classes at Pratt start in January, but don't worry. I'll take care of the holiday performances. I'll just need to go to New York a couple of times early in December."

"Fine." She feigned a yawn. "I'm really tired, Jake. I need to go to bed."

"Of course. You had a long day." He sprang to his feet and went to the door. "Thanks for understanding, Bee."

Understanding? She didn't understand, but she couldn't stop Jake from leaving, anymore than she could undo the accident that had killed her family thirteen years ago. Unlucky thirteen. `

She should have known this year would be horrific. Nine weeks to go.

What other nightmares were in store for her?

He opened the top drawer of Belinda's dresser and gazed at her panties: pale pink, pastel yellow, baby blue, white with lace trim. He ran his fingers over the silky fabric. He liked the black ones best. Sexy.

He couldn't wait to see her in them. Already he had an erection.

Too bad she wasn't here to enjoy it.

He pulled off the latex gloves, raised the panties to his nose and sniffed the crotch. And smelled laundry detergent, not the sexy scent of his beloved. He dropped them in the drawer and went to the clothes hamper in the corner of the room. Inside he found a pair of pastel-blue panties with a faint stain on the crotch. He raised it to his nose and inhaled the scent of her sex. Bliss!

His erection throbbed with a wild yearning.

How could she be so mean? Humiliating him when he demonstrated his knowledge of pianos and chamber music repertoire. Rejecting his suggestion to transcribe the Busoni *Violin Sonata* for flute. Laughing when he invited her to play duets with him. Laughing!

She wasn't ready to satisfy him yet, and he had his needs, as all men did.

Like Pa. He fingered the acne pits on his cheek, recalling the night Rachel had revealed her dark secret.

Twice a week Pa took his talented daughter to Boston Symphony concerts. Forget *his* talent, Rachel was the star. He had to stay home with Ma, wasting away in her wheelchair. Late one night he heard Rachel tiptoe past his room. Two minutes later he crept down the hall to her room and walked in on her. She was sitting at her makeup table, admiring her sharp-featured face in the mirror as she brushed her long blue-black hair.

"Did you ever hear of knocking?"

"Why do you and Pa get home so late? It's after midnight. Concerts don't last that long."

"None of your business, Zit-face." Stroking the brush through her lustrous blue-black hair, gazing at him in the mirror with her glittery-green eyes.

"You don't really go to symphony concerts, do you?"

Pink rose on her cheeks. "Of course we do. If Pa didn't take me to concerts, I wouldn't do it."

"Do what?"

A brittle smile. "After the concert we go to a motel and Pa fucks my brains out."

Shocked, he stared at her. Pictured his father, naked and hairy, screwing his fifteen-year-old sister. Strangely, the image excited him. Rachel lied a lot, but not this time, he was certain.

"What if . . ." he said, trying to act cool, "what if you get pregnant?"

"Duh!! I've been on the pill since I was twelve."

"Twelve? You and Pa have been doing this since you were . . . ?"

Her mouth twisted into a terrible smile. "Before that."

"You're disgusting!"

"And you're jealous. Pa loves me more than he loves you. How could anyone love you? You're the disgusting one, all those pimples. Mr. Zit-face with the puny dick," she said, unerringly finding his vulnerability. "Pa's is bigger. Big and fat and—"

"Shut up!"

He wanted to strangle her with his bare hands, wanted to see her face turn purple, wanted to watch those glittery-green eyes bug out of her head.

"You know it's true," she said, smirking at him in the mirror. "Remember when we used to take baths together when we were little? I can't believe how puny your dick is compared to Pa's."

His face turned crimson with embarrassment.

"Shut up or I'll tell the social worker." The woman visited twice a week to see how Ma was doing, as if she expected some miracle would allow Ma to rise from her wheelchair and walk like a normal human being.

Like a normal mother. The normal mother he'd never had.

"If you tell, I'll say you're a liar. I'll tell Pa about your porn magazines."

She'd been in his room! His hands clenched into fists. He took a step toward her. He wanted to fuck her, like his loutish excuse-for-a-father had fucked her, wanted to punch that smirk off her face and rip off her clothes and throw her on the bed and—

"Don't come near me! I'll tell Pa you attacked me."

His rage escalated. An impotent rage. Pa would believe Rachel, not him. Pa would beat his naked butt with a belt, jeering if he cried, telling him to *take it like a man*. Defeated, he turned and left. Rachel's triumphant laugh had followed him down the hall to his room.

Shaking with remembered rage, he sniffed Belinda's panties and touched his throbbing cock. Later, he would jerk off on them.

His wretched substitute for her love.

He pulled a pillowcase off a bed pillow and dropped in the panties, went to her bureau and opened her jewelry case. What would a thief steal? The pearl necklace and matching earrings for sure, the gold pins and diamond earrings, too. He dropped them in the pillowcase.

Belinda's flutes were the most valuable items in the house. She'd taken her platinum Haynes flute to Cincinnati, but others worth thousands were in her safe. No. If he stole them Belinda would be devastated. Still, he should take something else. A portable CD player and four compact discs lay on her bedside table, her favorites no doubt. He stuffed the disc player and CDs in the pillowcase, shut off the light and went downstairs.

He opened the door to Belinda's studio and gazed longingly at her Steinway. Ziegler had rebuked him for playing it, had said she never allowed anyone in her studio. Bullshit. Once his beloved realized how talented he was, she would love playing duets with him.

But he didn't dare play it now. If her neighbors heard someone playing her piano it might fuck up his plan. He shut the door and crossed the hall to Ziegler's office. The window shades were down so he turned on the desk lamp and riffled the file cabinets. Press clippings? No, he had all of those. Contacts for possible gigs? Of no interest to him.

A folder labeled Press Kit Photos. He took it out and opened it. His cock throbbed as he studied the photographs, his beloved in various poses: provocative and smiling, demure and businesslike.

Perfect for his late-night longings. He slid the folder into the pillowcase.

Another file cabinet held folders labeled Utility Bills, Tax Returns, Concert Payments and CD Royalties. He dumped them on the floor, scattering papers everywhere.

Fuck-all! If anyone did that to him, he'd kill them. He hated it when things were out of place, especially his Belinda collection.

A folder on the desk held receipts for the Cincinnati flight and the hotel. They had booked separate rooms. That didn't fool him. He knew they were lovers. He'd put an end to that soon enough. Then he would show his beloved the orgasmic delights of having sex with someone who adored her.

Someone who knew how to fuck her.

A snifter full of M&Ms sat on Ziegler's desk. He picked it up and threw it against the wall. The glass shattered and M&Ms scattered across the floor, a multi-colored *fuck-you*. Another dish held Hershey miniatures. He flung the candy on the floor and shut off the light.

He'd been here forty minutes. After entering the house, he'd used the code Ziegler had given him to disable the alarm. Let Ziegler take the heat for failing to arm the security system. No one could blame it on him.

He had the perfect alibi.

CHAPTER 20

Sunday, 5 November

The resonant voices of the African Baptist Gospel Church choir rolled over him like a tidal wave. Made him think about Chantelle.

His stomach cramped and his eyes welled up.

Praise the Lord! sang the choir, sending a shiver down his spine.

Beside him in the wooden pew, Uncle Jonas was clapping on the backbeat, swaying to and fro like the rest of the congregation. Dressed in their maroon and gold robes, the choir did their best to belt out a joyous hymn, only twenty-five strong now, unlike the fifty-voice choir before Katrina.

When the church reopened, he'd tried to persuade Chantelle to sing in the choir, but she wouldn't. "Got no decent clothes, Antoine, got no money to buy any. Besides, I don't want folks to see me. Somebody drops a dime they'll send me to Houston to be with my Mom."

Goin' to . . . CLAP Praise the Lord.

Goin' to . . . CLAP Join the Lord.

Goin' to Heaven, Al-le-lu-lia, goin' to . . . CLAP Be with the Lord!

Was Chantelle in Heaven, he wondered? Uncle Jonas thought so.

He blinked back tears and began clapping. He couldn't cry now, not in front of the Reverend Samuel Goines. He stared at Marcus, sitting beside his mother in the front pew. Marcus, the rat.

When the music ended Reverend Goines left his elegant carved-wood throne on the altar and marched to the pulpit to deliver his sermon, an imposing presence in his flowing gold robe, his kinky gray hair neatly combed, the pecan-brown skin on his face clean-shaven.

Today's sermon was Demon Drugs and Alcohol. To Antoine they all sounded alike, the Reverend shaking his finger at folks in the pews.

"Do not allow drugs and alcohol to derail your life," Reverend Goines thundered in his deep bass voice. "Do not allow those twin devil demons to keep you from the good graces of the Lord!"

Antoine wondered what Reverend Goines would do if he found out his son was dealing drugs. Drugs supplied by AK, which meant AK had a hold on him. Marcus was probably the one who'd told AK about Antoine talking to a cop. For the next forty minutes, he meditated on this, sitting blank-faced beside his uncle, shouting *Amen!* at the proper intervals, all the while feeling the heat of anger rise inside him.

When the service ended, the congregation filed into Fellowship Hall next to the sanctuary. Uncle Jonas headed for the coffee urn. Antoine hung back and leaned against a side wall. He didn't drink coffee, had no appetite for the home-baked cookies and frosted slices of sweet bread that filled the platters on the table beside the big shiny coffee urn.

His mind was on Marcus.

The last stragglers entered Fellowship Hall, followed by Mrs. Goines, Marcus, and Reverend Goines. The Reverend saw him and said, "Morning, Antoine, how you doing today?"

He summoned a smile. "Doing just fine, thank you, sir."

The Goines family forged deeper into Fellowship Hall, greeting one clump of parishioners after another, Marcus glancing around, casual-like. Antoine knew what he was doing: Keeping an eye on Antoine Carter. A spurt of anger stabbed his gut. He strode across the room to Marcus. The little rat's face was set in a belligerent expression, but traces of fear showed in his eyes.

"We need to talk," Antoine said in a low voice. "Outside. Now."

He strode to the side door, went out on the porch, leaned a hip against porch railing and waited, vengeful thoughts churning his mind.

A minute later Marcus came out the door in his navy-blue Sunday-go-to-meeting suit. Acting cool, but wary-eyed.

"What you been telling AK about me?"

The little rat's eyes hardened. "Ain't been telling him nuthin'."

"Yeah? Then how come he jumped me the other day, accused me of talking to a cop?"

"I dunno. Got nuthin' to do with me."

"Georgette told you they called me down the office on Friday, right?"

Marcus rolled his fleshy lips together and glowered at him.

"Don't be spying on me for AK. You do, I'll blow the whistle on the drug deals you got goin' on that street corner near NOCCA. Your daddy won't be too happy about that."

"You do and I'll tell AK, AK take care of you." Marcus gave him a nasty look, turned and went back inside.

AK take care of you. A chill ran down his spine like a jug full of ice water.

Big mistake, threatening Marcus. Should have kept his mouth shut. Damn that cop anyway, wanting him to snitch, saying they'd protect him.

The cops hadn't stopped AK from killing Chantelle.

Wouldn't stop AK from killing *him*, either.

———

Humming a fragment of her Gershwin encore, she unlocked the door, wheeled her suitcase into the foyer and stopped. Her neck prickled.

Why wasn't the alarm on?

Then she saw the M&Ms scattered over the floor in the hall, felt the eerie quiet of her house. She ran to the office and gasped. Sheets of paper, M&Ms, Hershey's mini-bars, and shattered glass from Jake's brandy snifter littered the floor. Someone had trashed her house. What about her flutes?

Her heart slammed her chest and the sour taste of fear flooded her mouth. She ran upstairs to her bedroom closet, shoved her clothes aside and knelt down in front of the large steel safe in the back of the closet. Her hands were shaking so badly it took her almost a minute to dial the combination.

Offering up a silent prayer, she opened the safe.

And saw her flute cases just as she'd left them. Weak with relief, she struggled to her feet, left the closet and looked around. No trash strewn around her bedroom, but one of her pillows lay on the floor, missing its pillowcase. She studied her bureau. The drawers were closed, but the lid of her jewelry box was open. Had someone stolen her jewelry? A few pieces were quite valuable. But she didn't have the strength to check them.

Sinking onto her bed, she rocked back and forth, overcome with hysterical laughter, laughter that ended in a choked sob.

Her stomach cramped, a vicious knife-like pain. Why was this happening now? She took a deep breath to steady her nerves and marshaled her thoughts. And her courage.

Get a grip, she thought. Lots of houses get burglarized in New Orleans, especially since Katrina. Over the weekend someone must have seen her dark house, assumed no one was home and taken advantage of it. But in the back of her mind, a question nagged her. Why wasn't the security alarm on?

Should she call Frank?

When she'd called him after the car accident, he'd been angry with her for not reporting it to the police. This time he would be furious. She gritted her teeth, picked up the phone on her bedside table and dialed 911.

"I called the police," she said, "but they didn't seem too hopeful about catching the burglar."

Frank said nothing, just looked at her. She felt safer now that he was here, a virile presence in her kitchen, leaning against the sink in a tan polo shirt and faded jeans, exuding vitality and strength. His dark probing eyes were incredibly sexy, regarding her steadily now.

She sank onto a chair at her butcher-block table, fighting the push-pull of sexual attraction and the irritation that festered in her mind. To break the silence, she said, "What good did it do to report it?"

He came to the table and sat down opposite her, his expression unreadable. "Someone broke into your house. That's a crime. Now there's a record of it. The alarm was off when you came in?"

"Yes. I don't understand it. Jake always arms it before we leave."

"Are you and Jake the only ones with the code?"

"A cleaning woman comes in once a week, but she doesn't have it. If I'm not here to let her in, Jake does. Mr. Silverman has the code, too. He's my new security man."

"What's his first name?"

"Barry."

"Did you check his credentials?"

"Yes. Well, I didn't, but Jake did. He'd been working for a London businessman. When Jake phoned him, the man was very enthusiastic. I forget his name, but Jake could tell you. Mr. Silverman is from New Orleans. He lives here."

"Uh-huh. And you know this how?"

"That's what he told me. Why? Does it matter?"

Frank gazed at her, clearly irritated. "I need to see his credentials."

"I doubt I could find them for you now. You saw the office. I'll ask Jake to find them when he comes in tomorrow." She raked her fingers through her hair. "Why didn't the policemen dust for fingerprints?"

"This is New Orleans not CSI. Tell me about Jake. Has he got a beef with you?"

"Of course not. Jake's my dearest friend. He helped me get through the accident and—" Hearing the tremor in her voice, she broke off. She would *not* cry, damn it!

"Somebody trashed the office. Not what you'd expect with a simple B&E. Are you and Jake getting along okay?"

"Yes. For the most part. Would you like something to drink?"

"No thanks. What's up with you and Jake?"

"I've got orange juice and Arizona Iced Tea."

"Belinda, what is it that you don't want to tell me?" Gazing at her with his incredibly sexy eyes, eyes that would probe her soul if she let them.

Her palms grew clammy. She didn't want to tell him that Jake was abandoning her. She didn't want to tell him any of her other secrets, either.

"What's going on with you and Jake?"

"Well, he's moving to New York in January, but that's hardly grounds for suspecting him. Besides, he was with me in Cincinnati."

"Why is he moving to New York?"

"Jake's a fantastic organist. He's got a Masters from New England Conservatory." She faked a smile, though her heart was a lump of lead. "He wants to pursue other opportunities. Isn't that how the saying goes?"

"Okay. Tell me about Silverman."

"I met him at the reception after my concert in London. He said he'd been working a security detail for a British businessman and if I ever needed a security driver, he'd be happy to do it. He gave me his card."

"You met him at a concert. And he just happened to be a security guy and gave you his card."

An angry flush flooded her cheeks. "Yes, and it's a good thing. After the NOCCA concert Friday night, a drunk accosted me in the parking lot. Mr. Silverman ran him off."

Frank's mouth quirked in annoyance. "Why didn't you tell me that before?"

Why didn't you come backstage after the concert? Then you could have protected me.

"It didn't seem that important."

"Describe the drunk."

"A big white man, big and scruffy looking. He looked like a lumberjack, dark beard, evil eyes. And a very foul mouth."

"Get Jake over here. Silverman, too. I want to talk to both of them."

First thing Monday morning Frank called London, sitting at his desk now with a phone clamped to his ear. Opposite him, Kenyon Miller frowned at his computer screen, not liking what he saw apparently. Meanwhile, the voice with the Brit accent droned on. Mr. Smythe-Jones.

Y in the middle, E at the end, the pompous ass had explained.

As if he gave a shit how the guy spelled his name. Vobitch would flip when he saw the phone bill, ten minutes to London and counting, the Brit rhapsodizing about Barry Silverman, who'd taken excellent care of his security, blah, blah, blah. He tried to picture the man, envisioning a fat old geezer with white hair sprouting from his ears. "Mr. Jones—"

"Smythe-Jones." The bigshot Brit correcting him.

"Uh-huh. What sort of business do you run?" Aware that Miller was listening now.

The line crackled with silence. Then, "I'm an entrepreneur."

He winked at Miller. "What sort of entrepreneur? Selling guns to Middle East rebels?" Miller gave a silent laugh and a thumbs-up, egging him on.

"Certainly not!" came the indignant reply. "I invest in stock futures, that sort of thing."

"Stock futures. That why you need security? You make a lot of money?"

"Detective Renzi, p'raps you haven't heard, but on *this* side of the pond, we've had several businessmen kidnapped for ransom. One bloke had a finger hacked off."

"Kidnapped for ransom and a finger hacked off," he repeated for Miller's benefit. "Were there any attempts to kidnap you when Silverman was guarding you?"

"Not a one. That's what I'm trying to tell you. His work was spot on for two years. Look here, Detective, I'm expecting a call from Tokyo, so if you're *quite* done . . ."

"Okay, Mr. Smythe-Jones, thanks for your time." He cradled the phone and rubbed the scar on his chin. Something felt wrong. The pompous Brit was just a voice on the phone, could be anybody. He needed to talk to Silverman. He'd interviewed Ziegler at Belinda's yesterday, but not Silverman. Belinda had phoned him and left a message, but Silverman never called back.

"Hoo-ee!" Miller said, his eyes gleeful. "Smith-Jones? What's up with that? Take the two most common names in the world, hook 'em together?"

"Hey, Mr. Know-Nothing. Not Smith, S-M-I-T-H. There's that all-important *Y* in the middle, that extra-special *E* at the end. Like he's an aristocrat or some fucking thing."

Miller cracked up, rumbling a laugh.

His cell phone rang and he grabbed it. "Renzi."

"Hey, Frank, it's Kelly. You got a minute?"

A minute? He had hours and days worth of minutes for Kelly O'Neil. A warm glow filled his chest as he pictured her entrancing sea-green eyes.

"Give me a minute, I'll call you back." He pushed back from his desk and said to Miller, "I gotta go check something. Back in five."

Focused on his computer, Miller waved a hand without looking up.

He hustled outside and sat on a stone bench between the Eighth District Station and the coffee joint next door, far enough from the outdoor tables so no one could overhear, and called Kelly.

"Sorry," he said. "It was noisy in the office. I had to go outside." A big fib. He didn't want to talk to her in front of Miller. They were on the verge of something. He felt it in his gut, the buzz he got before he slept with a woman.

Kelly responded with a derisive laugh. "Your office wasn't noisy. You just didn't want to talk to me in front of Kenyon Miller. I'm outside too."

"Yeah?" he said, grinning. "Close encounters with Warren getting to you? Can't stand being cooped up in a trailer Mr. Sexist-Pig?"

Fifteen months post-Katrina, the badly damaged District-Three station remained closed, the D-3 detectives working out of a trailer in cubicles barely big enough to hold a computer station.

"How'd you guess?" she said, with a lilt in her voice. "I'm sitting under a big oak tree enjoying the fresh air and sunshine, figured I'd give you a call and make sure you're busting your butt."

He could feel her smiling. "I am. I just finished talking to a snotty old fart in London."

"London? How come? Something to do with the Lakeview case?"

"No. How about we have dinner tonight and I'll tell you about it?"

"Uh, not tonight. Sorry. I've got something planned."

"Uh-huh," he said, thinking: What plans and with whom?

"How about tomorrow? I could meet you at seven."

His heart soared. "Perfect. Let's meet at Zea's on Magazine Street. My treat." Hinting this wasn't about work to see how she'd react.

She uttered a low throaty laugh. "Sounds great. See you then."

His heart thrummed. Dinner with Kelly O'Neil tomorrow night.

After dinner, anything could happen.

When it came to women, he liked to think positive.

At ten-thirty he unlocked Belinda's door and stepped into the foyer, carrying a foil-covered plate. Agitated voices came from the office. His heart surged, fueled by delicious anticipation. Now he would demonstrate his expertise to his beloved and make her understand how indispensable he was.

And Ziegler would get his comeuppance.

Belinda came out to the foyer, sporting a worried frown. "Hello, Mr. Silverman. Someone broke in while we were gone."

"Broke in!" he exclaimed, feigning astonishment and concern.

Ziegler came out of the office and stood beside Belinda.

He had to use all his willpower not to laugh. The asshole's bearded face was puckered in the mother of all frowns.

"Someone trashed the place," Ziegler said, glaring at him.

He set the foil-covered plate on the foyer table and adopted a stern expression. "That's not good. Tell me what happened, Belinda."

"I got home around three and came inside and saw the mess—"

"Hold it. Didn't the police come when the alarm went off?"

After a quick glance at Ziegler, she said, "The alarm wasn't on."

"I armed it before we left," Ziegler said, and gnawed at his thumbnail.

He smiled, emulating the condescending smile Ziegler often gave him. "Are you sure? You were in a rush. It's easy to forget something when—"

"I wasn't in a rush. I didn't *forget*. I set the alarm before I left."

Feigning concern, he said to Belinda, "You came in the house by yourself? What if the robbers were still here? If I had driven you home, I could have protected you."

If I'd come with you to Cincinnati none of this would have been necessary.

"She called you yesterday and left a message," Ziegler said. "Where were you?"

"Really? My answering service said nothing about a message." To Belinda he said, "Was anything stolen? What about your flutes?"

"My flutes weren't stolen, just some jewelry and my CD player."

And four CDs, and a pair of your sexy-smelling panties.

"Did you call the police?"

"Yes. For all the good it did. They didn't seem hopeful about catching the burglar."

"Did you notify your insurance company?"

"Yes. They told me to make a list of everything that's missing."

Ziegler skewered him a look, a vindictive squinty-eyed look. "Where were you yesterday?"

"At an Atlanta Symphony concert. My sis—" He caught himself in time. "My girlfriend plays in the orchestra. It was a terrific concert. I really enjoyed it." *Except for watching my bitch-sister Rachel sawing away on her violin.*

"When we're out of town," Ziegler said, "you're supposed to be here to cover the alarm in case something happens. That's why I gave you the code."

He gave the asshole a self-righteous smile. "I paid for a plane ticket to Cincinnati, Jake, but you told me I wasn't needed. The ticket wasn't refundable, so I exchanged it for a round-trip flight to Atlanta. I flew back early this morning."

Belinda glanced at Ziegler. His beloved appeared sympathetic, unlike Ziegler, who glared at him, his baleful eyes full of disdain.

"Only three people have the code, Mr. Silverman. Belinda has it, I have it, and you have it."

"Wait. Are you accusing *me*?" He turned to Belinda and made his eyes go wide. "You think *I* had something to do with this?"

"No, I don't." She wouldn't meet his gaze, however. A bad sign.

"Well, I do!" Ziegler said. "Your services are no longer required, Mr. Silverman. Send me an invoice for your time, including today, and I'll mail you a check."

An angry flush burned his cheeks. This was totally unfair. He couldn't allow this to happen. "Is that what you want, Belinda?"

She continued to stare at the floor. "I'm sorry, Mr. Silverman."

He clenched his fists and took a step toward Ziegler. The asshole stood his ground, smirking at him. He wanted to punch the smirk off his face, wanted to ram a fist into his gut and show Belinda how impotent and helpless Loverboy was. But that wouldn't do.

He looked at Belinda. "Well, if that's the way it is . . ."

"Yes, that's the way it is!" Ziegler said.

He picked up the foil-wrapped plate from the table and offered it to her. "My girlfriend baked some brownies and I saved some for you, Belinda."

"Take your fucking brownies and get out!" Ziegler shouted.

Rage hotter than a blazing inferno exploded inside him. With a colossal effort, he maintained control. "No need to get testy, Mr. Ziegler."

You'll get what's coming to you soon enough.

CHAPTER 21

Wednesday, 8 November

Kelly unlocked her front door and led him into her living room. She flashed a smile, but she seemed edgy. Maybe she was having second thoughts about inviting him home for a nightcap after their dinner at Zea's.

"Have a seat while I get the Baileys, Frank."

He put his arms around her and pulled her close. She exhaled a puff of air against his cheek, tipped her head back and looked at him, her sea-green eyes liquid pools. He took her face in his hands and kissed her, gently at first, more deeply when she opened her lips and pressed her body against him.

When they came up for air, she said, "Mmm. That was good."

He raised her top and caressed her back with his fingertips.

"Too many clothes," he said. "I want to feel your skin."

She pulled off her low-cut top and tossed it on the sofa. He undid her bra, brushed the straps from her shoulders and it fell to the floor.

"Take off your shirt," she whispered.

He feathered her nipples with his fingers and kissed her. When he took off his shirt and dropped it on the floor, she pressed against him. Her skin felt warm against his, her nipples hard against his chest. He felt her heartbeat, thrumming almost as fast as his.

His cell phone went off, a jarring interruption.

"I should have turned the damn thing off," he muttered. He didn't want to answer, but when his cell rang this late, it was usually urgent.

When he answered, Belinda screamed, "Frank, I don't know what to do! Jake is dead!"

His heart jolted. "Hold on, slow down. Tell me what happened."

"H-h-he felt sick this afternoon so he went home but then he felt worse, so he went to the hospital and now he's dead, Frank! Jake is dead! Can you come to the hospital?"

He glanced at Kelly, gazing at him now with a somber expression. "Which hospital?"

"Touro Infirmary. It's on—"

"I know where it is. I'll be there as soon as I can."

"Thank you, Frank. Please hurry!"

He punched off. "Sorry, Kelly. This woman's hysterical. I've got to go calm her down."

Vertical frown lines appeared between Kelly's eyebrows.

"It's not personal, it's business. She's had a lot of problems, a car accident, a B&E at her house, and now her manager's dead. It's more complicated than that, but I haven't got time to explain."

He bent down to retrieve his polo shirt. Inspired by a sudden idea, he said, "Would you mind coming with me? Maybe you can calm her down. You're good at that."

"I guess so, if you want." But her expression remained skeptical.

He drew her to him and kissed her. "What I want is to make love to you, but this won't wait. I'll explain in the car."

The look in her eyes said: *Not okay, but I'll go with it. For now.*

———

With Kelly at his side, he strode to the reception desk and flashed his ID badge at a tired-looking older woman in a white uniform.

"We're here to see Belinda Scully. She came in with a patient named Jake Ziegler. Can you tell me where to find her?"

"She's waiting for you in the Family Center. Do you know—?"

"I know where it is." He'd interviewed plenty of victims' families in the Family Center, the room where they parked relatives so the doctor could deliver bad news in private. He tilted his head at Kelly and they walked down a hall decorated with cheery watercolors of pink pelicans and various wildlife.

They came to a door with a metal faceplate: Family Center. He tapped on the door and stepped inside. Slumped in a wingchair with blue-flowered upholstery, Belinda looked up. Her eyes were bloodshot, surrounded by puffy skin. Her facial pallor matched the institutional-ivory walls. She leaped out of the chair, crossed the room in two long strides and threw her arms around him. "Thank God you're here, Frank. I don't know what I'm going to do."

Her ribs heaved—she was hyperventilating—and he smelled an unpleasant odor, as if she'd run a marathon and hadn't showered.

He eased her away and gestured at Kelly. "This is Detective Kelly O'Neil. I brought her along because, well, you seemed upset."

Belinda studied Kelly, a head-to-toe examination that took in Kelly's low-cut top and mini-skirt. Not exactly NOPD regulation, he realized.

She clamped her lips together and stepped back, shoulders clenched, neck corded. Held together by a slender thread of iron will.

"Tell me what happened," he said.

"Jake . . ." Her eyes welled with tears and her chest heaved. She shook her head and turned away.

He said to Kelly, "Stay with her while I talk to the doctor, okay?"

Kelly sent him a message with her eyes, one he couldn't fathom. "Sure, Frank. We'll be fine."

He returned to the desk and asked to speak to the attending physician.

The gray-haired woman stifled a yawn. "That would be Doctor Perez. A young gunshot victim came in a half hour ago. Doctor Perez is working on him in the Trauma Center, should be done soon."

He waited impatiently outside the Trauma Center with an elderly black woman in a faded-pink housecoat, sobbing quietly in a chair. Ten minutes later a man with dark hair and a mocha complexion pushed through a double door, dressed in green scrubs. He adjusted his horn-rimmed glasses and approached the sobbing woman. "Your grandson will be okay, Mrs. Jackson. The bullet nicked an artery in his thigh. That's why there was so much blood, but we've got him stabilized."

"Praise the Lord!" The grandmother leaped to her feet and clasped the doctor's hands. "Thank you, Doctor. Thank you for saving my boy!"

"A nurse will be out in a minute to give you the details."

Seemingly embarrassed by the woman's emotional outburst, the doctor turned to leave. Frank intercepted him and flashed his ID.

"I know you're busy, Doctor Perez, but could you tell me what happened to Jacob Ziegler?" Knowing the grandmother was listening, he lowered his voice. "Ziegler and Ms. Scully have had some problems lately."

In a Spanish-tinged accent, Perez said, "Come with me. We can talk in the physician's lounge."

The dim-lit cubicle had a metal coffee urn and two vending machines, one with bottled juice and soda, another with candy bars, packages of crackers and granola bars. Perez sank onto a green-plastic chair, removed his horn-rimmed glasses and rubbed his eyes. After polishing his spectacles with a handkerchief, he put them back on.

"Mr. Ziegler presented some odd symptoms when he arrived."

Frank got out his spiral notebook. "What time was that?"

Perez puffed his cheeks and blew a stream of air. "Tell you the truth they come in so fas' tonight I'm not sure. Beverly—she's on the desk—she could give you the exact time."

"Okay. I'm more interested in the COD. Ziegler wasn't that old."

"True. He was thirty-six. I cannot tell you the cause of death because I don't know. He was barely conscious on arrival. The triage nurse took his vital signs and sent him straight to the Trauma Center."

"That bad, huh?"

"Yes. We were concerned about his heart rate. It was very slow and irregular. Also, he complained about blurred vision and stomach pain."

"Could it have been a heart attack?"

"It is possible. We had no time to do an EKG. His condition deteriorated and then his heart stopped. We tried to save him." The doctor's expression grew pained. "We did what we could."

"But the patient died," Frank said, and cursed himself for the unthinking remark.

Clearly irritated, the doctor said, "Yes. Sometimes the patient dies."

"Forgive me, Doctor Perez, I'm not criticizing. I assume you've never met Ziegler, but I have. And I have information, which I'm not allowed to divulge . . ." Bullshitting the man now, anything to get information. "I believe his death might involve foul play."

Perez gazed at him, his eyes large and dark behind the horn-rimmed glasses. "I see. Back in my country—" He gave a tight smile. "I grew up in Panama but took my advanced medical training in the United States. Back in Panama I recall a similar case. Mr. Ziegler's partner said he came home from work feeling nauseated and—"

"Hold on," Frank said. "His partner? You mean Ms. Scully?"

"No. His *partner*. Mr. Ziegler was gay. His partner brought him to the hospital."

That stopped him. He'd figured Ziegler was gay but hadn't considered that he might have a partner. He had assumed Belinda brought him to the hospital. "What's the partner's name?"

"Dean Silva." The doctor checked his watch and stifled a yawn. "Excuse me, but I must get back to work."

"Before you go, could you elaborate on that case you had in Panama?"

"Ah. Yes. When I interned at a hospital in Panama City, I saw an interesting case. People think poisoning involves arsenic or cyanide or strychnine, but there are many toxic substances. Each year in the United States, seven hundred people die of poisoning. Most of them are adults. Many of those deaths are not accidental."

"What happened to the person you treated in Panama?"

"He died. From the autopsy and toxicology tests we concluded that he had eaten pokeweed. It's a plant. Some of the poor people eat the berries and leaves, but they must be thoroughly cooked." Perez smiled faintly. "Perhaps his wife was not a culinary expert."

Amused, Frank said, "Food for thought, huh?"

The doctor's professional demeanor reappeared as he rose to his feet. "I have ordered a full toxicology exam, including screens for alcohol, narcotics, sedatives, amphetamines, cocaine and marijuana. And a detailed report on the contents of Mr. Ziegler's stomach. Perhaps that will tell us something."

"Thank you, Doctor. And thanks for the poison lecture."

He headed back to the Family Room, thinking: Who would want Ziegler dead badly enough to poison him? And why?

By the time they left the hospital it was two in the morning. Judging by Kelly's eye-roll when he returned to the Family Center, her comment—*We'll be fine*—had been wishful thinking, a notion reinforced by the aversive body language as they walked Belinda to her car.

She seemed calmer now, holding herself rigid as though she was fighting for control. When they reached her blue Infiniti coup, he said, "I can drive you home and bring you back tomorrow to get your car."

"That won't be necessary," Belinda said.

He gave his car keys to Kelly. "Can you wait in my car? I'll be there in a minute." Without a word, Kelly took the keys and left.

Belinda opened her car door and looked at him. Her eyes had a glazed, dull look. Lifeless, no spark in them at all. She was still in shock.

"What's your schedule this week? Any concerts?"

"I have one in Baton Rouge on Sunday afternoon, but I'm going to cancel. I can't think about performing right now."

"So you'll be here? No out of town trips?"

She regarded him warily. No flirting tonight. "Why do you ask?"

"Once we get the autopsy report I might have questions."

Her eyes glistened with tears, a rare glimpse of vulnerability trumping her usual iron-willed demeanor. He felt bad for her, but he still thought she was hiding something.

"I have to call Jake's parents. They live on Long Island. They'll want to hold the funeral there, and I intend to go." Her mouth twisted in anguish. "What shall I tell them? I don't understand how Jake could get sick and . . . ."

"The doctor ordered an autopsy and full toxicology screens. That may tell us something. Why didn't you tell me Jake was gay?"

Her eyes flashed, remnants of the old fire. "I didn't think it was relevant. Jake was a very private person. His parents . . ." She trailed off and shrugged.

"They didn't know Jake was gay."

"No. Jake didn't feel he could tell them. Poor Dean."

"His partner, right? Can you give me his address and phone number?"

She reached in her purse, handed him a business card and said curtly, "I'm tired. I need to rest."

"Of course. Go home and get some sleep. Call me if you need me."

After giving him an odd look, she got in her car and slammed the door.

He watched her drive off, processing what she'd said. Jake's parents lived on Long Island and didn't know their son was gay. Jake had a partner. Did they have a spat? It wouldn't be the first time a gay man killed his partner. Tomorrow would be a busy day. He needed to talk to Dean Silva. And Belinda. And Barry Silverman.

When he got to his car, Kelly was sitting in the passenger seat. She handed him the keys. "How's the grieving celebrity?"

"Still in shock, but she'll survive. She's tough."

He cranked the car and drove out of the parking lot, wondering if Kelly was a wired as he was. "I take it you two didn't become bosom buddies while I was talking to the doctor."

She gave him a droll smile. "The Master Detective scores a bull's eye."

"What did she say?"

"She put on her Prima-Donna hat and listed her credentials. You know, flute soloist extraordinaire, protégé of Guy St. Cyr, whoever the hell he is—"

"Big time flute soloist."

"Whatever. When it comes to classical music, I never got beyond *Peter and the Wolf*."

The comment struck him funny and he cracked up. "If you'd stuck with the nuns . . ."

"Yeah, yeah," she said, waving a hand. "I mean, I feel for her, you know? Having someone she cared about die unexpectedly. But it's not like he was her husband."

"And he wasn't her boyfriend either. Ziegler's gay."

"Really? Did you know he was gay?"

"I figured it out a while ago, but I didn't know he had a partner."

"Are you going to talk to him?"

"Tomorrow I hope. Belinda too, once she's over the shock."

Five minutes later he pulled into Kelly's driveway, shut off the engine and draped his arm over the seat.

"What's your impression of Belinda? Other than prima-donna flutist."

"She's into image management. When we walked into that room, she was on the verge of hysteria, but the minute you left she got it together fast, no more tears, no hand wringing. To me, it felt like a performance. That's about it. Well, except for one thing."

"What's that?"

Her lips widened in a grin.

"What?"

"Belinda Scully is infatuated with Frank Renzi."

"Yeah?" He ran his fingers down her forearm.

"Yeah, and you know it."

He leaned over the console to kiss her, but she pushed him away.

"Not so fast. Her infatuation with you was my first observation. Here's another one."

He knew better than to interrupt, knew better than to make any wise-ass remarks, too.

"She knows we were making out before we came here."

"Get out. How could she?"

Kelly shook her head. "Men are so clueless. Women know these things, Frank. She probably smelled my perfume on you."

He loved the way she analyzed it, loved the way she said it so matter-of-factly. She was probably right and he didn't care. He wanted to take her inside and take her to bed. Would have if work hadn't been a scant five hours away.

He took her face in his hands and kissed her.

"I'll tell you what I know, Kelly O'Neil. You're a terrific woman and a savvy detective and I can't wait to make love to you."

CHAPTER 22

Thursday 9 November

Oz woke him at dawn. When the first rays of sunlight filtered into the room, his bunny had begun hopping around his cage, tossing his water dish in a frenzy of joy. The woman at the animal shelter had warned him that rabbits were sun-greeters, and Oz was no exception.

Now, bleary eyed and exhausted, he'd been awake for hours, a crucial question festering in his mind. What happened to Ziegler?

The man who loved chocolate. The man who'd fired him.

Rage clogged his throat. His plan had seemed foolproof, but now, in the cold light of day, he wasn't so sure.

He strode to the file cabinet. The photos he'd stolen lay on top, Belinda with her mouth open, lips moist, as though she'd licked them in anticipation of his kiss. He unzipped his fly and stroked his cock. Soon they would be together. Soon he would touch the silky skin of her breasts and stroke her nipples, erect with desire. For him. He pumped his hand faster, his breathing ragged, his erection a fierce ache. Felt the wondrous glow . . .

His cell phone chimed. Fuck-all! Who was calling when he was about to climax with his beloved? Then he thought: *It's Belinda calling me!*

Euphoric, he grabbed his cell phone, punched on and answered.

"Mr. Nickerson? This is Greg from Collections Unlimited. According to our records, you're three months behind on your American Express Card payments. We need to talk about a payment plan."

"Fuck you and your payment plan!" He snapped the phone shut.

To hell with Collections Unlimited. His glorious dream was about to come true. When he moved in with Belinda, he would have no rent to pay, and his new salary—one commensurate with his new duties—would allow him to pay off his debts.

He returned to the file cabinet and turned his Belinda photos over. He never fantasized about his beloved when he was angry. For that he used his bitch sister, visualizing her and Pa fucking like dogs all those years, picturing Rachel's dark hair draped over Pa's hairy chest, hearing their ugly grunts and cries. He stroked harder. Imagined his cock pounding into Rachel. Enjoying the terror in her eyes. Hearing her scream.

He tried to climax. Impossible. Not knowing what happened to Ziegler was driving him crazy. Shaking with rage, he punched Belinda's number into his cell phone and waited. Five rings . . . six . . .

He gripped the phone. Why didn't she answer?

"Hello."

Her soft voice made the hairs on his forearms stand at attention.

"Did I wake you, Belinda?" He slapped his forehead. How stupid! From his frequent observations, he knew Belinda rose at six-thirty every day to do a five mile run, followed by an hour of scales, arpeggios and finger exercises on her flute, then breakfast. When she didn't respond, he said, "It's Barry Silverman. Is something wrong?"

"Yes, Mr. Silverman, something is very wrong."

He did a festive dance beside the futon.

"Jake," she said in a dull voice. "It's Jake."

"What's wrong with Jake?" Hoping his ingenious plan had worked.

"Jake is dead."

His heart sang a Beethovian whoop of joy. He heard her faint breathing and realized he had to say something. "How terrible! What happened?"

"He went home sick yesterday and then he went to the hospital and they tried to save him, but—" A choked sob. "They couldn't."

Part of him resented the fact that she had such deep feelings for that asshole. But he couldn't ignore her distress.

"I'm shocked, Belinda. Jake was . . ." *Jake was an asshole and he deserved to die.* "You must be terribly upset. I'll come over right now and help you."

"Thank you, Mr. Silverman, you're very kind, but—"

"No buts, Belinda. I'll come over straightaway."

Come over and fuck your brains out.

"No, please, I don't—"

"This is no time to be stoic, Belinda. I'll be there in ten minutes."

A faint sigh. "All right." A soft click told him she'd hung up.

"Yahoo!" he screamed. "That asshole is dead, Oz! Belinda wants me to come over and console her." He glanced at Oz, cowering in the corner of his cage. Oz hated loud noises. Rabbits were prey, always watchful, ever fearful.

He sniffed his armpit. Disgusting. He couldn't go to his beloved smelling like a pig. He ran to the bathroom and got in the shower. As the steamy water beat against his body, his mind spun like a gerbil in a cage.

Belinda would need him to drive her to her concert in Baton Rouge on Sunday. She had another concert next weekend in Lexington, Kentucky. For that he would need money. But he was short of cash and his one remaining credit card was almost maxed-out. He couldn't use the cash in the storage locker he'd rented. That was for dire emergencies.

He soaped his groin and smiled. What was he thinking? Now that Ziegler was dead, Belinda was certain to rehire him.

Then his money problems would be over.

On the way to the house Ziegler had shared with his partner Frank drove past NOCCA. He couldn't stop thinking about Antoine Carter. Last Wednesday at the meeting with Vobitch, he'd voiced his suspicion that Antoine might have been the getaway driver for the Lakeview robbery. Vobitch had told him to lean on the kid. On Friday he had, but the kid had stonewalled him again. Antoine was scared.

You're gonna get me killed, he'd said. Twice.

With Antoine's words echoing in his mind, he parked in front of a small Creole cottage painted forest-green with white trim. He wasn't looking forward to interviewing Ziegler's partner, but if there were problems in the relationship, he needed to know.

Well-tended shrubs bordered the front walk and a planter of orange marigolds hung from a hook on the porch roof. He pushed the doorbell and waited. Heavy drapes covered the windows beside the door. A minute passed. He rang the bell again. Maybe Silva was out. He had chosen not to call first. In his experience, surprise visits usually brought the best results.

The sounds of a bolt being drawn and clicking locks told him he was about to meet Ziegler's partner. The door opened, revealing a young man with rumpled hair and red-rimmed eyes. "Mr. Silva? I'm Detective Frank Renzi, NOPD. Belinda Scully gave me your address. Can I come in? I've got a few questions."

Silva stared at him silently. He seemed dazed. A man in his early thirties, five-seven, slender but well built. His dark hair looked like it hadn't been washed and his chocolate-brown eyes were bloodshot.

"I know this is a difficult time, Mr. Silva, but the questions won't wait."

With a resigned sigh, Silva showed him into the living room. A mélange of odors permeated the air, some sort of spicy food he couldn't identify and a pungent aroma he knew quite well. Darkened by heavy drapes, the only light in the room came from a small table lamp. A brown leather couch faced a big-screen TV and an elaborate stereo system. He took a seat on the couch.

Silva hesitated, then perched on the other end.

"Belinda told me you were Jake's partner. I spoke with him a few times, and he seemed like a nice guy. I'm sorry for your loss."

"Thank you." Silva's eyes teared up and his Adam's apple bobbed.

"The doctor said you brought him to the hospital. Could you tell me what happened?"

Silva took a pack of Marlboros off the coffee table, shook one out and lighted it. Took a drag and blew smoke. To Frank, it seemed like Silva was buying time to construct his story. He'd seen that a few times. But maybe not.

At last Silva said, "Jake left for work around eight. I was off yesterday so I didn't . . ." His eyes teared up again. He swallowed hard. "I didn't have breakfast with him."

"You were off yesterday. Off from work?"

"Yes. I'm a medical courier. I deliver blood and tissue samples for Beta Diagnostics. If I work on a weekend, I get to take a weekday off."

He made a mental note to check this with Silva's employer.

"Jake called me at three-thirty and said he felt sick. I told him to come home, but he said he had too much work to do." Silva took jagged puffs on his cigarette and blew smoke. "For Belinda. She's got a concert in Baton Rouge on Sunday and another one in Kentucky next Saturday."

Silva's body language sent a clear message: He wasn't fond of Belinda.

"So Jake didn't come home?"

More jagged puffs, more plumes of smoke. "Not till four-thirty. He'd vomited twice at the office. I made him a cup of tea. Sometimes that settles your stomach, but it didn't help. Jake had a terrible headache. I wanted to take him to the emergency room, but he just wanted to lie down and sleep. He said he couldn't afford to get sick. He had to go to the concerts in Baton Rouge and Louisville with Belinda." A tick pulsed in Silva's cheek.

"Seems like Belinda Scully is a demanding employer."

"You can say that again!" Silva's eyes blazed with anger. "She'd call him all hours of the night, even on weekends. Not about anything important. Things she could have done for herself."

Silva seemed jealous of Ziegler's relationship with Belinda. But that didn't mean he wanted Ziegler dead. His grief seemed genuine.

"How were you and Jake getting along?"

Silva gazed at him, sullen and squinty-eyed. "We've been together for sixteen years. We got along fine."

"No arguments? No disagreements about the time he spent at work?"

"A few spats, maybe. Nothing serious. It was more about—" Silva snubbed out his cigarette.

"More about what?"

The tick in Silva's cheek pulsed rapidly. "Jake was in the closet. He was afraid to tell his parents, afraid they'd disown him or some goddam thing. I begged him to tell them, but he wouldn't. Now I can't even go to the funeral. It's like I'm nothing." His eyes glistened with unshed tears. "Sixteen years together, and this is how it ends."

Frank felt a pang of sympathy. He'd worked with a Boston cop in a similar situation. Ron was out, but his partner, the only son of Irish-Catholic parents, wasn't. "I'm sorry, Dean. Maybe society will wake up someday and figure out that if two people love each other, they should be together, no matter what."

Dean's attempt at an appreciative smile failed.

"What did Jake have for breakfast yesterday?"

"Orange juice, black coffee, and a bowl of cereal with a banana."

"What kind of cereal?"

Dean's eyes widened. "Why? You think I poisoned him?"

"I'm trying to figure out what made him sick. Food poisoning is one possibility." But not the only one.

"Cocoa Puffs. I hate that crap, but Jake loved it. That's all he ever ate for breakfast. Except when I made pancakes on the weekend."

"How about the orange juice? Did you drink some?"

"Yes, and it wasn't the coffee." Dean shot him a belligerent look. "Jake made a big pot of dark roast with chicory. I drank the rest and didn't get sick, so you can cross that off the list."

"Belinda said you and Jake planned to move to New York."

"She did? Amazing. She wasn't happy about it, I can tell you that. I got accepted into the masters program at Pratt. Classes start in January. It was going to be great. We'd be in a big city. A city that isn't full of religious bigots like New Orleans. We could go places together like we used to." He broke off and stared into space.

"Where was that?"

"Providence. We met at an organ recital at Brown University. Jake's a terrific organist. He was looking forward to finding another job in New York." Dean's mouth twisted. "And now he's dead."

"The plans were still on for you to move to New York?"

"Yes," Dean snapped. "I loved Jake. Why would I poison him?"

"Take it easy, Dean. With an unexplained death, we have to cover all the bases. I don't have the autopsy report yet. Or the toxicology results." He studied Dean's reaction. Dean appeared unperturbed. Maybe he didn't understand how thorough toxicology tests could be.

"It may have been something Jake ate, spoiled food maybe." But thanks to Doctor Perez's poison tutorial, he doubted it. He closed his notepad and stood. "Thanks, Dean. I'm sorry to bother you at a time like this."

"Will you call me when you get the autopsy results?"

"I will." He smiled. "By the way, who's your supplier?"

Dean looked at him, blank-faced. "Supplier?"

He tapped his nose. "The minute I came inside your house my pot detector went off."

Dean's body tensed and the nervous tick in his cheek jumped like crazy.

"I'm not looking to bust you for smoking pot in your own house, Dean. But I'd like to know who your supplier is."

A small shrug. "Just some kid."

"What's his name?"

"Name? These guys don't give you names. I call him Shorty. It's not like he gave me his business card. I think he goes to NOCCA."

His neck prickled. "What makes you think that?"

"I meet him two blocks from the school after classes get out. He parks at the corner and we . . . do what we do."

"What kind of car does he drive?"

"I don't know. An old Chevy, I think. I'm not into cars. Dark blue."

Not Antoine, Frank thought, relieved. Antoine drove a bronze Ford Tempo. "Describe him."

"A black kid with a chubby face and short dark hair. Short and kinky."

Definitely not Antoine. Antoine had dreads. "Was Jake into pot, too?"

"Not really. We'd share a blunt now and then."

"Did Belinda know about it?"

Dean Silva's liquid-brown eyes hardened. "Belinda didn't have a clue."

CHAPTER 23

"Dean, I know you're hurting right now—"

"Hurting? Christ, Belinda, Jake is dead! How am I supposed to feel?"

Hunched over Jake's desk, she gripped the phone in one hand, massaged her forehead with the other. This was the call she'd been dreading. Tension gripped her stomach in a stranglehold.

"I know how much you loved him. I just wanted to—"

"Wanted to what? Console me? Be serious. You don't give a shit about me or anyone else. Jake did everything for you! And what did he get from you? Nothing. No consideration that he might have a life of his own. You expected him to work his ass off for you. That's all you care about. Yourself and your fucking career."

Stunned by the ferocity of his attack, she blinked back tears. Still, in her heart, she knew Dean was right. She had been inconsiderate. Laying guilt trips on Jake for wanting to move to New York. To be with Dean.

I love him, Bee. I don't want to lose him.

A tear ran down her cheek. She brushed it away. Regained a semblance of control. "His parents plan to hold the funeral on Long Island where they live. They hired a funeral director to—" She stifled a sob as tears ran down her cheeks. "They hired a local funeral director to make arrangements to transport Jake's body to Long Island by train."

"When? I'll ride up with you."

"Saturday morning. I'm flying up on Sunday."

"Fine, but I'm going on the train. With Jake."

A vicious click in her ear and Dean was gone. She grabbed a tissue, blew her nose and wandered into her studio. Music was her only refuge, her one escape from grief. But she was too upset to play her flute.

Her eyes welled with tears, tears that streamed down her cheeks and dripped into her mouth, salty and bitter. A torrent of grief.

Sobbing uncontrollably, she slumped into her mother's rocking chair.

What would she do without Jake? Losing his emotional support was bad enough. She was beginning to realize all the work he'd done to manage her career, work she knew nothing about. When she'd called to cancel Sunday's performance, the Baton Rouge orchestra manager seemed annoyed until she told him about Jake. Then he had rhapsodized over how wonderful Jake was.

The memory brought fresh tears. Yes, Jake was wonderful, good and kind and thoughtful, all that and more. After the call to Baton Rouge, she'd sat there for an hour, trying to decide what to do about her other engagements. In the end, she'd done nothing. Sitting in Jake's chair brought home the utter finality of his death. Everything in the office reminded her of him: the concert posters on the walls, the folder with her concert schedule, even the bowls of M&Ms and Hershey's Mini-bars and the plate of brownies her student had given her, sweet reminders of Jake's chocoholic tendencies.

Jake had loved her, but she never showed her appreciation, never thanked him for all the things he did for her. Had done for her. Past tense.

She would never see his sweet smile again, never feel his arms around her, never hear his congratulations after a performance.

Jake was dead. She was all alone. Again. Her throat closed up.

First Mother and Dad and Blaine. Now Jake, her dearest friend.

No one else cared about her. Her audiences cheered, but that was for her performance. Even her mother's love had been conditional. To win Mother's love she had to be perfect: all A's in school, perfect auditions and performances. No one loved her for herself.

Not once since she'd left Boston had Ramon called. In fact, other than business, no one called. She had no family, no friends. Frank didn't care about her, either. He was smitten with that woman he'd brought to the hospital, looking like a streetwalker in her low-cut top. If she let her hair grow and used some makeup, she might even be attractive. It was obvious that she and Frank were lovers. Inside that hospital room, the sexual heat had radiated from them in palpable waves. Their knowing glances had confirmed it.

The clang of the doorbell cut into her thoughts. She massaged her temples. What now? Then she remembered. Mr. Silverman. She didn't want to deal with him, but she had to stop thinking of herself. She'd been inconsiderate of him too, belittling his attempt to impress her, dismissing his knowledge of chamber music.

Besides, he seemed quite worried about her.

She rose from the rocking chair and headed for the front door.

―――

He caressed the keys as tenderly as if they were his beloved's flesh, playing chords with his left hand, teasing out the melancholy melody with his right. He didn't dare look at her, sitting ten feet away in her rocking chair as he'd asked. At first she objected, but he had insisted, saying it was his tribute to Jake. He felt her eyes on him as he played his gift of love. He had no trouble recalling the simple melody, the first of Satie's *Trois Gymnopedies*.

His tribute to *her*, not the insufferable Ziegler.

As the last chord died away he sat motionless, aching to take her upstairs and make love to her. After a moment he turned to look. She sat in the chair, as still as a statue, as pale and wan as a woman in a Pre-Raphaelite painting. Tears streamed down her cheeks. With a shuddering sob, she met his gaze. "Thank you. What a beautiful tribute to Jake."

He rose from the piano and approached her. "My pleasure, Belinda. I know how much you loved Jake." Knew it and hated it.

She wiped tears from her eyes, balled up the tissue and stood. "I have something for you in the office."

He followed her into the hall. "Would you like your muffin now? We could sit in the kitchen and enjoy them together."

Or we could go to bed and I could suck your nipples and . . .

"Thanks, but I'm not hungry. Wait here and I'll get your check."

Stung by disappointment, he watched her enter the office. He needed the check desperately, but he'd bought two of her favorite muffins thinking they would enjoy them together. She came out of the office, shut the door and handed him an envelope. "Thank you for everything, Mr. Silverman. You've been very thoughtful and I really appreciate it."

A crumb of gratitude. Why wouldn't she use his first name?

"We should talk about the Baton Rouge concert. You'll need me to drive you, of course."

"I cancelled it. I couldn't possibly perform so soon after Jake—" She let out a heavy sigh and stared at the floor.

Anger roiled his gut. How could she cancel the concert? But he couldn't stay angry, not when she looked so exhausted, dark circles under her bloodshot eyes. "Of course. You're too distraught. I could have waited for the check." He gave her a smile, not a big joyful smile, a sympathetic one. "There's no reason I can't keep working for you. You need me more than ever now."

"I don't know. I'll have to ask Frank."

"Frank? Who's Frank?"

"Frank Renzi, the detective I talked to after my car accident. He's been very helpful."

His anger returned, blossomed into rage. "But he can't look after you every day like I can. You shouldn't be here by yourself. Remember that drunk? No telling what he might have done if I hadn't been there to protect you. Why don't I come over tomorrow and help with your concert schedule? You can't let your fans down, Belinda. You know how much they love you."

How much I love you, even if you won't acknowledge it.

"I'm sorry, Mr. Silverman, I can't think about that now."

A clear dismissal. Reluctantly, he turned and went to the foyer. Draped over the settee were two dresses and two pairs of slacks. He picked them up and draped them over his arm. "Let me take these to the dry cleaners."

"Oh, you don't need to—"

"Nonsense. It's no trouble at all." In fact, it gave him the perfect excuse to see her again. He'd order one-day service and bring it back tomorrow. Now that he had a new rival, he intended to visit her every day.

Detective Renzi might have been helpful, but not half as helpful as Barry Silverman intended to be.

———

"I don't know which NOCCA student sells pot to Ziegler's partner, but it's not Antoine Carter." Frank set his beer mug on the Bulldog bar and looked at Kelly, awaiting her reaction.

"That's good," she said tonelessly, avoiding his gaze.

"Antoine's got dreads and drives a bronze Ford Tempo. Dean gets his pot from a black kid with short hair, drives a dark-blue Chevy."

Kelly nodded absently, fussing with her cocktail napkin. Clearly she had things on her mind, things that didn't include the Lakeview case or Antoine or the death of Jake Ziegler. Earlier, she'd called and asked him to meet her at the Bulldog after work. He had happily agreed. Now he was getting bad vibes. This wasn't the woman he almost made love to last night, the woman who'd kissed him passionately and told him to take off his shirt.

The Bulldog had the usual hip ambiance, low-voiced chatter, jazz playing over the sound system, but Kelly's demeanor was different. Edgy. Tense. And her tailored suit and turtleneck screamed hands-off. The weather was chilly for November, but not as chilly as the vibes she was sending him.

To fill the silence, he said, "Last Friday Antoine stonewalled me again. He's scared. He said he's not the only NOCCA student that knows AK."

She twisted a lock of hair around her finger and looked at him. "You think the kid that sells pot to Ziegler's partner gets his supply from AK?"

"Ace Detective Kelly O'Neil scores a bull's-eye." He grinned at her, got no response. "What's up, Kelly? You seem preoccupied."

Her gaze drifted away. "Work's getting me down."

"That's not good. But police work is tough, Kelly. You've been a cop long enough to know that. Your father and brother are cops."

"But Homicide is different. Every night I go home with a headache. They pushed me into it after Katrina. When I worked Domestic Violence I didn't get headaches every night. I was helping women in bad situations leave the assholes that beat them. Now I feel like I'm beating my head against a wall. Even if we get a witness to a murder, half the time they won't testify."

She was right. The NOPD homicide conviction rate was abysmal. But it wasn't great for domestic violence cases either. Kelly empathized with the victims. She wanted to comfort them. He wanted to push the scumbags against a wall and punch them out.

"Have you talked to Morgan Vobitch about it?"

"Not yet, but as soon as we solve the Lakeview case I will."

"Maybe you should stop working overtime, counseling rape victims."

Her mouth quirked in annoyance. "That's the only thing that keeps me going." She tilted her head from side to side. No Big-Z earrings tonight.

Was she sending him a message? "What about the jewelry business?"

"Right now that seems like an impossible dream. I'm too tired to think about it." She drank some beer and stared at the liquor bottles behind the bar.

"Is that all that's bothering you? Work? Come on. Talk to me."

She gulped some beer, gnawed her lip. "I'm not sure this is a good idea."

"This being . . . ?"

"You know. You and me."

"Seemed like a good idea last night. To me anyway. I got the impression you thought so too. What changed? The phone call from Belinda and the weird scene at the hospital?"

Kelly looked at him. "Three times we've been together, Frank. Three dates, if you want to call it that. Each time you got a phone call."

"I'm a detective. It's not a nine-to-five job. You know that."

"Right. I was married to a cop, remember?"

He remembered all too well. Maybe she was right. He didn't feel like competing with a dead husband. Or an ex-husband, like Dana Swenson's.

"For you the job always comes first, Frank. That's what got Terry killed, stopping to help somebody."

Heat rose on his neck, irritation verging on anger. It wouldn't take much to push him over the edge. "You think that's bad? Wanting to help people?"

"But you take it to the edge. You're an adrenaline junkie. You take every fucking murder personally. Chantelle Wilson? You want to bust AK for that so bad you want to rip off his balls."

"Bet your ass I do."

"You don't have time for a relationship. The job always comes first."

I had time for Audrey and Gina. But he didn't want to talk about that, or think about it. His long-term affairs with both women had ended badly.

"Maybe you're the one that's not ready for a relationship. Two years since Terry died and you're still hurting. Maybe you'll always be hurting." He touched her hand. "Don't waste your life, Kelly. You deserve to be happy with someone, even if it isn't me."

She polished invisible spots on the bar with her napkin. "I just don't think this is a good idea. Work and all."

"Nobody will hear about us from me." He'd never told anyone about Audrey or Gina, not his Boston PD colleagues, not the guys he played hoop with, no one.

"Some cop is sure to run into us sooner or later."

He drank some beer, flashing on the night his wife's girlfriend saw him with Gina and told Evelyn about it, precipitating their ugly divorce.

"Frank, we've got the same boss! sooner or later someone will figure it out." Her eyes glinted with anger. "You think you're so cool, but you can't hide your feelings about women. Remember what I said last night? Belinda knew we were involved. Women know these things. Guys pick up on it too, guys like your sidekick Kenyon Miller. He knows you."

He touched a finger to her lips. "I don't want to fight. You need to think things through and figure out what you want. It's okay. I can wait."

But not forever. Not if she was too conflicted over her dead husband to figure out she needed sex like every normal woman her age. He eased into sardonic mode a la Morgan Vobitch. Things were going great: Dana back with her ex-husband, Kelly dazed and confused, no leads on Chantelle's murder, Jake Ziegler dead, possibly murdered.

Kelly touched his arm and smiled, not the mischievous smile that made her eyes light up, but a smile nevertheless. "Thanks for understanding."

He nodded, blank-faced. He didn't feel like making nice. "Let's head out. I've got an early appointment tomorrow."

CHAPTER 24

Friday morning, 10 November

"You can't even tell me why Jake died?" she said, outraged.

Frank met her gaze, blank-faced, but she caught of flicker of something in his eyes. Seated opposite her at her kitchen table, he looked strong and muscular and sexy as hell. But she wasn't going to get sucked into that trap again. He was screwing that woman cop.

"I got the autopsy results this morning," he said. "Cause of death inconclusive. Jake's kidney and liver functions were abnormal. We're waiting for the toxicology results. I need to talk to Silverman."

"Why?"

"I wanted to interview him the day of the burglary, but I never got the chance. He didn't call you back."

"He stopped by yesterday to offer his condolences."

"I thought he didn't work for you anymore."

"He doesn't, but he's been quite helpful since Jake died. I think Jake was a bit hard on him. All he did was visit his girlfriend in Atlanta. Unfortunately, that was the night of the burglary."

"What's the girlfriend's name?"

"He didn't say. They went to an Atlanta Symphony concert."

"Why didn't you tell me that before?"

She gave him an icy stare. "I didn't want to bother you. I'm sure you and your partner are busy with other things."

He held her gaze, digesting the word *partner*, no doubt. He knew what she really meant: Your girlfriend.

After a moment he said, "Do you have a picture of Silverman?"

"Jake made a copy of his driver's license. It's probably in a file cabinet. Jake spent hours reorganizing the files after the break-in."

"Let's find it. I need a picture of Silverman. The DL will do."

They left the kitchen and went to the office. Unlike the day of the burglary, it was neat and orderly now. Tears misted her eyes. Neat and orderly because Jake had cleaned up the mess. She opened the top drawer of a file cabinet, took out a folder labeled Silverman and gave it to Frank.

"He's been very helpful, running errands and such."

"What kind of errands?" Frank said, thumbing through the file.

"Odds and ends, trips to the cleaners. He's concerned about me."

Unlike you. You're too busy screwing your cop girlfriend.

Frank looked up from Silverman's file. "If I were you, I wouldn't let Barry Silverman run any more errands for you."

"Why not?"

"Jake died under suspicious circumstances. Might have been foul play. Right now, everyone is a suspect."

The statement shocked her. "Everyone? Including me?"

He gazed at her, expressionless. "*Everyone*. Can you tell me what Jake ate on Wednesday?"

"Not really. I was teaching at NOCCA. One of my students cancelled so I got home around one." She frowned. "Wait. My last student gave me some homemade brownies. I hate chocolate, but I didn't have the heart to refuse them. Jake loves chocolate, so I gave them to him."

Frank reacted as if he'd been jolted with electricity. "Where are they?"

"I put them down the garbage disposal with Jake's M&Ms and Hershey Mini-bars."

"Why the hell did you do that?" His dark eyes were squinty with anger.

"Every time I went in the office they reminded me that I'd never see Jake again. I couldn't stand seeing them. It was too upsetting."

"How many brownies were left?"

"Not many. Four or five."

"Out of how many?"

"I don't know," she snapped. "They were brownies, cut into squares."

"Who's the student?"

"Marcus Goines. He's a senior. Talented, but he lacks confidence."

Frank gazed at her with his dark penetrating eyes. "Any reason why Marcus Goines would want Jake dead?"

"Of course not. He's never even met Jake."

"Any reason why Marcus would want *you* dead?"

With an effort fine-tuned over hundreds of performances, she maintained a calm façade. Marcus didn't want her dead, but someone else might. Ramon's wife. A prickle of fear scraped her spine. The Spanish spitfire would do anything to keep her man.

But she wasn't about to tell Frank the sordid details: that she'd been seduced and abandoned by Ramon and blackmailed by his wife.

Aware of Frank's gaze, she maintained her cool demeanor. Damned if she'd give him the satisfaction of knowing how frightened she was.

"Absolutely not," she said.

Frank took Marcus Goines into the NOCCA conference room where he'd interviewed Antoine. Marcus didn't look any happier than Antoine had. He was built like a bowling ball, slumped in a folding chair, a worried frown on his chubby dark-skinned face.

"Belinda Scully tells me you're a talented flute player." Loosen him up, then drop the bomb.

The kid's lips twitched, almost a smile. "She did?"

"Yes. How long have you been studying with her?"

"Two years. Did she tell you I suggested the Gershwin encore?"

He nodded. A harmless fib to make the kid feel good. "Great piece. I heard her play it."

"She's a fabulous flute player," Marcus said, and lapsed into silence, staring at the floor as if it had just occurred to him that an NOPD detective hadn't pulled him out of class to talk about music.

"Tell me about the brownies."

The kid jerked as though he'd been hit with a stun gun and rubbed his hands on his chunky thighs. Nervous. Sweaty palms.

Frank waited, letting the silence build.

"I jus' gave her some brownies, no harm in that."

"Did you know that Belinda Scully doesn't eat chocolate?"

The kid shrugged. "I guess. I don't know."

"Okay, so you gave her the brownies. Any particular reason?"

"My mother . . ." Marcus licked his lips. "My mother made them."

As sure as big oak trees grew from little acorns, the kid was lying.

"And she would confirm that, right?"

Marcus jutted his chin. "What's the big deal? I gave my teacher some brownies. So what?"

"The big deal is this. Ms. Scully gave them to her manager and he got sick. So sick he had to go to the hospital. And then he died."

The kid gaped at him, eyes wide, mouth working.

"Jacob Ziegler. You know him?"

Marcus shook his head, and his knee started bobbing up and down.

"We've got a problem, Marcus. You gave Ms. Scully some brownies. She gave them to Ziegler. Ziegler ate them and died. Maybe I better ask your mother what ingredients she used."

"No!" Marcus waved his hands. "Please, don't talk to my mom!"

"Why not? You said she made them."

"That's what the guy tol' me to say."

He leaned forward and got in the kid's face. "What guy?"

"This guy I met. Barry. I don't know his last name."

He wanted to shout: *Barry Silverman*. Restrained himself. "Tell me the story from the beginning. Don't leave anything out and *don't lie to me*."

"Wednesday morning he asked me to give her the brownies."

"Some stranger asked you to give your teacher some brownies? Come on, Marcus."

"Not some stranger. I met him a while ago. He drives for Ms. Scully."

Barry Silverman. "Okay, so you knew him. How did that happen?"

"We got talking one day after school. He said he might be able to get me a scholarship to New England Conservatory. He knows some lady that works there." Marcus looked at him, eyes pleading. "I didn't mean to do nothing wrong, honest! Wednesday morning he said he talked to this lady and she might give me a scholarship. My folks don't have a lot of money, and New England Conservatory's a great school. I looked it up on the Internet."

"And then Barry asked you to give the brownies to Belinda?"

"Yes, sir. He said he meant to give them to her before but he forgot, and he wasn't driving her that day, so he asked me to do it."

Wasn't driving her, because Ziegler fired him. He almost felt sorry for the kid. Silverman had manipulated him. But Marcus might not be as innocent as he seemed. "What kind of car do you drive, Marcus?"

"An old Chevy. My folks got it for me so's I could drive to school."

"What color is it?"

"Dark blue. Can I go now?" Marcus half-rose from his chair.

"Sit down. We're not done. Did Barry tell you to say the brownies were from your mother?"

A vigorous nod. "Yes, sir, he did."

"And you didn't think that was odd?"

The kid's eyes shifted away. "Sort of. But he did me a favor, you know, recommending me to that lady at New England Conservatory, so I felt like, you know, I owed him one back."

"Okay, here's the deal. Talk to your parents tonight and tell them what happened with the brownies. I'll call your father tomorrow and have him bring you to the station so you can sign a statement about what you told me."

Not what he wanted, but Marcus was a juvenile. This time he would play by the rules. He'd interviewed Chantelle without calling her parents, and now she was dead. When Marcus came to the station with his father, he'd get him to sign the statement about the brownies first. Then he'd question him about the dope deals. At that point the father might lawyer-up. But maybe not.

Marcus didn't look too thrilled about the deal, frowning and fidgeting in his chair. "What do you think happened to Ms. Scully's manager?"

"That's what we're trying to find out. Go on back to class, Marcus. I'll see you and your father tomorrow at the station."

When Belinda opened the door, he stepped into the foyer. He'd tried to open the door with his key, but she must have changed the locks after the burglary. Not that this could stop him. If he wanted to get into her house, he could do it easily enough.

He held up her dry cleaning order, the hangers bunched together at the top, her clothes encased in clear filmy plastic. "Shall I take these upstairs?"

"No, thank you, I can do that. Wait here while I get my wallet."

He draped the clothes over the settee and watched her walk down the hall. She had on shorts today, displaying her long sexy legs, and the sinuous motion of her hips aroused him. He wanted to take her upstairs, rip off her clothes and fuck her brains out.

She returned from the kitchen and held out a twenty. "Is this enough?"

"It was only eighteen dollars. Let me give you the change—"

"No, no, you've done enough already." She favored him with a full-fledged smile. "It was very thoughtful of you and I appreciate it."

Heat flamed his groin. At last she was starting to appreciate how hard he worked to please her. Soon he would be indispensable.

"I'm happy to do it, but I'm concerned about you being here alone after that burglary. I'd feel better if I were here to protect you."

Vertical frown lines appeared between her eyes, little roadblocks that said NO. "I can't think about that today, Mr. Silverman."

He gritted his teeth. Why wouldn't she call him Barry?

"I could help with your schedule. You're no ordinary musician, Belinda. You're a famous flute soloist. Now is not the time to let your career falter."

Her blue eyes turned icy. Now she was angry. He couldn't have that. "You know how it is these days. If you're not constantly in the public eye, people forget how talented you are. I could help with your publicity."

"Not now. Thank you for collecting my dry cleaning."

A clear dismissal. Unwilling to leave, he said, "Did you like the muffins?"

"Muffins?" A perplexed frown.

"The blueberry muffins I brought yesterday. Were they good?"

"Oh. Yes. Thank you for being so thoughtful." She smiled.

His heart sang with joy. Two smiles in five minutes. But now she was yawning. His beloved wasn't sleeping very well. If she were sleeping with him, she would. After their sexual orgies, she would fall into a contented slumber. She wasn't quite ready for that. Not yet, but soon.

"Have the police told you what caused Jake's death?"

"No. Frank said they're waiting for the results of the toxicology tests."

That sounded ominous. "What sort of toxicology tests?"

"I don't know. I'm sorry, but I can't talk right now. I need to call the funeral director."

"When's the funeral?"

"Mr. Silverman," she said, raising her voice. "I can't talk now.

Wounded by her shrill tone, he left the house in an icy rage and got in his van. After all he'd done for her—bringing her muffins, playing one of her favorite pieces, tending to her dry cleaning, offering sympathy and support—she couldn't even be courteous. Had she told him when the funeral was? No.

But she'd told him about the toxicology tests. Tests that might reveal what Ziegler had eaten. He slammed his palms against the wheel. He hated it when things didn't go his way. By this time Belinda must have told Renzi his name. Not his real name, the name he was using now. What if she told Renzi who gave her the brownies? Then Renzi would talk to Marcus. And Marcus, the wretched little wuss, would tell Renzi where the brownies had come from. Acid burned his gut like a blowtorch.

DIVA

He pulled away from the curb and headed for NOCCA.

CHAPTER 25

Saturday, 11 November

At nine-thirty Frank drifted through a Mid-City neighborhood, hunting for the address on Barry Silverman's DL. The early morning rain had tapered to a misty drizzle, swished away by his windshield wipers. This part of town had been hard-hit by Katrina. Many of the houses were boarded-up hulks with piles of rubbish and moldy furniture piled outside.

He slowed to a crawl, passed a small cottage with the number 846 over the front door and came to an intersection. Silverman's house—848— should have been on the corner. It wasn't. No house, no cement slab, no FEMA trailer, just a weedy lot full of trash bags, rusty car parts and two discarded refrigerators wrapped with duct tape.

He continued through the intersection. The number on the first house was 850. The address on Silverman's license was bogus. He pulled to the curb and sat there thinking. Silverman had asked Marcus to give some brownies to Belinda. Ziegler ate them and wound up dead. Silverman had been in Atlanta the night Belinda's house had been burglarized. Or so he'd told Belinda.

When he talked to her yesterday, she'd been far more composed than she'd been at the hospital. On the verge of a nervous breakdown one night, an iceberg two days later. Needling him. *You and your partner.* She assumed he and Kelly were lovers, just as Kelly had said Belinda was jealous. She was also a VIP, and he didn't want her causing trouble, for him or for Kelly. One phone call was all it would take. When he asked her if Marcus might want her dead, she had flinched. A tell of fear, quickly suppressed. For a moment, she stood there, frozen, as if she was trying to solve a complicated math problem.

Then, eyes distant, she had said: *Absolutely not.*

Belinda was hiding something. And she seemed oddly protective of Silverman, a man she'd met in London who supposedly hailed from New Orleans. He wouldn't bet the farm on it. In fact, he wouldn't be surprised if

Silverman was the one who had forced her off the road the night of the accident. A calculated ploy to make Belinda hire him.

He studied the photocopy of Silverman's license. Age, 36. Height, 6 feet. Weight, 185. Eyes: blue. Hair: brown. Eyeglasses: no.

The man in the photo had small, close-set eyes and a high forehead accentuated by a receding hairline. No smile.

He punched a number into his cell phone. One ring and a message came on: *Silverman Associates. We're out working a case right now. Leave a message.*

A male voice: no regional accent, no inflection, flat and unemotional. Not the sort of message likely to drum up business.

He decided to wait until Monday to check Silverman's phone records. Bad enough he was working on his birthday. And Chantelle's. A wave of sadness welled up inside him. If she'd lived to celebrate it, Chantelle would have turned sixteen today. And now he was forty-four.

No birthday celebrations for him, either. Kelly had killed that Thursday night. After leaving the Bulldog, he'd driven home and poured himself a big belt of scotch, something he rarely did. His Glenfiddich was reserved for celebrations and holidays. And consolation when his love life tanked.

After an auspicious beginning, their relationship had fizzled. Maybe Kelly was right. Until Chantelle's murder was solved, he had no time for a relationship. And the danger that someone would figure out they were dating was real. Cops were notorious gossips.

Still, he found her enormously attractive. He loved her eyes, loved the way she bantered with him. She seemed comfortable with men, probably because she had three brothers and a father who doted on her. Her assessment of Belinda had been uncannily accurate: Belinda was into image management, on and off stage. Belinda was infatuated with him.

Feeling weary and vaguely depressed, he put the car in gear and drove off. Now he had to call Marcus Goines' parents and persuade them to bring him to the station. Another unpleasant chore. The father was pastor of the African Baptist Gospel Choir Church. He couldn't understand why a Baptist minister's son was dealing dope. Most of the dope dealers in town were kids from the projects with single mothers who couldn't control them. Marcus was a talented music student, the only child of an upstanding two-parent family.

His cell phone rang, jolting him out of his ruminations. He checked the caller-ID. Shocked, he pulled to the curb and answered.

"What's up, Frank? Taking it easy on a Saturday?"

A curveball from Kelly O'Neil, acting as though their discussion at the Bulldog hadn't happened. Playing along, he said, "No, busting my butt and getting nowhere fast."

"What are you working on?" Sticking to a safe topic. Work.

"Hunting for Belinda Scully's security man, the one Jake Ziegler fired. I got a copy of his DL, decided to pay him a visit. The address is bogus, no house, just a vacant lot."

"The plot thickens," Kelly said in her familiar droll tone.

He loved the sound of her voice, low-pitched and throaty. "What are you doing? Did you sleep in this morning?"

"No. I had a lot of things to do. The yard's a mess and uh, while I was raking up leaves I started thinking about you, and I was wondering if you'd like to come over for dinner tonight."

Another curveball. Sometimes women mystified him.

"I'm not much of a cook," she said. "Grilled salmon and vegetables is the best—"

"Sounds great. Don't try to be Betty Crocker."

She burst out laughing. "Betty Crocker. Jeez, Frank, where do you get these images?"

My vivid imagination, picturing us in bed together celebrating my birthday.

"Can I bring the wine?"

"A bottle of red would be great. How does six-thirty sound?"

"Great. See you then." He clicked off and smiled.

Maybe his birthday wouldn't be such a downer after all.

After forcing down a lunch of chicken soup and oyster crackers, Belinda went upstairs to her bedroom closet. All of her black outfits were designed for performances, not funerals. She pulled out a beige pantsuit. The outfit was plain and drab. Not terribly flattering.

Tears stung her eyes. What was she thinking? This wasn't about her. This was for Jake, the man who'd consoled her after her family was killed. The man who'd stuck by her through the lean years, the dreary small town recitals and the solo concerts with amateur orchestras, all those years when she'd worked her ass off to distinguish herself from the millions of other talented flute soloists. Talented, but without her tenacity and will to succeed.

And now, just as she was on the verge of stardom, her world had come crashing down.

Resolutely, she packed the beige pantsuit in her suitcase. She was dreading the funeral, but she had to comfort Jake's parents in their hour of grief, just as Jake had comforted her. It was the least she could do. The last thing she would ever do for Jake.

Early this morning she had driven to the train station to meet the funeral director and make sure Jake's casket was safely aboard the train. His parents would meet the train at Penn Station. Dean had insisted on riding with the casket. She would fly to Long Island tomorrow. The funeral service was Monday at eleven. Later that afternoon she would fly back to New Orleans.

The phone on her bedside table rang, jangling her nerves. On the way to answer it she glimpsed her image in the wall mirror. Her eyes were bloodshot, and gritty from lack of sleep.

"Hello, Belinda. How are you feeling this morning?"

Mr. Silverman. The man was beginning to annoy her. This morning when she went out to get the newspaper, she'd found a box of muffins on the doorstep. Still, he seemed concerned about her and eager to please, running errands. Maybe she would rehire him.

Jake worked his ass off for you and what did he get in return?

"Thank you for calling. I'm a bit tired, but I'll be okay."

"Stress is bad for your immune system. You should take some extra vitamin C."

She tried to quell her annoyance. He sounded like Mother, nagging her to eat right and be sure to get eight hours sleep a night and drink plenty of milk so she'd have strong bones.

"Did you get the muffins I left for you?"

"Yes. Thank you. That was very thoughtful of you." She'd thrown them in the garbage.

"I'm going out to run some errands. Do you need any groceries?"

The thought of food made her gag. All she'd eaten for two days was chicken soup. Mother's cure for everything. Her mother, dead and gone for thirteen years. Unlucky thirteen.

"No. I'm getting ready to fly to New York for the funeral."

"You must be feeling sad and lonely. I can drive you to the airport."

"Thank you, but that's not necessary. I prefer to drive myself."

After a short silence, he said, "All right, but be careful. You know what happened the last time you drove home from the airport."

A chill skittered down her spine. She remembered all right. Someone had forced her off the road, one in a series of ugly events: weird fan mail, a whispered voicemail threat, a creepy note on her doorstep, a burglary. And

Jake's sudden death. All within weeks of the thirteenth anniversary of the accident that had decimated her family. Would this unlucky year never end?

She gave herself a pep talk. She was no ordinary woman. She was Belinda Scully, a survivor, a confident performer with an unshakable will.

"I'm packing for my trip, Mr. Silverman, so if you'll excuse me . . ."

"When will you be back?"

"Next week," she said firmly, and hung up. If he didn't know when she'd be back, he couldn't call and pester her.

You only care about yourself. And your career. Dean's stinging rebuke.

She clenched her teeth. Silverman was annoying but he was right.

She was stressed-out, not eating right, not sleeping. And the only person who seemed concerned about her was Barry Silverman.

On his way back to the station Frank cruised through the Bayou St. John neighborhood. Setting aside his blissful anticipation of dinner with Kelly, he turned onto a side street and focused on Antoine Carter. According to the clerk in the NOCCA office, his parents were still living in Houston. Prior to Katrina, they had driven there with Antoine and his eleven-year-old sister to stay with relatives. When NOCCA reopened, Antoine, a scholarship student, had returned to New Orleans to live with his uncle, Jonas Carter.

He parked across the street from Jonas Carter's house, a shotgun double with mocha-brown shingles and gleaming white trim. Twin driveways bordered the house, Antoine's bronze Ford Tempo in one, a black Ford 150 pickup in the other. The window shades were down, and not to keep out the sun. The sky was still overcast after the heavy rain that had pounded the area.

Was Antoine was inside grieving for his girlfriend? Or hiding from AK?

He lowered the car window, hoping to hear Antoine practicing. No music, just chirping robins and squawking blue jays. He continued down the street at a leisurely pace, picturing the NOPD artist's sketch: a young black male with dreadlocks, large wide-set eyes and a broad nose. Like Antoine.

The Lakeview Residents Association was hounding NOPD. Lakeview had been decimated by Katrina. Only a third of the residents had returned. Many were still living in FEMA trailers. Others occupied re-built homes surrounded by gutted houses with knee-high weeds out front. Few businesses had reopened. Lakeview residents didn't want thugs robbing the few that had.

His eyes flicked to the rearview. A dark-blue Lincoln Town Car was behind him, driven by a young black male, another one riding shotgun. Impossible to tell if anyone else was in the car.

He slowed down to see what they would do. The Lincoln settled in ten feet from his bumper. He turned right at the next corner. The Lincoln followed. He took the next right, stomped the gas pedal and raced to the next intersection. The Lincoln sped after him.

In the rearview, he saw a black kid lean out the passenger side window. Holding a shotgun. Adrenaline blasted his heart rate. What the hell? Broad daylight on a Saturday and a car full of gunslingers was after him?

He stomped the accelerator. Gripped the wheel with one hand. Dug out his SIG-Sauer. Not that he'd shoot at them. That was Hollywood nonsense. There were too many civilians around. Holding the weapon reassured him, but his heart drummed his ribs like the hooves of a runaway horse.

Thirty yards ahead of him, a maroon Toyota turned a corner and approached him. He blew past it. Glimpsed the woman driver's face. Saw astonishment, then fear. In the rearview, he saw her pull over.

The thugs kept coming. The Lincoln was gaining on him. He wheeled left and rocketed down a street, hoping some little kid on a bike wouldn't zoom out into his path. Hoping the street didn't dead-end at a canal.

Blam! A slug ripped into the trunk of his car. Cursing aloud, he took the next left. Floored the accelerator. Zoomed past an elderly black man carrying groceries into a house. At the next cross street, he slowed and checked the rearview. No Lincoln. He turned left again and completed the circuit back to where the thugs had begun chasing him. The street where Antoine Carter lived with his uncle. No sign of the Lincoln.

He holstered his weapon and waited for his heart rate to return to what passed for normal. Twelve days ago he'd caught AK and his goons in the NOCCA parking lot, threatening Antoine. Last week, he had pulled Antoine out of class to interview him. *You gonna get me killed,* Antoine had said. *I'm not the only NOCCA student that knows AK.* Was Marcus the other student? Had Marcus told AK that Detective Frank Renzi had interviewed Antoine? Someone had. Why else would AK's thugs be watching Antoine's house?

Seething with anger, he headed for Iberville. New Orleans housing projects were no different from the projects in Boston. Ghettos of poverty, race and crime, ruled by vicious punks with no regard for life. An image flashed in his mind: eleven-year-old Janelle Robinson lying dead on a grungy carpet, killed by a cop's bullet—his own or his partner's—a black girl caught in the crossfire of a bust gone bad. His gut twisted in a sickening freefall.

Bile rose in his throat as he pictured the tears on the chocolate skin of Janelle Robinson's face. Chantelle had been caught in the crossfire too. He couldn't imagine how scared she must have felt, all alone in that apartment, knowing addicts used vacant units as crack houses, copping drugs from the evil excuse for a man that ran the place. AK-47, the King of Iberville.

It took him less than ten minutes to get there. He got out of his car and examined the trunk. A hole was punched through the metal beside the Mazda logo. Anger burned a hole in his gut, and his mind seethed with ugly thoughts as he marched into the complex to the building where Chantelle had lived.

He leaned against the door and waited.

Crawl out from under your rock, scumbag. I know you're here.

Sure enough, a minute later AK sauntered around the corner of the next building. "Wha's up, my man?" Flashing his gold-toothed smile.

"I just played a game of tag with your homeboys."

"That right? Y'all have a good time?"

"What were they doing in Antoine Carter's neighborhood?"

AK's eyes hardened and his smile faded. "What was *you* doing there?"

He stepped closer, invading AK's space, looming over the shorter man. "Seems like every time I get anywhere near Antoine you and your homeboys turn up. Why's that?"

"Me and Antoine, we *buddies*."

"Were you *buddies* with Chantelle Wilson, too?"

"Who?" Frowning. "Oh, the bitch got killed a couple weeks ago?"

It took all his willpower not to throttle the bastard.

"No. The girl someone murdered to keep her from talking."

AK backed up two paces. "Talkin' 'bout what?"

"The Lakeview murder. Why did you push that woman out of the car?"

"Did no such thing. Who tol' you that?" AK said, eyes cold as ice and hard as granite.

"We got the getaway car. We got evidence."

"You got evidence why don't you arrest me?" His gold-toothed smile reappeared. "You got no evidence. You got nuthin', 'cuz I got nuthin' to do with what went down in that lily-white neighborhood."

Frank gave him a hard-eyed stare—*I'll get you, scumbag*—and returned to his car. AK and his thugs were watching Antoine. Sooner or later they'd kill him, just like they'd killed Chantelle.

Now he had to call Marcus's parents. His gut churned like a blender chopping nails. Talking to Marcus and his folks right now might be a bad idea. Any bullshit from Marcus and he'd blow up. And blow his chances of tying Marcus and his drug deals to AK.

Screw it. He'd call them tomorrow after he had a chance to calm down.

After he celebrated his birthday with Kelly O'Neil.

CHAPTER 26

Saturday 7:45 P.M.

"I wasn't sure I could do this," Kelly said, lying on her side facing him, her eyes luminous in the glow from her bedside table lamp.

Frank snuggled closer, relishing the feel of her skin against his. They'd been in bed for an hour, an exquisite exploration of touching, tasting and melding. So far he'd seen her in gym shorts, work clothes, and a miniskirt. Naked was better. Her body was gorgeous, long and lean, rounded breasts above a trim waist, tanned muscular legs. And she was a fireball in bed.

He traced a finger down her cheek to the curve of her jaw.

"But you did. So?"

"So it was very good, Frank. Scary good." Gazing at him with those irresistible eyes, sea-green and deep as the ocean, sucking him closer.

"Nothing to be scared about. Just enjoy."

"Enjoy isn't the problem."

He caressed curve of her waist. "What's the problem?"

"I don't know. Like, where do we go from here?"

Were all women like this, he wondered. First time in bed with a guy, they wanted a roadmap for the next five years.

"I'm happy you liked me enough to invite me over for dinner," he said, adding with a mischievous grin, "So you could seduce me."

She mock-punched his arm. "That's what I like about you, Frank. Your quirky sense of humor."

"Damn. Here I was thinking it was my sex appeal."

"Oooh," she teased. "Fishing for compliments?"

"No, but I'll give you one. You're comfortable with your body. Lots of women aren't."

Her expression grew thoughtful. "Like your wife maybe?"

He could see her mind working. Any police force was a hotbed of gossip. She had to have heard the rumors about why he had resigned from Boston PD and moved to New Orleans. "Ex-wife," he said.

"Okay, ex-wife. So? What happened?"

Reflexively, he fingered the scar on his chin. He didn't want to talk about the painful weeks and months when he had functioned only by burying himself in the Boston crime scene. "It's complicated and I refuse to trash my ex-wife. Let's just say we had certain incompatibilities. I was seeing someone else. Someone I cared about a lot. Evelyn found out and filed for divorce."

"There's a mouthful. If you weren't compatible, why didn't you get a divorce?"

"I couldn't stand not seeing Maureen every day. That's what happened with two of my friends. You get divorced and start out thinking you'll see your kid every weekend and then there's reasons why you don't and I couldn't . . ." He stopped, feeling the knife-sharp pain all over again.

Kelly touched his cheek. "You don't have to explain. I get it. You loved your daughter more than you loved your wife and you couldn't leave her. Your daughter."

A great weight came off his shoulders. "I couldn't abandon Maureen. Not then, not ever."

"Where's Maureen now?"

"Now? All grown up. She's twenty-four, doing a residency in orthopedic surgery at Johns Hopkins in Baltimore."

"Impressive. You must be proud of her."

He smiled. "Yeah, Mo's great. I wish I could see her more often, but we're both busy, you know? Since Katrina it's been tough for me to get up there. But we talk on the phone."

Kelly nodded, but her eyes had that speculative look again. "That's what scares me. You're divorced and my husband is dead. I don't think I could go through that again. I mean, I worried about Terry, patrolling the mean streets of New Orleans and all, but then he's driving home on a rainy Saturday night and . . ." Her eyes welled with tears.

He pulled her close, felt her heartbeat against his chest. "You didn't deserve to have—I'm not going to say your husband—that's too impersonal. You didn't deserve to have the man you loved get killed in a senseless accident. But he was and I'm sorry for your loss."

"Wow. A soft-hearted tough guy that knows how to charm women."

He grinned. "Want to go for round two?"

She kissed his lips. "Not so fast, Renzi. Time for dinner."

He put on the heavy molded-plastic ear pads and strapped on the clear Plexiglas eye protectors. Squinted at the target 100 yards away and squeezed off a round. The gun range was in Kenner near the airport. Nine o'clock at night he pretty much had the place to himself.

An acid bath churned in his gut, impossible to ignore.

Nothing was going right.

He couldn't understand why Belinda had refused his offer to drive her to the airport. Two hours ago he'd driven past her house. Her blue Infiniti stood in the driveway. He'd thought about disabling it, decided not push his luck. Not after his talk with Marcus yesterday afternoon.

Ignoring the stabbing pain in his gut, he squeezed off another round. The kid had lied to him. He hated that. People who doubted his intelligence infuriated him. Eventually, Marcus had admitted he'd told the cop about the brownies. Not just any cop, Detective Frank Renzi.

Belinda's new savior. His new rival.

His anger became a fulminating rage. He fired four shots at the target in quick succession. Ziegler's death was causing problems, problems he had failed to anticipate. When Renzi got the toxicology report listing the curious substance in Ziegler's body—his potion of oleander, ubiquitous in New Orleans, the poisonous leaves there for the plucking—Renzi would put him at the top of his suspect list.

Another problem to solve, one of many.

The Diva was treating him like dirt. Refusing a ride to the airport. Refusing to say when she'd be back. How could he persuade her to rehire him if she was in New York? What if she stayed for a week? By then Renzi might have the toxicology report.

He hit the button on the automatic retrieval system and slammed another clip into his Ruger semi-automatic as the target shimmied toward him. He pulled the target off the clip and studied it.

Perfect: every shot in the kill zone. When everything clicked, it was like a Mozart symphony, perfect from start to finish. That's how it would be when Belinda gave in to her secret desires: She'd take off her clothes and do a sexy dance and beg him to fuck her. Unlike Rachel, his cock-tease sister.

He pictured her on stage in Atlanta dressed in her high-necked black dress with the long skirt, sawing away on her violin. Forget all those years of fucking Daddy-O. Rachel had found God. Six months after winning a seat in the Atlanta Symphony in 2000, she had joined one of those born-again Christian churches. The night she'd called to tell him this, he had to pinch his nose to keep from laughing.

Unaware of his amusement, she had prattled on about Pa, saying he'd moved back to Rhode Island and was working at a furniture store. He knew why she stayed in touch with Pa. She was obsessed with finding her birth parents. By then Ma was dead, so Pa was the only one who could tell her, something he'd refused to do, even when he was fucking her. The night she'd called him, he had just mustered out of the Army. Six years ago, but he remembered it like it was yesterday. Two days before Thanksgiving.

But Rachel wasn't feeling very thankful, lamenting: *Why won't Pa tell me?*

Because Pa's a prick, he'd said. Not saying what he was thinking.

It's the one hold he's got over you and he still wants to fuck you.

He attached another target to the clip and hit the button to send it back to the far wall, ruminating about the screwed-up flakes that adopted them.

Ma was smart at least, and college educated, unlike Pa who'd barely made it through high school. A talented violinist, Plain Jane had dreamed of a career in music until her father died of Parkinson's disease—a portent of things to come as it turned out. To support herself Plain Jane had majored in music education at a state college. Her dream was over.

Pa had no interest in college. He was into cars and guns. Good thing. The Army drafted him and sent him to Vietnam. Before he shipped out he met Plain Jane and got her pregnant. Wedding bells coming up. But while Pa was in Vietnam, Ma had a miscarriage, and Pa came home sterile, because of Agent Orange. Or so he'd said. That's why they had adopted him and Rachel.

He clenched his fingers around the Ruger, recalling the humiliations he'd suffered, the things he'd been forced to do for Ma, the beatings from Pa, the taunts from Rachel. The favored child who'd won Pa's love by fucking him. His bitch sister had bested him in every possible way, achieving her goal to play in an orchestra, surpassing him as a musician, while he had found only failure. But not when it came to Pa. Pa was crafty, but not crafty enough. In the end he had settled the score with his miserable excuse for a father.

He laughed aloud, recalling their final conversation and the sweet aftermath. Maybe he'd tell Rachel about it someday. That would be a kick.

He studied the target. Raised his weapon. Took aim and squeezed off one round after another, a barrage of hatred.

Seated in Kelly's kitchen, Frank sipped some of the Shiraz he'd brought, watching her move around the room, long-legged and sexy in her coral-blue top and cutoff jeans.

"What does your father do?" she asked, glancing at him over her shoulder as she took salads out of the refrigerator. "Is he still in Boston?"

"Yes. Seventy-two and still going strong. He's an appellate court judge."

Earlier his father had called to wish him a happy birthday. A nice gesture, but their stilted conversation brought pangs of regret. After his divorce, their relationship, once close, had deteriorated. Judge Salvatore Renzi had no use for adulterers, and Frank made no attempt to explain, knowing it would be fruitless. Over time the rift had lessened, but the freewheeling gab-sessions they had once enjoyed, ranging from legal and law enforcement issues to the Boston Celtics, had not resumed. At the end of today's conversation Frank had promised to visit, no specific date stated. And no suggestions from Judge Salvatore Renzi.

Kelly set platters of asparagus and salmon on the table and flashed a mischievous grin. "I had a Betty Crocker moment this afternoon."

He laughed. "I don't believe it. The witness is lying."

His cell phone rang and Kelly rolled her eyes. *For you, the job always comes first, Frank.* He wanted to shut the damn thing off. It was his birthday. Let someone else handle the emergency. But he couldn't.

When he answered, Otis Jones said, "Sorry to bother you on a Saturday night, but we got a situation I think you should know about. Got a missing NOCCA student, a kid named Marcus Goines."

His first reaction was relief. It wasn't Antoine. But if Marcus was missing, that was also bad news. Very bad news if his drug-dealing theory was accurate. "Since when?"

"His parents said he never came home from school yesterday. They thought he might be out with his friends, got concerned when he didn't show up for dinner. They started calling his friends but nobody'd seen him. They reported him missing early this morning. His father's a preacher. Half the congregation's out looking for him. You know this kid?"

He looked at Kelly, who gazed at him, blank-faced.

"Yes. I interviewed him yesterday about another case. I think he might be dealing drugs. He knows Antoine Carter. Probably knows AK, too."

"If he's messin' with drugs and knows AK," Otis said, "that puts a whole new twist on it. We put out a BOLO on his car. It's not in the NOCCA lot, so he must have driven somewhere after school."

"Meet you at the District-One station in half an hour."

He shut the phone and braced himself for Kelly's reaction.

To his surprise, she said, "Give me ten minutes to put away the food and change my clothes. I'm coming with you."

It was midnight by the time they left the District-One station. Reverend Goines was still there, a forlorn figure slumped on a wooden bench, looking like a horse had kicked him. Mrs. Goines was at home with friends, hoping for a phone call from Marcus. When they got to the station Frank had told Otis about his interview with Marcus but said nothing to Reverend Goines. The man didn't need to hear about tainted brownies and drug deals now. His only child was missing. Otis had dispatched three squad cars to Iberville, but at eleven-thirty they had reported back: No one at Iberville had seen him. None who would admit to it, anyway.

A NOCCA classmate had seen Marcus leave school after classes ended Friday afternoon. No sign of him since. And plenty of people might want Marcus dead. Silverman, for one, AK for another. If Marcus was dealing drugs and crossed AK for some reason, AK wouldn't hesitate to kill him. And then there was Antoine. If Antoine believed Marcus had ratted him out to AK, Antoine might have decided to get rid of him.

He pulled into Kelly's driveway at twelve-thirty. Earlier, they had eaten the Subway sandwiches Otis had ordered for them. A far cry from Kelly's grilled salmon, but it was too late to eat now.

"Come on in, Frank," she said, opening her door. "I've got something for you."

"Uh-oh. You're not gonna shoot me for ruining dinner are you?"

She left the car without answering. Mystified, he followed her inside. The faint aroma of Teriyaki salmon still permeated her kitchen.

"Have a seat," she said, gesturing at the table.

She poured two glasses of wine and brought them to the table. "I'm glad you came over, even if we didn't get to eat dinner. Cooking for one all the time gets boring."

A troubled look flitted over her face. He knew what she was thinking. Two years ago she was cooking for her husband. "It's okay," he said.

"No it isn't." She touched his hand and smiled. "I like you, Frank. Have you noticed?"

He smiled back. "I noticed. I like you, too. When you called this morning it made my day. Unfortunately, things went downhill after that."

"What happened?" She shook her head. "Wait. Scratch that. We don't have to talk about work. That was just my excuse to call you."

"You don't need an excuse to call me."

"Yeah, well, I like to pick your brains, oh brilliant one, master of all detectives."

He laughed aloud. "You keep slinging bull like that and I might have to take you to bed." She grinned, but he could tell she had more to say.

His gut tightened.

"You never stop being a detective, Frank. I, on the other hand, get bogged down with other things. I was pretty blunt when we talked at the Bulldog Thursday night."

"About needing space because of Terry?" *Or about me not having time for a relationship,* he thought but didn't say. Why ask for trouble?

"I need to stop thinking about Terry," she said, gazing at him with her beautiful sea-green eyes. "I need to stop living in the past and enjoy the present. And that includes you. Tell me what happened after I called you."

"I drove past Antoine's house. His parents are still in Houston so he lives with his uncle."

"You're worried about him because of AK, right?"

"Big time. I saw Antoine's car and figured he was inside with his uncle, safe and sound."

"I keep thinking about his girlfriend. Chantelle." Kelly shook her head. "Murdered at fifteen."

"Today would have been her sixteenth birthday."

Kelly raised an eyebrow. "And you know that how?"

"The memorial T-shirts at the funeral. And your next question?"

She spread her hands in a gesture of defeat. "Sorry, Great One. I have no clue."

"Why did I remember Chantelle's birthday?" He grinned. "And the answer is . . . it's the same day as mine."

Her lips parted in a smile. She rose from her chair, went to a cupboard, took out a plate and brought it to the table. On the plate was a chocolate frosted cupcake with one candle in it.

She brushed his lips with a kiss. "Happy birthday, Frank."

He stared at her, dumbfounded. "How'd you know it was my birthday?"

"Frank. I'm a detective. You think you're the only genius in the room?"

He pulled her onto his lap. "I'm not the only wise-ass, either."

She ruffled his hair. "No cake till you tell me what happened today."

"Okay." But he didn't want to. Digging up his birth date was one thing. Surprising him with a cupcake was another. He hadn't had a birthday cake in years, not since before the divorce when Maureen and Evelyn would serenade him and make him blow out the candles.

"After I drove past Antoine's house I spotted a Lincoln Town Car with two desperados behind me. One had a shotgun. I figure they were AK's thugs, keeping an eye on Antoine."

Kelly gripped his arm. Her fingers were icy. "What happened?"

This is a bad idea, he thought, *too reminiscent of her husband not coming home one night.* But he was into it now, too late to stop.

"They must have recognized my car. I've been at Iberville at least three times in the past two weeks. They put a bullet in the trunk of my car. Pissed me off, big time. So I drove to Iberville to talk to AK."

"By yourself?" Kelly stared at him, aghast. "These punks would as soon kill you as look at you. Why didn't you call me?"

"What, and mess up your dinner preparations?"

Her face worked with emotion. "Don't joke about stuff like that."

He hugged her. "You're right. But the maggots pissed me off."

"Jesus, Frank, you're worse than my brothers. They take no shit from anyone, but when they settle a score, they go together, all three of them."

"Huh," he said, deadpan. "You think they'd whup my ass?"

She grinned. "I'm not touching that one with a ten-foot pole."

He pulled her close. "I got a ten-foot pole for you."

"Yeah, yeah, you wish," she said. But her eyes were ripe with invitation.

"Want to take advantage of it or would you rather stay here and share my cupcake?"

"Cupcake or bed. Geez, Frank, these are tough choices." She frowned in mock-concentration but a mischievous smile tugged at the corner of her lips. Then she pulled him close and whispered, "Bed first, cupcake later."

CHAPTER 27

Sunday 12:20 P.M.

Antoine paid for the CD at the register, boogied on out of the Louisiana Music Factory and ambled down Decatur Street, basking in the warmth of the midday sun. Way better than listening to Reverend Goines rant about sin. This morning he'd told Uncle Jonas he felt sick, must have caught a bug or something. Got back a dubious look. Uncle Jonas took his responsibilities seriously, had promised Antoine's parents he'd make sure Antoine went to school every day and take him to church every Sunday.

He'd refused his uncle's usual Sunday breakfast—fried eggs, grits and toast—said his stomach felt like a meat grinder. And it did. Go to church, he'd run into Marcus. Out of sight, out of mind be the best thing. Five minutes after Uncle Jonas left, he'd hopped in his car and drove to the French Quarter, got to the music store right when it opened at noon.

Clutching the yellow plastic bag with Antonio Hart's latest CD in his left hand, he dug out his car keys, fantasizing about his future, imagining himself onstage at Snug Harbor with his own quartet, or playing lead sax in the Dizzy Gillespie Reunion Band like Antonio Hart.

A bleak vision shattered his joyful mood.

Chantelle at the microphone singing with his quartet.

His heart crumbled into a thousand pieces like a broken mirror. Yesterday was her birthday, sweet sixteen. Would have been, if she wasn't dead. Chantelle would never sing with his group, would never sing again except in Heaven maybe. He couldn't get her out his mind. Even when he played along with one of his CDs, a vision of Chantelle might blindside him, his eyes filling with tears at the sight of her beautiful face and sparkling eyes.

Oblivious to passing cars, he put his head down and trudged along the sidewalk, not much traffic at this hour on a Sunday, everybody sleeping in after a night of partying. Across the street, the sun bounced off the gleaming tower of Canal Place, a swanky shopping center, a young couple going in the back entrance to catch an early movie at the Canal Place Theater probably.

Hearing voices behind him, he turned to look. He saw no one and kept walking, hurrying now. Uncle Jonas be home from church by one, he'd better be there if he knew what was good for him. Better hide the CD, too. If Uncle Jonas heard a new CD, he'd have to explain where he got it. He smiled as a solution came to him: Take the wrapper off in his car, listen to Antonio Hart on the way home, Uncle Jonas be none the wiser.

"Yo," called a deep voice behind him. "Antoine."

He turned to look and his heart jumped into his throat. AK and his homeboys, Spider and Dead-Eye, jogging toward him a block away.

Sweet Jesus! He turned and ran like hell. If he could get to his car …

No. They were too close, footsteps pounding the sidewalk behind him. He ducked down an alley lined with smelly trash containers, risked a glance over his shoulder. They were gaining on him.

"Yo, Antoine! Stop! I just wanna talk to you."

Just wanna talk to you. Bullshit. AK wanted to beat the crap out of him because Marcus, the little rat, had told AK that cop had pulled him out of Jazz Harmony class. He ran faster, arms flailing, clutching the bag with the CD, bolted out of the alley onto Chartres Street.

Hadn't told the cop nothing, but AK would never believe it.

He ran faster, feet slamming the pavement, heart pounding so hard it made his teeth hurt. He dodged a man and a woman walking along the sidewalk. White tourists. No help there. Maybe he'd go to the District-Eight police station on Royal Street where Detective Renzi worked.

But Renzi wouldn't be there on a Sunday. And AK and his thugs would catch him long before he got there.

"Antoine! Wait up!"

Powered by adrenaline, he ran faster. But he couldn't outrun them forever. He zigged left and ran up Conti Street, breathing hard. Maybe he'd go in a store. But a lot of stores were still closed after Katrina and some of the others didn't open on Sunday. This end of the Quarter was full of upscale shops that catered to tourists. Nobody gonna help a black kid running from three 'bangers in cargo pants and hoodies. Go in a store, they would corner him like a mouse in a trap.

Maybe he could make it to Harrah's. The gambling casino at the foot of Canal Street was open 24-7. Plenty of security there. No. Forget that. They wouldn't let him in the door, see some wild-eyed black kid run inside, they might even call the cops. Maybe that be the best thing.

He glanced over his shoulder. Saw Dead-Eye but not AK and Spider.

Jesus! Dead-Eye was driving him into a trap. Then he saw what was in Dead-Eye's hand. His heart almost stopped. A mean-looking gun.

He kept running. If he could get to the next street, maybe he could hide out in a store for a while, then sneak back to his car. Uncle Jonas would be pissed, coming home from church to an empty house.

But that was the least of his worries.

Most important thing now was to stay alive.

A stitch in his side slowed him to a trot. The pain stabbed his ribs like a steak knife. He swiped sweat off his brow. Risked another glance over his shoulder. Dead-Eye was still behind him, but not gaining on him. Dead-Eye was winded, too. If he could get to the Royal Café, he'd be safe. People went there to drink coffee and eat pastries while they read the Sunday paper outside in the long narrow courtyard.

AK wouldn't dare shoot him in front of all those people, would he?

And then, his worst fear. AK and Spider sprang out of an alley ahead of him packing killer hardware. Jesus God, they were going to kill him!

Panic-stricken, he ducked into the recessed doorway of a jewelry store and yanked the door open. A white lady in a polka-dot dress stood behind a waist-high display case.

Her head jerked up and she looked at him, eyes fearful.

"I won't hurt you," he gasped. "Just let me out the back. There's three guys chasing me. If I don't get away, they'll kill me."

"Works going great, Dad. Last week I assisted one of the orthopedic surgeons on a broken leg with a compound fracture."

Enjoying the trill of enthusiasm in his daughter's voice, Frank sank onto Kelly's sofa with his cell phone. Kelly had made him use the bathroom first. After a quick shower and shave, he'd found a message from Maureen on his cell phone. Which he'd shut off last night before he and Kelly went to bed.

No message from Otis, though. No news on Marcus.

"Sounds like you're knocking 'em dead, Mo." He grinned. "Well, you know what I mean."

"Yeah, Dad, I know. You and your dark humor."

He pictured her: hazel eyes, auburn hair and a big grin when she was happy, which was most of the time, unlike her mother. Maureen was the light of his life. Damn, he missed her. "Other than work, how are things?"

"I spent last weekend with Mom. It was nice to be home."

"How's she doing? She doing okay?" He assumed so. He hadn't had a late-night panic call from his ex-wife for almost a month.

"I guess. She's got that teacher's aide job, but she doesn't go out much."

Doesn't go out much. Meaning what, he wondered.

"Do you think she could be a lesbian?"

The question bowled him over, not the fact that Maureen thought Evelyn could be a lesbian, the fact that she had voiced the idea to him.

"No, I don't. What makes you think that?"

"I don't know." Sounding like she wished she hadn't brought it up. "She doesn't seem interested in meeting . . . you know, guys."

Of course not. His ex-wife wasn't interested in sex with anyone, male or female.

"She's only forty-two, Dad. And she's in good shape, attractive. She could be dating. You go out on dates, don't you?"

He couldn't believe he was having this conversation. His daughter, a twenty-four-year-old resident in orthopedic surgery, asking about his sex life?

"I mean . . . you did it before, right?"

The subtle reproach brought back the aching sadness he'd felt during the divorce, a bitter fight that had driven a wedge between him and his daughter that had only recently begun to heal.

"Your mother's fine, Mo. You worry too much." He wasn't about to tell her that after she was born Evelyn decided she'd had enough of sex. A year later he'd begun a long-term affair with Audrey. But he wasn't going to discuss this with his daughter. He hadn't when Evelyn filed for divorce, citing adultery, and he wasn't going to do it now.

"Any chance you can fly to Baltimore for a weekend, Dad?"

"I'd love to, but I doubt it'll be anytime soon. We're still shorthanded since Katrina."

"Okay." The disappointment in her voice made him ache.

"I'll get up there soon, I promise. How's the riding going?"

"Great! Jeremy and I got picked to ride in the state competition. I am totally psyched!"

He smiled, picturing her beaming face. She'd met Jeremy, a show horse rider, at the Baltimore Hunt Club three years ago. Now Jeremy was her steady boyfriend. He heard Kelly's footsteps coming down the hall.

"Congratulations. When is it? Maybe I'll come up and watch you."

"Second Saturday in January. I already got that weekend off."

"I'll try to get off, too. But we'll see each other before that, right?"

"I hope so. Are you coming to Boston for the holidays?" Tension in her voice now, the bone of contention being: Where would she spend Thanksgiving and Christmas, with him or with her mother?

"I haven't had time to think about it, but we'll work it out."

Kelly entered the room dressed in black slacks, a V-necked gold top and a pair of Big-Z earrings. He gave her a thumbs-up. She looked more like a model than a cop, dark hair fringed around her face, tailored slacks accentuating her slender but curvy figure.

"Where were you when I called last night?" Mo asked. "Out celebrating your birthday?"

"Tell you all about it when I see you, Mo," he said, and saw Kelly react to his daughter's name. "Thanks for the card. It was great."

Her handwritten note had made him melt: *You're the best, Dad. Thanks for always being there for me.*

"You sound happy. Were you out with your girlfriend last night when I called? The one that lives in Omaha?"

"No," he said, meeting Kelly's gaze. "I was with one of my detective friends. We're about to go out for brunch."

"Oh, a *female* detective friend," Maureen said, her voice tinged with amusement. "Good for you. I guess the Omaha lady didn't work out, huh?"

"Right." He didn't want to talk about it. "Sent me an email about the riding meet, okay?"

"Okay, Dad. Love you."

"Love you too." He closed his cell phone and rose from the couch. "My daughter," he said.

"Like I couldn't guess from your proud-poppa expression. I bet you're a great dad. I love watching men interact with their kids. I know it's a cliché, but it's so . . . heartwarming."

He wrapped his arms around her, inhaling her vanilla-spice scent. "That's because you and your dad had a good relationship."

She tilted her head and her earrings swung back and forth. "Well, now that we've established that, let's go get some breakfast. Man, you wore me out last night."

"Takes two to tango." He grinned. "Shall we take your car or mine?"

"Mine. Yours has a bullet hole in the trunk. But you can drive if you want."

"What? You think I'm one of those macho guys that can't stand to ride with a woman driver? You drive. I'll relax and enjoy the scenery."

Gasping for breath, Antoine took another step into the store, so winded he felt dizzy. The lady looked panicky, eyes wide, mouth gaped open, frozen behind a waist-high case full of antique jewelry, ivory cameos set into earrings, pendants and brooches. *Jesus, stop gawking at the jewelry!*

He reached behind him and pulled the door shut.

And saw the woman's hand disappear beneath the counter.

"You got an alarm button, hit it," he said. "Get the cops over here."

The woman licked her lips, looked even more terrified.

"There's three guys out there fixin' to shoot me. You got a safety lock for the door? Hit the button to lock it and let me out the back. I gotta get away from those guys."

Guys that would be outside the door with the big glass window any second. Guys that would shoot him in the back. He wanted to turn and see if this was so, but he didn't dare. What if the woman had gun? Lots of French Quarter merchants kept guns in their stores. And dogs.

Fear clawed his throat. Jesus, what if she had a dog?

"I want you to leave," she said, her voice high and tight with fear.

"I will! But I can't go out the front—"

Blam! The window in the door shattered into a million pieces, little glass rocks cascading over the carpet, scattering everywhere like sparkly diamonds.

He dropped to the floor and squirmed forward on his belly. Said in a loud whisper, "Call the police."

"I am," she said in a quavery voice.

Inching forward on his belly, he squirmed toward the rear of the shop. Saw the woman hunkered down behind the display case.

"Can I get out the back?" he whispered.

Crouched on the floor behind the counter, holding a cell phone to her ear, she nodded vigorously.

"Antoine! You don't come outta there we come in and shoot you daid!"

The woman frantically motioned him toward the back.

"Hurry," she said. "Hurry."

CHAPTER 28

They were lucky to get a table at the Marigny Brasserie. Located on Frenchman's Street two blocks from the French Quarter, the restaurant drew both locals and tourists to its celebrated Sunday brunch. The place was packed, close to a hundred people digging the Pfister Sisters, a hip vocal trio that sang 1940 swing tunes, *Boogie-woogie Bugle Boy* being their specialty.

Frank ordered the Brasserie Breakfast, an omelet with mushrooms and peppers. Kelly went with scrambled eggs and a side order of bacon. And a pitcher of Mimosas. Kelly's idea. He liked most of her ideas, so why not?

He leaned back against the padded seat, enjoying the tangy orange juice and champagne, enjoying the sight of Kelly O'Neil even more. His kind of woman. Italian with a twist of Irish: Olive skin, short dark hair framing an oval face, and those beautiful Irish eyes.

She raised her glass in a mock-toast. "Nice to relax for a change."

"Sure is. No shoptalk today. What shall we do after brunch?"

"There's an interesting exhibit at Fine Arts Photography." She grinned. "Or we could go back to my house. But I wouldn't want to wear you out."

Before he could think of a suitable retort, the waiter delivered their breakfast, and the Pfister Sisters began a toe-tapping version of the Boswell Sister's *What'd You Do to Me*. Appropriate, he thought, watching Kelly crunch a piece of bacon, looking happy and content.

Man, he could get used to this. Then his cell phone rang.

Kelly pulled hers out, realized it was his and rolled her eyes. He checked the ID. A cell phone number, one he didn't recognize. Hoping it was Otis calling with news about the Goines kid, he clicked on and said, "Renzi."

"Help me."

The whisper sent chills down his neck. He signaled Kelly, who frowned and mouthed: *What?*

"Who's this? Antoine?" he said, keeping his voice low.

Silence on the other end, except for the sound of labored breathing.

"Talk to me. That you, Antoine?"

"Yes." A single syllable, barely audible.

"Where are you?"

"Royal Street, behind a store. AK's after me."

Frank signaled a passing waiter.

The waiter stopped at their booth, frowning, and said, "Is everything—"

Kelly shushed him and flashed her wallet.

"Antoine," he said into the phone, "I'm on Frenchman Street near the Quarter. I'll come get you. Tell me what block of Royal Street. Tell me the name of the store. Anything."

"Three blocks from Canal. Behind a jewelry store. Hurry. They're coming—"

The line went dead. He pushed back his chair and said to Kelly in a low voice, "AK's got Antoine cornered. Are we set?"

"We're good," she said, rising to her feet.

Heads turned as they rushed out of the restaurant. Kelly tossed him her car keys. "You drive. You know where we're going."

They ducked around the corner and broke into a run, got to her car in thirty seconds flat. He got behind the wheel and cranked the engine. Kelly jumped in and he rocketed away from the curb. "Royal Street, third block. Is there a jewelry store there?"

"There's a jewelry story near Café Beignet."

His cell phone rang and he grabbed it. "Renzi."

"They got guns." A whisper. "They shot out the store window."

"Where are you? Are you safe?"

"Hiding in an alley. Behind the Hotel Monteleone."

He gripped the wheel and turned onto Esplanade. Royal was the next cross street. The wrong end of Royal, unfortunately. Antoine was seven blocks away. Hiding from AK and his gunslinger thugs.

"Stay where you are, Antoine. I'm on Royal now, be there in a minute."

"Hurry." A faint whisper.

He peered into the steamy mirror above his bathroom sink. His face was a ghostly image slathered with shaving cream. With great care, he drew the razor around two zits on his cheek. Fuck-all! Zits were for teenagers.

How could a thirty-six year old man get zits?

Easy. Too much stress, too much junk food, and too little sleep.

Last night he'd maintained his vigil outside of Belinda's house. Snacking on Doritos and sipping from a large container of black coffee, he waited until the light in her bedroom window winked out at one-thirty. Exhausted, he had driven home and slept for five hours.

He rinsed the razor under the hot water and continued his careful, methodical strokes. Today she would fly to New York to attend Ziegler's funeral. But when would she be back?

The question vexed him so much he almost cut himself. Using a damp facecloth, he patted shaving cream from his face, wiped the fog off the mirror and examined his cheek. The two zits stood out like angry red flares.

Fuck-all! Worse than a teenager.

He put on his last clean shirt, went down the hall to the kitchen and opened the refrigerator. Nothing but empty shelves. He needed food, but he was short on cash. His boss at the limo service was giving him four-hour shifts, saying he had to get in line, others were ahead of him. Same thing when he asked for his check. Wait.

He slammed his fist on the counter. All he did these days was wait. Wait for decent tips. Wait for his paycheck. Wait for Belinda to come home so he could introduce her to his orgasmic delights.

His groin stirred, a delicious tingle.

Inside his cage beside the kitchen, Oz gazed up at him with his pretty blue eyes. "I had a rough night last night, Oz."

And the night before, and the night before that. Belinda had cast him into tortured limbo, wondering when she would return.

He looked down at his Wizard of Oz, gazing up at him with longing. Poor bunny. These days he had no time for him. He chopped up the last two carrots, opened the cage door and dropped them in the food dish.

Oz pounced on them with enthusiasm, jaws working.

"Be a good boy, Oz. I've got to go buy us some food. When I get home I'll let you out and stroke you and pet you and make you feel loved."

But who would make *him* feel loved? His throat closed up. His beloved was going to New York. What if she never came back? The idea crushed him.

He touched his crotch.

He might have to find another substitute.

The one last night hadn't been very cooperative.

When they reached the alley behind the Hotel Monteleone, he parked Kelly's car across the opening to prevent any cars from entering or leaving. Sweat dampened his shirt and the palms of his hands.

Where the hell was Antoine? Was he still alive?

He dug his SIG out of the holster and looked over at Kelly. Saw her pull up one trouser leg and yank a Glock-9 out an ankle holster.

Despite the tension, he smiled as a catchy phrase popped into his mind. *Two cops on a date, armed and dangerous.*

She gave him a steely look, her expression grim. "What?"

Gunshots shattered the rear window, spewing glass over the back seat.

"Get down! They're behind us!" he yelled, and slid lower in the seat.

Crouched in the foot-well of the passenger seat, Kelly gripped her Glock, her face tight with tension. "We're sitting ducks in the car."

She was right. No telling what kind of ammo AK and his thugs were using. Some of the slugs they sold these days could penetrate steel. They couldn't stay in the car. "Get out and run to the alley. I'll follow you."

Without a word, she jumped out and bolted into the alley. No gunshots.

He waited five seconds and opened the car door. Still no gunshots.

Crouching low, he sprinted to the alley.

Kelly stood with her back against the brick wall of the building, holding her Glock with both hands. "You think they're still there?"

"If they are, they're in one of the doorways along the side street. AK doesn't know your car, but they might have seen me when we drove by."

"Want me to call for backup?"

During their frantic drive through the French Quarter, Kelly had called the District Eight station to report a problem at the jewelry store on Royal Street. But that was three blocks away. Frank looked down the alley. No sign of Antoine. Twenty yards from their position at the end of the alleyway, two columns of empty milk crates were stacked against the side of a brick building. Beside the milk crates were two large green Dumpsters.

"No," he said. "If they were still there, they'd have shot at us when we left the car. Stay here and cover me while I look for Antoine."

He forged deeper into the alley, his SIG at the ready. Fifteen yards into the alley he stopped. "Antoine," he called softly. "It's Renzi. Where are you?"

A long moment passed. Then Antoine's head appeared behind one of the big green Dumpsters. When he saw Frank, he hauled himself erect, his expression a mixture of anxiety and relief. He came out from behind the Dumpster. Dirt caked his shirt, and both pant legs were ripped.

Clutching a yellow plastic bag in one hand, he brushed dreadlocks from his face, fear evident in his large dark eyes. "Thank you. They were gonna kill me," Antoine said. Then he frowned. "I heard shots."

"They shot out our car window. Come on. We'll drive you home."

"Okay, but . . ."

"But what?" he snapped. Now that the crisis was over his quota of patience was gone.

"Could you take me to my car? It's parked over on Canal Street."

"Forget the car. We're driving you to your uncle's house. Let's go."

They walked back to the alleyway entrance. Kelly stood with her back against the brick wall, grim-faced, holding her Glock-9 in both hands. Seeing the amazement on Antoine's face, Frank stifled a grin, imagining the kid's thoughts: *Nobody better mess with that woman.*

Grim-faced and squinty-eyed, Kelly motioned Antoine into the front passenger seat. After Antoine got in the car, she said, "You drive, Frank. I'll ride in back and keep an eye on things."

He nodded, thinking: *This is a first, having a girlfriend watch my back.*

Ten silent minutes later he pulled to a stop outside Jonas Carter's house and said to Antoine, "I want you to go in the house and stay there."

The kid looked at him, the saddest face he'd ever seen, Antoine's large dark eyes bright with tears. "Yessir. Go in the house and deal with my uncle."

"Deal with him however you want, but *do not leave that house.* I need to go get my car, but I'll be back. Then you and your uncle and I are going to sit down and have a long talk. Go."

Antoine got out and trudged to the door of the shotgun double, went in and shut the door.

Kelly took his place in the front passenger seat. "I don't mind waiting, Frank. Go talk to them."

He traced a finger down her cheek. "No. You've done enough already. I'm just sorry we can't kick back and relax like we planned."

"Shit happens. We'll have other Sundays."

"Music to my ears. I'll make it up to you next Sunday, I promise."

"Yeah, well, we'll see. A lot could happen before then."

What did that mean? A lot could happen with their relationship? A lot could happen at work that might make him break his promise?

"It was great having a pistol-packing partner with me today," he said. "Thanks for helping out."

Kelly grinned. "Frank. I'm a *cop*. What did you expect?"

CHAPTER 29

"Man, I never been so scared in my life."

Frank watched fear wash over Antoine's face and settle in his eyes.

They were seated at the dining room table in his uncle's spic-and-span house, not a speck of dust anywhere, the maple tabletop gleaming, looked like it had been polished with Pledge. Antoine faced him across the table. Jonas Carter sat beside his nephew, a distinguished-looking man with chiseled features and gray hair, looked a bit like Ossie Davis.

A very unhappy Ossie Davis.

"AK and his boys musta seen me coming out of the Louisiana Music Factory. When they yelled at me, I took off. They were gonna kill me."

"Tell me about the Lakeview robbery," Frank said. "Chantelle was there, right?"

Antoine stared at the table top. "Yeah, but she ran away when the cop came out the store. I told her before we went there. Anything happens, I said, you run away. Don't worry 'bout me."

"Why you go and do somethin' stupid like that, boy?" Jonas Carter said, his voice full of disappointment, dark eyes fixed on Antoine. "Your parents brought you up better'n that."

Antoine sat there with his eyes downcast as though he was studying the molecules of wood on the tabletop. "Worried about Chantelle," he mumbled.

"Be better off worrying 'bout yourself," said the uncle. "That girl's trouble from the get go."

"Was not! Chantelle was—" Antoine bit his lip. "Wasn't none of it her fault. Her crackhead mom's in Houston ever since Katrina, step-daddy took *his* kid to Atlanta, left Chantelle to fend for herself." He looked at Frank. "Like you said, right Detective Renzi?"

Choosing his words carefully, he said. "I think Chantelle was a victim of circumstances. But that doesn't excuse you for helping AK rob that store."

"Exactly," Jonas Carter declared. "No excuse for it a'tall."

"Mr. Carter, I know you mean well, but I'd appreciate it if you'd let Antoine talk." Shifting his gaze to the miserable teenager, he said, "I need you to tell me exactly what happened."

Jonas Carter nodded. "Tell the man what happened, Antoine."

"Chantelle was living at Iberville 'cuz she don't have no place else to live. But AK was bothering her." Lacing his slender fingers together, Antoine stared at the tabletop. "He wanted to, you know, get in her pants. But she told AK we were, you know, involved. One day I was there AK says 'You got to help me, prove you not gonna turn on me.'"

"Blackmailing you," Frank said.

"Exactly!" Antoine exclaimed. "No way would I go and rob that store. But AK said if I didn't—" He turned to his uncle. "I was afraid, Uncle Jonas. Not for myself, for Chantelle. You don't know how bad things are at Iberville."

Carter opened his mouth to speak, but Frank cut him off. "We know how bad it is. So AK made you go with him to rob the store. Then what?" Deliberately choosing words that cast Antoine in a more favorable light. Antoine didn't go on his own; AK forced him.

After Kelly drove him back to his car, he had asked if she had a tape recorder. Her mini-recorder was in the middle of the table now, recording everything, including his suggestion to Jonas Carter that he call a lawyer, an offer Carter had declined. So he'd read Antoine the Miranda warning and stated that Antoine's uncle, Jonas Carter, was present.

"We meet up in Chantelle's apartment, but then AK says Chantelle gotta come with us, be the lookout." Antoine shrugged. "What could I do? AK's got his posse with him."

"The two thugs that were chasing you today?"

"Yeah. The ones at NOCCA that day, in the parking lot."

"Okay, tell me their names."

Antoine looked away and heaved a sigh. "Man, I dunno . . ."

"I need names, Antoine. If you want me to help you, give me names."

"Antoine," Jonas Carter said in a warning tone.

The kid slumped lower in his chair. "Don't know their real names, just street names."

Frank said nothing, just stared at him.

"Spider," Antoine mumbled. "And Dead-Eye."

"Okay, so you and Chantelle and AK get in the Cadillac and drive to the store in Lakeview. Then what happened?"

Antoine licked his lips. Looked at his uncle. "Can I have some water?"

Without a word, Jonas Carter left the table, went in the kitchen and returned with three bottles of Aquafina. He handed one to Frank—company first—one to Antoine, and opened his own.

The three of them slugged down water in silence.

Antoine set his half-empty bottle on the table. Heaved a sigh. "Okay, so we get to the store and get out the car. AK tells Chantelle to hide around the corner of the store and watch for cop cars."

"What happened when you and AK went in the store?"

"Man, I was shaking like a leaf. We go inside and there's a white lady at the counter talking to the clerk. AK tells me go down the back, like I'm looking for something. So I go to the refrigerator cases along the back wall. Then I hear the lady scream. Not loud, just kind of surprised. Then AK says, 'Gimme the money in the register, muthafucka.'"

Antoine ducked his head, as though he expected his uncle to box his ears for the foul language. But Jonas Carter sat there like a bronze statue, his expression pained. Full of misery and despair. A world of hurt.

"Then what?" Frank said. The next part was crucial.

"I creep down an aisle, almost died when I see AK holding a gun to the lady's head. Jesus-Lord, I told him before we went inside, 'No guns, right?' And AK said, 'No guns.' Shouda known he was lyin', gives me his evil smile. Anyway, the clerk opens the register, you know, and AK tells him to put the money in a plastic bag. The guy does what he's told. But then . . !."

Antoine drank some water and wiped his mouth with the back of his hand. "Then the door opens and this guy walks in. I knew right off he was a cop. Didn't have no uniform on, but I could tell. He had to know what's going down 'cuz AK's got his gun on the lady. He shouts 'Police, put the gun down.' And AK shoots him. Lord-A'mighty, thought I'd wet my pants! Then AK grabs the bag with the money and says, 'Yo, partner, we outta here.'"

Antoine shook his head. "Like I'm his partner. But I wasn't." He looked Frank in the eye. "I didn't wanna be there, I swear to you. I ain't friends with AK. I hate his guts. What he did to Chantelle."

"What did he do to Chantelle?" Frank said quietly.

"He made her . . . made her *do* him, you know? She didn't wanna tell me, but I knew something's wrong one night, she's crying." His hands clenched and his eyes brimmed with tears. "AK put a gun on her, made her give him a blow job. Said if I don't do this robbery, he make her do it again."

A sob wracked him and tears ran down his cheeks.

Outraged darkened Jonas Carter's face. He put his arm around Antoine and said, "It's okay, Antoine. You hear? It's okay."

Antoine brushed away the tears and straightened in his chair, mouth set in a grim line. "I couldn't let him do that. So, I did what I did."

Why didn't you get her out of there? Frank thought. But the kid was already in pain, no point second guessing him and making him feel worse.

"What happened with the cop?"

"He staggers outside, yells at us to drop the guns and come out with our hands on our head. AK makes clerk get on the floor and says don't call the cops. Then AK shoots at him." Antoine looked at Frank. "Not to hit him. If AK wanted to kill him, you know, he'd a done it. He shot up a bottle of booze on the shelf behind the counter to scare the guy. Then he grabs the white lady and says 'We outta here.'"

Frank said, "For the record, Antoine, did you have a gun?"

"No!" Antoine stared at him, wide-eyed. "I never had a gun, never carried a gun, never shot a gun, don't want to!"

"Okay. Then what happened?"

Antoine gulped some water. "I was scared the cop would shoot us. When I go out, I see the lady—she's just a little bitty thing—clamped against AK's chest. AK's got the gun against her head, got the back door of the Caddy open, tells me get in and drive. So I did."

"Okay, so you were driving. Where were AK and the woman?"

"In the back seat."

"Where on the back seat? Behind you or on the passenger side?"

A crucial detail. The crime-scene techs had taken prints off the rear door behind the driver's seat.

"First off they be laying across the back seat 'cuz the lady's struggling, begging AK to let her go. Then AK hit her in the head with the gun. I saw him in the rearview. After that she's quiet." Antoine heaved a sigh. "Then AK shoves her toward the door behind me. I'm scared he's gonna shoot me if I don't do what he says, so I drive like hell, turn this way and that. Then I hear sirens, see lights flashing behind us, and AK's opens the door."

"Which door?" Frank said.

"The one behind me. He tells me go faster, take the next right, and when I turn right, Jesus-Lord, we had to be going sixty, he opens the door and . . ." Antoine shut his eyes, whispered, "He pushed the lady out."

"AK pushed the woman out of the car?" Frank said.

Antoine nodded, his face clenched. "He pushed her out."

"While your hands were on the steering wheel."

"Yessir. I be holding onto that wheel for dear life. When I turn that corner, the door swings open and AK shoves the lady out the car, and I hear this thump. I wanted to stop, but AK puts the gun to my neck, says *Step on it, we gotta lose these cops.* So I did."

Looking miserable and unhappy, Antoine sank back in his chair, sucked down some water and stared at the table.

Frank checked his watch, announced that the interview had ended at three-twenty P.M. and shut off the tape recorder.

"What happens now?" asked Jonas Carter, eyes full of concern. "Antoine done wrong, but it don't seem like it was all his fault."

"I can't promise what will happen, but I can tell you this: We need Antoine to testify to this in court. If he testifies, the D.A. and the judge might cut him some slack."

Antoine raised his head and looked at him, grim-faced and hard-eyed. "Testify against AK you mean?"

"That's exactly what I mean. If you do, we'll protect you."

"Not much protection you come to NOCCA and call me down the office. AK knew I talked to you. Marcus told him. He's in my jazz harmony class. Marcus been dealing pot, gets it from AK."

"Marcus Goines?" Jonas Carter gasped. "Reverend Goines' son?"

Antoine nodded. "Marcus. No doubt about it."

Jonas Carter frowned. "The boy's missing."

Antoine gaped at his uncle, then at Frank. "Marcus is missing?"

His surprise seemed genuine. Scratch Antoine from the suspect list. Forty-eight hours and no sign of the kid. Frank figured it would be a miracle if Marcus turned up alive. AK and his thugs had tried to kill Antoine today. Wouldn't surprise him if they had already killed Marcus.

"Marcus has been missing since Friday," Frank said. "He never came home from school. Will you testify against AK?"

Antoine clenched his hands into fists. "I'll testify, no doubt about that. Bad enough he pushed that lady out the car. Him and his buddies killed Chantelle. Nobody gonna rat 'em out for it, but I know they did." Antoine drilled him with a look. "AK gonna get the chair for killing that lady?"

"He will if I have anything to say about it."

An imperfect form of justice for Chantelle, but it might be the best he could do. He couldn't prove AK killed her and if AK's thugs ratted on him, they might never live to testify.

CHAPTER 30

Monday, 13 November

With a palpable sense of relief, she turned onto her street. Almost home. She massaged the tense knot that had taken up residence in her neck during the plane ride. Meeting Jake's parents, their dark eyes hollow with grief, had been an ordeal. Their funeral arrangements—the music, the tributes from Jake's cousins, the rabbi's poignant speech—had been beautiful. Everything had been perfect, except for the fact that Jake was dead.

She was all alone. Again. Unwilling to sink into self-pity, she gripped the wheel and gritted her teeth. Facing adversity alone was nothing new. She had survived the loss of her family, an unintended pregnancy and two heartbreaking affairs with married men. But now, thanks to her determination and talent and hard work, her career was about to take off.

She noticed a black van parked in a driveway three houses down from hers on the opposite side of the street. ACE PLUMBERS, according to the white letters on the side. Nothing new there, either. Since Katrina everyone on her street had experienced intermittent sewage or water problems.

She pulled into the circular driveway in front of her house, got out and rolled her suitcase up the walk. A box sat on the floor of the porch, pastries from Mr. Silverman probably. Why did he do it? He knew she'd be away. They would be stale and even if they weren't, she wouldn't eat them. She left her suitcase in the foyer, went in the kitchen and put the box in the trash.

Home at last. She kicked off her shoes, took a bottle of iced tea out of the refrigerator and gulped half the contents, her mind racing with things to do. For some reason she felt more energized than she had in years, as though she'd shed several layers of skin and the real Belinda Scully had emerged.

She wandered down the hall to the office. Not Jake's office, her office. She was looking forward to the concert in Louisville. Music had always been her salvation, a soothing balm for emotional turmoil. Just what she needed to survive the holidays: Thanksgiving, Christmas and New Years. Family holidays, and she had no family. Fortunately she would be busy. She opened the folder that lay on the desk and checked her schedule: ten concerts.

The phone rang. She picked up and answered crisply, "Belinda Scully. May I help you?"

"Hello, Belinda, it's Barry. I'm happy you're home safe and sound, but I didn't expect you to answer. You need to rest. You've suffered a terrible loss. That takes a toll on you."

She made a face. She hated it when people dragged her down with negativity. "I'm fine. It's time I got back to work."

"Then we need to talk about your security arrangements."

A dull ache pulsed behind her eyes. "Not now. I have work to do—"

"You're alone in that house, Belinda. You need someone to protect you, someone to take over Jake's duties. My schedule is quite flexible. I can come over right now and—"

"No. It's kind of you to offer, but I'm fine. Really."

"You say you're fine, but Jake's death had to be a shock. I don't blame you for feeling down. One doesn't expect one's friends to die so young."

She frowned. Jake's death was a shock, and Frank's statement last Friday had been equally shocking. *Jake's death was suspicious. Everyone is a suspect.*

"I'm sorry, but I can't talk right now. I've got to unpack and—"

"Did you find the muffins? I thought you might appreciate a treat when you got home."

She rolled her eyes. "Yes, I did. Thank you, Mr. Silverman."

"Barry." His voice hit her ear like a pistol shot.

Shocked, she held the receiver away from her ear. She didn't want to call him Barry. That implied they were friends. They weren't, and they weren't going to be. She did need help with the business until she hired a new manager, but Silverman seemed to think he had a lock on the job.

You only think about yourself. And your career. Dean's words.

She took a deep breath. Let it out. Kept her voice even. "It was very thoughtful of you to buy the pastries. Thank you."

"What are your plans for the Louisville concert?"

Irritated, she snapped, "I plan to play a magnificent performance."

"Of course you will. You're the best young flute soloist in the world. But you need a security plan. We can fly to Louisville together—"

"Stop!" she shouted. "Didn't you hear what I said? I'm *busy*. I've already made my arrangements for Louisville. I don't need you to go with me."

A brief silence. Then, "That's a decision you might regret. You must be tired. I'll speak with you later. Welcome home, Belinda."

Forcing herself not to yell, she said, "Goodbye, Mr. Silverman."

Just as she was getting back on track a new problem surfaced. But she refused to let Mr. Silverman ruin her upbeat mood. She was playing the Zwilich *Flute Concerto* and the Gershwin in Louisville.

She shut her eyes and recited her mantra. *Never give in to fear. Act successful and you will be successful. Believe in yourself and you cannot fail.*

She opened her eyes and smiled.

The concert in Louisville would be perfect.

"You sure the kid will testify?" A.D.A. Eddie Rouzan, a tired-looking black man, shot a skeptical look at Frank, another at Vobitch, the three of them huddled inside Vobitch's office with the door closed. "Half these kids are no-shows when the court date arrives."

Frank glanced at Vobitch. He looked as tired as Rouzan and way more annoyed. The media frenzy over the Lakeview case continued unabated. In fact it was getting worse.

"Antoine will testify," Frank said. "He thinks AK murdered his girlfriend to keep her quiet. I think so too, but we don't have any evidence on the Chantelle Wilson murder."

"You got evidence AK did the Lakeview woman?" Rouzan said.

"We got the getaway car," Vobitch snarled. "We got prints off the steering wheel and the back door. We got the wounded cop's description of the robbers."

Frank gestured at the tape deck. "I taped Antoine's confession."

"You read him the Miranda, right? No coercion."

"It's on the tape! You heard me do it."

"Yeah, but the judge might not like it. The kid refused an attorney."

"I told his uncle they could call one. They declined." When that failed to erase Rouzan's skeptical expression, he said, "How about a lineup? Haul AK in and have Officer Robichard identify him."

Rouzan yawned. Fifteen months post-Katrina the overworked D.A.'s office was short of prosecutors and plagued by a skyrocketing crime rate.

"We pull in AK and his thugs," Vobitch said, "one of 'em might flip."

"I doubt it," Rouzan said. "These 'bangers turn in their mama 'fore they rat on a brother. Morgan, I know you want to clear this one. We're under pressure, too, but I won't go to court with a weak case, hang it on a witness that might split." He rose from his chair. "This case is high-profile. I don't want it to blow up in my face. Get me a match on the prints. Get me a solid ID from the cop. Get me some evidence so I can win the case."

As soon as Rouzan left, Vobitch exploded. "Fuck Rouzan and the DA's office! All these prosecutors want everything tied in a nice pink bow. Let's get an arrest warrant."

He loved it when Vobitch went ballistic. They sometimes had their differences, but when the chips were down, Vobitch usually did what Frank considered to be the right thing. Not necessarily the most prudent thing, the one most likely to get results.

His cell phone rang. He checked the ID and held up a wait-a-minute finger. Vobitch nodded and raked stubby fingers through his silvery hair.

When he answered, Kelly said, "Hi Frank, you busy?"

"You mean that interview I told you about?"

Speaking in the low husky voice he found so enchanting, she said, "Oh, you can't talk now, huh?"

Nice to know they were on the same wavelength. "Right," he said, aware that Vobitch was waiting, impatiently tapping a pen on his desk. He felt a zing of adrenaline, talking to his lover while his boss was waiting, the thrill of the forbidden.

"I'm working topless today."

He couldn't believe she'd said it. Maintaining a serious expression, a major effort, he said, "I'd better check that out ASAP."

A seductive chuckle. "I'll set a timer, see how long it takes you."

He punched off, wiped his sweaty palm on his pant leg. Talk about living dangerously.

"I'll write the fucking warrant myself," Vobitch said, "hand it to the judge personally! If he doesn't okay it I'll stick a gun in his fucking ear."

"Bad idea, Morgan. Play it safe and send it by courier."

Vobitch glowered at him. "You're not the one taking phone calls from pissed-off Lakeview residents. And when *they're* not calling me, I got some bleeding-heart social worker on the line, wants to play hug-a-thug, make sure we don't railroad some innocent black kid."

"I might have a new angle on the case."

"Good news I hope," Vobitch said, wearily rubbing his eyes.

"Remember that hit-and-run incident with the VIP?"

"The one where you called London and talked for twenty minutes on account of some flute player got in an accident?" Vobitch said, icing him with another look, his slate-gray eyes full of fury.

"Right. Belinda Scully. Last Wednesday her manager died under suspicious circumstances. The emergency room doc thinks he might have been poisoned. We're waiting on the tox report."

"So? You got a suspect?"

"Yes. Scully's driver. Ziegler fired him two days before he died."

"Well, you got motive. What's this got to do with the Lakeview case?"

"Ziegler's autopsy indicated he'd eaten chocolate. One of Scully's flute students gave her brownies. She hates chocolate, gave them to Ziegler. I interviewed the student on Friday. He said Scully's driver asked him to give them to her. I was planning to have the kid come in with his father to sign a statement, but that's out the window now. His name is Marcus Goines."

Vobitch's eyes went wide as a satellite dish. "The kid that's missing?"

"Bingo. Here's the Lakeview connection. Turns out Marcus has been dealing pot. AK is his supplier. Antoine confirmed it, but I didn't want to bring it up while Rouzan was here."

"Right. He'd have blown it off as hearsay or some fucking thing. You think AK whacked the Goines kid?"

"That's one possibility. Scully's driver is another. I need to call London again and get a better handle on the guy."

"Okay, but keep it short," Vobitch said. "I gotta find a friendly reporter, plant a bug in his ear that we got something going on the Lakeview case."

Vobitch was desperate to clear the Lakeview case, but even if they got the warrant, nailing AK for murder would be tough. Being an NOPD cop these days was like Jelly Roll Morton playing piano in a Storyville brothel. The Jellyman couldn't control what happened in the rooms upstairs any more than Vobitch could control what the DA did.

Frank went outside to his car and dialed Kelly's cell phone.

"Is this the deceptive detective who speaks in riddles?" she said.

"Is this the temptress that blindsides me with phone sex while I'm in a meeting with my boss?"

A low throaty laugh. "That's where you were when I called?"

"Yes. Morgan and I were telling ADA Rouzan about Antoine and the Lakeview case. Rouzan's afraid Antoine won't testify. Morgan's gonna go for an arrest warrant, grab AK and put him in a lineup. If the judge goes for it."

"He will if it relates to the Lakeview case."

"I hope so. Why'd you call me? Pining for my irresistible voice?"

"Yowza, listen to the man's ego! Your irresistible voice is nice, but I had other reasons. A woman got raped Saturday night and Violent Crimes asked me to interview her."

"Your serial rapist?"

"No. Different MO. The asshole beat her up and broke her nose. The good news is she identified his vehicle. She used to work at her father's Ford dealership. She said she's positive it was a Ford E-series van."

"Hold it. Silverman drives a Ford E-series van."

"A black one?"

"No, his is white."

"Uh-oh, Warren just came out and spotted me. Listen, I can't meet you tonight after work. I forgot I promised to have dinner with Terry's mother. Can we do it tomorrow night instead?"

Unwilling to show his disappointment, he said, "Sure, no problem. I'll see you tomorrow anyway. Morgan's calling a meeting so we can set up a plan to nab AK and his thugs."

He went back to his office. Kelly was hot on her latest rape case, but his mind was on Ziegler. He dialed a number and waited.

"State Toxicology Lab, Annette speaking."

"Hi, Annette, Detective Renzi, NOPD. I'm waiting on a tox report for Jacob Ziegler, died last Wednesday. Could you check the status for me?"

"Hold on." He heard papers rustling as she muttered, "Everyone wants their tox reports yesterday. And we're working fourteen hours a day on Katrina bodies."

After Katrina the state had set up a temporary lab at the hospital in Carville that had once housed victims of Hanson's Disease. The hospital had closed years ago, but many still called it the leper hospital. Hundreds of Katrina victims remained there, awaiting identification.

"Sorry," Annette said. "The Ziegler report isn't back yet. I'll put a pink sticky on it, might have it for you by the end of the week."

He thanked her, rang off, and punched a string of numbers into the phone: country and city code, then the six-digit number of Smythe-Jones, former employer of Barry Silverman. He heard the doop-doop ring of the international call. Then a mechanical voice: *The number you dialed has been disconnected. No further information is available.*

He slammed the phone in the cradle. Smythe-Jones was a phony and so was Barry Silverman. Silverman was no security expert, he was a stalker. He might also be a killer. And so far all their attempts to find him had failed.

CHAPTER 31

Humming a snippet of *I Got Rhythm,* she fixed a salad to go with the barbequed chicken she'd bought for dinner. Twenty minutes ago, after a perfect run-through of the Zwilich, she'd put the chicken in the oven to reheat, returned to her studio and played her *Gershwin Variations* twice, flawlessly. The Louisville audience was sure to love it. A limo would meet her at the airport Friday afternoon and drive her to the hotel. The only rehearsal was at seven, but she wasn't worried. The Louisville Orchestra was topnotch.

She cut a plum tomato into quarters, dropped them on a salad plate of greens and drained the broccoli in the sink. Hearing the long rolling rumble of distant thunder, she leaned over the sink and looked out the window. The setting sun had disappeared behind sullen gray clouds.

The phone rang, shrill and insistent in the silence of her kitchen.

Her pulse pounded. She checked the Caller ID. *Unavailable.*

Her neck tensed and her diaphragm tightened. She massaged her icy fingers. The phone had rung twice while she was practicing, but she had ignored it. After she finished, she had checked her voicemail.

No message from the five o'clock caller, but at six there had been.

Why don't you answer, Belinda? I know you're there. Your car's out front and the office light is on. She had run to the window and scanned the street. Silverman's van was nowhere in sight, but she was no longer sure its absence meant anything. No longer sure she was safe.

Her eyes flicked to the wall calendar beside the refrigerator. Today's date was circled. Monday, the thirteenth of November. Unlucky thirteen.

More thunder, an ominous rumble. But nowhere near as ominous as her ringing telephone. Now it was seven o'clock. It had to be him.

She rubbed the goose bumps on her arms, aware of how empty her house was. Aware of how alone she was without Jake. And Frank was no help. He was busy with work, busy romancing that woman detective.

The ringing stopped as her voicemail kicked in. Not wanting to listen, afraid not to, she ran to the office and heard the tone sound. Then his voice.

What a wonderful rendition of the Gershwin you just played, Belinda. Note perfect.

She felt like a horse had kicked her in the gut. He'd been outside her house, close enough to hear her.

Pick up the phone and talk to me, Belinda. I've got a great surprise for you.

Surprise? She didn't need surprises. She needed peace and quiet. She needed to get her life back on track and play a perfect performance in Louisville and . . .

Why won't you talk to me? After all I've done for you it's the least you can do. Maybe you're nervous about your concert in Louisville. It's your first since Jake died.

She clapped a hand over her mouth. How could he be so cruel?

Jake won't be with you, but I will. I'll be in the front row so don't slip up. Don't let your fingers freeze in the middle of the Gershwin. Everything would be perfect if you'd just pick up the phone. Then I'd come over and we'd have a glass of wine with dinner. You're having barbequed chicken, right?

Her heart slammed her chest. How did he know?

I wish you'd talk to me, Belinda. I hate talking to machines. But have it your way. I'll call you later.

A click and the line went dead. But for how long? Would he call again at eight? Bile filled her throat and tremors wracked her body. She felt like a prisoner in her own house.

With a terrible feeling of dread, she returned to the kitchen and took the chicken out of the oven. The greasy odor nauseated her. How could she eat when this horrible man kept calling every hour on the hour?

She was at his mercy. Helpless.

She leaned against the kitchen counter and massaged her throbbing forehead, eyeing the telephone. Normally an innocuous convenience, it had now become an instrument of evil.

Then it dawned on her. She wasn't helpless.

She grabbed the phone plug, yanked it out of the socket, ran to the office and did the same. Two down, one more in her bedroom. Energized, she raced upstairs, traced the wires from the phone on her bedside table to the phone jack and pulled the plug. Now Silverman could call to his heart's content, but her phone wouldn't ring.

Still, not having a phone by her bed made her nervous. But Silverman didn't have her cell phone number. With her cell phone on her bedside table, she could climb into bed and have a secure restful sleep, uninterrupted by disturbing phone calls.

DIVA

2:45 A.M.

It was a perfect night for a break-in. A thick blanket of clouds obscured the moon. He shut off his headlights and drifted past Belinda's Victorian. Not a speck of light seeped through the windows. Every house on the street was dark, not even a porch light on.

Two blocks over he parked on a narrow street with an upscale market, a coffee shop, and a French bakery with baguettes in the display window. He slipped out of the van, blending into the darkness in his black sweat suit, a black-knit cap pulled low over his forehead. Standard attire for Special Ops night missions. He hadn't darkened the skin on his face. He doubted that he'd run into anyone at this hour, but if he did, a man in blackface would draw unwanted attention.

The Army had turned him into a lean-mean fighting machine, a far cry from his pudgy physique in high school. After leaving the Army he had maintained a daily routine of pushups, sit-ups and a five-mile run. Even now he could cover a hundred yards as fast as an NFL running back and not break a sweat. His long determined strides got him to her house in two minutes.

Moving silently in rubber-soled shoes, he skulked along the side of her house, antsy with anticipation. He couldn't wait to watch her, a vision of loveliness tucked safely in her bed.

The adjacent house was silent and dark, no light showing inside or out. His heart pounded as he crept up the steps to her back door. He stood still. Listened. Heard nothing. The Diva was fast asleep upstairs.

He peeped through the window beside the door. The kitchen was dark. Darkness was his friend. He'd chosen the back door for his entry. It had only one lock. The front door had a Yale lock and a two-pronged deadbolt. It also faced the street where anyone driving by might see him.

Holding the lock pick in his right hand, gripping his right hand with his left, he guided the pick into the lock. Earlier he had greased it with lard. That would lubricate the lock mechanism and muffle any metal-to-metal sounds.

The pick slipped in easily, no telltale clicks.

Although he had done this many times in the service of his country, his nerves chattered like castanets. His biggest concern was the alarm. After he opened the door, he would have only twenty seconds to disable the security system. He worked the pick, felt the tumbler give and pushed.

The door opened with a faint *chink*. He stepped inside.

His heart was a wild thing in his chest. He quickly closed the door and turned to the alarm system keypad on the wall beside the door. A red light blinked insistently, keeping time with his pounding heart. If she had changed the code, he was fucked.

With a gloved fingertip, he punched in the code. Held his breath.

The red light winked out and the green Ready light came on.

He let out the breath he'd been holding. Now he wouldn't have to use his clippers to cut the wires. Special Ops Rules: Always have a fallback plan. Cutting the wires would have allowed him to escape before the security service called to ask why her alarm was ringing.

But not enough time to complete his mission.

Her kitchen smelled of coffee and cinnamon, and he had a sudden urge to smoke. During his military days he'd smoked a pack a day. Cigarettes were cheap at the PX, but not in the civilian world. Four years ago they got so expensive he'd quit. He needed the money for more important things: following Belinda, flying around the country to attend her concerts, moving to New Orleans after she decided to relocate here.

Silent as smoke, he drifted through the kitchen to the hall. No need to worry about the motion detectors with the alarm disabled. Now he could focus on his mission. A drumbeat of anger pulsed his temples. None of this would have been necessary if The Diva had deigned to answer the telephone and talk to him. But she hadn't. Worse, when he'd called at eight and nine and ten, the phone rang, but nothing happened, no voicemail, nothing.

The Diva had disconnected her telephone.

He could not allow her to dismiss him like that.

He tiptoed down the pitch-dark hall beside the stairs. Testing each step lest the wood creak and wake her, he crept up to the second floor landing. Her bedroom was across the hall, six feet away. He stood there, motionless. His years in Special Ops had made him ultra sensitive to sounds and odors. Her bedroom door was open.

Even from here he could smell her sexy perfume.

Intoxicated by her scent, he stepped into the room.

The curtains were open, and light filtered in from the streetlamp outside her house. As his eyes adjusted to the gloom, he was able to pick out her dresser and her bed. Still he waited, enjoying the sweet sexy smell of her, the faint sound of her even breathing.

His vision sharpened. Now he could see her clearly. She had thrown off the sheet and lay on her side, curled up in her pale-blue satin baby-dolls. Exquisite. He licked his lips, enthralled by the tendrils of coppery hair spread over her pillow. Her cheek gleamed ivory in the streetlamp's pale light. Her left hand rested on her stomach. His eyes drifted to her crotch, imagining her pubic hair, a dark triangle below her hand. Imagining her nipples, pink and erect. Pure fantasy of course. Her genitals and nipples were hidden beneath the pajamas. But soon he would see them.

See them and fondle them and lick them.

The idea excited him so much he almost forgot why he was here. He edged to the bedside table. And saw her cell phone. Just like he'd figured. His darling Diva couldn't bear to sleep without a phone beside her. Thinking it would keep her safe.

She shifted her position and moaned softly.

His heart hammered his ribs. He froze. Held his breath. Let it out when her eyes remained shut. She stirred once more, then relaxed, her breathing even, too deep in slumber to wake up.

He moved closer. Close enough to reach out and touch her.

Oh, how he wanted to touch her. Transfixed, he gazed at her naked legs, her ivory-skinned face, her pink sensual lips. Her magnificent Victorian had a double-locked front door and a state-of-the-art security system with motion detectors and electronic contacts pasted to every window.

The Diva thought she was safe. She wasn't. Ignoring his pleas, she had thwarted his repeated attempts to talk to her. Now she would pay.

He took the cell phone off the bedside table and slid it in his pocket. Moved silently to her dresser. Studied the sensuous curved bottle beside her jewel case. Mambo for Women by Liz Claiborne. Upon learning this was her favorite perfume, he had gone to the Liz Claiborne website and read the description: *Mambo captures the flirty spirit of the women who wear it.*

Exactly! The Diva was flirty. The personification of the sexy sales pitch: succulent Mango, seductive red Hibiscus, romanced by Vanilla and Musk. Succulent and seductive. The sensuous curved bottle beckoned, seducing him. Another keepsake to cherish. Tempting, but she would miss it right away.

He edged back to the bed and admired her high cheekbones. Her magnificent breasts, round and prominent, pressed against the fabric of her baby-dolls. Her arched light-brown eyebrows were much nicer than his reddish-brown ones. Burning with desire, he watched her. His groin ached and his throat was dry and parched. He licked his lips.

No. He mustn't touch her. Not yet. But soon.

He crept to the door, padded downstairs to the safety of her kitchen, and powered up her cell phone. With a faint chime, the faceplate lit up. He chose Menu, then Account. *Please tell me the number.*

It did. He memorized the number, pressed Contacts and scrolled through the names. There weren't many. Five men were listed.

One was Frank Renzi. His rival. Her new savior. Or so she thought.

He memorized Renzi's number, too.

A sudden flash of swirling blue light burst through the kitchen window.

He froze. A police car outside her house.

He flattened himself against the wall.

Sweat dampened his forehead. He waited.

When the flashing blue light went away, he peeked out the window. Saw the cruiser continue down the street. That was a relief. But why was a cop car flashing a light on the Diva's house?

He'd been in here too long. He had to return the cell phone to Belinda's bedside table, reset the security alarm and get out of her house before the police cruiser came back. He crept upstairs and entered her bedroom.

Spellbound, he stared at her.

Illuminated by the pale light of the streetlamp, the Diva lay in her bed, blissfully unaware she was being watched. He could take her right now. His need was palpable, a heaviness in his gut, a tight feeling in his chest, a monstrous ache in his groin.

He wanted to touch her. Wanted to lick her. Wanted to fuck her.

But that would ruin his plan. He wanted to fuck her all right, not just tonight, every night. Forever.

Endless days and nights with the Diva.

She stirred and murmured something, an indistinct mutter.

His heart hammered his chest like a howitzer.

Get out before she wakes up!

Special Ops Rules: Get in and get out. If things go bad, run like hell.

But there was no need to panic. She had gone back to sleep.

Silently, he left the room and went downstairs.

In the kitchen, he re-armed the security system, stepped out into the darkness and closed the door. Euphoric, he walked away. A perfect mission.

His heart sang like an operatic soprano soaring above an orchestra. Watching the Diva sleep within the supposed safety of her house gave him an incredible sense of power. Better than any high he'd ever experienced.

He was in control. She wasn't.

A feeling like no other.

CHAPTER 32

Wednesday, 15 November

His cell phone jolted him awake. Not his Belinda phone. That one played a lovely bit of Mozart. His other phone was blasting Wagner's *Ride of the Valkyries*. He sat up on the futon and looked at his watch. Ten-thirty.

Fuck-all! He was due at work an hour ago.

When he answered, his boss screamed, "Where the hell are you? I got three pissed off customers calling me, asking where's their ride."

"I'm on my way. I had a flat tire and—"

"Flat tire, my ass! Why the hell didn't you *call* me?"

"I'm sorry, sir. I'll be there in a jiffy." Groveling and hating it.

"No you won't, asshole. You're fired. Your services are no longer required."

A resounding click and Mr. Nasty was gone. And so was his job.

He flopped back on the futon and rubbed his eyes. What would he do for money? He was damn near broke. He struggled to his feet and stretched his arms over his head. Disgusting odors wafted from his armpits. After his hours-long vigil outside Belinda's house last night, he'd been too tired to shower when he got home, had instead fallen into a deep sleep.

Too deep as it turned out.

He let Oz out of his cage, scooped him up and petted him. "What a sweet boy you are, Oz. Unlike my boss. The fucking asshole just fired me."

―――――

When Frank mentioned Kelly's father, Detective Inspector Ian Attaway was eager to help. Yesterday, when he told Kelly that Smythe-Jones's phone had been disconnected, she said her father had a friend on the London police force. Last night after work she'd called her father, got the man's name and phone number, and called him with the information.

Now Detective Inspector Attaway was explaining how Chicago Police Captain Rico Zavarella had helped him "nab the bugger who'd been fleecing British tourists," a tale of intrigue involving a Chicago street thug ripping off British passengers at O'Hare Airport.

Interesting story, but Vobitch would go ballistic if the call ran too long.

To his relief, Attaway finally wrapped up the story and said, "How can I be helping you?"

"I'm tracking a suspect, might be a killer. He used to be a security driver for Belinda Scully and—"

"The flute soloist? She played a marvelous concert at the Royal Festival Hall not long ago. Has something happened to her?"

"Not yet, but this guy is stalking her. Scully's manager fired him, wound up dead two days later under suspicious circumstances." He glanced at his watch. "I'll email you the details. Here's where I need help. My suspect met her at that Royal Festival Hall concert and said he worked security for some big-shot London businessman, a guy named Thaddeus Smythe-Jones."

"What a load of crap. Smythe-Jones is a businessman all right. Monkey business."

"That doesn't surprise me. The first time I called, he said my suspect was a terrific security expert, satisfied his every need, blah, blah, blah."

Attaway chuckled. "Smythe-Jones does tend to run on. He used to be a skip-tracer, rounding up dads that skip out on child support, folks with delinquent credit card accounts and such. Five years ago he got into more lucrative pursuits, put up a website and started selling fake ID's. You know the drill: *Get a New Identity and Start a New Life*."

"My suspect uses the name Barry Silverman. You think it's a fake?"

"Almost certainly. These skip-tracers know all the tricks. Must do or they'd never find the blokes. What better man to have in your corner if you want to ditch your old identity?"

"Last time I called Smythe-Jones his number it was disconnected."

"Probably a pay-as-you-go cell. He tells all his clients to use them, so don't count on tracing your man through his cell records. But here's a bit of good news. Smythe-Jones is a convicted felon out on parole. He reports to his control officer every week. Want me to talk to him?"

"That would be great. I need Silverman's real name and anything else you can get ASAP."

"Right-O," Ian said. "I'll ring you after I talk to him."

He hung up and checked the time. Eleven minutes. That should satisfy Vobitch. He thought about having another cup of coffee, decided against it. His stomach was too jumpy. Too many worries and unanswered questions.

Having scored the warrant for AK, Vobitch had been jubilant at yesterday's meeting. The Chief of Detectives had assigned a SWAT team to the operation. Anything to solve the Lakeview case. The homicide detectives from Districts One, Three and Eight had devised a plan. An hour from now they would execute the warrant and grab AK and his thugs. Or try to.

But he couldn't stop thinking about Silverman. Yesterday he'd put out a BOLO on Silverman's van. Once entered into the system, the tag and description would be electronically transmitted to laptops in the cruisers and unmarked cars. Every cop on duty would have it. With that many eyes looking for Silverman's van, it shouldn't take long to locate him.

Or so he hoped. If Attaway was correct, Silverman had a fake ID. What had he been in his previous life? A murderer? He was a stalker for sure, Belinda being the current object of his obsessive attention. A major worry.

He dialed her house, got shunted into voicemail and left a message for her to call him. Restless with energy, he went outside to get some fresh air.

———

Nauseated by the stench of too many bodies in a confined space, Antoine pressed the cell phone against his ear. Sweat dripped down his face. Detective Renzi sat beside him on a large upended milk crate, a reassuring presence. Stooped over in the van's rear compartment, two more detectives were eyeballing him, white guys with hard faces. The guy in charge, another white guy, leaned against the back door. He was built like a Sherman tank, had a big hooked nose and laser-beam gray eyes.

Eyes that sent a clear message. *Do what we say or I'll rip out your throat.*

Had no problem doing what they said, had a problem with what AK might say.

A voice spoke into his ear "Yo, speak to me."

"AK, we gotta talk, man."

"Heh, heh, heh." AK's evil chuckle. "How you doin', Antoine? How come you didn't wanna talk to me on Sunday, went and run off like that?"

He glanced at Renzi, who motioned with his hand, reminding him to repeat what AK said so they'd know what was happening. "Didn't wanna talk to you on Sunday, seemed like you was fixin' to kill me."

"No such thing! We just wanted to talk."

"You wanna talk, let's do it now. How come you done what you done to Chantelle?"

"You wanna talk, come on over to Iberville."

"Talk at Iberville?" he said, and looked at Renzi.

Renzi shook his head, scissored his hands back and forth. The cops had already told him: *No meet at the project. Meet him at City Park.*

"No way I be meeting you at Iberville, your posse be there. Got to be someplace neutral."

"You fixin' for a fight?"

"Damn straight. Meet me in the sculpture garden at the art museum in City Park. No guns, no backup, just you and me." His hand clenched in a fist. He wanted to ram it down AK's throat, take some teeth with it. "Let's see if you man enough to come by yourself and not hide behind your homeboys. I'll whup yo ass."

"Fuck you, Antoine. I don't need no help to whup yo ass. Meet me behind the Shell Station, corner of North Rampart and Esplanade, half an hour."

"North Rampart and . . ." Feeling four pairs of eyes on him, he tried to tell the location, realized the time factor was more important.

"Wait. Half an hour? That's too soon—"

Heard a loud click in his ear.

He looked at the hard-eyed cops. "AK says meet him behind the Shell Station, corner of North Rampart and Esplanade in half an hour."

"Fuck!" said the head honcho. "That's too soon! We need more time to set up."

———

Three loud thumps interrupted his pushups.

He glanced at Oz, cowering in his cage.

More thumps. Louder. Insistent. Then a deep voice. "I know you in there. Paint your van black don't fool me none. Open up!"

He scrambled to his feet and grabbed his wallet, composing excuses on his way to the door. When he opened it a dark presence confronted him.

Six-foot-six Aristide Ortiz, with a big frown on his ugly ebony-skinned puss. "You ain't paid your rent in three months."

He took a wad of bills out of his wallet, two hundred dollars, all that remained of Belinda's check. "I'm sorry, Mr. Ortiz. I've been too busy to get over to your house and pay you."

Got back an implacable stare. "You owe me twelve-hundred bucks."

The man's menacing eyes gave him pause. His buck knife was in the van. Useless. His arsenal was in a storage locker. He set his palm against the door, about to slam it shut.

A mean-looking Glock-9 appeared in Ortiz's hand.

"Lemme in, 'less you want a muthafuckin' hole in your chest."

He backed away and Ortiz followed him into the bed-sitting room.

"The fuck is this?" Gesturing at the cage with his Glock. "I tol' you no pets!"

Terrified by the man's loud voice, Oz cowered in a corner.

"It's just a rabbit to keep me company. He stays in his cage. He won't damage anything."

The landlord's nostrils flared. "Whole place stinks of shit. Where's the money?"

He thrust the cash at him. "Here's two hundred. I'll have to go to the bank for the rest."

Ortiz snatched the bills. "Two hundred ain't jackshit. A thousand bucks you still owe me."

"I told you. I'll go to the bank and get it."

"Bet yo ass you will or you be full of more holes than that rabbit cage. Noon tomorrow I be back with my sons. You don't have the loot, we bust your balls, truck yo stuff to the dump." He gestured at Oz. "Take yo rabbit home and have us some boiled bunny for dinner."

He wanted to punch the man's ugly puss, would have if a Glock-9 hadn't been aimed at his heart. He forced a smile. "I'll have it tomorrow, Mr. Ortiz, don't you worry."

"I ain't the one needs to worry. That be *you*." Ortiz turned and stomped out of the apartment.

A fierce ache pounded his temples. Ortiz was bad enough. His sons were probably just as big and twice as ugly. Go to the bank and get the cash? What a joke. He had no bank account. His only cash was in his storage locker. Special Ops Rules: Always prepare a Doomsday Plan in case things turn ugly. Like now.

He massaged his temples, his mind churning. Then he smiled.

What was he thinking? He didn't need a doomsday plan. Belinda hadn't been her usual gracious self lately, but this was an emergency. Once she understood the danger he was in, she was certain to help him.

After all he had done for her, how could she not?

CHAPTER 33

Frank jumped into Miller's unmarked Chevy Caprice.

"Get going," he said. "AK told Antoine to meet him at the Shell Station, North Rampart and Esplanade, half an hour."

Two more unmarked cars idled at the curb behind them: Kelly and Warren Wood in one, Otis Jones and Sam Wallace in another. The SWAT team Hummer was parked around the corner out of sight.

Miller pulled away from the curb, cutting off a startled motorist. "Don't leave us much time to set up. That's fourteen blocks from here."

"No kidding. Too many lights on Rampart. Take Burgundy. It's only got stop signs. Lean on the horn, we can blow through them."

Miller slewed right on Burgundy and floored the accelerator.

A woman on the sidewalk sprang back, glaring at them as they passed. In the wing mirror, he glimpsed Warren's car speeding north on Canal Street. Vobitch, riding in front with Warren, would coordinate the operation. Kelly was riding in back. She'd be safe with Vobitch. His big worry: Chuck Duncan was driving Antoine to the meet in the surveillance van. Antoine wouldn't be involved in the takedown, but Vobitch wanted him nearby in case AK didn't show and Antoine had to call him again.

His radio crackled to life. Vobitch with an update. "The phone tech pinpointed AK's cell phone location, corner of North Rampart and Esplanade, must have been at the Shell Station when he took the call. All units proceed with caution. No lights, no sirens. Chuck, park the van at the corner of Esplanade and Burgundy, get in back and stay there. Out."

Miller shook his head. "Bad news."

Frank nodded as they zoomed east on Burgundy toward Esplanade, Miller touching the brakes before each intersection and leaning on the horn.

Five blocks down, nine to go. The radio crackled to life again.

Vobitch: "Dispatch says two D-Eight patrol cars are in the vicinity of the Shell Station. I told Dispatch to send those units as backup. Out."

Bad idea, Frank thought. The patrol cops hadn't been briefed. But it wasn't his call. Vobitch was running the show. No matter how well you planned an operation, shit happened.

Miller slewed to a stop at the next intersection, horn blaring as a yellow taxi crossed in front of them. Four blocks to Esplanade. Ten minutes to get in position. Their hastily revised plan: Block the escape routes. Warren, Kelly and Vobitch would park two blocks west of the Shell Station. Otis and Sam would park on Rampart across from the station. Miller would park their car one block south of the station on Burgundy.

That eased his mind somewhat. They would be near the surveillance van so he could watch out for Antoine. Or so he hoped.

When they reached Esplanade, the black surveillance van was already parked on the corner of Burgundy, headed north toward the Shell Station.

"Chuck made good time," Miller said.

He nodded. Tension clawed his gut like a jungle cat tearing meat.

Miller eased the Chevy across Esplanade. This part of Burgundy was one-way west and they were driving east. Fortunately, no cars were approaching. Miller wheeled into a driveway, reversed direction and pulled into a vacant space a half block down from Esplanade. From here, Frank could just make out the rear fender of the surveillance van.

An adrenaline rush jumped his heart rate, the buzz he always got before the action. He racked his SIG. Miller did the same with his Glock.

As they left the car a bald man with a gray beard came out of the house across the street and gawked at them. Like Miller, Frank wore loose-fitting navy-blue sweats, but Miller was an imposing presence: a six-foot-six black man with a shaven pate and a soul patch. Both of them were bulked out with body armor and packing semi-automatics.

Not your average Joes in the 'hood. The gray-bearded man jumped into a lemon yellow VW Bug and drove off.

Frank gestured at the small white cottage with green shutters beside their car. "Let's cut through the backyard and check out the Shell Station."

With guns drawn, they crept alongside the one-story house. In the backyard, two white bed-sheets on a clothesline flapped in the breeze. Near the back fence, flies buzzed the lids of four black trashcans.

Off in the distance, a siren sounded.

"Damn," Miller said. "AK hears that, he might run."

A flash of motion exploded off to their left. His heart jolted.

Three men with automatic rifles, AK and his goons racing toward Esplanade. And the surveillance van.

He took off running. If they made the surveillance van, Antoine was dead. The van looked innocuous enough, chipped black paint, dark-tinted windows, a blacked out rear window.

But if AK spotted the telltale antennas on the roof . . .

A giant fist gripped his gut. He ran faster. Beside him, Miller matched his speed, their feet pounding the sidewalk as they raced toward the corner.

The surveillance van was moving. Good, he thought. Get Antoine out of there. He saw it back up, then pull forward. Then, a burst of shots.

The van lurched to a stop and rocked back and forth. More shots.

His heart slammed his chest. He rounded the corner and stopped, horrified. Dancing alongside the van, AK raked it with automatic weapon fire, heavy-duty slugs penetrating the van like a hot knife cutting butter.

He fired three rounds. Saw AK's baggy pants jerk as a slug hit them. Miller was firing too, but AK whirled and ran behind a row of hedges in front of the next house.

More automatic fire, directed at them now.

They ran for cover, charged across the lawn of the two-story house on the corner and ducked behind the porch. He motioned at Miller to circle the house and studied the van. Even from here, thirty yards away, he could see blood on the windshield. Chuck was hit. No telling about Antoine.

He keyed his handset: "Officer down at Burgundy and Esplanade. AK shot up the surveillance van. Renzi and Miller in pursuit."

He wanted to check the van and see if Antoine was okay, but another burst of automatic fire came at him, too many rounds to count. He dropped to the ground and crawled under the porch.

More shots, AK's thugs pinning him down with AK-47s. A fine weapon, fast and accurate, easy to use. Load the 30-round magazine with 7.62x39 caliber hollow-point slugs and it was a killer.

Shrill sirens filled the air, approaching from all directions.

Hugging the ground, he crawled to the other end of the porch. No more shots, lots of sirens. He squirmed out from under the porch. Eased his torso up until his head was level with the porch floor. Looked around the corner.

Twenty yards away AK stood on the sidewalk, wearing a white shirt and baggy cargo pants. Acting like he didn't have a care in the world, he reached into his pocket and pulled out a fresh magazine.

Frank heard a faint chink as AK rammed the clip into his AK-47.

The street was deserted. Hearing this many shots, anyone in the houses along the street knew enough to stay inside.

A District-Eight squad car with flashing lights barreled down the street, siren screaming. AK opened up on it with his automatic, smoke rising from the barrel. The sound was deafening.

He saw spent brass casings scatter over the sidewalk. Saw the left front tire of the squad car blow out, an explosion of black rubber spiraling along the pavement. The car slewed to a stop. He took aim at AK, but AK broke left, firing as he zigzagged down the sidewalk.

One of the patrol cops went down and lay still beside the squad, arms flung out. AK strolled toward the cop and raised his weapon.

Frank braced his shooting hand on his left forearm, took careful aim and fired. Saw AK spin left, drop his weapon and clutch his shoulder.

A barrage of bullets came at him. AK's goons pinning him down again.

He dove under the porch.

The giant cat clawed his gut, and guilty thoughts churned his mind.

Was Antoine okay? Antoine was the innocent bystander inside the van, because Frank had talked him into helping them corral AK. And what about Chuck? He'd seen a lot of blood on the van windshield.

He flattened himself on the ground. Inched forward under the porch. Saw AK run through the yard beside the next house.

He took aim and fired.

Verging on panic, he clamped the cell phone to his ear, silently begging his beloved to answer. *Please answer, just this once.*

Her voicemail came on again. Enraged, he clenched his fist. He'd called four times in the last thirty minutes. His stomach was an acid bath, eating him alive, killing him slowly. He had to talk to her.

"Belinda, it's Barry. Please pick up. I need to talk to you. It's an emergency!" He scratched his cheek, willing her to answer. "Please answer the phone, Belinda. I have to talk to you. It's an emergency."

His fingernails dug into his cheek.

She'd pay for this, making him grovel.

"Stop calling me, Mr. Silverman. I don't want to talk to you."

His heart soared at the sound of her voice. "I'm sorry to disturb you, Belinda, but my landlord was just here, threatening me. I'm behind on my rent. He's coming back tomorrow and—"

"That's your problem. Call the police. Let them handle—"

"Wait, you don't understand. He had a gun. If you give me back my job, even for a few hours a day, I can pay him and everything will be fine."

The acid in his gut came to a full rolling boil. She was making him beg. How could she do this to him? How could she be so mean?

"I don't want you working for me. Ever since I got home from New York you've done nothing but upset me. If you don't stop calling, I'll go to court and get a restraining order."

Red-hot pokers of rage ripped his gut.

After all he'd done for her, the bitch was threatening him.

"Belinda, how can you say that? I'm your biggest fan. I've gone the extra mile for you. How can you be so ungrateful?"

"Stop calling me. Stop watching my house. I don't want to talk to you."

Humiliation flamed his cheeks like a blowtorch. "Your fans won't think much of you when I tell them how mean you've been to me."

"*I'm not being mean!*" she shouted. "*Leave me alone!*"

He felt something sticky and examined his hand. Bright red blood smeared his fingers. He touched his cheek. Thanks to her hateful words he'd scratched the zit beside his nose until it bled. How could she be so cruel? Didn't she feel even a shred of sympathy?

"I didn't mean that, Belinda. I'd never do anything to hurt you—"

"Don't call here again. I don't want to talk to you ever again. I don't want to see you again, either. Not ever. Find someone else to bother."

A click louder than a gunshot on a rifle range sounded in his ear.

A message of utter finality. The Diva never wanted to talk to him again.

Never wanted to see him again.

Vengeful thoughts flitted through his mind like furry gray bats.

To escape the withering firepower, Frank dove underneath the porch, muscled forward on his elbows and scrambled out the other end. Miller, crouched beside the house, crawled closer and said, "AK's goons left their car at the station. We got 'em boxed in."

"Fine, but AK hit one of the uniforms." He heard sirens, more backup and medics to tend the wounded. "You think it's just the three of them?"

"Christ, I hope so."

"I think I winged AK in the shoulder." He got on his radio. "Attention all units, this is Renzi. Officer down on Burgundy between Esplanade and

Kerlerec. Get SWAT over here. One subject is wounded. They've got automatic weapons. Miller and I are in pursuit."

Static on the radio. Then Vobitch: "SWAT's on their way, Frank. Stay put and wait for them."

"Tell them to hurry. Out."

He looked at Miller. "Fuck waiting. Did you check the van?"

"No. Too busy chasing AK's goon—"

Miller broke off at the sound of automatic fire. They bolted toward the street. As they reached the corner of the house a blue-on-white squad with two uniforms inside flashed by, siren screaming, light bar flashing.

A burst of gunfire. The windshield of the squad car disintegrated.

"Fuckers are two houses up, across the street," Miller said. "I saw the muzzle flash."

The patrol car doors opened like butterfly wings, and the driver dived to the pavement. Blood dripped down his face. He pulled his weapon and crouched behind the car door.

Frank motioned to Miller, and they circled the adjacent Creole cottage, footsteps muffled by weedy grass. He registered motion at a window as a curtain fell back into place. Christ, there were people inside. If AK took hostages, this would be a clusterfuck.

More gunfire. They ran toward the street and stopped at the corner of the house. Diagonally ahead to their left, two uniforms knelt beside a patrol car, firing at a house across the street.

"AK, I'm hit! The motherfuckers hit me!"

"One down," Miller said. "Look!"

AK and Dead-Eye raced across the street. No sign of Spider. AK had no weapon, clutching his shoulder with one hand. Dead-Eye sprayed the squad car with his AK-47. One officer flopped on the ground and his partner squirmed over to help him. Crouched beside the house, Frank and Miller fired continuously at AK and Dead-Eye, but they were zigzagging targets.

AK shouted something and they split up. AK veered east, away from them, Dead-Eye ran north toward the Shell Station.

"Take Dead-Eye," Frank said. "I'll go after AK. Be careful!"

Miller took off as ear-splitting sirens filled the air. Frank rammed a fresh magazine into his SIG. If he cornered AK, he wanted a full clip. He vaulted a low split-rail fence between two cottages, entered the backyard and stopped. Blood smeared a six-foot rustic pine fence, no telling what was on the other side. AK might not have his AK-47, but that didn't mean he was unarmed.

A softball-sized rock lay on the ground near a downspout on the house. He ran over and grabbed it and lobbed the rock over the fence.

Bam-bam-bam. Three shots in rapid succession hit the fence.

On his hands and knees, he crawled to the spot where the fence met the house. Put one eye to the two-inch gap.

AK sat on the ground, back pressed against a tree trunk, legs splayed. Bright red blood soaked his white shirt. The maggot held a semi-automatic pistol in one hand, clutched his shoulder with the other.

He heard more sirens. Help was on the way, SWAT probably, and more patrol cars. He could call in AK's location and wait for backup.

But screw that. He wanted to take the fucker himself.

"Put the gun on the ground and put your hands on your head."

"Fuck you!" A bullet shattered one of the pine slats.

"You're surrounded by cops. Put the gun down."

"That you, Renzi?"

"Right. Give it up, AK. Put down the gun."

"What then? You gonna shoot me?"

"Not if you put down the gun."

But he had no way of knowing if the bastard did or not. He saw a loose knot in a pine board two feet ahead of him, crawled forward and punched it with his fist. The knot fell into the yard.

Blam! A shot penetrated the wood above his head.

"Drop the gun, AK. I can see you. If that gun's not ten feet away from you in five seconds, you're gonna lose your fucking gold tooth."

Five seconds passed. Ten. Fifteen seconds of silence. He gave it another thirty seconds and cautiously peeped through the knothole.

AK's head lolled forward on his chest, eyes closed. His right hand lay in his lap, fingers curled around the semi-automatic. Tempting. AK was holding a recently fired gun, GSR on his hands. No wits, no worries.

The King of Iberville had slaughtered Chantelle and disfigured her face, had suckered Antoine into a crime he would never have committed on his own. Now Antoine might be dead. But if he shot AK, he would be no better than the lawless little maggots that were roaming the streets, administering their twisted brand of justice and terrorizing innocent people.

He hauled himself upward, rolled over the top of the rustic-pine fence and dropped to the ground on the other side. AK opened his eyes. Raised his blood-smeared hand. Tossed the semi-automatic on the ground.

"Don't shoot, man. I give up."

CHAPTER 34

10:02 P.M.

"Today New Orleans police arrested the man they believe robbed a Lakeview convenience store last month," said the television reporter, a somber-eyed woman with long dark hair and a narrow face. "Twenty-two-year-old Atticus Kroll has a lengthy arrest record, but no convictions. The woman taken hostage during the robbery later died."

Speaking over footage of the bullet-riddled NOPD surveillance van, she said, "Kroll's arrest came at significant cost. One police officer died and three others were wounded, one seriously. Another man, believed to be a member of Kroll's gang, also died. Police have not released his name."

When footage of NOPD officers taking AK and Dead-Eye into the lockup appeared, Frank grabbed the clicker and shut off the television.

"I hate when they put my picture on TV."

Beside him on the sofa, Kelly curled a leg underneath her and faced him. "They were shooting at you with fucking AK-47s. It's a miracle you're alive."

He felt a flick of anger, then a twist of guilt. He didn't consider it a miracle, but he felt bad about Chuck Duncan. Thirty slugs had penetrated the surveillance van. Duncan had died at the hospital.

With an angry motion Kelly drank from a bottle of Bud Light and set it on her coffee table. "These little shits kill people for no reason."

And drag innocent people into their muck-filled orbit, Frank thought, recalling Antoine's terror-filled eyes when he threw a blanket over his head to shield his face from the cameras and hustled him into Miller's car.

"AK and his thugs were gunning for us. I think AK's posse saw the van drive past Iberville and tipped him off. Antoine said Chuck saw AK coming, pushed him on the floor, climbed forward and got behind the wheel."

"And they shot him. Jesus, he's got a wife and three kids."

"He didn't deserve to die, and I'm sorry he did. But at least we got AK and two of his thugs off the street."

Her mouth quirked. "Right. Spider's dead, and Kenyon captured Dead-Eye while you were doing your hero act with AK."

"What do you mean, hero act? I was doing my job."

He hated it when people second-guessed him. His ex-wife had done it for years: *Why do you take these dangerous assignments? If you cared about me and Maureen, you'd stop trying to be a hero.* Conveniently forgetting that she'd known he was a cop when she married him.

"Why didn't you wait for backup?" Kelly said. "AK wasn't going anywhere, bleeding the way he was. He could have shot you!"

And I could have shot him, Frank thought. He was glad he had resisted the temptation. Split-second decisions made in the heat of battle could give you nightmares for the rest of your life.

She touched his cheek. "I was worried about you."

"I base my decisions on the situation. You're a cop, Kelly. You should understand that."

"I understand the cop part, but I'm not sure I understand you. You act like you're the only one that wants to get the badasses off the street. I do too, but I don't go one-on-one with an armed killer when other cops are around."

"Lighten up, okay? It's the testosterone factor." He grinned. "Back in the dark ages, the guys inherited the go-for-the-jugular-gene."

No smile, but her expression softened. "What did the girls get?"

"They got to go home with the hero and make love and enjoy life."

They didn't expect the hero to hide from the bad guys.

"I did that before, Frank. That's not how it turned out."

Acid roiled his gut. She couldn't forget what happened to Terry. Now she was afraid it might happen to him. If this continued to be an issue, they were in serious trouble. Cops were trained to run toward danger, not away from it. His basic nature was to take risks, not play it safe. He wasn't going to stop doing what made him feel most alive, flirting with danger and winning.

"I can't change who I am, Kelly. I took a risk today and lived to tell the tale." He traced her lips with his finger. "You might do it too someday, if someone you care about is in danger. We all take risks. You took a risk when you invited me over for dinner last Saturday. That turned out okay, didn't it?"

A smile played over her lips. "I can't argue with that."

"No reason to argue. This was a rough day. We're alive. Let's enjoy it."

She pulled him close and said, "You're right, Frank. Let's enjoy it."

Belinda shut down the computer and yawned. Almost eleven. Where had the time gone? Still, this had been a productive day. After lunch she had emailed her prospective business agents, noting the dates she would be in New York to interview them. Then she'd phoned the managers of the orchestras she would solo with during the holidays and asked them to send the rehearsal schedule.

She was taking charge of her life and it felt good. Her confidence was growing. It was like learning a new solo. The first time through, there were mistakes, but after hours of practice she perfected the piece.

This afternoon she had played the Zwilich and the Gershwin twice, perfectly. Anticipating the reaction to her performance, she smiled. The Louisville audience was certain to love both pieces.

She rose from the desk, made sure the curtains were closed, shut off the light and left the office. Checking the curtains was now a nightly habit. The only unpleasant part of her day had been the call from Silverman, begging her to answer, saying it was an emergency.

Nonsense. It was a ploy to get her to talk to him. And she had.

In no uncertain terms she had told him he couldn't have his job back. His threat to tell her fans she'd been mean to him was ludicrous. And she had no intention of taking out a restraining order. According to an article she'd read, that might make things worse. No, she had handled it perfectly.

Calmly and politely, she had told him she didn't want to talk to him, didn't want to see him ever again. Well, maybe not so calmly. She recalled raising her voice at one point, something she tried not to do, even when she got exasperated with a clerk over a bill.

But Silverman was worse than any clerk, begging and pleading, saying he needed money. How pathetic. She pictured his acne scarred cheeks, pale blue eyes and frizzy brown hair. Silverman clearly had problems with women. She couldn't believe she had ever considered rehiring him.

Frank had left a message asking her to call him. She hadn't. She wasn't going to obsess about Frank and his girlfriend. Frank was history. There were plenty of attractive men out there. She might even meet one in Louisville.

She checked to make sure the security system was armed, shut off the lights in the foyer and went upstairs to her bedroom. Encased in clear plastic, her royal-blue performance gown hung from the hook on her closet door. She still hadn't decided which of the outfits spread out on her bed to bring to Louisville. She picked up the aqua pantsuit. A silk outfit might be too light and frothy. Kentucky could be cold in November.

An odd sound sent her stomach into sickening freefall.

There it was again. A loud thump.

Her mouth went dry and her heart pounded in terror. She dropped the pantsuit on the bed and massaged her fingers. They were icy cold and goose bumps ran up and down her arms. Willing herself to be calm, she expanded her diaphragm and drew a deep breath the way she did before performances to control her breathing.

All the doors were locked. The security system was armed.

No one could get in her house without her knowing it.

Padding barefoot over the rug, she went to the bedroom door and stuck her head into the hall. Silence. No thumps, no bumps.

"You're being silly," she said aloud. "Stop imagining things."

She returned to her bed and studied her outfits.

Stop dithering. Make a decision, go to bed and get some rest. Her teal-green dress would be perfect for the after-party. She would take two pairs of slacks, one for the plane, one for rehearsal, and two light-weight tops to go with them.

An image of Jake sprang into her mind: his dark eyes and sweet smile. Unwilling to give in to grief, she shook her head. Her dearest friend was gone, but if Jake were here, he would be proud of her. His untimely death had forced her to grow up and take control of her life. Now, a week later, she was not only mastering it, she was enjoying it.

Everything would be perfect in Louisville.

Thursday, 16 November 2:10 A.M.

He scooped ringlets of brown hair out of the sink, flushed them down the toilet and studied his image in the medicine cabinet mirror. With his head shaved, he looked a bit like Robert DeNiro in *Taxi Driver*. "Who you talking to?" he said to his reflection in the mirror. "Are you talkin' to me?"

He uttered a sardonic laugh. Maybe he'd run that line past Belinda.

Are you talkin' to me?

The Diva didn't want to talk to him, but she would.

Her fans could eat their hearts out. From now on the only person she'd be playing for would be him. Once she came to her senses and realized they were meant for each other, she would kiss him and fondle him and rub her luscious body against him and beg him to fuck her.

He took a bottle of extra-strength ibuprofen out of the medicine cabinet and dry-swallowed four capsules, hoping to ease the massive headache that pounded his temples. He scooped the other meds in the cabinet into a plastic bag, shut out the light, walked down the hall to the kitchen and opened the refrigerator. Nothing but bare shelves. Only a half-empty quart of orange juice and plastic containers of catsup and mustard remained.

Earlier he had shredded the Belinda memorabilia he'd collected over the years. His painstaking labor of love. Twenty folders full of concert reviews, newspaper and magazine articles, and his handwritten notes about items on her website. He had even shredded her photographs, glossy full-color prints that reminded him of happier days. Days when his beloved was only a yearning in his heart. Days when he'd finally made her notice him. Days when he had happily served in her employ.

But she had dismissed him as if he were a cockroach.

After all he'd done for her.

I don't want to talk to you ever again. I don't want to see you again, either. Not ever.

How could she abandon him in his hour of desperate need?

The pain of unrequited love crushed his chest like a boa constrictor. That's what love was about: pain. Pain worse than a root-canal without Novocain. The few times in his life he'd grown to love someone, the result had always been the same. Rejection and pain.

He checked the file cabinet to make sure it was empty. No more worries about utility bills and credit cards now. Turning to the CD rack, he removed his Belinda CDs and four of his other favorites, and tucked them into his knapsack. The safe house he'd found had no electricity, but he had bought a battery-powered boom-box at a drug store. The water was disconnected, too. He'd be roughing it, but he had endured worse on Special Ops missions.

He had also emptied his Doomsday storage locker. The cash and his survival kit were locked in the van. His arsenal was hidden at his new abode. Recalling his landlord's threat, he smiled a grim smile of satisfaction.

Ortiz would find nothing of value here, just ratty furniture and the Oz droppings he'd taken pleasure in scattering over the carpet. Ortiz would probably take his remaining classical CDs and sell them, but so what? He had the ones he wanted. The Diva's CDs would keep him company until he had the real thing. He pulled a black-knit cap over his newly shaven head. From inside his cage, the Wizard of Oz gazed up at him with his sky-blue eyes.

His precious little bunny. Alert. Ever watchful for predators.

At this hour Oz was usually asleep, but this was a special night.

"Time to hit the road, Oz." He picked up the cage and left.

CHAPTER 35

Thursday, 16 November

When the phone rang, she lowered the spoonful of cottage cheese and pineapple into the dish. Unwilling to miss any business calls, she had reconnected her landline this morning. Each time it rang, her heart jolted and her palms dampened with sweat.

She rose from the table, went to the wall-phone and checked Caller ID. Not Silverman, but not someone she wanted to talk to, either.

"Hello," she said crisply, "Belinda Scully speaking."

"Belinda, it's Frank Renzi. How are you doing?"

I'd be fine if I didn't keep getting phone calls from people I don't want to talk to.

"Okay. I'm eating lunch."

"I called you yesterday. Didn't you get my message?"

She gritted her teeth. He was acting like an inquisitor, badgering her. If he started an argument, she'd hang up on him.

"I've been busy."

"I just found out Silverman isn't who he says he is. His real name is Benjamin Stoltz. Do you know anyone by that name?"

Her headache throbbed. She rued the day she'd met the man.

"I don't think so."

"Think, Belinda. It might be important."

"I meet a lot of people. I don't remember a Benjamin Stoltz."

Still, the name did sound familiar. Nagged by a vague recollection, she closed her eyes. In a flash it came to her.

"I knew a violinist named Stoltz. We played in an All-State orchestra together in high school. I forget her first name. Ruth, maybe? Roberta? No, I think it was Rachael."

"Rachael Stoltz?"

"Yes. I didn't know her well. I think she had a brother, but he wasn't in the orchestra."

"Did you ever meet him?"

"If I did, I don't remember it. That was ages ago."

"What did Rachael look like?"

"She was very attractive. Long dark hair, green eyes. All the boys were gaga about her."

"No resemblance to Barry Silverman?"

She laughed aloud. "None. He's got frizzy brown hair and blue eyes."

"Remember that voicemail message you told me about, the one with the threat?"

Chills danced down her spine. She would never forget it. "I remember."

"Did he ever call again?"

"No, just that one call."

"Tell me about the voice."

"It's hard to describe. A raspy whisper, sort of like one of those mafia mobsters in a B-movie."

"What about Silverman? Have you heard from him?"

"Yes. He called me Monday afternoon after I got home from New York."

"New York?"

"Yes," she said, irritated. "I went to Long Island for Jake's funeral."

"Oh. Sorry. I forgot. That must have been difficult."

Difficult? Was that all he could say? How about an emotional ordeal that she'd carry with her the rest of her life? Jake's parents grief-stricken over the death of their only child.

"It was. Did you get the results of the toxicology tests?"

"Not yet. What did Silverman say when he called?

"I didn't answer, but he kept leaving messages. He said he knew I was home because my car was out front and the lights were on in the office. I looked outside but I didn't see his van. Later he called and left another message. He knew I was having chicken for dinner. I bought a barbequed chicken. He must have seen me."

"He's watching your house and following you. You need to hire a security team."

"Not now! I've got a concert this weekend. Besides, I took care of him." She felt a burst of pride. She didn't need Frank to solve her problems. "He called again later. I was sick of hearing his messages so I picked up and told him not to call me anymore. I told him I never wanted to see him again."

"How did he take it? What did he say?"

She twisted the telephone cord around her fingers. Think about the concert. Think about the music. Think about anything but Barry Silverman. Stoltz. Whatever his name was.

"I can't waste time worrying about him. I've got a concert this weekend. My flight to Louisville leaves tomorrow at ten-thirty."

"How are you getting to the airport?"

"I'll drive myself and leave my car in short term parking. I'll only be gone three days."

"I'd feel better if you checked into a hotel tonight."

A chill wracked her. *Maybe you're nervous about your concert in Louisville, Belinda. After all, it's the first one you'll play since Jake died. Jake won't be with you, but I will. I'll be in the front row so don't slip up.*

Silverman's words had frightened her badly. The thought of seeing him terrified her. Damned if she'd admit that to Frank, though. She wasn't some helpless little girl.

"I am not checking into a hotel. I'm staying right here in my own house. I'll be fine."

"You blew Silverman off. He's dangerous—"

"Frank, I'm not staying in a hotel and I'm not going to argue about it."

A long silence. Then, "Okay, but lock your doors when you're home. If Silverman shows up, do not let him in. Call me right away. If *anything* unusual happens, call me."

Frank seemed awfully worried about her all of a sudden. Maybe his detective girlfriend was giving him problems. But that was his worry, not hers.

"Nothing's going to happen, Frank. I'll be fine."

―――

Unsettled by what Belinda had said, Frank tapped his pen on the desk. Yesterday she'd blown Silverman off. She didn't get it. Silverman was a stalker, and stalkers didn't go away quietly when women rejected them, they escalated. Tomorrow she would fly to Louisville, but for the next twenty-four hours she'd be on her own with no one to protect her. And he had no clue where Silverman was. The BOLO on his van had drawn a blank.

He fingered the scar on his chin. Belinda's description of the voicemail threat she'd received was also worrisome. A raspy whisper. Kelly's rape victim had said her attacker spoke in a raspy whisper. She had also identified his vehicle. An E-Series Ford van like Silverman's. But the rapist's van was black.

He punched Kelly's work number into his cell phone.

"Kelly O'Neil."

The sound of her voice brought a smile to his face. "Hi, Kelly. Your father's London cop connection helped a lot."

"That's good," she said, her tone listless.

"You sound kind of down. Are you okay?"

"I keep thinking about Chuck. The funeral's on Saturday, cops coming in from all over."

Another funeral with cops coming in from all over. Had many had come for Terry's funeral, he wondered. "I'm sorry. That must bring back painful memories."

When she didn't respond, he said, "Ian Attaway called me with Silverman's real name. Benjamin Stoltz. S-T-O-L-T-Z. Any chance you could run the name through the data bases? I'd do it, but I have to write the Incident Report on yesterday's craziness."

Miller had taken four days off to visit his family in Atlanta, which left him to write the report. He hated writing reports, and this one was crucial. Every detail had to be precise or the judge might dismiss the case. Chuck would have died for nothing.

"I'll give it a shot," Kelly said. "I have to interview a witness on another case this afternoon."

"Thanks, that would be great. I just called Belinda. She didn't remember Benjamin Stoltz, but she played in an orchestra with a violinist named Rachael Stoltz. Could you run that name too?"

"Sure. Same last name, I'll probably get lots of hits. Want me to call if I find something?"

"Yes. Call my cell in case I'm out of the office. This guy's a ticking time-bomb. Belinda blew him off yesterday. I tried to get her to stay in a hotel tonight, but she won't. She's got a concert in Louisville this weekend."

"Maybe we'll find him while she's in Louisville. I'll run those names. You never know what the damsel detective might find."

Amused by her playful comment, he smiled but quickly sobered.

No sign of Silverman's van. Nothing on the Goines kid, either. And Silverman was out there, a stalker rejected by the object of his obsession. Dangerous. Rejected stalkers could be deadly.

CHAPTER 36

Her eyes fluttered open. Pale sunlight was creeping through her window.

With a vague sense of foreboding, she rolled over and looked at her clock radio—6:30—and her alarm went off, an insistent beep. She silenced the alarm and threw off the sheet. Her flight wasn't until ten-thirty, but she wanted to leave the house by eight-thirty. That would give her plenty of time to get through security, find her gate and relax.

She heard a faint sigh. Her skin prickled.

"Good morning, Belinda."

For an instant, she thought she had imagined the voice.

Fear jolted her wide awake. She gasped.

Silverman stood in the doorway, smiling. No, not a smile, a suggestive leer. But where was his hair? His frizzy brown hair was gone. He looked like some futuristic militiaman in a sci-fi movie. His head was hairless. Even his eyebrows were gone, which accentuated his pale-blue eyes.

Predatory eyes, fixed on her.

"What's the matter, Belinda? You seem frightened."

Her heart slammed her ribs. "I'm not frightened."

"Good. No reason to be afraid of me."

"I'm not." She wasn't frightened, she was terrified.

"Of course not. We're friends, aren't we, Belinda." Delivered in a flat voice edged with anger.

"I have to go to the airport."

He smiled, baring his teeth like a crocodile about to devour a flamingo. "But how will you get there? I offered to drive you, but you refused."

Her mind scrabbled for a way out. "I ordered a cab, but they'll call first."

"Will they?" He smiled. "What time are they coming?"

Realizing that defense was futile, she swung her legs over the side of the bed. Her naked legs. Aware of her filmy-thin baby-dolls, she hugged her arms against her chest, felt the rapid thud of her heartbeat. "How did you get in?"

"That's not important. Now that you've had a nice restful sleep, I bet you're raring to go. Ready to go knock 'em dead in Louisville?"

Fighting the rigidity of her cheek muscles, she forced a smile. "Yes."

"Gee, can I come with you?"

Her stomach cramped, a sickening jolt of fear. "Is that what you want?"

"Of course," he snapped. "But you don't seem to want me with you."

She said nothing. What could she say? *I don't want you with me. I want you out of my bedroom, out of my house, out of my life.*

"Gee, Belinda, you're not a very good hostess. You haven't offered me anything to eat, not even a cup of coffee."

She stared at him. Why was he acting as though he was her guest?

"Let's have breakfast. It's not good to travel on an empty stomach."

She parsed the words. Was he going to let her go to the airport?

In an angry gesture, he jerked his thumb. "Downstairs, Belinda."

"Let me put on my robe." Keeping her voice even, though she wanted to scream.

"No." His pale-blue eyes were shards of ice. "I like you better in your sexy baby-dolls."

Do what he wants. Placate him and maybe he'll leave. Numbly, she rose from the bed and approached the door. Shrank back as she passed him, disgusted by his rank odor. Gripping the cherry-wood banister, she descended the stairs, aware of his presence behind her, so close she could feel his breath on her neck. At the foot of the stairs, she hesitated.

The front door was twelve feet away. Maybe she could run for it.

No. He would catch her and be furious. Better to keep up a pretense of civility and wait for a better opportunity to escape. Clinging to this slender thread of hope, she preceded him into the kitchen. She leaned against the counter and faced him, clutching her arms over her breasts.

She forced a smile. "What would you like for breakfast?"

"Scrambled eggs. Make enough for two so we can eat together."

"I don't usually eat a big breakfast. Just orange juice and some fruit yogurt. And tea."

"Well, I wouldn't want to make you do anything you don't *want* to do." With a mocking smile, he said, "Make me some scrambled eggs and coffee. After watching you sleep all night, I'm ravenous."

All night? She felt like a cockroach had crawled down her neck.

She gave herself a silent pep talk. *Concentrate! This is a performance, and you know how to perform. Lull him into a false sense of security and figure out how to escape.*

Aware of his malodorous presence ten feet away, feeling his rapacious eyes on her scantily clad body, she went to the refrigerator. Took out three eggs, milk and butter. Set butter in a frying pan to melt. Beat the eggs and added milk. The activity soothed her. Keep busy and don't look at him.

If she looked at him she might dissolve into helpless tears.

When the scrambled eggs were done she scooped them onto a plate and carried it to her butcher-block table.

"That looks good, Belinda. Get your OJ and yogurt and sit down."

She did as she was told and sat down opposite him. But there was no way she could eat. Dread seethed in her gut like a giant mass of maggots.

He forked scrambled eggs into his mouth, chewed hungrily and swallowed. "What do you want, Belinda?"

"Want?"

"Yes. Right now. What do you want?"

She wiped her sweaty palms on a napkin. "I want you to leave."

"Aw, gee. That's not very nice."

"I need to get ready." She checked the time. Amazing. It was only ten before seven. He'd been here twenty minutes. Correction. He'd been here all night, watching her while she slept. Only twenty minutes ago had she discovered his disgusting presence.

"If I leave now, will you invite me back sometime?"

"Yes."

He chuckled, an evil grating sound. "Don't lie to me, Belinda."

She studied his outfit. He didn't appear to have a weapon, but his black coveralls had a lot of pockets, enough to conceal a gun or a knife. Even if he had no weapon, he had his fists. He was bigger than she was. And stronger.

"I need to shower and get dressed so I can go to the airport."

He forked eggs into his mouth and stared at her. "The airport," he said.

"Yes."

"Your flight to Louisville."

"Yes."

"But I don't have a ticket. You didn't get one for me, did you?"

"No." *And you know it,* she wanted to scream. *Stop baiting me!*

"Well, I guess we'll just stay here and spend a nice weekend together."

The mass of maggots in her stomach turned to molten lava, seething and heaving. He had no intention of letting her go to Louisville. She should have done what Frank said and stayed at a hotel. But it was too late for that now. Too late to call Frank. Silverman was in her house.

No, not Silverman. Benjamin Stoltz. Rachael's brother.

"Have you ever taken it in the ass, Belinda?"

Panic gushed into her throat, a geyser of horror.

"Have you?"

Unable to look at him, she stared at the floor.

"It's a simple enough question, Belinda. Either you have or you haven't. Which is it?"

Fighting to stay calm, she dug her fingernails into her palms.

"No, Mr. Silverman."

"Barry." His eyes were pale-blue marbles of rage. "Say it! Barry!"

She worked up some saliva and forced out the word. "Barry."

"That's better. Why don't you take off your PJs and we'll go upstairs and have a good time."

Her mouth was so dry she couldn't speak. She shook her head: No.

"Why not? You've got a great body. Why not show it to me?"

"I don't want to." Tears flooded her eyes.

"What do you want?"

"I want you out of my house." She clenched her fists. "Please. Leave."

"Just like that? After all I've done for you?"

As his voracious eyes devoured her body she fought the rising tide of panic inside her. She was trapped inside her own house. Her body shook with tremors. She feared she would faint.

He drank from his coffee mug, frowning as if he were considering something. "All right," he said.

A kernel of hope blossomed. "You'll go?"

"Yes. On one condition. I want you to kiss me goodbye."

She couldn't believe her ears.

"Come on, Belinda. One goodbye kiss and I'll go."

"No." A whisper. Her chest muscles were so tight she couldn't breath.

"Well, then, I guess I'll have to stay for the weekend. It'll be fun. I'll introduce you to the pleasure of taking it in the ass. I know you'll like it." He winked. "I've got a big one."

Bile flooded her throat. She forced herself to swallow. Would he really go if she kissed him? She took a deep breath. "Just one kiss?"

"One kiss and I'll go. I promise."

"One kiss and you'll go." Hearing the telltale tremor in her voice. Hating herself for showing fear.

"Exactly right."

Gripping the table to steady herself, she rose from her chair. He sprang to his feet and stepped closer, a fearsome malodorous presence. She made her mind go blank. This would be over soon. If she kissed him goodbye he would leave. She closed her eyes. She couldn't bear to look at his rubbery-red lips.

"No, no, no. Belinda, I want *you* to kiss *me*, not the other way around."

She wanted to ram her knee in his crotch and crush his testicles. But the rational part of her mind told her not to. Enraged, he might hurt her. Or kill her. Sickened by his odor, she stood on tiptoe and set her lips against his.

His hand clamped her head, locking it in place. Then his tongue forced its way into her mouth, rough and slimy, probing her gumline. His other hand pressed her buttocks against him. She felt his erection, hot and hard against her pubic bone. The kiss seemed to go on forever. An endless nightmare.

When he released her, she stumbled to the sink, certain she would vomit. She worked her tongue around her mouth to erase the ugly taste and the filth of his saliva. She spat into the sink.

"That was great, Belinda. You sure do know how to kiss."

Dear God please let him leave, please make him go out the door and—

"Okay, Belinda, guess I'll be going."

Tears of relief flooded her eyes. In a minute this hideous nightmare would be over. She could be strong for a minute, couldn't she? Maybe not. Her legs felt rubbery, her heart was racing, and the sight of him made her want to puke.

"Walk me to the door," he said, gesturing for her to precede him.

She didn't want to, didn't want him behind her. But she had to do what he said, had to get him out of her house. Acutely aware of his presence behind her, she walked down the hall to the foyer.

Suddenly she was flat on her back on the floor. She screamed, a piercing shriek of absolute terror. He struck her face, two brutal slaps that brought tears to her eyes. "Don't scream, Belinda. No one can hear you."

He straddled her, pinned her arms to her sides with his knees, pulled down her baby-dolls and ran his fingers over her pubic hair.

"Pretty baby," he said, and licked her lips with his horrible red tongue.

CHAPTER 37

He pinned her against the desk in her office. Her body shook with violent tremors and her chest heaved, like a dog panting. Her outgoing voicemail message ended and the tone sounded. Then, a male voice.

Belinda, it's Frank. Pick up if you're still there. I need to tell you something.

Setting the serrated buck knife against her throat, he whispered, "Does that phone have a speaker?"

Two quick jerks of her head. More panicky breathing.

He pricked her throat with the blade. "Turn it on and be careful what you say. If you fuck up, I'll slit your lovely throat."

She extended her hand. Pressed a button on the console.

"Tell him you were in the shower," he whispered.

"Hello, Frank? Sorry, I was . . . taking a shower."

Renzi's voice boomed over the speaker: *Glad I caught you before you left. I just got Jake's toxicology report. He was poisoned.*

Anger shot through him like heat-lightning.

"Act surprised," he whispered. Beneath his arm, her body trembled.

"Oh . . . goodness. That's awful, Frank."

I think Silverman put poison in the brownies he gave to your student.

Rage bubbled into his throat. Renzi had figured it out.

"Get rid of him," he whispered.

"Frank, I'm sorry, but I have to go now."

Right. I don't want you to miss your flight. How're you doing? Any more problems?

She hesitated, and he pricked her neck with the knife.

"No, Frank. No problems. Not even a whisper."

I'm glad to hear it. Well, have a good concert.

"Thank you, Frank."

He broke the connection and spun her around to face him.

"I know you're dying to fuck me, Belinda, but your lover-boy knows too much. We'll have to have our orgy somewhere else."

Seated at his desk, Frank sipped his coffee, mulling over his conversation with Belinda. Yesterday she'd sounded feisty, describing how she dumped Silverman, saying she planned to play a perfect performance in Louisville. Today she sounded passive. Distracted.

Goodness, that's awful. Her lame response when he said Jake had been poisoned. No reaction to his theory about Silverman, either. When he asked if she was okay, she said she was.

No problems. Not even a whisper.

Whisper. Raspy whisper. He slammed his coffee mug on his desk.

Silverman was there!

He leaped from his chair, ran down the hall and burst into Vobitch's office. Vobitch looked up, his eyes wide at the sudden intrusion.

"Mobilize a SWAT team! Silverman's at Belinda's house. He's got her!"

"How do you—"

"He's there, trust me. Get SWAT over there."

He bolted from the office and ran outside to his car. His gut was an acid bath, his mind churning with what-ifs. If Silverman had heard his end of the conversation, he'd know they were onto him. No telling what he'd do to Belinda. Or anyone else who got in his way.

Two minutes later he was barreling down the I-10 in the high speed lane, zooming past slower cars. His cell rang.

When he answered, Kelly said, "How you doing, Frank?"

"Not good. Silverman's holding Belinda hostage at her house. I'm headed there now."

"Jesus, Frank. Be careful. The guy's a nutcase, you said so yourself. I called to tell you I got a hit on a Carl Stoltz."

He leaned on the horn and a dawdling Honda moved over.

"He got a Section-Eight discharge from the Army, served in Vietnam, got busted for selling drugs. The discharge was dated 1970, which makes Carl Stoltz too old to be our guy."

"If he was in his twenties back then he'd be almost sixty now. Maybe it's the father. Thanks for tracking him down." He cut across two lanes and exited onto City Park Avenue. Five minutes and he'd be at Belinda's house.

"Wait, there's more. I got hits on Rachel Stoltz, too. She plays violin for the Atlanta Symphony. Want me to call them and get her phone number?"

"ASAP. Anything you get on Benjamin Stoltz will be a huge help."

"Right." And after a moment's hesitation, "Be careful, Frank."

"I will. Call me soon as you get anything."

Thirty minutes later he stood at the foot of Belinda's bed, his gut churning worse than before. Tangled sheets lay in a heap at the foot of the bed. Five minutes ago a SWAT team had powered their way into her house. Nobody home, no sign of a struggle anywhere. And no tips from the bulletin Vobitch had given the radio and TV stations about an armed man with a female hostage driving a white Ford E-series van.

Morgan Vobitch stomped into the room, his head thrust forward like a silvery-haired buffalo, his face a study in frustration. "Dirty skillet in the sink, two mugs on the table, looks like they had breakfast. Fucker might have been here a while."

He didn't want to think about what that meant. They left the bedroom and went downstairs. Voices floated through the house, members of the SWAT team and other police officers. When they entered the kitchen, a crime scene technician was dusting Belinda's butcher-block table for prints. Two ceramic mugs in clear plastic evidence bags stood on the kitchen counter. A Teflon-coated frying pan with bits of egg sat in the sink.

The sight of it made him sick. Rejected stalkers were unpredictable. Volatile and dangerous. Silverman had broken into Belinda's house and forced her to cook breakfast for him. Had poisoned Ziegler for firing him. Given the slightest provocation, he's kill Belinda too.

But why hadn't he killed her here?

"He must have heard what I said to her," Frank said. "He knows we're onto him. He's taking her someplace so he can fuck with her."

Vobitch raked fingers through his thatch of silvery hair. "Yeah, but where? Maybe someone will spot the van and call us."

Frank's cell rang. He checked the ID and answered.

"I just talked to the sister," Kelly said. "Benjamin is her brother, but she said they're not close. She hasn't seen him in years."

"What about the rest of the family? Any other siblings?"

"No, just the two of them. Rachel said her mother died in 1990."

"Her mother died of what?" he said, eyeing Vobitch, who was listening intently.

"Parkinson's Disease. Rachel said she'd been in a wheelchair for years."

"What about the father?"

"When I asked if Carl Stoltz was her father, she hemmed and hawed at first. After I pressed her, she admitted he was. But he's dead, too. Rachael said he died six years ago in 2000."

"She tell you how the father died?" he said, eyeing Vobitch.

"She said he was an alcoholic. This family is royally fucked up."

"Her brother is that's for sure. What else did she say?"

"She kept asking why I was calling her. I said we needed to get in touch with Benjamin. I asked for his phone number, but she said she didn't have it. Sorry I couldn't get more."

A cloud of disappointment engulfed him. "Thanks Kelly. You did what you could."

"What's the situation there?"

"The house is empty. No sign of a struggle. They're gone."

"Not good," Kelly said.

"Not good," he echoed. "Gotta go. Keep in touch."

To Vobitch he said, "Kelly talked to the sister. Not much help there. Both parents are dead. She's not in touch with the brother."

Vobitch raked his fingers through his hair. "So now we wait."

Acid chewed his gut. Waiting was not an option.

Silverman had Belinda. He would torture and rape her first.

Then he would kill her.

CHAPTER 38

She wiped herself with the toilet paper he'd given her, grateful for an amenity she normally took for granted. But nothing was normal now. He'd told her not to flush the toilet. The water was disconnected. No electricity either. The hot humid air inside the bathroom reeked of mold, and the sweatshirt she'd pulled over her pajama top gave off the sour stink of fear.

She wished she'd put on sensible clothes and shoes, but she'd been too terrified. He had threatened to put her in his van in her pajamas if she didn't dress fast enough. He didn't even have the decency to let her change in the bathroom, so she'd slipped her feet into the worn leather sandals she used for slippers and pulled a sweatshirt and a pair of shorts over her baby-dolls.

The man was insane. Shaving his head. Wearing black paramilitary garb like a soldier in a war movie. But this wasn't a movie. It was real. Tears stung her eyes. The thirteenth anniversary of the accident that killed her family had brought nothing but disaster. Her premonition was about to come true: She would die before achieving her musical goals like her brother.

She struggled to calm herself. She had to escape. Five minutes ago when he'd dragged her inside through a side door, sullen gray clouds obscured the sun. A fence bordering the driveway blocked any view of the adjacent house. This one, a two-story structure with a central staircase, had been gutted. A five-foot-high watermark from the Katrina floodwaters darkened the mold-blackened studs, and debris littered the floor of the uninhabited house.

Uninhabited. She shuddered. That's why Silverman had chosen it.

If she screamed would anyone hear?

Every muscle in her body ached. Her fingers were shards of ice and her mouth felt like burnt toast. She ran her tongue over her teeth, trying to get rid of the disgusting taste, and stared at her image in the grime-streaked mirror over the sink. Tangled hair and sallow cheeks, barely visible in the faint light filtering through a frosted-glass window high on the wall beside the toilet.

Maybe she could break the window and escape.

"Hurry up, Belinda. I'm waiting for you."

His sing-song voice, outside the door. No way could she break the window, climb through it and run. He would hear the glass break and catch her before she could escape. She didn't dare make him angry. If she did, he might watch her the next time she used the bathroom.

She opened the door. Her stomach lurched.

Her captor was leaning against a stud opposite the door, leering at her. "Too bad your boyfriend called. We could have had our fun at your house."

She tried to swallow, but her mouth was a thick ball of cotton.

"He's not my boyfriend."

His eyes blinked slowly like a Gila monster. "Seems like you've got lots of boyfriends. Renzi, for one. Who was the guy at the train station?"

"Train station?" What was he talking about?

"The good-looking young guy with the dark hair and beard."

Sweat trickled down her back. He had followed her to the train station on Saturday morning. "That was Dean Silva, Jake's partner."

"Partner? Ziegler was gay?" said the man who called himself Barry Silverman. The man Frank said was Benjamin Stoltz. Rachel Stoltz's brother.

"Yes." Her legs trembled and her body sagged. She gripped the doorjamb to keep from falling.

"You look kinda shaky, Belinda. Come sit down and tell me about Jake and his faggot partner." Gesturing for her to walk in front of him.

Bile rose in her throat. The last time she walked in front of him she had wound up on the floor. Vile memories assaulted her. His disgusting tongue in her mouth. His fingers probing her crotch. His rubbery-red lips kissing her.

He was crazy. Crazy enough to kill her. She had to get away.

"Could I please have some water? I'm very thirsty."

His pale blue eyes hardened. "I'll get you some water in a minute. Go."

She walked down the hall, eyes focused on the floor to make sure she didn't trip. A creepy sensation crawled down her neck: his evil presence behind her. At the end of the hall she entered a large open space.

Venetian blinds covered windows on two of the walls. In the center of the concrete slab floor, two boxy chairs without legs faced each other, the foam-filled kind that unfolded into beds. When she was at Julliard she'd bought one in case a friend wanted to stay over.

No one had. She'd had no friends at Julliard, only competitors.

He shoved her toward one of the chairs. She sank down on it, grateful to rest. Grateful he hadn't unfolded the chairs into beds. Grateful he wasn't asking her to kiss him. Or worse.

He strode to a Styrofoam ice chest on the floor, raised the lid and took out two bottles of water. Beside the ice chest was a large olive-green knapsack. An ugly-looking rifle stood in the corner, its muzzle aimed at the ceiling. It looked like the ones she'd seen terrorists use on TV. A sick feeling soured her stomach. She knew he had a knife. Now she knew he had a rifle.

Maybe he had other weapons. She didn't want to think about what weapons he had. Or what he might do with them.

He came over and handed her a bottle of water. "There you go, Belinda. All the comforts of home." He sat down on the other chair and stared at her.

"Thank you." With trembling hands, she unscrewed the cap.

"Barry. Did you forget my name?" His pale blue eyes bored into her, laser-beams of anger.

"No, Barry, I didn't forget." She gulped some water. She had to be smart, had to placate him. Had to take his mind off sex.

"Tell me how you learned to play the piano so well . . . Barry."

His eyes lit up and he smiled. "You really think I play well?"

"Very well. Where did you study?"

"I started lessons when we lived in Rhode Island," he said, nodding his head as if he were listening to some sort of music.

"Whereabouts in Rhode Island?" *Keep him talking.*

"Just a rinky-dink little town. I'm sure you've never heard of it."

"Was that where you and Rachael—" She stopped.

He gazed at her, expressionless. "You remember Rachael, huh?"

She forced a smile, worked hard to make it seem genuine. "You must have started young, playing as well as you do."

"Rachael started violin when she was five." He smiled, but his pale-blue eyes were cold and full of rage. "I didn't start till I was ten. If I'd started at five, I might have been another Van Cliburn. He started piano when he was three, soloed with the Houston Symphony when he was twelve. You think I'd have been as good as Cliburn?" He held up his hands and spread his fingers. "I can reach and octave and a half."

She didn't want to look at his fingers, didn't want to remember them probing her crotch. Without thinking, she said, "Cliburn was a natural."

And silently cursed herself for the careless remark.

His smile disappeared. "That's what they said about Rachael. Bullshit. She's nothing like you, Belinda. You put your heart and soul into the music. Rachael's got no heart. Got no soul either."

What an odd remark. It sounded like he hated his sister. Why was that, she wondered. And realized he was staring at her, waiting for her to speak. "You started piano lessons when you were ten?"

"Bet your ass I did. Ma got me a teacher. Pa didn't like it. He loved listening to Rachael play. She was way ahead of me, years of lessons and a prodigy to boot. Pa used to call me a sissy. Boys aren't supposed to play piano, they're supposed to play with—"

He gulped some water and gazed at her, expressionless.

"You went to school in Rhode Island?" Anything to keep him talking. Her hands dampened with sweat. She had to kill time until someone rescued her. But how would they find her? Even if Frank understood the clue she'd given him about the whisper, he would be looking for Silverman's white van.

But his van wasn't white now, it was black.

"Yes, and it sucked. All the kids in my school were stupid. They hated classical music. They were into country. *Hee-haw!*"

His sing-song voice was driving her crazy, and no one was going to save her from him. She had to save herself. And she would. Or die trying. Anger welled up inside her. She would not allow this evil man to defeat her. She knew how to manage fear, had done it many times. She focused on her breathing, took deep breaths down to her diaphragm. Her heartbeat slowed.

"Later we moved to Boston," he said, wiping his mouth with the back of his hand. "Rachael had a great violin teacher. She got into the New England Conservatory prep division when she was ten. Not me. Daddy-O said I wasn't good enough."

"Were your parents musical?"

He burst out laughing. "Well, that is the question, isn't it?" He stared into the distance, seemingly lost in thought. "On Saturdays me and Ma used to listen to the Met Opera on the radio."

"What about your father? What did he do for a living?"

Fury darkened his face. "None of your fucking business."

She reeled back as though he had slapped her. One minute he was laughing, the next he was an enraged bull.

He brayed a laugh. "Gol-ly! That wasn't very nice of me, was it? Here you are asking about my family, and I go and bite your head off."

He rose and extended his hand. "Come on. Let's have some fun."

Her mind flooded with vile images, and her heart pounded her ribs like a panic-stricken animal.

CHAPTER 39

Albert Schumacher raised one slat of the Venetian blind and studied the black van in Joe Landry's driveway across the street. Joe and the missus had flown to Chicago to escape Katrina, paid a contractor to gut their house, said they'd never be back. It wasn't on the market yet. Last week when Joe called, he'd said he was waiting on the Road Home people to settle their claim.

Twelve houses on their block had taken five feet of water. Now only three were occupied, so Albert had to stay vigilant, looters roaming around looking for vacant homes to rob. Here it was broad daylight and some thug was in Joe's house doing God knows what.

He went to the hall closet and got out his shotgun. He might be seventy-two, but he was no pushover, not with his Winchester Select Model 101 with the lightweight barrels and the brass-bead front sight. He took the shotgun in the kitchen, poured himself another cup of coffee and glanced at the small TV on the counter. He kept it on all day, tuned to a local channel, the voices keeping him company.

The Young and the Restless ended and a commercial came on, one of those sappy Viagra ads, a gray-haired older couple acting lovey-dovey. Watch TV too much, you'd think every man on Earth was ready to get it on every minute of the day. God knows he wasn't. His wife had passed two years before Katrina, thank the Lord. She'd have thrown a hissy-fit, coming home like he had to find the house they'd occupied for thirty years—the house where they'd raised two great kids—filled with muck and moldy furniture and a refrigerator full of bugs.

A bold graphic on the TV caught his eye: NEWS BULLETIN.

Albert went over and upped the volume.

"New Orleans police say a man broke into a house and kidnapped a woman today. He's described as a white male in his thirties, six feet tall and slender. Police believe he's driving a white Ford E-series van. If you see the van, call the number on the bottom of your screen. Do not approach this man. Police say he is armed and extremely dangerous."

Albert adjusted the bottom plate of his dentures with his tongue. Some nut was out there, armed and dangerous. He set his coffee mug in the sink and returned to the front room, cradling his Winchester in the crook of his arm. He sidled up to the window, raised one slat of the blind and looked across the street.

The van was still there. Looked like a Ford to him. He squinted.

Yup, had that distinctive Ford logo on the back. A black Ford van.

The announcer had said the guy was driving a white van, hadn't she? Albert fingered the stubble on his jaw. Damned if he could remember. But that van had no business being in Joe's driveway. Of that he was certain.

He returned to the kitchen, picked up the phone and dialed 9-1-1.

A woman came on the line, asking what was his emergency.

"That nutcase that kidnapped the women. I think he might be in my neighborhood."

"Could you tell me your name and your location, sir?"

Albert stated his name and address. "I got a gutted house across the street from me, and there's a Ford van parked in the driveway."

"Is it a white van?"

Lord-a-Mighty, here he was being a good citizen and this dumbbell was grilling him like he was a suspect. "No, it isn't. But it's a Ford van and it's big and it's parked where it ain't supposed to be."

"Thank you, sir. I'll notify the detectives."

"You want the plate number?"

"Yes, sir. Do you have it?"

"Nope, but if you hold on a second, I'll get it for you."

He watched the Diva listen to the music coming from his boom box.

Prelude to the Afternoon of a Faun, Charles Munch conducting the Boston Symphony back in the '60s, recently reissued on CD. He had asked her to identify the flutist on the opening solo. His version of Name That Tune.

She seemed enthralled, sitting as still as a Rodin sculpture, eyes closed, lips curved in a smile. A far cry from when he tried to make love to her this morning. When she resisted, he'd slapped her. He hadn't meant to. It just happened. Since then she'd been much nicer, asking about his music background, complimenting his playing.

Maybe they could work things out after all.

His cell phone ripped into *Ride of the Valkyries*. Startled, he pulled it out and studied the faceplate. The Diva opened her eyes, watching him as the music soared to a lush climax. "Stay there, Belinda. I need to take this call in the other room, but I'll be watching you."

She nodded, dreamy-faced, like she was in a trance.

He went down the hall to the gutted kitchen. The stench was awful, the sink full of moldy rags. He could see The Diva through the spaces between the studs, but she couldn't hear him. He punched on. "What."

"Ben?"

"Why are you calling me?"

"Are you in trouble? A New Orleans police officer called this morning asking about you."

His neck felt like spiders were crawling over it. How could that be? They didn't know his real name. "What did he say?"

"It was a woman. She was asking about you, and Ma and Pa."

"What did you tell her?"

"I told her Ma and Pa were dead."

"What did you tell her about *me*, Rachael?"

"Nothing. I said I hadn't seen you for years. Where are you? Why are the cops calling me?"

"I'm in N'awlins. It's a fun town. Y'all come and see me, y'hear?"

"Stop it, Ben. The cop got my number from the orchestra manager. I don't know what you're doing, but you better stop or you'll get me in trouble!"

"As if you never got *me* in trouble. You got me in trouble every chance you got. Daddy-O used to beat the shit out of me, remember?"

Silence on the other end. He turned to monitor Belinda. What a good girl, sitting on his makeshift loveseat, eyes closed, listening to the music.

A sharp crack sounded, brilliant light flashed outside the window, then deep rolling thunder.

"Ben, why did that policewoman call me?"

Poor Rachael. She didn't want to get in trouble. When she was fucking Pa, she didn't worry about getting in trouble. But that was then and this was now. Rachel had stayed in touch with Pa right up until he died. He knew why. She wanted to know who her birth parents were. Didn't want to know bad enough to keep fucking him, though.

"Remember Belinda Scully?" he said. This was going to be fun.

"The girl that played principal flute in the All-State orchestra? What about her?"

"The cops think I kidnapped her, but I didn't. Turn on the TV and watch the news. You'll see."

He closed the phone and rubbed his eyes. He'd been up all night, watching Belinda sleep, anticipating her reaction when she woke up. And then, his reward. The kiss. The sweetness of her mouth.

Until lover-boy Renzi called.

On the way here in the van, he'd heard the radio bulletin. The cops were hunting for a white Ford E-series van. *Do not approach this man. Police say he's armed and they consider him very dangerous.*

He laughed aloud. He was dangerous all right. Dangerous and armed to the teeth. If anyone approached him, he'd blow their fucking heads off. And now the cops knew his true identity. He smiled.

Doomsday, coming soon to a theater near you. He was going to be famous and he didn't need to shoot a president like Hinckley, in his pathetic attempt to impress Jody Foster. The most important person in *his* world was sitting right there on his loveseat. Now they were alone.

Well, Oz was here, but Oz didn't count.

Anticipating the sweetness of her mouth, he started down the hall.

Frank paced Belinda's driveway, waiting impatiently while Vobitch talked on his cell phone. The crime scene techs had finished and gone.

Vobitch signaled him, mouthed: *We got a tip on the van.*

His heart thrummed his chest. About time they caught a break.

Vobitch's gleeful expression faded and he punched off.

"The tipster says the van's black. Probably a dead-end, but they'll check it. They're running the plate now, shouldn't take long."

Not a white van, a black one. An errant thought plinked his mind and flitted away. He raked his fingers through his hair. They had to find Belinda.

He closed his eyes and concentrated. A movie scene blossomed in his mind: the assassin in *Day of the Jackal*, spray-painting his white sports car blue.

"What's the address?"

"Frank, I'm not sending SWAT until I'm sure it's Stoltz."

"Fuck waiting! Give me the address."

Terrified by her captor's bizarre behavior, she tried to calm her wildly beating heart. After the phone call, he had returned, muttering to himself. When the music ended she'd heard loud cracks of thunder, and flashes of lightning had filtered through the window blinds. Then Silverman asked her to identify the flutist who'd played the seductive flute solo.

When she said she couldn't, he said, "Play it for me. That's why I let you bring your flute, Belinda. So you could play for me. Just for me."

Every flutist at Julliard knew the solo by heart. Debussy's *Prelude to an Afternoon of a Faun* was required repertoire for every orchestral audition.

Now she had to play it in this stinking hellhole. Not for an audition, to placate an evil monster with a shaven head. If she didn't, he might kill her.

She raised the platinum Haynes flute to her mouth and took an enormous breath. Gazing at the floor, she played the solo on autopilot, her fingers moving effortlessly, her mind alive with possibility.

Something in her flute case had given her a glimmer of hope.

If she was very careful and very brave, maybe she could escape.

She finished, lowered her flute and forced herself to look at him.

He clapped his hands and his rubbery-red lips spread in a smile. The monster with the shaven-head and piggish blue eyes looked positively ecstatic. "Gorgeous! You're a fabulous flutist, Belinda. Play something else for me."

She took a deep breath the way she did before a big performance to steady her nerves. "Would you like me to play the Gershwin Variations?"

He leered at her, devouring her with his eyes. "Would you *like* to play it for me?"

She mentally rehearsed what she had to do. No one was going to save her. She had to save herself.

"I'd love to, Barry. But first I have to adjust the tension on the keys."

He frowned. "Why?"

"Because of all the trills," she explained, working to keep her voice calm. "I do it when I go offstage, during the applause." She dredged up a smile, the charismatic smile she used to charm her audiences. "Want me to show you how I do it? It will be our little secret."

He clapped his hands like a delighted child. "Show me, show me!"

"Don't get up, Barry. Let me get the screwdriver and I'll show you."

She went to the foam-filled chair where her flute case lay open. Her palms were wet with sweat and her heart was jumping like a jackrabbit inside her chest. She wiped her palms on her jeans. *Don't think about it. Just do it.*

She picked up the tiny screwdriver she used to adjust the tension on the keys of her flute. Attached to the one-inch molded-plastic handle was a two-inch metal rod that ended in a sharp flat edge.

Holding the flute in her left hand, she showed him the screwdriver. "See? The screws are tiny, so this tool is perfect. Watch how I do it."

He leaned forward in his chair, smiling and eager. "I'm watching!"

She stood by his chair, slightly behind him. Now came the difficult part.

The terrifying part. If she failed, she was dead.

"Keep your eye on this tiny screw." She touched it with the tip of the screwdriver. "I'm just going to give it a half-twist."

Gripping the screwdriver in her hand, she thrust the blade at his eye, but at the last instant he turned his head. She tried to alter her thrust. Too late.

Instead of piercing his eye, the screwdriver plunged into the bridge of his nose, ripping flesh as she thrust it upward with all her strength.

"Arrrrgh!" he screamed, clasping his hands to his face.

She whirled and ran down the hall toward the door where they had entered the house. *Dear God, let it be unlocked, let me out of here!*

Behind her, she heard him moaning.

Then, footsteps, thundering toward her. "You traitorous bitch!"

Consumed by panic, she froze.

She couldn't think. Couldn't breath. Couldn't move.

She had to move!

Holding the flute in her left hand, she grabbed the doorknob with her right and twisted. The door creaked and groaned. Opened an inch and stuck.

The door was warped from the flooding. She was trapped.

"I'll make you wish you'd never been born!"

She thought her heart would explode.

Desperate, she yanked at the door. It moved another inch.

Footsteps behind her. Closer and closer. "I'll fix you, bitch!"

She turned and looked. Saw a horrifying vision staggering toward her, blood spurting from the gash on his brow. The eye below it was shut. The other eye was fixed on her like a pale-blue laser beam from hell.

Now he was only ten yards away, arms extended, his claw-like fingers outstretched to grab her.

She dropped her flute, stuck her fingers in the opening and yanked as hard as she could.

CHAPTER 40

Albert brushed crumbs off his mustache and set the red Fiestaware plate in the sink. He wasn't given to bragging, but in his opinion he made the best grilled cheese and bologna sandwich anywhere: two thick slices each of German bologna and Munster cheese on whole-wheat bread, toasted in a frying pan till it was crispy brown.

Now that he'd finished lunch, he'd better go see what was going on at Joe Landry's house across the street.

He grabbed his Winchester, went in the parlor and tilted the blinds.

The storm was worse. Jagged bolts of lightning flashed, quickly followed by the boom of rolling thunder. Wind drove sheets of rain sideways, pelting the street and the sidewalk like buckshot.

The van was still in Joe's driveway. Where the hell were the cops?

A flash of motion caught his eye: a woman running down the sidewalk across the street. Running as if the harpies from hell were after her, arms flailing, legs pumping, hair plastered to her head.

She had sandals on her feet.

Piss-poor shoes for running in a torrential downpour.

He fingered his mustache. Not many of his neighbors were runners and of the few he'd seen, this woman wasn't one of them. He'd have remembered that reddish-gold hair.

Too many weird things were happening today. A woman out running in a violent rainstorm, a van parked where it shouldn't be. He'd called to report that van twenty minutes ago.

No wonder folks didn't respond when the cops asked for help. Call in with important information and they paid no attention.

He went back to the kitchen, got on the phone and dialed 9-1-1.

Frank slewed around the corner of the rain-slicked street and stomped his brakes, unable to believe his eyes. Belinda Scully was running down the middle of the street. He jumped out of the car and grabbed her.

She collapsed in his arms and clung to him, trembling. "Frank! Thank God you're here. H-h-he was in my bedroom when I woke up and I couldn't make him leave and . . . he made me . . . h-h-he's a maniac!"

Ignoring the pelting rain, he rubbed her back, eyeballing the area behind her. The street was deserted, the gutters flooded with rainwater. No cars, no people, no sign of Stoltz. "It's okay, Belinda. You're safe now."

He helped her into his car and got behind the wheel. Rain drummed the roof, cascading down the windshield. Belinda slumped in the passenger seat, arms hugging her chest, staring straight ahead. Stringy strands of hair were plastered to her forehead. After a moment she turned her head and looked at him. Her eyes had that hollow vacant look, the thousand-yard stare he'd seen in the eyes of people who had narrowly escaped death.

"I stabbed him with a screwdriver."

"Where is he? Someplace near here?"

She made a vague gesture with her hand. "Back there in a gutted house. I don't know which one. When I got out, I just ran away as fast as I could."

He squeezed her shoulder, felt the fragility of her bones through her sodden sweatshirt. "Don't worry, we'll get him."

He did a U-turn, got on his radio and called Dispatch. He told the dispatcher that Belinda was safe in his car, but the subject might be holed up in a nearby house. He gave the location and told the dispatcher to send a SWAT team ASAP.

"He's got a gun," Belinda said.

He looked over and saw her shudder. "A hand gun?"

"No, a rifle." In a flat listless voice, she said, "This has been the longest day of my life."

"I'm sure it has." And it wasn't over. He felt less frantic now that Belinda was safe in his car, but Stoltz was still at large, armed with a rifle. And way more dangerous now that his love object had escaped.

The worst possible scenario.

"I dropped my flute," she said tonelessly. "Back in that house."

Amazed that she was worried about a flute, he studied her slack expression. She was in shock. He'd seen it before, traumatized survivors worrying about inconsequential details. She was lucky to be alive.

"Forget the flute. You can buy another one."

She gave him an unfathomable look, then leaned back against the headrest, frowning as though she was working out a complicated puzzle.

The sky darkened to a deep charcoal-gray and a deluge of rain splattered the windshield. In the distance he heard sirens amidst claps of thunder.

"Is there someone you want to call? You can use my cell phone."

Anguish twisted her mouth and a muscle bunched in her jaw. She took a deep breath, and her face settled into a familiar mask of tranquility. "No, but thanks for the offer."

Her matter-of-fact tone tore at his heart. Belinda had no family to call. No friends. A sad commentary on the life of a beautiful and celebrated flute soloist. Ziegler had been her only friend, but Ziegler was dead.

Audiences adored her, but when disaster struck and she needed someone, Belinda Scully was all alone.

Excruciating pain ripped his forehead. Fuck-all! He could barely see.

Blood was still oozing from the wound, dripping into his eye.

Damn that bitch to hell! Everything she'd said had been a lie, everything she'd done a deception. Even the music she'd played had been designed to make him think she cared for him. His cherished dream that she might come to love him as much as he loved her had been a grand delusion.

She didn't give a flying fuck about him. To her he was nothing. Less than nothing. A cipher. The traitorous bitch had ripped a three-inch gash from the bridge of his nose through the flesh of his shaven eyebrow. Thanks to his survival kit, he had staunched the worst of the bleeding.

Survival 101: Tend your wounds and retaliate. Fury flamed his cheeks.

He might not be able to settle the score with The Diva, but before this day was done, she would know how powerful he was. The whole fucking world would know how deadly he could be, cops included.

They were already here. From his sniper perch at the second floor window, he watched them barricade the end of the street to keep out curious onlookers and television crews. If he wanted to go out in a blaze of glory, it wouldn't be hard, not with his handy-dandy Bushmaster M4 Carbine and high-powered Nikon scope. It was raining like hell, but he'd taken out targets at two hundred yards in worse weather during Special Ops exercises. His marksmanship scores had been excellent.

But not as high as Pa's, a fact the prick had taken great pleasure in cramming down his throat.

His forehead throbbed, a kaleidoscope of pain: bright yellow, brilliant red and dark magenta. He should have killed the bitch as soon as they got here. An icy rage settled over him. She'd tried to blind him, had missed his eye by less than a half inch. Then, while he stood there in agony, she had escaped. And told the cops where to find him.

He looked out the window. Reinforcements had arrived, two big black Hummers rolling down the street toward the house.

"Benjamin Stoltz." An electronically magnified voice floating through the window. "You're surrounded. Put down your weapon and come out with your hands up and you won't be hurt!"

Won't be hurt. The cops giving him the Big Lie.

He peered out the window. Forewarned by the Belinda-bitch, the cops would be wearing body armor. That would lower the body count. He needed a better victim pool. And pain meds. He wiped blood from the bridge of his nose and laughed aloud, delighted at the conjunction of needs. His mind fizzed like Coke shaken in a can, foaming with possibilities.

Time to leave this filthy gutted house and go to a hospital.

He raced downstairs to the cupboard below the smelly sink where his arsenal was hidden. Those cops were in for a surprise.

Five minutes later he opened one of the second floor windows that faced the back yard. Two uniforms were creeping alongside the one-story house behind this one. Pelted with rain and drenched to the skin, the lead officer, a tall rugged-looking guy bulked out with body armor, reached the corner of the neighboring house and stopped. The cop behind him was wearing body armor too, but he was short and stocky, with a thick neck.

Perfect. Special Ops rules: In an ambush, pick off the rear man first.

He took out an all-carbon Blackhawk-4000 arrow and set it onto his crossbow. The 30-inch projectile had three yellow feathers at one end, a killer hunting tip at the other. The shot would be tricky due to the wind and rain, but he had confidence in his ability. Months of practice at the Special Ops target range had prepared him.

He took a deep breath, held it and released the arrow.

The short stocky cop fell to the ground with an arrow through his neck.

The first cop heard him fall and turned to look. No chance at that cop's neck. He set another Blackhawk onto the crossbow, took aim and let it go.

His target went down, clutching his thigh. The other one wasn't moving.

Excellent. The bow had served its purpose, a silent deadly weapon to create a diversion so he could escape. But he didn't have much time.

He ran downstairs to the side door. The Diva's flute lay on the floor. He planted his foot on one end, grabbed the other end with his hand and yanked. The Diva's precious flute bent in half like a platinum Gummy Bear. With a grim smile, he threw it on the floor.

"The bitch will never play *this* flute again, Oz."

Inside the wire-mesh cage, his precious little bunny gazed up at him.

His heart melted. Oz had been his faithful companion for the last three years. Always overjoyed to see him. Delighted to snuggle against him. Always wanting to be petted and stroked. Someone else would have to take care of his Wizard of Oz now.

"I hate to leave you, Oz. You've been my one true companion, the only creature in the world that loves me. But you can't come with me."

Couldn't come with him because he was on a mission, the most important mission of his life and probably the last.

He broke down the Bushmaster, jammed it into his knapsack with the ammo and other supplies. Holding the Ruger, he ran to the back of the house and looked out a window. Forty yards to his right, pelted by rain, a crowd of cops encircled the two men he'd shot with the crossbow, dismayed and distracted, all thought of capturing the fugitive forgotten. For now.

He eased open the window. Rain stung his face. Levering himself over the sill, he dropped to the ground and took off running, the knapsack in one hand, the Ruger in the other. Seconds later he vaulted a low cedar-plank fence and sprinted to the street that paralleled the rear of the gutted house.

The safe-house that was no longer safe, thanks to the Belinda-bitch.

Pain pounded his forehead. She would pay for this. He didn't know how, but he intended to find her and make her pay. His final mission.

He heard more sirens approaching, an undulating wail. He sprinted across the street and ran alongside a house with boarded-up windows, feet squishing in the rain-soaked grass. This was the danger point. He didn't know how wide a perimeter the cops had established. If he ran into a patrol car, he would have to shoot it out and he didn't want to do that. Not yet.

Breathing hard, he raced through tall weeds between two gutted houses, slowed as he approached the next street. Solid sheets of rain had drenched his clothes, and his skin felt clammy. His mind churned, ordering priorities.

First, he needed a vehicle. During the torrential rains that often hit New Orleans, most residents stayed inside unless they had urgent business. All he had to do was find someone who *did* have urgent business.

Someone in a vehicle. Someone to drive him to a hospital.

Then, badaboom. Doomsday in New Orleans.

CHAPTER 41

Frank flipped through an old issue of *Sports Illustrated* with unseeing eyes. The hall door was closed, but faint announcements from the PA system filtered into the small windowless waiting room. City Hospital had replaced Charity as the go-to facility for trauma victims. Charity was much larger but it had sustained massive damage during Katrina and hadn't reopened.

A lamp on the corner table gave off a cheery glow, but he didn't feel cheery. He felt stymied. Frustrated. He wanted to go capture Stoltz.

A rap on the hall door, then Kelly's voice: "Frank, you in there?"

About time. He set the magazine on a table and stood. "Come on in."

Dressed in a rain-soaked hooded sweatshirt and a pair of jeans tucked into all-weather boots, Kelly stepped into the room, tracking mud over the institutional-gray carpet. "Where's Belinda? How is she?"

He gestured at an inner door that faced the hall. "In there with the doctor. When I picked her up she looked like a war refuge, face streaked with dirt, hair matted to her head. I snuck her in through the side entrance. A nurse brought us up here to wait for the doctor."

"Who's the doctor?" Kelly said.

"Iris Golden."

"Excellent. She does a lot of the rape exams. How's Belinda?"

"Hard to tell. When the nurse asked if she wanted to wash up and brush her hair, Belinda said she just wanted to sleep. I think she wants to pretend this is all a bad dream, but Stoltz is still out there. She's lucky to be alive."

"That's for sure. His sister said he served in the military."

"Yeah? You didn't mention that before."

Kelly flashed a cool-your-jets grin. "The damsel detective did her due diligence, called Rachel back and questioned her. She said they lived in Rhode Island until 1985. Then they moved to Massachusetts."

"That's where Belinda met Rachel, in an All-State Orchestra. Maybe he spotted her then. But his parents are dead now, and Rachael lives in Atlanta."

"So Rachael said, but who knows? I could tell she didn't want to talk to me. If Stoltz was in the military, he'd have had weapons training. We need a warrant to access the military data base."

He raked his fingers through his hair, imagining various scenarios, none of them good. His cell phone rang. When he answered, Vobitch yelled, "He shot two cops with a fucking bow! One's got an arrow through his neck. The other cop took one in the thigh. SWAT's ready to enter the house, but I'm not sure he's still there."

His gut lurched, a sickening freefall. "Did anyone see him leave?"

"No, but the cops he shot were behind the house. It was fucking chaos back there. He might have escaped during the confusion."

"What about the van?"

"Still there. If he split, he's on foot, but who knows for how long?"

"Kelly's here. I asked her to come to the hospital in case we needed a female cop in the exam room. She talked to the sister again. Stoltz served in the military. Can we get a warrant to get into the military data base?"

"Military. Jesus-fucking-Christ! Frank, I saw some bad shit in Harlem, but I've never seen anything like this. The fucking arrow's embedded in his *neck!* In one side and out the other."

His stomach churned like a coffee-grinder. "We need that warrant. If we access his military records, we might get a better handle on him."

"I'll take care of it. I already put out another bulletin to the radio and TV stations. Where's the Scully woman?"

"In a critical-care suite on the top floor of City Hospital. A doctor's with her now. Kelly and I are right outside in a waiting room."

"Let's keep in touch by cell phone," Vobitch said. "The radio chatter will be fierce once SWAT enters the house."

He closed his cell and said to Kelly, "He shot two cops. One's got an arrow in his neck. Another one took it in the leg. Vobitch thinks Stoltz might have left the house."

"Arrows?" Her face paled and her eyes widened. "This guy's a maniac."

"Right. A well-prepared maniac."

"It could have been you," she said, gazing at him, horror-stricken.

"Well, it wasn't." But she was right: it could have been his neck with an arrow in it.

"Want to call Rachael? Maybe you can get more out of her."

"Good idea." He opened his cell phone. "Give me the number."

He loped through the rain, splashing through puddles, laboring under the weight of the knapsack that held his Bushmaster M4, extra ammo and other supplies. He rounded the corner of a house and stopped.

Twenty yards away, a tan Mazda MPV stood at a traffic light.

Rain pelted the pavement, driven sideways by the gusty wind. The street was deserted, not another car in sight. Approaching from the rear, he trotted to the MPV and peered through the back window. A woman alone in the car. Perfect. Gripping the Ruger in one hand, he crept to the passenger side door and dropped the knapsack.

In one swift motion he yanked open the door and leveled the Ruger at the woman's head. "Freeze or you're dead."

Her head swiveled, her mouth sagged open, and he was inside.

Training the Ruger on her with one hand, he hauled the knapsack inside with the other and slammed the door. Paralyzed by fear, she gaped at him, a chubby-faced woman, early twenties, her dirty-blond hair twisted into twin ponytails that flopped over her ears.

"Don't do anything stupid and you'll be fine. We're taking a ride."

Her chest rose and fell rapidly. "Please don't hurt me. My baby's in the backseat."

Fuck-all! He turned and saw the kid, about a year old, bright-red cheeks, staring at him with dull glazed eyes.

"Do what I say, and you and junior will be fine."

"Lucy," the woman said in a high-pitched voice. "Her name is Lucy."

"Whatever." He didn't give a damn what the kid's name was. She wasn't old enough to talk, much less cause trouble.

He saw the traffic light turn green.

"Drive to the nearest I-10 entrance and get on heading west."

The woman gnawed her lip. "I have to take Lucy to the doctor. She's got a bad fever."

"Not now you don't. You're gonna take me where I want to go. Drive like your life depends on it because it does. Yours and the kid's."

Her mouth contorted in anguish. She gripped the wheel and accelerated. At the next corner she turned onto a wide boulevard, following a sign for the I-10 entrance.

He heard sirens. Looked in the side-view mirror. Saw flashing blue lights behind them. "Pull over and let them go by." He touched the muzzle of the

Ruger to her head to make sure she did. Then he squirmed into the foot-well beside the knapsack and ducked below the dash.

The woman pulled over.

The sirens grew louder and a police car flew by, lights flashing.

"Very good. Now get going. Take me to Lakeside Hospital. My wife's having a baby." This was almost fun, making things up on the fly.

The woman glanced at him and quickly looked away. "Why didn't you call a cab?"

"Shut up and drive."

The kid in the back seat whimpered, a soft petulant sound.

"Please, you can have the car. Just let us out and take it."

"No, keep going."

Her face puckered and tears rolled down her cheeks.

She swerved, and they hit something.

"If you crash this car, you and the kid are history."

"It was a trash can. I couldn't help—"

"Shut up and drive!"

The kid shrieked as if stabbed by a knife.

"No answer," Frank said, and closed his cell phone.

"You think she's in cahoots with the brother?" Kelly said.

"Could be. I think he's been stalking Belinda for years. He was savvy enough to get a fake ID from the guy in London, ruthless enough to run her off the road to get her to hire him. After Jake fired him, he poisoned the brownies and got the Goines kid to deliver them. He claimed he was in Atlanta during the supposed break-in at Belinda's house. The sister lives in Atlanta. She's stonewalling you and—"

He broke off as the door to Belinda's room opened. Doctor Iris Golden stepped into the anteroom and shut Belinda's door. A handsome woman in her fifties, Golden was tall and slender, with warm brown eyes and dark hair streaked with gray. She beamed Kelly a smile. "Hi, Kelly, how are you?"

"I'm good, Doctor. Have you met Frank?"

"Briefly, before I examined Belinda."

No high-wattage smile for him, Frank noticed. "How's she doing?"

"Reasonably well, given the circumstances. Her heart-rate, pulse and blood pressure are elevated, but that's to be expected. I was going to do a rape-kit exam, but she said it wasn't necessary." Golden gave him a grim look. "He was about to rape her when you phoned this morning."

"Jesus," he muttered. If he hadn't called . . .

"She wouldn't tell me about what happened later. She's in shock and I didn't want to push it. I asked if there was anyone she wanted to call, but she said no."

"Her family died in a car accident years ago," he said. No need to mention that Belinda had no friends to call in an emergency. The doctor was smart enough to figure that out.

"I'm going to admit her," Golden said, jotting notes on a form clamped to her clipboard. "I want to observe her for twenty-four hours in case she has any adverse reactions."

"Can I talk to her?"

Golden gave him a stern look. "Not now. She needs to rest. I've given her a sedative to help her sleep. When she wakes up, she might need to talk to someone. Will you be here, Kelly?"

"Frank and I will stay with her," Kelly said.

Frank said nothing. Kelly could stay, but he wouldn't. Not with Stoltz out there. Stoltz was a ticking time bomb with an arsenal, packing a rifle, shooting cops with arrows, no telling what he'd do next.

The woman kept crying, great gulping sobs, tears pouring down her cheeks. Traffic on the Interstate was light, cars creeping along, splashing through puddles, windshield wipers working furiously. The kid had settled into a continuous whimper, a grating sound that aggravated his headache.

To drown out the whimper he punched on the radio. A commercial was on, touting Extra-strength Excedrin for headaches. He smiled at the irony.

He had the mother of all headaches.

Because The Diva had gored him with her fucking screwdriver.

The commercial ended and a news-bulletin jingle sounded.

"Updating the hostage crisis we reported earlier," said a male voice, "the woman escaped. Police have taken her to a hospital, no word on her condition. SWAT teams have surrounded a house where they believe the kidnapper is hiding. He's described as a white male, six feet tall, with reddish-brown hair. If you see this man, police ask you to call 9-1-1. Do not approach him. He is armed and extremely dangerous."

The woman made a keening sound in her throat, and the kid let out an ear-splitting scream.

"Shut up!" How could he think with them blubbering? He shut off the radio. The cops thought he was still in the house. Good. The Diva hadn't told them he'd shaved his head. Also good. Police had taken her to a hospital. No news on her condition. But what about *his* condition?

He pressed a hand to his forehead, his excruciatingly *painful* forehead. He lowered his hand. Saw blood on his fingers. Clenched his fist.

If he knew where that bitch was, he'd go there and kill her.

Think, you idiot. Where would they take her?

To a trauma center of course, but not Charity. Charity was closed.

Then he recalled the newspaper article about his Belinda-substitute—the one whose nose he'd broken.

"Change in plans," he said. "Take the next exit."

Gripping the wheel, the woman eased into the exit lane, still sobbing, but quieter now. Rain thundered on the MPV roof. They passed a strip mall with a Blockbuster and a Sears Auto Center. Two blocks later he spotted a bus stop with a plexi-glass waiting area.

"Pull over at that bus stop. You and junior are getting out."

She looked at him, a quick glance, then away.

"Your forehead is bleeding," she said in a shaky voice.

"Well, aren't you sweet, worrying about my bloody forehead."

She parked beside the bus stop and shot him another quick glance. Was she worried about the gash on his brow? No, she was looking at his gun.

"You got a cell phone?" he said.

"Yes. In my purse." She sniffled, sucking snot down her throat.

"Throw the purse over here by my feet."

She took a big leather pouch off the center console and tossed it into the foot-well at his feet.

"When you get out, I'll have my gun on junior. You do anything stupid, I'll *shoot* him."

"I won't do anything stupid. Please don't hurt my baby."

He smiled. "See how nice I am, finding you a nice dry place to wait out of the rain? Go."

She jumped out, slammed the door, ran around the hood, opened the back door and fumbled with the car-seat release. The red-faced kid shrieked and waved its tiny fists.

"Wait in the shelter until a bus comes. Don't call the cops. If you do, I will track you down and I will kill you and your kid."

She yanked the squalling kid out of the car seat, slammed the door and ran. He clambered over the center console into the driver's seat and watched her, clutching the kid to her chest, probably thought she'd died and gone to heaven, rescuing her kid from the big scary man with the bloody forehead.

Good riddance. He had bigger fish to fry. The Diva-bitch. He put the MPV in gear and touched his forehead. His fingers came away sticky with blood, and the merciless pain continued unabated. He pulled a Belinda CD out of his knapsack and put it in the disc player.

Maybe Belinda and her magic flute would sooth his headache.

The magic flute she would never play again.

Vengeance was going to be sweet.

She watched the rain pelt the window, pinging against the glass, felt her heart thump inside her chest. The doctor had given her a shot to make her sleep, but it wasn't working. Every muscle in her body quivered with tension. She shut her eyes. Saw visions of Silverman. His ghastly shaven head. Those horrible lips. Those voracious eyes.

She moaned into the pillow. She had escaped, but her beloved Haynes flute was back in that hellhole.

Music had been the center of her world forever. During the dark days after the wrong-way driver decimated her family, music had kept her from self-destructing. Lonely and heartsick, she had even considered suicide. The music had saved her. She couldn't remember a time when she wasn't playing her flute. Nothing was more important to her.

Until her life was at stake.

Then, without hesitation, she had dropped her flute on the floor.

Dropped it. On the floor. An unthinkable act. Until today.

And now she was alive. She was in a hospital. Surrounded by people who cared about her, people like the doctor. She tried to remember the woman's name but her brain was fried.

Her eyes closed. She was safe now.

Frank was right outside. Frank would protect her.

CHAPTER 42

He parked in a No-Parking zone near the side entrance of City Hospital and hopped out of the MPV. The torrential rain had slackened to a drizzle. Droplets of rain glistened on the green shrubbery beside the entrance, but the area behind them was dry, protected by the overhanging roof. He retrieved the knapsack from the MPV and hid it behind the shrubs. Hiding the Ruger behind his thigh, he mounted the steps to the glass double doors.

He felt like Rambo. Rambo on a mission. Kill some cops, including Renzi, and make The Diva wish she'd never been born.

He took the blood-soaked bandage out of his pocket, held it to his forehead and stepped inside. A uniformed security guard sat inside a glassed-in booth beside the door.

"I need help," he said, making it sound urgent.

Without hesitation, the guard came out of the booth. And saw the gun.

"Turn around and go out the door."

The guard's eyes hardened. "Fuck you."

He slammed the Ruger against the bridge of the guard's nose. The man reeled back, bounced off the wall and slid into a seated position. He clubbed him again, two hard blows to the head. The guard flopped sideways onto the floor. He ran outside and grabbed his knapsack and raced back inside.

The guard lay motionless, eyes closed. Blood pooled on the gray-tile floor beneath his head. The wannabe-hero was down for the count.

He loped down the hall to the lobby. Four women looked up, gaping at him. A woman with a towheaded toddler in her lap. Two black women, one pregnant, the other one older with kinky gray hair. A pasty-faced teenager slumped in a chair, obviously pregnant, reading a paperback novel.

The woman behind the reception desk saw him and gasped.

"Nobody moves, nobody gets hurt." To the receptionist he said, "Where's Belinda Scully?" Got back a rabbity look, the woman looking like she wanted to run, hands fluttering to her mouth.

"Tell me or I will kill you right now." He aimed the gun at her head.

"I don't—" Reacting to his murderous glare, she said, "S-s-somewhere on Level Three."

"Very good. Go sit with the patients."

Eyes wide, she came around the desk. He hit her with the gun butt, and she went down, shrieking. The teenaged girl yelped and clapped a hand over her mouth. The black women watched him, flat-eyed and expressionless. They knew not to fuck with a guy with a gun.

"Anyone calls the cops I'll come back and kill you. Believe it."

He trotted down the hall to a pair of elevators, hit the call button, set the knapsack on the floor and checked his wristwatch. Not bad. He'd been inside the hospital less than two minutes.

When the elevator on the right arrived, he trained the Ruger on the metal doors, tensed when the ping sounded.

The doors opened. An empty car.

He grabbed the knapsack, got in and hit the button for Three.

In the waiting area, the black women and the pregnant teenager bolted for the door. The woman with the toddler did too, but paused at a fire alarm long enough to pull the handle.

———

Cursing under his breath, Frank opened the door to the hall. The alarm was deafening. A door opposite Belinda's suite opened onto a stairwell. Their only escape route. Elevators weren't an option now. Her suite was at the end of a short hall that intersected the main corridor thirty yards to his left. Beyond the right-angle turn were two delivery suites, a nurse's station and a pair of elevators. Shouts and urgent voices came from that direction.

He shut the door and said to Kelly, "Go check on Belinda. Tell her not to worry."

She gave him a look—*Don't worry? Are you crazy?*—opened Belinda's door and went inside.

She was right. He was frantic, his fears fueled by the clanging alarm. He called Vobitch, told him the situation and they made a quick decision. As he closed his cell phone, Kelly came out of Belinda's room, shaking her head.

"I can't believe she's sleeping through this."

"We think Stoltz is here."

"Here?" Her sea-green eyes widened with dismay.

The alarm raked his nerves like a buzz saw. "Vobitch said SWAT got in the house, but it was empty. I think Stoltz came here to kill Belinda."

"But how would he know she's—"

"I don't know, but he knows we made him for the Ziegler murder. He's got nothing to lose. Belinda got away. He wants revenge. Vobitch wants us to stay with her until more cops get here. It's too dangerous to take her down the stairs. Stoltz could be anywhere."

The hall door opened and Frank raised his SIG.

A security guard in an NOPD uniform saw the gun and said, "Hey, don't get excited! We're evacuating the hospital."

Frank showed his NOPD badge. "We're staying."

"I got orders to evacuate everybody who can move."

"We've got orders to stay here with Belinda Scully. The kidnapper may be in the hospital. Get everyone else out fast."

Get them out so Stoltz doesn't have too many targets.

The ear-splitting alarm drove nails into his aching head. As the elevator passed Level Two he aimed the Ruger at the door. No telling what awaited him on Level Three. He'd wanted to find The Diva-bitch before the cops arrived, but that might not be possible now.

The elevator stopped, and the doors slowly rolled open.

Two men stood five feet away, an NOPD cop and a light-skinned black man, who was saying, "I can't leave! What about my wife?"

The cop glanced his way and his hand twitched toward his belt.

"Don't even think about it. Hands up, both of you."

The black man gaped at him stupidly. "My wife's having a baby!"

"Shut up." To the cop he said, "You gonna evacuate the hospital?"

The cop, a grim-faced man with hard blue eyes, held his hands at shoulder level palms out. "That's what I'm doing now."

He risked a quick glance down the hall, saw a vacant nursing station, beyond it a pair of double-doors. "What's behind those doors?"

"My wife is in labor!" the man shouted, wild-eyed.

"I told you to shut up." To the cop he said, "What's behind the doors?"

"Two delivery suites. This guy's wife is in one. The other one's vacant."

Should he kill them? It hardly seemed sporting. Too much like shooting chickens in a coop. "Okay, Daddy, get out of here."

The man's face puckered. "I'm not going anywhere. My wife—"

"Move or I'll kill you! Use those stairs over there."

"Do what he says," the cop said.

"Exactly right. Move or you're dead." The man gave him a nasty look, shuffled slowly to the door, opened it and started downstairs. He leveled the Ruger at the cop. "How come there's nobody on the nursing station?"

"There's no patient rooms on Level Three, and the delivery room doors lock automatically. Doctors and nurses are in there with the woman in labor."

"Uh-huh. Where's Belinda Scully?"

The guard's eyes shifted down and away toward the floor.

"Answer me!" A muscle jumped in the guard's jaw. Another cop with a hero complex. The bitch was here on Level Three, with Renzi probably. But the alarm was blaring and time was running out. "Do those keys on your belt open any closets?"

"Yes."

"Take me to the nearest one. And no funny stuff. I mean business."

I mean business. That was a Rambo line if he ever heard one.

With the ear-splitting alarm clanging in their ears, they walked down the corridor past the nurse's station until the cop stopped at a door.

"If that's not a closet, you're dead. Open the door."

The cop looked at the Ruger. Took out a key and opened the door of what appeared to be a supply closet, bed linens and pillows lining the shelves.

The alarm stopped. Unnerved by the sudden quiet, he glanced behind him. The hall was empty. No cops with guns drawn. Not yet anyway.

"Stand still while I take your weapon out of the holster."

He set the knapsack on the floor, touched the Ruger to the guard's neck and pulled the Glock-9mm out of the guard's holster. And realized the radio handset on the cop's belt was emitting faint voices.

"Hand me the keys and that radio. Don't screw up or I'll kill you."

"Don't shoot me. I got a wife and three kids."

"Do what I say and you'll be fine."

The cop handed him the metal key ring, then the radio handset.

"Get in the closet and take off your shirt and pants."

The cop stepped into the closet. Stripped off his dark-blue shirt and dropped it on the floor. Took off his belt. "My shoes. I don't think I can get my pants over them."

"Don't worry about it. Just drop your pants to your ankles."

The cop shoved his pants down to his ankles.

He set the Ruger against the cop's head and pulled the trigger. The cop fell as if he'd been pole-axed. His legs twitched, two quick spasms, and went still. Blood gushed from his head onto the closet floor.

Fuck-all! His ears were ringing, first the alarm, now the gunshot. He pulled off the cop's shoes and trousers, grabbed the uniform shirt and backed out of the closet. And heard sirens. Many sirens.

The Diva was somewhere on Level Three, but he had no time to find her now. And when he did find her, he intended to spend some time with her. No quick mercy killing for the Diva-bitch.

He locked the closet, hooked the police radio on his belt, stuffed the uniform in his knapsack and ran down the hall to a sign that said: LEVEL THREE PARKING GARAGE. He sprinted down a long glassed-in walkway into the garage. Now the sirens were louder, and closer. Ten yards to his left, a lighted sign above a door said: STAIRS. He took them two at a time, grunting under the weight of the knapsack. His forehead throbbed, but he ignored it. Focus on the mission. Get to the roof, take out some cops, and call Renzi. Renzi's cell number was burned into his brain.

Hey loverboy. Give me Belinda or I'll kill more cops.

On Level Four he entered the garage and saw a half dozen parked cars. Yellow arrows on the cement floor pointed to an up-ramp. He loped up the ramp to Level Five. Three cars were angle-parked in an area sheltered by the roof. He ran up the next ramp to the roof. No cars. Perfect. Except for the excruciating pain in his head and the sirens approaching the hospital.

A four-foot cement wall lined the perimeter of the roof. He ran to one corner and peeked over the wall. The street below bordered the eastern end of the garage with the entry and exit ramps. No cop cars, but soon there would be. Through the misty drizzle, he walked the perimeter. At the northwest corner he found the perfect sniper position. Six stories below him, four fire trucks idled in front of the hospital entrance. Firemen in yellow helmets were already rushing into the hospital.

Might as well get in some target practice before the cops arrived.

He removed the two sections of the Bushmaster M4 carbine from his knapsack and assembled it with practiced speed. Adjusted the 6-position stock. Dry-fired the weapon to make sure it was ready. It was.

He clipped on the Nikon Monarch scope, raised the carbine above the top of the wall and peered through the scope. Not quite right.

He adjusted the scope and sighted again. Much better.

That fireman was crystal clear in the scope's crosshairs.

CHAPTER 43

She swung her legs over the side of the bed. A minute ago she'd heard fireworks outside. She turned and looked out the window. How could it be fireworks? It wasn't dark enough. Turning her head made her dizzy.

Bracing her palms on the mattress to steady herself, she eased off the bed. The tile floor felt icy beneath her bare feet. She adjusted the hospital robe and belted it around her waist. Stuck her feet into the foam slippers on the floor beside the bed. Shuffled toward the door.

Waves of nausea and dizziness hit her. She lurched forward, grabbed the handle and opened the door. And bit back a scream.

Frank had a gun in his hand and so did the woman beside him.

She braced her hand on the doorjamb to keep from falling. "What's wrong? I woke up and heard fireworks."

"Someone pulled a fire alarm," Frank said. "You were asleep. We didn't want to wake you. Nothing to worry about. Kelly, help her back to bed."

Something was wrong. She could see it in his eyes. "I don't want to go back to bed. I want you to tell me what's wrong."

His cell phone rang. He checked the faceplate. His eyes crinkled, not in a good way. "Kelly will explain. I need to talk to someone."

"I don't want *Kelly* to explain." But Frank turned and left with the gun in his hand. The woman with the short dark hair took her arm and guided her back to her room.

"You look woozy, Belinda. You need to lie down."

She sat on the side of the bed. She felt woozy all right. Woozy and frightened. Something was wrong. Very wrong.

The woman holstered her gun and approached the bed. "I'm Kelly O'Neil. We met a couple of weeks ago at another hospital."

"I remember," she said, picturing the woman who'd waltzed into the room with Frank the night Jake died. The woman dressed in shorts and a halter-top, smelling of sex.

Kelly smiled faintly. "I figured you would. You're smart, Belinda. I'm amazed that you got away from this guy. He's a tough hombre."

Tough hombre? Kelly O'Neil couldn't begin to imagine what that monster had done to her.

"Tell me what's wrong! Why were you and Frank standing outside my room with guns? He got away, didn't he." Hoping she was wrong, but knowing in her heart she was right.

Kelly O'Neil sucked her lower lip into her mouth, frowning. Thinking.

An ice pick of fear stabbed her chest. "Is he here?"

"It would help if you could describe him and tell us what he's wearing."

An icy calm settled over her. "I'll tell you the only thing you need to know. If he's here, he'll kill me." She studied the woman at the foot of the bed, regarding her with cool green eyes. "You're worried about Frank."

"Yes. He wants to get this guy and I'm afraid—"

"You're in love with him."

Kelly blinked her no-longer-cool eyes. Now her eyes were deep pools of emotion.

"Frank seems like a nice guy," she said. What an inane comment. If Frank hadn't come along and put her in his car, she'd be dead. The monster would have caught her and killed her.

Kelly raised her hand—the hand that wasn't holding the gun—and wiped sweat off her forehead. "Yes, he is. But I'm not in love with him."

Not yet, but you will be soon. "He's a monster."

Kelly's eyes widened.

"Not Frank. Silverman. Stoltz. Whatever his name is."

"Did he rape you?" Kelly's expression softened. "You can tell me if you want. Sometimes it helps to talk about it, get it out of your system."

She rubbed her arms. Nothing could erase the horror of that monster.

"When I woke up this morning—" Was it only this morning? It seemed like this nightmare had begun days ago. Eons ago. "When I woke up he was in my bedroom. I asked him to leave but he wouldn't. He made me go downstairs and cook him breakfast."

"That's disgusting." Kelly glanced at the door, tense, vigilant.

She plucked at her tangled hair. "I made him scrambled eggs and coffee. I thought if I did what he asked he'd leave." She sucked in a ragged breath, felt the cold hard needles of horror all over again. "How stupid."

"Was that when Frank called you?"

She shut her eyes. Saw the nightmare unspool again in vivid color. "No, that was later. When he finished eating, he asked me what I wanted." She opened her eyes and looked at Kelly. "I said I wanted him to leave. And he said he would if I kissed him goodbye."

Kelly gasped. "What a sick fuck! You're right. He is a monster."

Her eyes welled with tears. "He promised to leave if I kissed him, and I thought: *What's one kiss? Kiss him and he'll go and this nightmare will be over.* But when I kissed him he stuck his tongue in my mouth." She gagged and clutched her stomach, nauseated by the memory of that disgusting slimy tongue inside her mouth.

Kelly rubbed her back. "It's okay, Belinda. I probably would have done the same thing. You did what you thought was right. How could you know he's a fucking creep?"

She couldn't believe that she'd just described the most hideous thing she'd ever experienced to this total stranger. Kelly O'Neil, who was in love with Frank Renzi, whether she wanted to admit it or not.

"I should have known. I should have stabbed him with a kitchen knife."

"No, no, no." Kelly rubbed her back in a circular motion. "Don't second guess yourself. You outsmarted the son-of-a bitch and got away. Not many women would have been brave enough to do what you did."

"Thank you." Strangely, she did feel better after talking about it.

Kelly smiled. "You're welcome. Tell me how you got away."

Standing behind the nurses' station in the main hall, he gripped his SIG in one hand, his cell phone in the other. The nurses had left in a hurry, papers and medical charts strewn over the desk. A small TV was still on, tuned to a local channel, volume muted. A grim-faced reporter was talking at the camera. A graphic at the bottom of the screen said: *City Hospital Under Siege.*

He raised the cell to his mouth, forced himself to be calm. That's what hostage negotiations were all about. Don't let the fucker rattle you. Stoltz no longer had Belinda, but dozens of patients, doctors and nurses inside City Hospital were, for all intents and purposes, hostages. "What do you want?"

"What took you so long, loverboy? You been making out with Belinda?"

"What do you want?"

"You know what I want. Belinda. Put her on. Let me talk to her."

"I can't. She's not here."

"You're a motherfucking liar! I know she's here."

On the TV screen, footage of the parking lot at the other end of the hospital appeared: civilian and police vehicles parked haphazardly, hospital workers and visitors milling around. Out of range of the nutcase with the rifle on the garage roof. The glassed-in walkway to the garage was ten feet away. He wanted to go up there and kill the bastard. But Stoltz was a sniper with a high-powered rifle. "She can't talk to you. The doctor sedated her."

"Bullshit! You got five minutes or I'll kill more cops. Call you in five."

A click sounded in his ear. Pain stabbed his gut.

Five minutes to make a plan. Or more people would die.

He trotted up the ramp toward the roof. Renzi didn't want him to talk to Belinda. Didn't want him killing people, either. He rounded the last turn and heard an ominous sound. *Whup-whup-whup.* Fuck-all! The cops had sent up a chopper. He ducked beside a support column as the sound drew closer. Eased his head around the column and scanned the sky. And laughed aloud.

A red-and-white news chopper with a Channel-Five logo hovered over the roof, filming the most exciting thing that ever happened in this town. But he couldn't have helicopters over-flying the roof. The cops might get ideas and send one of theirs. The chopper receded into the distance, circled and came back. He let loose with the carbine, ten, twenty, thirty rounds. The chopper dipped and swooped and flew away. He hadn't hit it, but he'd scared them off. Rambo couldn't have done better.

He descended the ramp, hunkered down in a corner of the Level 5 garage and dug a power bar out of his knapsack. The driving rain had stopped, but the drizzle continued and the temperature had fallen. His commando outfit was drenched, and the sharp wind gusting through the garage was giving him chills. He was tired and hungry. But he'd survived worse. Beatings from Pa. Humiliations from Rachael. Betrayal from Belinda.

Renzi was probably pacing her room right now, waiting for his call. Fuck Renzi. The Diva was on Level Three. It shouldn't be hard to find her. Kill Renzi and hoo-eee, let the vengeance begin!

He swallowed the last of the power bar, ran up the ramp to the northwest corner of the roof and peeped over the cement wall. Two NOPD squad cars sat kitty-cornered across an intersection, light racks flashing. Two more blocked the garage entrance. Two cops in each car.

Not smart if a sniper with a Bushmaster M-4 was on the roof.

He sited through the Nikon scope. The cops were crystal clear inside their cars. Hell, one was smoking a cigarette, taking a drag right now . . .

CHAPTER 44

He ran down the main corridor, turned left at the end and saw Kelly in the hall outside Belinda's suite holding her Glock with both hands. "Where the hell have you been? Jesus! I was worried about you."

An angry woman, half-Irish, half-Italian. He knew what that meant. Full-blown fury was a heartbeat away. But he had no time to placate her.

"Let me use your cell. I need to call Vobitch. That call I got was from Stoltz. He wants to talk to Belinda. He's going to call me back on mine in five minutes. If we don't let him talk to Belinda, he said he'd kill more cops."

Wordlessly, Kelly handed him her cell. He called Vobitch, told him what Stoltz had said and checked his watch. Two minutes gone already.

"He's dicking you around," Vobitch said. "He just shot at the squads blocking the garage entrance, hit both drivers. SWAT's on the way. Captain Martin wants to talk to you, channel-three on the radio."

Martin was the NOPD Deputy Chief in charge of the operation. Operation Sniper. Frank got on his radio and called him.

Martin: *I'm sending four detectives up the stairs outside your room, two to guard the stairwell and two to guard the main corridor where it intersects your hall. The SWAT team is on their way. Stay alert and keep me informed.*

"Roger, Captain. Thanks." He hooked the radio on his belt and said to Kelly, "We better check Belinda. How are you two getting along?"

She gave him an odd look. "Not great, but better than before."

He tapped on the inner door. "Belinda? It's Frank and Kelly."

When they went inside, Belinda's face was ashen. Suspended from the ceiling above the bed was a television set, picture on, sound muted.

"I don't want you watching news updates on TV," he said.

"Stop treating me like a child. He's shooting at firemen and policemen!" Her voice rose in a crescendo of anger. "Jake would still be alive if it wasn't for me. He *told* me Silverman was weird, but I was too stupid to see it. Now he's killing people. And it's my fault."

"Stop." Kelly went over and put her arm around Belinda. "None of this is your fault. He's crazy. You are not responsible for this."

"Kelly's right," he said. "He kidnapped you and held you in that house."

"I want to talk to him."

"Talking to him won't do any good."

Belinda glared at him, her eyes blazing fury. "Frank, he's killing innocent people. I know how to make him stop. Let me talk to him."

He saw the fierce intensity in her eyes, knew that if she set her mind on something, she wouldn't quit. She wanted to talk to Stoltz. No way in hell was he going to let her.

"We can't let him kill people," she snapped. "We have to do something."

"We are doing something," he said. "He's surrounded. He's not getting out of this hospital." Not alive, anyway. But she was right. They had to do something or more cops might die.

"Maybe Belinda can help us get him," Kelly said. "If we lured him down here to talk to her—"

"Lure him down here? This is exactly where he wants to be. He's up on the roof right now trying to figure out how to get to Belinda. And if he does, he'll kill her. Or die trying."

Belinda flinched, but he wasn't going to sugarcoat the pill. Stoltz had nothing to lose. He wanted to go out in a blaze of glory, but his main objective was Belinda. He'd have fun with her first, his idea of fun anyway, rape, torture and humiliate her. Then he would kill her.

"You could hide in the bathroom," Belinda said. "When he comes in the room you could arrest him."

"*Arrest* him? The only way to stop this guy is to kill him."

"Frank," Kelly said, "I still think we could use her to get to him."

"What? You want me to run up there and invite him down?"

Kelly's eyes flashed in anger, but he didn't care. He had no time for this. The bastard was roaming the roof, shooting cops. SWAT was on the way, but Stoltz was perfectly positioned to deal out more death and destruction.

"Stay here with Belinda," he said. "I need to talk to the reinforcements."

He peeked over the wall at the cop cars blocking the garage entrance. Both windshields were blown out, the drivers slumped in their seats. Their partners were hunkered outside the squads, using the doors for protection. He fired a burst to keep them in position. Then, stooping low so they couldn't see him, he ran to the northeast corner. Parked catty-cornered at an intersection were two more squad cars. He jammed in a fresh clip, drew a bead on one car and fired in short bursts. *Tat-tat-tat, tat-tat-tat.*

Keep the cops busy so they wouldn't get any ideas about coming up the ramp to ambush him. He fired again. When he paused to look, the cops outside the squads fired at him. He raked them with a merciless hail of bullets. The recoil punched his shoulder and the sound hurt his ears.

His headache returned with a vengeance.

Frank stepped into the hall just as the stairwell door opposite Belinda's suite opened. Warren Wood stepped into the hall, chest thrust out, cheeks pale against his dark Fu Manchu. Larry Nixon, Chuck Duncan's replacement, was behind him. Nixon was stocky and several inches shorter than Warren. His smooth pink-cheeked face looked like he'd just shaved, and his eyes, unlike Warren's, were full of apprehension.

"Me and Larry will set up at the corner of the main hall," Wood said. "We'll protect your flank." He turned and swaggered down the hall.

"Be careful," Frank said. Wood acted confident, but to him it seemed like false bravado. Nixon looked worried, and rightfully so. The nutcase on the roof had already shot two firemen and several cops.

Otis Jones and Sam Wallace entered the hallway. Unlike Warren, the two black detectives displayed no bravado, just grim determination. They had faced armed killers before. "A helluva mess," Otis said, his dark eyes somber.

"Damn straight," Sam said, gripping a radio handset in one hand, his service weapon in the other. "The bastard's up there shooting cops."

Otis ran a hand over his gray-speckled hair. "Reminds me of the sniper on the roof of the Howard Johnson's Hotel back in seventy-three. He killed nine people, five of 'em cops. That was before I joined the force, but some of the older guys still talk about it."

He was glad to see Otis. Otis had worked District-One for years, where shots were fired every day. He'd be steady in a crisis. Sam was younger, but he had a steely resolve about him. Sam would be okay.

He wished he felt as confident about Wood and Nixon. He turned and watched them disappear around the corner into the main hall.

If Stoltz figured out where Belinda was, that's the way he would come.

His head throbbed, a relentless crescendo of pain. He took his meds out of the knapsack and dry-swallowed them. Big showdown with the Diva-bitch and Renzi coming up. Too bad he couldn't kill Rachel, too.

Had she really said that to Pa? *Ben wants to fuck me.*

Giving Pa another reason to hate him. He took out his cell phone.

He'd given up any idea of getting out of here alive. Why not settle the score with Rachel too? Tell her about his final conversation with Pa.

His sweet moment of truth, crystal clear in his mind even now.

A week after Rachel called to tell him about her born-again experience, lamenting that Pa wouldn't tell her about her birth parents, he'd called the asshole. Pa was shocked to hear from him, got over it quick when he invited him out for dinner. He picked him up and took him to a swanky restaurant in Providence. The place was jammed so they had to park on the top level of the adjacent parking garage. Pa's hair had more gray streaks than he remembered, but he hadn't seen the man for a long time.

Figuring his plan would go easier if Pa was soused, he got him drunk. It wasn't hard. Pa sucked down four Jack Daniels, hardly touched his dinner. Didn't want to hear about his exploits with Special Ops, either.

Pa always had to be the center of attention.

After dinner, he asked about his birth parents.

"You don't wanna know," Pa said.

"Yes, I do," he said, "and so does Rachel."

But Pa just sucked up more Jack Daniels and turned maudlin, feeling sorry for himself, Ma was gone, Rachel was gone, blah, blah, blah.

"What about me?" he said. "I just bought you a nice dinner. But you never gave a shit about me, did you Pa? It was always about Rachel."

He paid the bill and they left. He had to help Pa to the elevator in the garage, grabbing his arm to steady him when he swayed. They were about the same height, but Pa was heavier, arms thick and muscular. Pa's obsessions in life were pumping iron and maintaining his marksmanship at a gun range.

And fucking Rachel.

When they got to his car, he didn't unlock the door.

"Come on, boy. Let's get in the car so you can take me home."

Not so fast. He had a plan, and taking Pa home wasn't part of it.

His heart pounded a frenzy of hammer-strokes. Time to deliver The Speech, the one he'd fantasized about for twenty years. His Ruger was in a holster inside his jacket. How easy it would be. One shot to the head and bye-bye Daddy-O. But that wasn't the ending he'd planned for this drama.

"Time we had a talk, Pops." His heart was beating so hard he thought his chest would explode.

"Talk?" Pa looked at him, bleary-eyed. "We got nothing to talk about. Take me home." So drunk he could barely stand and still giving orders, still thinking he was in charge.

He took out the Ruger and aimed it at his father.

"The hell you doin', boy? Put that thing down."

"No. That's what you did to me my whole life. Put me down. Nothing I ever did was good enough to suit you. Rachel was perfect. I was dog shit."

Pa worked his lips, not saying anything but thinking, all shifty-eyed now.

"You and Rachel were pretty tight back then, right, Pops? Real tight."

Pa's piggish eyes went cold. "Don't talk to me like that, boy."

"Why not? It's true. You were fucking her."

"Shut up. You got no idea what was goin' on back then."

"Yes I do. Rachel told me. You know what they call it when a father fucks his daughter, Pops? Incest."

"She's not my blood." Clamping his lips together, glaring at him.

"Bullshit. You and Ma raised her like a daughter."

"But she ain't my *blood,* boy, and you ain't neither. Get that fuckin' gun out of my face."

"Right. I'm not your blood, and thank God for that. You started fucking your daughter when she was eleven. You turned her into a cocktease."

"That what you call it? Cocktease?" An ugly chuckle. "Rachel told me you wanted to fuck her. That right, boy?"

"She's not my sister."

"Don't be so sure. You got the same mother."

The statement took his breath away.

"I don't believe it. Who?"

Got back a big wolfish grin. "Your mama's a fuckin' whore, slept with any guy that came along, didn't have the sense to protect herself, kept getting pregnant. We adopted you first, then Rachael. God knows who your daddies were. Rachel turned into a looker, but you? Hell, you were ugly from the git-go, stayed ugly your whole miserable worthless life."

Recalling Pa's final insult, he leaned against the cement wall and massaged his aching head. Felt the hatred all over again.

He punched Rachel's number into his cell and hit Send.

CHAPTER 45

He was ready to explode. After making sure Otis and Sam were set up to guard the stairwell opposite the door to Belinda's suite, he had returned to her room. He felt like a lion in a cage, prodded by an angry zookeeper. Stoltz was shooting cops from the roof, and Belinda was pissed off because he wouldn't let her talk to him. Another minute and he'd blow up at her.

Kelly's cell phone rang. She checked the ID, gave him a warning look and answered the call. "Hello, Rachel?"

Letting him know it was the sister. He mouthed: *Let me talk to her.*

She waved him off. "Calm down, Rachel. He did what?" Her eyes widened, "My God, that's awful."

Belinda grabbed his arm. "Is that his sister on the phone?"

He shushed her and whispered, "Kelly talked to her earlier today."

"Rachel," Kelly said, "if you can help us—" And after a pause, "Great! Give me the number." Signaling him to write it down.

He grabbed a pen and wrote down numbers as Kelly spoke them aloud.

"Thank you, Rachael. We'll keep you informed." Kelly clicked off and beamed him a triumphant smile. "That's his cell phone number."

"Call him," Belinda said in a steely voice. "I want to talk to him."

"Hold it," he said. To Kelly, he said, "Why was Rachael so upset?"

"I could barely understand her at first. She was hysterical, crying and screaming. Stoltz called her and said horrible things about her birth mother. She said they were adopted. She's bullshit at him, called him every vile name in the book. She wants us to kill him."

Belinda's mouth gaped open. "Kill him?"

Kelly nodded. "*Kill him,* she said. *He doesn't deserve to live.*"

Fuzzy-headed with pain, he crept to the corner of the roof.

But no pain in the world could dampen his euphoria. Telling Rachel what Pa had said was almost as good as killing her. *You're my half-sister, Rachel. We had the same mommy, and mommy-dearest was a prostitute.*

"Liar!" she'd screamed. Poor Rachel, fucking Pa all those years, then staying in touch with him, hoping he'd reveal the names of her birth parents. All that anticipation only to learn that her birth mother—the mother they'd shared, God knows who their fathers were—all that hope and expectation only to find out that mommy-dearest was a slut.

He smiled. Did that piss Rachael off or what? Raging at him, calling him vile names. But what could she do? Pa was dead.

He hadn't told her that part of the story. Pa hadn't been prepared for his Big Speech that night. Hadn't been prepared for what happened next, either.

He massaged his aching forehead.

You were ugly from the get-go, stayed ugly your whole miserable worthless life.

Pa's final insult. His first impulse was to shoot him. Then he'd decided a bullet was too good for the asshole. He took Pa by the shoulders, muscled him over to the cement wall of the parking garage, heaved him up and over.

Hanging over the side, four stories up, Pa clung to the wall with both hands, mouth open to expose yellow cigarette-stained teeth, skin taut around his eyes. Eyes full of fury. "Quit fucking around, boy. Pull me up."

"Not a chance. You always loved to put me down, did it every chance you got. Now I'm going to put you down. Way down."

He hit Pa's left hand with the butt of the Ruger, saw panic blossom in Pa's eyes as he lost his grip, clinging to the wall with one hand now.

"Have a nice trip." He hit the other hand and watched him fall.

Then he got in his car. When he exited the garage, he saw a crowd of people around Pa's body. He kept going. They ruled it an accidental death. No one had seen it happen, and the alcohol level in Pa's blood was five times the legal limit. When the cops interviewed him, he said he had offered his father a ride home, but his father refused, so he'd left.

What was it the fire-and-brimstone preachers said? *Vengeance is mine.*

Seeing the panic in Pa's eyes before he fell was priceless, better than any orgasm he'd ever had. He smiled at the memory.

Vengeance had been sweet. Now he was ready for more. That sobered him up. Special Ops Rule: Always protect your flank.

Sooner or later the cops would come up the garage ramp. But they knew he had an automatic weapon, knew he'd kill lots of cops if they did. Captain

Marvel had a marvelous plan. A SWAT team was on its way, men in body armor, armed with flashbangs and grenades.

The second flashpoint was the Level Three walkway into the hospital. He figured they hadn't come after him that way for the same reason. Trapped in the corridor, they'd be vulnerable, exposed to his high-powered weapon.

But it was only a matter of time. Soon they would mount a full-scale assault. Maybe they'd wait until dark. Leaden gray clouds hung low in the sky, blocking the sun, but there were a couple of hours of daylight left.

He eased his head above the wall, saw a big black Hummer lumbering down the street. Captain Marvel's SWAT team. He grabbed the Bushmaster and checked the magazine. Half-full. That should do it. He sighted through the scope at the Hummer's windshield and fired. The windshield exploded, splintering into fragments.

That would hold them for a while. But time was running out. He ran down the ramp to Level Four and did a careful reconnaissance. No cops. He ran down to Level Three. All clear there, too.

Alive with anticipation he headed for the walkway.

The Wagnerian ring-tone of his cell stopped him, echoing through the cavernous garage. He punched on to silence it, but said nothing.

"Give it up, Stoltz. You're surrounded. Put your weapons down and walk out of there now. Nobody else has to die."

Oh yes they do. As many as possible.

"You keeping track of the body count, Renzi?"

Silence on the phone. Renzi had no answer for that one.

Feeling the delicious anticipation in his groin, he said, "How's Belinda?"

"She's okay. It's good that you didn't hurt her. That will count in your favor if you surrender."

Hurt her? He should have killed the bitch. Soon he would and he'd take his time doing it. He'd put his hands around her lovely neck and squeeze until her eyes rolled up in her head. But not right away.

He had other delights to inflict upon her first.

"Belinda wants to talk to you," Renzi said.

Incredulous, he laughed aloud. "She does? How sweet."

"Wait a second and I'll put her on."

"No fucking way. Send her up to the roof so I can talk to her up close and personal." *Up close and personal.* There was a Rambo line.

Silence on the other end. "What's the matter, Renzi? Doesn't Belinda wanna talk to me up close and personal?"

"You're not in any position to be setting conditions."

Mr. All-Powerful, thinking he was in charge. He'd find out soon enough who had the upper hand.

"Come on up to the roof and take me out yourself, Renzi. I dare you."

He shut the cell phone. Rachael, the other traitorous bitch, must have given Renzi the number.

Then he thought: GPS. They could pinpoint his position through his cell phone. He ran to an outside wall and dropped it over the side.

"Did you hear me?" Frank gripped his cell phone in his sweaty hand, aware that Kelly and Belinda were listening. Nothing from Stoltz. He closed the cell and shook his head at Kelly. "He's gone."

Kelly's cell phone rang. "Vobitch," she said, and handed him the phone.

"He just shot up the SWAT team Hummer," Vobitch said, "blew out the windshield."

"Damn! I just talked to him on his cell. He wants Belinda to come to the roof. When I nixed that, he dared me to come up there." He rubbed the scar on his chin. "Let me go up and divert him, buy time for SWAT to set up."

"Hold on," Vobitch said. "Let me check with Captain Martin."

He waited, avoiding Kelly's eyes, knowing what he'd see in them: Fear and fury. Seconds later Vobitch came back on the line and outlined the plan.

Adrenaline zinged his veins, boosting his heart rate. Finally, some action. He motioned Kelly out of the room. "Stay here, while I talk to Kelly."

"Tell me what's going on!" Belinda shouted.

He shut the door to Belinda's room and told Kelly the plan. "Wood and Nixon guard the main hall. Sam Wallace guards the stairwell. You stay with Belinda. Otis and I will go through the walkway to the garage and pin Stoltz down on the roof while SWAT mobilizes on the ground floor. Captain Martin will send them up as soon as I call in a visual on Stoltz."

Kelly gazed at him, eyes full of dread. "Don't try to be a hero."

"I won't. Put Belinda on the floor behind the bed and don't open the door for anyone." He squeezed her arm. "Hey, we'll get this guy and go out for a beer later."

Her eyes glistened with tears. "Frank. No more jokes."

He put his arms around her, felt her arms clench around him. "Take care of yourself," he said, his voice thick with emotion.

Her feeble attempt at a smile failed. "You too," she whispered.

CHAPTER 46

Frank braced himself against the wall beside the walkway entrance. Felt the nervous buzz hit his gut. He racked his SIG-Sauer and locked eyes with Otis, poised at the other side of the glassed-in hallway.

"We gonna be sitting ducks," Otis said.

"I'll go first, you cover me. When I get halfway, run like hell."

He doubted Stoltz was waiting at the far end. Stoltz had plenty of targets to shoot at from the roof. But his thumping heart, racing pulse and sweaty palms said otherwise. His mind was rationalizing.

His body was preparing for extreme danger.

Come up to the roof and take me out yourself, Renzi. I dare you.

"If he shoots," Otis said, "hit the deck so's I can pop him without hitting you."

He nodded and stared down the glassed-in corridor. Thirty yards long, about the length of a basketball court. As point guard of his high school team, he'd stolen the ball at one end lots of times, raced the length of the court and for a lay-up. But not with an armed lunatic waiting under the hoop.

Buzzed with adrenaline, he got into a zone of concentration. Took a deep breath and took off, arms extended, SIG aimed at the dark maw of the parking garage entrance. The thud of his footsteps bounced off the walls, reverberating inside the enclosed walkway.

Time collapsed into slow motion. Legs pumping. Eyes focused. Mouth sucking air. No gunman in sight. No shots. No killer slugs. Yet.

Halfway there, he heard Otis's feet pounding behind him.

He ran faster, stomach tight, lungs burning.

Still no shots. No sign of Stoltz.

With an adrenaline-fueled burst of speed, he reached the far end and flattened his back against the wall outside the entrance, gasping for breath, his heart hammering his chest. He eyeballed the dark interior of the garage, a shadowy concrete jungle of thick support beams, waist-high walls and slanted ramps. No one in sight. So far.

Otis pounded down the hallway, flattened himself against the opposite wall, eyes darting everywhere, his Glock aimed at the garage.

"Clear in that direction," Frank whispered, pointing with his head.

"Same over there."

"I'm going in. Cover me." He crouched and sprang into the garage, arms extended, sweeping the area left to right.

Nothing. No motion. No sounds. No Stoltz.

Six cars were nosed against the cement wall of the up-ramp to the next level. He waved Otis into the garage. "Let's check those cars," he said. "They look empty, but you never know."

Otis swiveled his body in a 360-degree appraisal of the garage. "Man, this place creeps me out. Lotta places for the fucker to hide."

His neck prickled. Was Stoltz watching them, ready to pounce?

Methodically, they checked each car. Found no one.

Otis crept over to the up-ramp that led to Level Four and called, "Big military-type knapsack over here."

He trotted over to Otis. A large olive-green knapsack sat on the cement floor. Blood stains darkened one of the shoulder straps.

Come on up to the roof and take me out yourself, Renzi.

"Looks like he's wounded," Otis said. "Maybe one of the cops hit him. Lord knows they been trying."

"Maybe." He scratched the scar on his jaw. According to Rachel, Stoltz had called her and said vile things about her birth mother. But Stoltz was a liar. Maybe Rachel was, too. If she wasn't in touch with her brother, how did he get her phone number? Certain things didn't add up.

But he had no time to figure it out. They'd been in the garage for five minutes and Captain Martin was waiting for a report. He got on his radio.

"Renzi reporting. We're in the garage on Level Three. No sign of Stoltz, but we found his knapsack on the ramp that leads to the roof."

Captain Martin: "Let the bomb squad handle it. Continue to the roof as planned, but be careful. Do not attempt to capture him. SWAT is in position at Ground Level. Report in as soon you see him. Out."

He hooked the handset on his belt and looked at Otis.

"Captain Martin says head for the roof. Let's go."

He eased open the door of the Level Three stairwell, stepped out and clipped the radio on his belt. Captain Marvel was calling this Operation Sniper. How about Operation Get Even, or Operation Settle the Score?

No, how about Operation Payback? That'd be good. Lightning bolts of multi-colored pain zapped his forehead. Before planting the knapsack on the ramp, he'd swallowed two Percocets. They would make him drowsy, but so what? In an hour this would be over.

From now on there would only be death and destruction.

He smiled. Renzi had taken his the challenge to come to the roof. Renzi thought he was smarter than his adversary. Renzi was in for a surprise. He'd left his Bushman M4 on the roof. His crossbow and Blackhawk arrows were back at the safe house. Silent and deadly, the all-carbon 30-inch arrows with the killer tips had facilitated his escape.

He took a metal cylinder out of his pocket and screwed it onto the muzzle of his Beretta Cheetah. Not as silent as the arrows but just as deadly. He'd saved his best weapon for last. The Beretta was loaded with ten .22 LR subsonic cartridges, minimum recoil, low noise. Quite accurate if the target was less than fifty yards away. And his targets would be closer than that.

The barrel was five and a half inches long. The sound suppressor added another five. It might give him the edge he needed. His Ruger was in the pocket of his coveralls in case he needed a backup weapon.

He leaned against the wall beside the walkway to the hospital. He felt woozy. Was it the pain meds or hunger? He tried to remember his last meal. The scrambled eggs Belinda had made him this morning. His throat constricted and tears stung his eyes. How could it end this way? For years Belinda had been the center of his world. His reason to get up in the morning. His consolation when other things in his life turned to shit.

How could she be so cruel? All he had ever wanted was to love her.

He visualized her, asleep in her bed, unaware of his presence. So gorgeous he almost came, just looking at her. He could have overpowered her while she slept, but he hadn't. He'd been considerate, had waited until she woke up. But did she show any appreciation?

No. Even her kiss was a burnt offering. She'd only kissed him because he'd promised to leave.

I don't want to talk to you. I don't want to see you again. Not ever.

Her words seared into his brain. And with those devastating words, her monumental perfection—her sensual beauty and exquisite musicality—had crumbled to ashes. So had his love.

He had bent over backwards to please her. Not any more. Now she would do exactly what he said. Anticipation fueled the fire in his groin.

The cop's uniform shirt was a tight fit, but from a distance it wouldn't matter. First impressions were what counted. For a few seconds, the uniform would give him an advantage. Long enough to inflict the necessary damage.

He tugged the black knit cap lower on his shaven head. Nothing could hide the gash on his brow. The gash inflicted by the traitorous Diva-bitch.

She would pay dearly for her betrayal.

First he'd take out a few cops. Then, sweet vengeance.

He peeked around the corner. No one was visible at the far end of the glassed-in walkway. But when he reached the halfway point anyone in the main hall on Level Three would see him. Should he slither down the corridor on his belly like a snake, or should he march down it like Rambo?

What would Rambo do?

He stepped into the corridor, walking with his head held high. That's how you got into places where you didn't belong. Dressed in his finery, he'd done it in London, conning his way into Belinda's reception at the Royal Trafalgar. Dress the part and act like you belong. Attitude was everything.

That, and knowing you were going to die. Nothing to lose, everything to gain. Kill some cops. Fuck with Belinda, then kill her.

Five yards from the end of the walkway he slowed. Edged to the corner and stopped. This was the danger point. But he felt no fear.

When you're not afraid to die, everything is easy.

He edged into the hall with the Beretta hidden behind his right leg.

Twenty yards to his right, a man with a bushy Fu Manchu stood with one hand on his hip. His other hand held a 9-millimeter Glock.

Walking steadily toward Fu Manchu, he said, "How's it going?"

The guy frowned. Eyeballed his police uniform. "Who are you?"

He raised the Berretta and shot Fu Manchu between the eyes.

Special Ops rule: If the enemy is less than twenty yards away, hit the center of mass for a takedown. But if they're wearing body armor, go for the head. By the time Fu Manchu hit the floor, he was braced against the wall five feet away. The suppressor had muffled the shot, but not completely.

He gripped the Beretta, poised to shoot whoever came around the corner from the hall to his left. Two seconds passed. Three . . .

Another cop burst around the corner and shouted, "Warren!"

He shot the cop in the head. No moans, just a thump as his body hit the floor. Two down with a minimum of fuss. But two more cops awaited him.

Thanks to Captain Marvel, he knew one was in the stairwell opposite The Diva's room. Officer O'Neil was inside the room, protecting Belinda.

Officer O'Neil was dead meat.

Two shots, two cops down. The big question: Had the two remaining cops heard his partially silenced gunshots? He'd need one more to kill the cop in the stairwell. Even if O'Neil heard them, he had the advantage of surprise, if only for a split second. He was wearing the cop's uniform.

No cop wanted to shoot another cop. He'd kill Officer O'Neil first. Then he would fuck with Belinda. What a glorious treat.

His groin was burning with anticipation. But time was short. When Renzi and his partner found no one on the roof, they would report to Captain Marvel and go back to Belinda's room. Maybe he'd have time to kill Officer O'Neil, take his revenge on Belinda, and kill Renzi too. A perfect trifecta.

Pa would have been proud. Then again, maybe not.

His miserable-excuse-for-a-father had never said anything good about him. So his adopted son had killed him. Sublime justice.

He heard sounds, soft footsteps around the corner.

The mice were stirring and Rambo was waiting.

Frank stopped at the Level Five up-ramp that led to the roof. He and Otis had checked every car on Level Four. All empty. So were the cars on Level Five. The garage was eerily quiet. No sirens. No gunshots. He realized he was holding his breath. Let out a sigh. Took a deep breath. Listened.

The squad cars outside the garage would be full of radio chatter, but he couldn't hear it. The hospital and the garage were surrounded by massive oak trees, home to dozens of bird's nests, but he heard no birds chirping, either. It was as if the whole world had been silenced by a mute button.

He looked up at the sky. The rain had stopped but leaden clouds hung low in the sky. Not a sound from the roof.

Was Stoltz up there waiting to kill him?

Come up to the roof and take me out yourself, Renzi.

"Quiet up there," Otis muttered. "What the hell's he doing?"

"I don't know. But there's no cover once we get to the roof."

"Go up the ramp one on each side, we might hit him before he sees us."

Ugly scenarios churned in Frank's mind. Should they wait for SWAT? The only way down from the roof was this ramp. If Stoltz tried to leave the roof, he and Otis could stop him.

An elusive thought plinked his mind and flitted away.

Stoltz was up on the roof, an ex-military man ready-willing-and-able to shoot the police officers positioned around the garage with his high-powered weapon. If they didn't stop him, there would be more dead and wounded. During this interminable standoff, Stoltz had killed one firefighter, critically wounded another, and shot several cops, no word on their condition.

So why wasn't he shooting? Nothing but silence from the roof.

He gripped the SIG and said to Otis, "Let's go. Shoot anything that moves. I'll take the left side, you take the right."

Hugging the cement wall, he inched up the ramp. Despite the chill in the air, sweat beaded his face. He crept upward, inch by inch. Glanced at Otis, on the other side of the ramp, arms extended, gripping the Glock in both hands as he moved upward toward the roof.

Halfway up the ramp, Frank stopped. From here he would have a clear view of the roof when he raised his head above the cement wall. And anyone on the roof would have a clear view of his head.

He made eye contact with Otis and nodded.

With his heart slamming his chest, he sprang to his feet. Did a rapid three-hundred-sixty-degree scan of the vast open space.

No Stoltz. Thirty yards away, an automatic rifle lay on the cement.

"Where the hell is he?" Otis said as they stepped onto the roof.

Frank shook his head, mystified. His muscles ached with tension and his pulse pounded a vicious drumbeat in his temples. Then he recalled an earlier report from Vobitch. A discussion they'd had hours ago. Eons ago.

After entering the hospital, Stoltz had overpowered an off-duty cop working a security detail on the first floor. What if there'd been another one?

It hit him like a sledgehammer in the gut. "He's got a police radio!"

He dug out his cell, speed-dialed Kelly's cell and gave it to Otis.

"Warn Kelly. Tell her Stoltz is coming. Then call Vobitch. Tell him everyone needs to stay off the radio!"

He whirled and raced down the ramp, whipping around turns like a slingshot. He had to get to Belinda's room before Stoltz did. No telling how much of a lead the bastard had.

Would Wood and Nixon stop him? He hadn't heard any gunshots.

He whipped around a corner onto Level Three and ran to the walkway. Kelly was in the most danger. Guarding the person Stoltz most wanted to kill.

He raced down the glassed-in walkway, feet pounding the cement, heart pounding like a howitzer. If Stoltz hurt Kelly or Belinda, he'd kill the bastard.

CHAPTER 47

The monster was in her room. Again.

Her heart was a wild beast inside her chest.

How could this be? She had escaped him once. Now he stood ten feet away, a terrifying presence, face caked with dirt and dried blood, leering at her, his disgusting stench filling the room. His terrible eyes pierced her like rapiers. His gun, long and lethal-looking, was aimed at Kelly.

Fearing her legs would collapse, she set her butt against the edge of the bed. Hunched her shoulders inside the hospital robe. Hugged her arms to her chest. She didn't dare look at Kelly.

When they heard popping sounds in the hall, Kelly had told her to get on the floor behind the bed. But there was no time. The monster burst into the room and shot at them, a strangely muted sound. Muted or not, it had shattered the window behind her.

Now damp air was blowing on the back of her neck.

Her body shook with tremors, icy chills radiating from her belly to her chest. Six feet to her left, Kelly stood with her feet apart, gripping her gun.

Somehow, Kelly had summoned the courage to raise her gun and aim it at the monster. To protect her.

"Ready to party, Belinda?" The monster's ice-pick eyes drilled into her.

Her stomach heaved. She feared her bladder would burst.

"We're not having any party," Kelly said, her voice edged with grit, a rasp on metal.

"Oh, yes we are." The monster smiled, a terrifying smile, a death's head smile. "We're going to have a great time, aren't we, Belinda?"

The wild beast ripped her chest.

She couldn't speak, couldn't breath. Couldn't bear his predatory eyes, devouring her like a piece of meat.

Summoning every ounce of resolve within her, she smiled at him. "I'm glad you're here, Barry. I wanted to speak to you before, but—"

"Bullshit! That's not what you wanted this morning." He shifted his stance to aim the gun at her. "You wanted me out of your house. That's what you said, Belinda. Admit it."

Her scalp tingled, prickles of fear. She tried to lick her lips, but her mouth was too dry. She bit her cheek to summon some saliva.

"I suppose I did. But you frightened me, Barry. I didn't expect to wake up and find you in my bedroom. It was . . . a shock."

"A shock. Is that the best you can do? You said you wanted to talk to me, but you don't have much to say. No more compliments for Barry, huh?"

His insatiable eyes devoured her. But his hands remained steady, aiming the long lethal-looking gun at her.

Kelly's cell phone rang, a shrill insistent sound.

"Don't even think about it. You answer that phone and you're dead. Shut the fuckin' thing off. Now."

Something stirred within her, some primal instinct, rising up to fight the fear that paralyzed her. *Never give in to fear. Act successful and you will be successful. Believe in yourself and you cannot fail.*

The words she chanted silently before performances as she waited to go onstage. Now she had to give a different sort of performance.

A perfect performance. The performance of her life.

Ignoring the chills that wracked her, she breathed down to her diaphragm. *Talk to him about music. And keep using his name. He likes that.*

"I liked your suggestion about the Busoni violin sonata, Barry. If you lend me the score, I'll transcribe it for flute and we can play it together."

An infinitesimal change in his expression told her she'd scored a hit.

Then his face clenched in a scowl and his neck corded. "We won't be playing any duets now and you know it. You think I'm stupid?"

"No, Barry. I don't think you're stupid. I think you're very smart."

"You got that right. Too smart to fall for any more of your fucking lies. You fooled me once with that bullshit about fixing your flute with that fucking screwdriver. And then you stabbed me. You don't think the cops are going to let me out of here alive, do you?"

"We will if you put down the gun," Kelly said. "Put the gun down and everything will be fine."

He laughed, a raucous braying sound that filled the room. "Listen to Little Miss Robo-Cop, thinks she's gonna take me in by herself." His gaze flicked to Kelly. "That what you think, Officer O'Neil?"

Belinda gasped. How did he know Kelly's name?

"I think you don't give a damn about anyone but yourself," Kelly said, her voice tense and shrill and full of determination.

"Shut up! Just 'cuz you got a gun doesn't give you the right to put me down. You want to shoot me? Go ahead. My finger's on the trigger and this Beretta's got a real light pull. You know what that means, Officer O'Neil? You shoot me, my finger hits the trigger and boom. Belinda's dead. Stop running your mouth or I'll shoot you."

"Barry," she said, desperate to distract him, "remember the piece you played on my piano that day when I came into the studio?"

"Sure. The Beethoven sonata. I played it for my Boston Conservatory audition. Not well enough to get accepted, though. Back then I couldn't do anything well enough." His lips twisted into a ferocious smile, the smile of a wolf about to pounce on its prey. "But now I can. Ask those cops out there. They'll tell you how good I am. The ones that are still talking."

The ones that are still talking.

She dug her nails into her arm. Was Frank dead?

Icy chills skittered down her neck. She had to keep him talking, had to keep him focused on music. Not killing cops. Or her.

"I thought your piano playing was quite fine—"

"Shut up! Don't feed me compliments thinking it'll get you out of here. It won't."

"I'm not trying to get out of here, Barry. I'm trying to talk to you. This morning you asked me what I wanted. Why don't you tell me what *you* want."

He studied her silently, his eyes cold and merciless. "Here's what I *used to* want, Belinda. I wanted you to like me. Back in high school, Rachel introduced us after a concert and you blew me off like I was nothing. You were the star even then, principal flute of the best high school orchestra in the state. Fifteen years old and you made the others sound like fifth graders."

Back in high school. Fear jolted her like an electric current.

"I'm sorry, Barry, but I don't remember meeting you."

"You blew me off in London, too. Belinda Scully didn't need a driver." An ugly smile parted his rubbery-red lips. "The accident changed that though. That got your attention." His gaze shifted to Kelly. "Don't shake your head, bitch. I should shoot you—"

"No, no, no! You don't have to shoot anyone, Barry. Let Kelly go. She can leave her gun here and walk out the door and you and I can talk privately—"

"No." Kelly's grim raspy voice. "I'm not going anywhere until he puts down the gun. I'm not leaving this room until Belinda walks out of here safe and sound."

Another braying laugh from the monster. "Hoo-eee, this little gal is a spitfire! Wish I'd met you sooner, Officer O'Neil. We could have had fun. Except for the fact that I've been in love with Belinda forever. Too bad Belinda didn't reciprocate."

He raised the lethal-looking gun and aimed it at her heart.

"Please don't point that gun at me, Barry. You wouldn't do that if you loved me."

His expression grew thoughtful, a ruminative expression that morphed into anger. "It's for your own good. That's what Daddy-O used to say when he beat me. It's for your own good, boy."

Her fingernails clawed her forearms. She couldn't keep this up much longer. "Barry, this morning you wanted me to kiss you goodbye." She forced herself to smile, forced herself to look him in the eye. "Will you let Kelly go if I kiss you?"

Bile rose in her throat, her body revolting at the thought of those lips on her mouth.

"Now there's an idea." A big wolfish grin. "I like that, Belinda. You want to kiss me? Great."

Her heart exploded in a paroxysm of fear and revulsion.

Kiss the monster? Feel that disgusting tongue inside her mouth again? Could she make herself do it? But if Kelly got away, she could get help.

"Let Kelly go first. Then we'll have some privacy so I can . . ." She steeled herself. "So I can kiss you the way you deserve to be kissed."

His face froze, a death mask of rage. "Kelly's not going anywhere. Get on your knees, Belinda. Forget playing kissy-face. It's time you kissed another part of my anatomy."

Frank burst from the walkway into the hospital corridor and stopped, shocked at the carnage. Warren Wood was down. Larry Nixon was down.

His gut plummeted like an elevator with cut cables. Holding his SIG in front of him, he advanced down the corridor. Warren lay on the floor in a pool of blood, eyes vacant and staring, a bullet hole between them.

But Nixon was alive. His eyes blinked shut. Slowly opened. Nixon saw him, and his mouth opened, but no sound came out, his tongue thrusting between his lips. Frank knelt down beside him. Saw the entry wound in the side of his head. Saw Nixon's eyes start to glaze over.

"Took my gun," Nixon gasped. "I think he got Sam, too."

"Don't try to talk. Otis is coming. He'll help you."

He rose. Took two strides. Flattened his back to the wall.

Peeked around the corner. Near the door to Belinda's room, Sam Wallace lay on the floor. Blood seeped from his neck.

Belinda's last line of defense. Fear clawed his throat.

He tried to get his breath. Forced air from his lungs. Inhaled.

The corridor was silent, a terrible eerie stillness, as if this were some post-apocalyptic world where everyone had died.

He crept down the hall to Sam. Saw the head wound and the vacant eyes. Sam was gone. His shirt clung to his back, soaked with sweat. Gripping the SIG in both hands, he inched closer to Belinda's suite.

His heart slammed his ribs so hard he could almost hear it.

The door to the anteroom was open.

"Don't do it, Belinda. He'll kill us both."

The hackles rose on his neck. Kelly's voice, shrill with panic.

Kelly was alive, and so was Belinda. But Stoltz was with them.

He edged into the anteroom. Bloody footprints on the carpet.

Straight ahead of him, the door to Belinda's room was ajar.

"Don't pay any attention to Little Miss Robo-cop, Belinda. Do what I tell you."

Stoltz. And Stoltz had a gun. A meat-cleaver of dread chopped his gut.

The carpet masked the sound of his footsteps as he inched to the door. Put his eye to the opening. The sight fried his brain.

He closed his eyes. Opened them. Saw the same horrific scene. Kelly, eyes wide, face frozen in a feral expression, arms raised in front of her. Holding her Glock in both hands. Aimed at someone he couldn't see.

Stoltz. Armed and dangerous and bent on revenge.

The door wasn't open wide enough for him to see Belinda. Or Stoltz.

But it wasn't hard to picture the scene. Kelly had her gun on Stoltz. And Stoltz had his gun on Belinda. Stalemate. Unless he did something.

Holding the SIG in his right hand, he put his left palm against the door.

Willing Kelly to notice and hoping Stoltz wouldn't, he gave the door a tiny shove. The door opened another inch. Then another. And Kelly saw it!

She didn't look his way, but he could tell by the way her jaw muscles bunched. Now he could see Stoltz, the right half of him anyway.

His back was to the door, feet spread, legs braced. Holding a Beretta fitted with a silencer. Aimed at Belinda's head. He could only see part of her. The part he could see was kneeling on the floor, facing Stoltz.

He waggled his fingers to attract Kelly's attention. Then, in rapid succession, he held up three fingers—one, two, three—then motioned downward with his hand. *One, two, three, drop to the floor.*

Kelly blinked twice. Two deliberate strokes of her eyelids.

His heart surged. Kelly got it. But Belinda didn't know he was here. Kelly would know enough to drop to the floor when he fired, but Belinda wouldn't. If he fired at Stoltz, he might hit her.

"Let's go, Belinda," Stoltz said. "You asked me what I wanted and I told you. Suck my dick, bitch. That's what you get for stabbing me."

The air left his lungs as if sucked out by a vacuum cleaner.

Situation critical.

He raised his left hand and waggled his fingers at Kelly.

He held up one finger. Two fingers. Three.

Kelly dropped to the floor and he burst into the room.

"Police! Drop the gun!"

Stoltz whirled, arms extended, both hands clamped on the Beretta. "Motherfuck—"

He shot Stoltz in the face.

Inside the small hospital room the blast was deafening. Time stretched out like a slow-motion video, a kaleidoscope of sounds and images.

Belinda eyes widened. Her mouth opened, but no sound came out.

In a reflex motion Stoltz threw up his hands. A shot from his Beretta pierced the ceiling. Blood spurted from the hole in his forehead.

But he stayed on his feet, teeth bared like a cornered animal. A guttural sound came from his mouth.

More sounds. Belinda's high-pitched wail.

More images. Kelly prone on the floor, gripping her Glock.

Stoltz's bloody hairless face.

Then, impossibly, Stoltz staggered toward him, hands outstretched, fingers like claws, eyes fixed on him. His face contorted with fury and hate.

Frank aimed at his heart and pulled the trigger.

Stoltz blinked, shuddered, and collapsed on the floor.

CHAPTER 48

"It was a righteous shoot, Frank. No question." Vobitch rattled the ice in his rocks glass, stone-faced as Mount Rushmore, gray eyes full of certainty.

He nodded, chewing a mouthful of cheeseburger. They were holed up in a dim-lit pub in Kenner, two towns away from the carnage at City Hospital.

"How'd it go with IAD?" Vobitch asked.

After the IAD interview, Vobitch had met him outside in the hall and said, "Come on, Frank, I'm taking you out for a pop."

Twenty feet from their booth, a TV set above the bar blared news of the New Orleans Massacre. Frank ignored it and mopped his cheeseburger in some catsup. Under stress, his appetite vanished, but now he was ravenous.

He hadn't eaten all day, the longest day of his life. But he was alive. Kelly was alive. Belinda was alive. And Stoltz was dead. The buzz-saw that had clawed his gut for the last twelve hours had subsided.

Vobitch raked fingers through his silvery mane of hair, outrage replacing the certainty in his eyes. "What? Did they lean on you? I'll blast those fuckheads—"

"It went okay. I've been through this before. In Boston."

Boston had been much worse. The bad guy died, but so had an innocent young girl. That interview had been a nightmare. Hard eyes, probing questions, police union and IAD tape-recorders running. He'd sat there for an hour picturing the dead girl, pain gnawing his gut.

He gulped some ice water, unable to quench his terrible thirst. "They put me on paid administrative leave and told me to write my report ASAP."

"You're okay with this, right?" Vobitch said, pressing him.

Touched, he studied the older man, not old enough to be his father, but old enough to express his concern in a fatherly way. Vobitch hadn't brought him here to be sociable. It was a gesture of solidarity: *You did the right thing, and I'm behind you a hundred percent.*

Had Judge Salvatore Renzi heard about the massacre, he wondered.

"I just wish we got Stoltz sooner," he said. "He killed a lot of people, wounded a lot more. He did a lot of damage."

Vobitch rattled the ice in his glass at the waitress, signaling for another round. "Hey, the guy was a fuckin' maniac. We get into the military data base, we'll probably find out he was a Green Beret or something. He had a fuckin' arsenal! SWAT found a crossbow in that house. Know what else they found?"

Overcome by exhaustion, he shook his head, too weary for words.

"A rabbit."

He studied his boss's face to see if he was joking. Vobitch often did that in tense situations to put people at ease. "A live rabbit?"

"Yeah. In a cage, like it was his pet or some fuckin' thing." Vobitch's lips formed a smile. "When one of the SWAT guys tried to take the rabbit out of the cage it bit him."

Laughter burst from his mouth. For a moment Vobitch stared at him. Then Vobitch started laughing too, thunderous gut-shaking guffaws. Nervous laughter after the unbearable tension.

"The rabbit," Frank said, shaking with laughter. "The rabbit bit him?"

Vobitch nodded. He couldn't stop laughing either.

The waitress brought their drinks—Dewars on the rocks for Vobitch, a Heineken for Frank—and hustled back to the bar, couldn't get away from her weirdo-customers fast enough.

Their laughter, a welcome release from the stress, finally subsided. Frank set aside his plate, all traces of cheeseburger gone. Now that he'd eaten he wanted to go home and sleep for twenty-four hours. Make that a week. He yawned, a prodigious crack-your-jaw yawn, exhausted by the day's frantic action and bone-crushing tension.

A ring-tone sounded. Vobitch took out his cell phone and answered, then listened, poker-faced.

Emotionally drained, Frank leaned back against the padded seat. Kelly's father and oldest brother had flown in from Chicago. He was glad the cops in her family had come down to support her, but that meant he wouldn't see her till Monday. Seventy-two interminable hours.

After Stoltz went down he'd wanted to hold her, wanted the reassurance of physical contact after his agonizing fear that Stoltz would kill her. But Belinda was screaming and Stoltz was twitching on the floor and four cops had burst into the room. Then, chaos.

Vobitch closed his cell. "They found the Goines kid up in Jackson, Mississippi. A businessman flew home from a trip, found a body in the trunk of his car in long-term parking."

It didn't surprise him, but he felt bad for the parents. Marcus had done something stupid, dealing dope and getting mixed up with AK, but he didn't deserve to die. "AK swore he didn't kill Marcus. Maybe he was telling the truth. If AK wanted to dump a body, he wouldn't go to Mississippi to do it."

"Sounds about right to me. Chalk up another victim to Stoltz." Vobitch grabbed the check and slid out of the booth. "Let's get out of here. You need to go home and crash."

He went home, took a hot shower and fell into an exhausted sleep. The next morning he woke up at five and went for a long run. When he returned to his apartment at six, the sun was peeping through the trees and his phone was ringing. The New Orleans Massacre had made the national news. He fielded calls from his daughter, his ex-wife, his father, and Kenyon Miller.

Even Dana Swenson called from Omaha.

Not a word from Belinda.

At noon, he got in his car and left. He needed to be by himself for a while, needed solitude to process the previous day's horror.

He got on the I-10 and headed west. At one-thirty he blew past Baton Rouge, crossed the Mississippi and drove through the Atchafalaya swamp.

But his mind kept flitting from one flashback to another. Hideous sights and horrible sounds. Belinda's terror-filled eyes. The shots from the hospital roof. The mind-blowing image of Stoltz holding a gun on Belinda and Kelly.

A Herbie Hancock CD got him to Lafayette. A Clark Terry CD got him to Lake Charles near the Texas border. At a rest stop, he filled the gas tank, bought a sandwich and a container of orange juice and got back on the road.

More flashbacks. Kelly, her face a grim mask of determination, her Glock aimed at Stoltz. He couldn't get that one out of his mind.

Had he arrived five minutes later, Kelly would be dead. Then Stoltz would have raped Belinda and killed her.

He made his mind go blank. He swigged some OJ and ate his turkey sandwich as he zoomed down the highway. His father's call had come at nine-twenty this morning. "Are you all right, Frank? I saw the news on CNN. Looked like a blood-bath."

He didn't want to discuss it, but his father had wormed the story out of him. And in the end Judge Salvatore Renzi said: *You did the right thing, Frank. I'm proud of you.* A reward better than any service medal or commendation.

He balled up the sandwich wrapper and chugged the last of the orange juice. A minute later he was crossing the sky-high bridge that swooped into

Texas, overlooking oil refinery smoke-stacks and the rows of storage tanks that bordered the city of Beaumont.

His cell phone rang. He checked the ID. He'd almost left it home. Good thing he hadn't. "Frank," Kelly said softly. "I can't talk long. Dad and my brother are in the other room. I just wanted to hear your voice."

"I'm glad," he said, his voice husky. "I'll see you Monday, right?"

"You bet," she said, and her voice had the lilt in it that he loved. "Come to my house after work. I'll be waiting."

On Monday morning Belinda walked into Frank's office at nine o'clock. A ceiling fan swirled cool air around the room, but her hands were damp with sweat. This would be difficult, but she was determined to do it. She owed Frank an apology. No. She owed him her life.

He sat at his desk staring at a computer monitor. A large black man with a shaven head sat at another desk. They looked up as she approached.

"Belinda," Frank said, and smiled. "How are you doing?"

The other man rose from his chair. She could tell he recognized her. "I gotta go interview a witness," he muttered, and hurried out of the office.

Frank rose to his feet, gave her a hug and gestured at a chair, inviting her to sit. "How are you doing?" he said again.

"I'm not sleeping very well, but I guess that will pass." She perched on the chair beside the desk. "I wanted to come and thank you in person. You were right, Frank. I should have taken your advice and stayed in a hotel—"

"Don't beat yourself up over it. None of this was your fault. Stoltz was fixated on you. He was a military man, ex-Army. He knew what he was doing, planned the whole thing, every step of the way."

She clasped her hands together, mustering her resolve.

"Kelly saved me. She was afraid he'd kill you. Kelly loves you."

Frank stared at her, slack-jawed. She almost laughed. But that would be rude. She didn't intend to be rude to anyone else ever again.

"She does, Frank. Even if she hasn't figured it out yet."

Seemingly flustered, he shuffled papers around his desk, which surprised her. She'd never seen him the least bit flustered before.

At last he said, "What are your plans? Will you stay in New Orleans?"

"No. One of my cousins called. She heard what happened and invited me to stay with her for a while. She lives in Baltimore. After that I'm not sure. I need to think about it." She needed to think about a lot of things.

"I'm glad you've got family to help you get through this," Frank said. "That's important."

"Yes, it is." She'd been without family and friends for a long time. Too long. "What about you, Frank? This must have been terrible for you."

"I'll be okay. I've got my daughter and my father."

"And Kelly." She rose from the chair, relieved that the conversation she had been dreading was over. "Thank you for everything, Frank. Can I call you sometime to see how you're doing?"

"Sure. Call me from your cousin's. Maybe you'll fall in love with Baltimore."

She smiled but said nothing, left the office with her back straight and her head high. She walked through the foyer and out into the sunlight.

The police had returned her custom-built flute, the flute Stoltz had forced her to play and then destroyed. She would never play it again, would have another one built, one that didn't involve hideous memories. She had cancelled her remaining performances for the year. In January she would resume her career with a new manager. But she would not allow it to dominate her life.

Recalling Frank's words, she smiled. She didn't want to fall in love with Baltimore. She wanted to fall in love with a man who loved her for herself, not her professional achievements. Guy St. Cyr had sent her an email asking if she was all right. She hadn't answered it. Not a word from Ramon.

The instant he entered Kelly's house they melded into a bear hug. "God, I missed you," she breathed in his ear.

"Mmm," he said, holding her close. "Feels like forever since I touched you." He kissed her, a long deep satisfying kiss. "Great to be alive, isn't it?"

Her eyes searched his face. "Yes."

"I'm glad your dad and your brother came down."

"Me, too. But I worried about you, alone in your apartment."

"I wasn't home alone," he said, and saw her grin at his play on the movie title. "I got sick of answering phone calls and questions so I drove to Houston. Did some thinking."

"Come tell me about it. I got us a nice bottle of red."

They went in the kitchen and he opened the wine. Kelly was wearing a pair of her big-Z earrings, silver etched with turquoise. He set their wine glasses on the table and sat down. She came over and climbed into his lap.

Things were definitely looking up. "You trying to get a rise out of me?"

She mussed his hair. "Yes, but you'll have to wait till after dinner to do anything about it."

"Who says?" He raised her shirt and caressed her back.

"Me." She brushed his lips with a kiss. "I've been thinking too. When Stoltz came in that room, I thought it was all over. All that stuff about seeing your life flash before your eyes? That's bullshit."

He knew exactly what she meant. Life-and-death situations altered your perspective on life. If you survived.

She gazed at him, eyes tinged with sadness. "Then everything changed. Belinda changed. She stood up for me. She knew Stoltz was going to kill me. She kept telling him to let me go and she'd do whatever he wanted. He told her to suck his dick." Kelly stuck a finger in her mouth in the universal puke-gesture. "It made me sick. I wanted to kill the son-of-a-bitch. I didn't care if he shot me. I wanted him *dead*."

He pulled her close, felt her heartbeat thrum against his chest.

"Now I know how you feel, Frank. Those times when you get that I'm-gonna-get-the-bad-guy look? That's how I felt about Stoltz. He said he'd let me go if Belinda gave him a blow job. What a crock. If you hadn't come in the room when you did, I'd have shot him myself."

Her mouth quivered and her eyes gleamed with tears.

He cupped her face in his hands and brushed her lips with a kiss. "I'm glad you understand me better, but I'm sorry you had to go through what you did to get there. I'm having flashbacks, are you?"

"Yes, but it will pass. Dad and my brother talked to me about that. They've been through some shit in Chicago. This morning I told Vobitch I want to transfer back to Domestic Violence. I'm done with Homicide."

She tilted her head and her big-Z earrings swung to and fro. "You think I'm a quitter?" she said, gazing at him, solemn-eyed.

"Are you kidding? After what you went through? Kelly, you're one of the bravest women I ever met. You're great with rape victims and battered women. Domestic Violence is lucky to get you."

She picked up her wine glass. "Well, now that we got that out of the way we can relax and have dinner."

He took the wine glass from her hand and set it on the table.

"Dinner can wait. I can't."

Her lips curled in a smile and her eyes crinkled at the corners. "You know what, Frank? Every now and then you come up with a great idea."

ABOUT THE AUTHOR

In her travels, Susan Fleet has worn many hats: trumpeter, college professor, music historian, radio host and award-winning author, to name a few. The Premier Book Awards named her first novel, *Absolution,* Best Mystery-Suspense-Thriller of 2009. She divides her time between Boston and New Orleans, the settings for her suspense thrillers.

Visit her at www.susanfleet.com

Keep reading for a sample of Susan Fleet's next exciting Frank Renzi thriller

NATALIE

October 1988   New Orleans

One night my mother didn't come home.

Every morning she came in my room and woke me with a kiss and said, "Rise and shine, Natalie. Your breakfast is ready."

Not today. Today, our apartment was silent and still, except for the rain splattering my bedroom window. Not only that, the clock radio beside my bed told me it was 8:35. I was late for school.

Sometimes I stay up late watching TV, but Mom always gets me up in time for school. Last night before Mom left she said, "Do your homework and go to bed and I'll see you tomorrow."

I shut my eyes tight and buried my face in the pillow and tried to pretend it was a dream. But down deep I knew it wasn't. I don't know why.

Last night Mom left for work at nine o'clock same as always, wearing a pretty dress and her favorite perfume. Mom's beautiful. She's got long chestnut-brown hair and big green eyes that she makes look even more beautiful with glittery eye shadow. Every night before she leaves, she always says the same thing: *Don't answer the phone. Don't open the door to anyone. Don't leave the apartment.* One night I snuck out to the corner store to buy a snack and the clerk told Mom the next day. Mom got mad and said if I ever did that again, I wouldn't get my allowance.

I clenched my teeth, hoping the horrible feeling of dread would go away. But it didn't. I threw off the sheet, got out of bed and went in the kitchen. Normally, my milk and cereal and fruit would be on the breakfast bar where we ate our meals. But nothing was normal now.

The futon in the living room where my mother slept was still upright, no sheet, no pillow. After I left for school Mom usually goes back to bed. She needs to sleep because she works late. She's a hostess at a fancy restaurant. Or so she said. I'd never been there. Lately, I'd begun to suspect this wasn't so. I'm only ten, but I watch TV, and I don't think hostesses wear fancy dresses and lots of makeup and smell the way I imagined the sexy women on TV smelled when they went out with important men.

A big blob of fear clogged my throat. I felt sick, like I might throw up, and my hands felt weird, hot and cold at the same time, and damp with sweat. Mom always said to call her cell phone if there was an emergency. And if this wasn't an emergency, what was? I went to the wall phone beside our boxy old refrigerator with the yellowed enamel. Mom's cell phone number is printed on a pink Post-It stuck to the fridge. Right beside is another pink Post-It with the numbers for police and fire and medical emergencies.

I started to reach for the phone, but the doorbell rang.

My heart stopped, at least it felt like it did. *Don't open the door to anyone.*

I crept to the door and looked through the peephole the way Mom taught me. My legs felt like Jell-O. A woman in a dark-blue police uniform was standing outside in the rain. Police meant trouble. That's what Mom always said. But I was already in trouble. Late for school. And Mom wasn't here. And a policewoman was ringing our doorbell. I looked through the peephole again. The policewoman's expression scared me. Frown lines grooved her forehead, the way Mom's did when she was worried about something, like when she didn't have enough money to pay the bills.

I worked all the locks and opened the door.

"Natalie?" the policewoman said. She didn't smile when she said it.

I nodded. I was too scared to think, too scared to breathe.

"I'm Detective Fontenot with the New Orleans Police Department. Your mother's been hurt."

My world crashed and burned like a spaceship without a parachute.

Mom was hurt. Badly hurt. Otherwise, she would have called me.

The policewoman said, "Someone shot your mother last night."

―――

July 2008   New Orleans

The stench was overpowering, worse than most corpses found in fancy hotels, a pungent mix of stale urine and rank body odor. Twenty-plus years as a cop, he'd seen his share. This one was spread-eagled naked on a king-sized four-poster bed, arms over his head, legs aimed at the footboard. Beneath his head was a blood-soaked pillow, and a large yellow urine stain soiled the sheet. Centered in his forehead was a gunshot entry-wound.

Whoever popped the guy had shut off the A/C, maybe after the shot, maybe before. Maybe the guy was into hot sex.

Sometime after midnight someone had called the Hotel Bienvenue desk to report a problem in Room 635. A big problem, big enough for the hotel security guard to call NOPD and have them roust Homicide Detective Frank Renzi out of bed at one A.M.

He eyeballed the corpse. No defense wounds, no visible bruises. No doubt about the cause of death. The person that called in the problem hadn't hung around. Now it was 1:35. He'd already called for the crime scene techs and a coroner's investigator, any kind of luck they'd be here soon and so would his partner. An NOPD uniform was posted outside the door of the room to fend off any unauthorized visitors.

The mahogany kneehole desk beside the window was squeaky clean, no dust, no notes. Heavy drapes covered the window, not that anyone could see into a room on the sixth floor. Beside the bed the victim's clothes lay in a heap on the floor, a pair of jockey shorts on top.

"Yo, Frank." His partner, Kenyon Miller, ambled into the room and wrinkled his nose. "What we got? A stinker?"

"A ripe one for sure. Feels like the A/C's been off for a while."

Miller eyed the corpse. "Mm, mm, mm. This'll cause a shitstorm."

"Why? You know him?"

"Yeah, and I'm not talking about his Yankee Doodle."

Frank grinned. Every black guy he'd ever worked with had an arsenal of terms for male genitalia. Yankee Doodle. That was a new one. "Who is he?"

"Arnold Peterson, but it ain't who he is, it's what he does." Miller mopped beads of sweat from his shaven pate with a handkerchief. "Be all kinds of pressure on this one. Peterson's marketing director for Harrah's, a high profile guy with big shot buddies, including the Saint's owner."

"You sure it's Peterson?"

"No doubt in my mind. I've seen him at Saint's games with the owner."

"Looks like a hit. One shot, middle of the forehead."

"Wouldn't surprise me. What I hear, Peterson's a real prick, screwed a few people to get the job, might have been screwing around on his wife, too."

"Maybe the wife found out and hired a hitter." He'd seen that once or twice. "The A/C's been off for a while, might complicate the TOD." He made a mental note to nail down the time of the "problem" call. "I'm going down to the desk and see who rented the room."

Miller shot him an aggrieved look. "Sure. Go down to the *delightfully* cool lobby while I sweat it out with the stinky corpse." Ramping up the sarcasm, he added, "While you're at it, why not have a pop in the nice air-conditioned lounge and ask the bartender if Peterson was there tonight?"

Miller, jiving him as usual. "Aw, you poor thing. Next thing you'll be weeping into your Miller Light. Here's the deal. I'll do the notification. That'll be fun. You canvas the guests on this floor to see if they heard anything."

On the way to the elevator, he spotted a security camera near the ceiling at the end of the hall. Maybe they'd catch a break with that. They might need one. VIP murders could be brutal. Summers in New Orleans were equally brutal: hot and humid, no telling when a hurricane might churn into the Gulf and spawn a massive evacuation with horrendous traffic jams. Add in a high-profile murder victim? Hell, just what he needed to spice up his life.

Made in the USA
San Bernardino, CA
21 November 2013